Tangled Vines

Tangled Vines

A Novel by

Janet Dailey

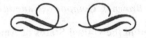

Little, Brown and Company

Boston   Toronto   London

ISBN 0-316-17156-5

Published simultaneously in Canada
by Little, Brown & Company (Canada) Limited

Printed in the United States of America

A television-satellite van bearing the "News Four" logo of the local NBC station in New York stood at the curb a short distance from Playmates Arch in Central Park. There, along the footpath, a camera crew was busy setting up for a remote telecast for the local "Live at Five" report. Behind portable barricades erected by park security, a horde of onlookers watched the proceedings in the steamy heat of an August afternoon.

Old-fashioned hurdy-gurdy music from the park's carousel drifted above the drone of the van's generator as Kelly Douglas stepped out of the air-conditioned vehicle. A co-anchor on the evening newscast at KNBC for almost two years now, she was in full makeup, her auburn hair drawn back in a French braid.

"Hey, Kelly." Eddy Michels, one of the tech crew, came trotting up, slowing to a stop when he reached her. "Man, you talk about hot." He wiped a sweaty cheek on the shoulder of his T-shirt. "It must be a hundred in the shade."

"At least," Kelly agreed and lifted her hands. "Welcome to New York, nature's summertime sauna."

"You've got that right." He started to turn away, then swung back. "I meant to tell you — I loved that interview you did with that bureaucrat Blaine the other day. You really had her squirming and stammering around for an answer when you pointed out all the discrepancies in her report. You shouldn't have taken pity on her, though, and backed off."

Kelly smiled and shook her head in friendly disagreement. "I learned back in Iowa not to have a battle of wits with an opponent who has run out of ammunition. Especially an opponent with powerful friends."

He chuckled and conceded, "You have a point there."

"I know I do." Her smile widened as she warned, "Deliberately making a fool of somebody is the quickest way to make an enemy for life."

"I suppose you learned that growing up in Iowa, too," he joked.

"Naturally," Kelly replied with a straight face, then laughed, and set off to join the camera crew on the footpath to the arch.

As she drew close to the crew, she was recognized and a male voice shouted from the gathering of onlookers, "Hey, Kelly, aren't you worried about coming here to Central Park?"

"Only with you," she countered quickly and smiled, automatically scanning the crowd to locate her caller.

An older man stood well apart from the others, his face turned in profile, his dark hair threaded with strands of gray. He was dressed in a plaid shirt and a faded pair of golf green slacks, sharply creased. The clothes, the cocky sneer of his lips . . .

Kelly went cold when she saw him, fear freezing her in place as images flashed — a hard-knuckled fist swinging with force, pain exploding in white-hot arcs, silencing a half-born cry, the jerk of brutal hands, the stench of whiskey breath, a small, frightened voice sobbing, "Don't hit me, Daddy. Don't hit me," a string of violent curses, the taste and smell of blood.

She stared, her face pale with shock, her mind racing in panic. How had he found her? How, after all these years? She had made a new life for herself. People liked her; they respected her. Dear God, she couldn't let him ruin that for her. She couldn't let him hurt her again. She couldn't.

"Kelly, what's wrong?" a voice asked. "You are white as a ghost."

She couldn't answer. She couldn't look away from him. Then the man turned, giving her a full view of his face. It wasn't him. Relief came in waves.

Finally Kelly was able to focus on the woman in front of her, one of the producer's assistants. "It's the heat," she lied, something she did with the skill of an expert. "I'll be fine."

Reassured by the color coming back to Kelly's face, the woman nodded. "Patty Cummins from the Central Park Zoo is here. I thought you might want to meet her before we go on the air."

"Of course." Kelly glanced back at the man, confirming again that it wasn't him. How could it be? He was still back in California. Back in Napa Valley. She was safe. She had nothing to worry about. Nothing at all.

*   *   *

The vineyard baked in the heat of an August sun, its vines strung along the mountain's rugged slope in orderly rows, their roots sunk deep in the rocky soil, drawing moisture and the distinctive taste of the earth from it. The land was poor, incapable of nourishing any other crop, yet from the grapes of this vineyard had come some of the finest wines in the whole of Napa Valley — some said the world.

Rutledge wine made from Rutledge vines grown on Rutledge land.

A tan Jeep with the insignia of the Rutledge Estate winery painted on its doors sat at one end of the vineyard, parked on the grassy shoulder of a dirt road. Sam Rutledge slowly made his way back to it, pausing now and then among the vines to examine a cluster of ripening grapes.

At thirty-six he had lines bracketing his mouth and fanning from the corners of his eyes in deep creases, but the years hadn't faded the faint smattering of freckles that showed beneath the dark tan of his broad, roughly planed face. He wore tan chinos and a blue chambray shirt, the cuffs rolled back exposing the corded muscles of his forearms. An old and weatherworn brown hat, the kind that had been in vogue in the forties, shaded his eyes from the full glare of the sun.

As he neared the end of the row and the Jeep, Sam Rutledge stopped and reached down to scoop up a handful of soil, a mixture of dust and pebbles.

It was Rutledge soil, the same as the vines. His life revolved around them. It was the way he wanted it.

Still holding the dirt in his hand, Sam lifted his head and turned to look across the narrow vineyard-strewn valley. The wild canyons and spiny ridges of the Mayacamas Mountains lay to the west, a twin to the coastal range that walled the valley on the east. The deep green of conifer and oak blanketed its slopes and contrasted sharply with the dull yellow of summer-parched pastures.

Mount St. Helena stood at the head of the valley, its rounded peak thrusting up to dominate the northern horizon. Over it all arched the blue canopy of an unclouded sky. It was a land of sparse rainfall and unrelenting sun, of cooling fogs from the Pacific and baking heat, of rock, volcanic ash, and the sediment of ancient marine life. Sam saw it as nature's crucible.

His fingers curled around the rocky dirt in his palm, holding it tightly for a moment, then opening as he turned his hand to let the soil fall back to the ground. As Sam dusted his hands off, he heard a vehicle on the road. He immediately wondered who had left the main gate open. Rutledge Estate wasn't open to the public. Tours of the winery were by appointment only and the schedule rarely permitted that.

The sound grew into the definite rumble of a car. A green-and-white Buick LeSabre rounded the bend in the road, trailing a thick cloud of dust. The staccato roar from its knocking engine shattered the quiet of the vineyard.

Sam recognized the ten-year-old car even before he saw the magnetic sign on the door panel that read REBECCA'S VINEYARD. There was only one car like it in the entire valley and it belonged to Len Dougherty, as did the ten acres that Dougherty called Rebecca's Vineyard. The last time Sam saw it, it had looked more like a jungle than a vineyard. He hadn't been surprised by that. Len Dougherty only masqueraded as a vintner; his true career was drinking, with brawling an occasional pastime.

Sam had no use for the man and no pity for his current financial problems. It showed in his face when the Buick shuddered to an abrupt stop with a screech of grinding brake shoes. Dust enveloped the car, then swept on.

"Where is she?" Len Dougherty stuck his head out the window, his heavily lined face twisted in anger. "Dammit, I said where is she?"

"I assume you mean Katherine." From long habit, Sam referred to his grandmother by her first name. As he approached his Jeep, he didn't have to guess at the reason Dougherty wanted to see her. Obviously he had been served with the foreclosure notice.

"You know damned well that's who I meant," the man snapped, his eyes narrowing into slits. "And I'm telling you the same as I'll tell her. You aren't taking my land from me." He averted his gaze, as usual unable to look anyone in the eye for long. "That vineyard is mine. You don't have the right to take it."

"Any lawyer in the county will tell you otherwise, Dougherty," Sam replied evenly. "You borrowed money from Rutledge Estate and gave a first mortgage on your land to secure the loan. Now you've fallen behind in the payments and we are foreclosing. It's as simple and legal as that."

"Legal thievery, you mean," Dougherty retorted and tromped on the gas, sending bald tires spinning, kicking up gravel and more dust before they gained traction and the car sped off.

Sam followed its dust wake with his gaze until the car disappeared over the rise. He swept off his hat and ran combing fingers through his thick hair, the color of khaki. He had expected Dougherty to react to the foreclosure notice with outrage and anger. But, in Sam's opinion, the real outrage was Dougherty's neglect of the land, the way he had let it go to seed.

The ten-acre parcel had once been part of Rutledge Estate. Then, some sixty years ago, Dougherty's father had been killed in a freak accident at the winery, leaving his pregnant widow without money or a place to live. Out of pity and a sense of duty, Katherine had given his widow a small house on the estate and its surrounding ten acres of vineyard.

As far as Sam was concerned, it was time that land was once again within the boundaries of Rutledge Estate. As he pushed the hat back on, he threw a glance at the sun. At this time of day, Dougherty would find Katherine at the winery with old Claude.

Sam climbed into the Jeep and folded his six-foot-one-inch frame into the driver's seat, then drove off in the same direction Dougherty had taken, but with no thought of rescuing his grandmother. Even at ninety, Katherine Rutledge was more than capable of dealing with Len Dougherty. Or anyone else, for that matter.

A grove of cinnamon-barked madrona trees shaded the dirt yard outside the winery of Rutledge Estate. Built more than one hundred years ago, it was a massive structure of weathered brick that stood three-and-a-half stories tall. The cupola atop the roof provided the lone embellishment to its otherwise severe lines.

A pair of huge wooden doors marked the main entrance to the winery. One stood open, and it was through it that Katherine Rutledge walked, a silver-topped ebony cane touching the ground with each stride. She was a petite woman, weighing barely one hundred pounds. She walked with shoulders perfectly squared, her posture always correct, a fact that had more than one person proclaiming she had a backbone of iron.

Time had turned her once black hair an immaculate white. As a bride, Katherine had worn it in a fashionable bob; now it was styled in an updated version that framed her face in soft waves. It was a face that remained relatively unlined despite her years. Her features seemed delicate, almost fragile . . . until one looked into her eyes. There was a kind of power in their dark blue depths, the kind that came from the merging of intelligence and determination.

Claude Broussard was at her side. Fifteen years younger than Katherine, he had been the cellar master at Rutledge Estate from the time Prohibition had ended. French by birth, he was a stocky man with big hands, big shoulders, and an even bigger chest. Age had thickened his girth and grayed his shock of hair, but his step, like Katherine's, remained firm and his legendary strength undiminished. As recently as this winter, after a full keg of wine had tumbled from its pallet on a forklift, workers at the winery had watched in awe as Claude hoisted the thirty-gallon keg onto his shoulder and set it back on the pallet.

"A man called Ferguson came by the winery this morning," he informed Katherine. "He has purchased the vineyard planted by Cooper. He wished to sell us his grapes."

"What nonsense." Her response was immediate, her voice still carrying the lilt of her European finishing school. "How could we possibly buy his grapes when we have no idea who their parents are? I planted every vine on this estate, tended them, watched them grow from cuttings into maturity. Rutledge wine is made only from Rutledge grapes. If this man should call again, inform him of that."

In full agreement, Claude Broussard nodded. "As you say, Madam."

He had always called her that, from the moment of their first meeting in France when he was a mere boy. Never Madam Rutledge. Certainly never Katherine. To him, she had been always and simply Madam. An appellation others had picked up years ago. It was not uncommon for those in the industry to refer to wines bottled under the label of Rutledge Estate as Madam's wine. In the decade following the repeal of Prohibition, it had been used in jest, mocking her attempts to produce a red wine to rival the great Bordeaux from France. When her wines began to win in blind tastings against those from famed châteaux, it was spoken with respect and, more often, envy.

No small amount of the credit belonged to him as *maître de chai*, master of the cellar. Aware of that, Claude lifted his head a little higher. But his pleased look faded when an old Buick swung into the winery yard and stopped, the engine backfiring. A fine film of dust coated the old car's highly waxed surface, dulling its sheen. Claude cast a worried glance at Katherine.

Distaste flickered through her expression when she saw Len Dougherty climb out of the driver's side. She smoothed all trace of it from her face as he approached.

Her glance skimmed his graying hair and lined face. His olive green trousers sported knife-sharp creases down the legs and his striped shirt was stiffly starched. Appearance was everything to Len Dougherty, even now.

"You can't do this." He halted before her. Aqua Velva had been applied to his smoothly shaven cheeks with a heavy hand, but not heavy enough to mask the smell of whiskey. "You can't take my vineyard away. That land is mine. It belongs to me."

"If you wish to eliminate my claim to the property, Mr. Dougherty, you have only to pay me the balance you owe, and the land is yours," Katherine informed him.

"But that's more than thirty-five thousand dollars." Dougherty looked away, a watery brightness to his eyes, jaw clenched, hands trembling. "I can't get my hands on that much money before the end of October. I need more time." The protest carried a familiar wheedling note. "It hasn't been easy for me since I lost my wife — "

"She died some twenty years ago." Katherine had a voice like cut crystal, sharp enough to slice to the bone when she chose. She chose now. "You have sufficiently milked her death. Do not expect to gain any more from it."

He reddened. The infusion of color briefly eliminated the unhealthy pallor of his skin. "You are a cold and heartless old bitch. No wonder your son Gil hates you."

Pain. It struck swiftly and sharply. The kind of pain only a mother can know when she is hated by her child. A pain that hadn't diminished with the passing years, but rather deepened, just as Gilbert's hatred of her had deepened with time.

Unable to deny Dougherty's claim, Katherine stiffened, holding herself even straighter. "My relationship with Gilbert is not a subject I intend to discuss with you, Mr. Dougherty."

Dougherty had scored, and he knew it. "It must gripe the hell out of you that his winery is every bit as successful as Rutledge Estate. Who knows — in a few years The Cloisters might even be bigger."

A tan Jeep pulled into the yard and parked in the shade of the madrona trees. Out of the corner of her eye, Katherine saw her grandson Sam Rutledge climb out.

"I fail to see the relevance of your remarks, Mr. Dougherty." With a lift of her cane, Katherine indicated the papers gripped in his hand. "You have been served with legal notice. Either you pay the full amount owed or you forfeit your vineyard. The choice is yours."

"Damn you," he cursed bitterly. "You think you got me beat, don't you? But you'll see. Before I let you get your hands on my place, I'll burn every inch of it."

"Do that," Sam said as he joined them. "It will save us from bringing in a bulldozer to clear it." To Katherine, he said, "I flew over his place last Saturday when I took the Cub up." The Cub was the antique, two-seat biplane Sam had restored to flying condition two years ago. "From the air, I could see he'd let the vineyard grow wild. It's nothing but a jungle of weeds, vines, and brush now."

"I couldn't help it," Dougherty protested quickly, and defensively. "My health hasn't been good lately."

"Go," Katherine ordered abruptly, treating Dougherty to an icy glare. "I am weary of your eternal grousing and I am too old to waste more of my precious time listening to you." She turned to Sam. "Take me to the house, Jonathon."

Inadvertently she called Sam by his father's name, and Sam didn't bother to correct her. He had been a boy of fourteen when his father died twenty-odd years ago. Ever since, Katherine would slip now and then and address him as Jonathon. Over the years, Sam had learned to ignore it.

He escorted Katherine to the Jeep and helped her into the passenger seat, then walked around to the driver's side. As he swung behind the wheel, he heard her sigh, a note of impatience in the sound.

"Thinking about Dougherty?" Sam ventured, throwing her a glance as he turned the wheel and steered the Jeep onto a tree-shaded drive. "I have the feeling he's going to cause some kind of trouble before this is over."

"Dougherty does not concern me. He can do nothing."

The crispness of her voice made it clear the subject was closed; there would be no further discussion. Her mind could shut doors like that, on things, feelings, or people. Just the way she'd shut his uncle Gilbert from her life, Sam recalled as the Jeep cruised up the narrow lane.

Sam had been away at boarding school at the time of the split. In the valley there had been a hundred versions of what happened, a hundred causes offered for it. Any of them could be true. His father had never discussed it with him, and Katherine certainly never spoke of it.

Through lawyers, she had bought out any interest that her son Gilbert had in the family business immediately following the breakup. Gil had used that money plus more from investors, bought some abandoned vineyard property not five miles from Rutledge Estate, built a monastic-style winery, dubbed it The Cloisters, and successfully launched a wine of the same name, going into direct and open competition with his mother.

More than once, Sam had observed chance meetings between

them at some wine function. A stranger would never suspect they were mother and son, let alone that they were estranged. No hostility or animosity was exhibited. Katherine treated him as she would any other vintner with whom she had a nodding acquaintance — when she deigned to acknowledge him at all. But the rivalry was there. It was a secret to no one.

"I spoke with Emile this morning," Katherine said. Emile was, of course, Baron Emile Fougère, owner of Château Noir in France's famed Médoc region. "He will be attending the wine auction in New York next week. I have arranged to meet him there."

Her fingers closed around the cane's carved handle. Its presence was a constant reminder of her own mortality, something Katherine had been forced to acknowledge last year after she had been immobilized for two weeks from a fall that left her with a severely bruised hip and thigh.

In the time she had left, Katherine was determined to ensure the future of Rutledge Estate. As painful as it was to admit, she doubted that it would be secure in the hands of her grandson.

She cast an assessing glance his way. Sam had his father's strong muscles, his height and build. There was a coolness to his light brown eyes and a hardness to his features. And yet, he had never shown any pride in the wines that bore the name Rutledge Estate. And without pride, there was no passion; without passion, the wine became merely a product.

Under such circumstances, she had no choice but to look outside the family. This past spring she had contacted the current baron of Château Noir and proposed a business arrangement that would link the two families in a venture to make one great wine at Rutledge Estate.

An agreement in principle would have been reached by now if Gil hadn't entered the picture, proposing a similar agreement to the baron. He had done it to thwart and irritate her, Katherine was sure.

"Naturally you will accompany me to New York," she told Sam when he stopped the Jeep in front of the house.

"Naturally." Sam came around to the passenger side and assisted her from the Jeep.

Katherine turned to the house and paused, her gaze running over it. An imposing structure, it had been built twenty years before the end of the century by her late husband's grandfather. Modeled after the great châteaux in France, it stood two-and-a-half stories tall. Creeper vines crawled over its walls of old rose brick, softening their severe lines. Chimneys punctuated the steep slope of the slate roof and the windows were mullioned long and narrow with leaded-glass panes. It spoke of old money and deep roots.

The entry door of heavy Honduran mahogany swung open and the ever-vigilant housekeeper, Mrs. Vargas, stepped out. Dressed in a starched black uniform, she wore her gray hair scraped back in a chignon.

"That man Dougherty was here earlier, demanding to see you," the housekeeper stated with a sniff, indicating what she thought of his demand. "He finally left after I informed him you weren't in."

Katherine merely nodded in response as Sam walked her to the marbled steps of the front entrance. "Have Han Li fix some tea and serve it on the terrace," she ordered, then glanced at Sam. "Will you be joining me?"

"No. I have some things to do." Unlike Katherine, Sam wasn't so quick to dismiss Len Dougherty.

Sober, the man was harmless enough. But drunk, he was known to turn violent, and that violence could be unleashed on property or people. Sam intended to make sure it wasn't Rutledge.

Traffic clogged downtown St. Helena. Its postcard-perfect Main Street was lined with turn-of-the-century buildings of stone and brick, a collection of quaint shops and trendy restaurants. A Toyota with Oregon plates pulled out from its parking space, directly into the path of Len Dougherty's Buick. Cursing, he slammed on the brakes and the horn.

"Damned tourists are thick as fruit flies," he muttered. "Think they own everything, just like the Rutledges."

That thought had the panic coming back, bringing with it the tinny taste of fear to his mouth and the desperate need for a drink.

With relief Dougherty spotted the Miller Beer sign in the window of a crumbling brick building. The faded lettering above the door identified the establishment as Ye Olde Tavern, but the locals who frequented the bar called it Big Eddie's.

Leaving his car parked in an empty space in front of the bar, Dougherty went inside. The air smelled of stale tobacco smoke and spilled drinks.

Big Eddie was behind the bar. He looked up when Dougherty walked in, then turned back to the television set mounted on the wall. There was a game show on. Big Eddie loved game shows.

Dougherty claimed his usual perch, the stool at the end of the bar. "I'll have a whiskey."

Big Eddie climbed off his stool, reached under the counter, and set a shot glass and a bottle of whiskey in front of Dougherty, then went back to his seat and the game show.

Dougherty bolted down the first shot in one swallow, feeling little of the burn. With a steadier hand, he filled the glass again. He gulped down half of it, then lowered the glass, the whiskey flowing down his throat like lava. The foreclosure notice he'd stuffed in his shirt pocket earlier poked him in the chest.

Thirty-five thousand dollars. It might as well be three hundred thousand for all the chance he had of getting his hands on that kind of money.

Damn her eyes, he thought, remembering Katherine Rutledge's steely gaze boring into him. He threw back the rest of his drink and topped the glass again, dragging it close to him.

He lost track of time sitting there, one hand clutching the bottle and the other around the glass. More of the regulars drifted in. Dougherty noticed his bottle was half empty about the same time he noticed the level of voices rising to compete with the television. Tom Brokaw's face was on the screen.

The legs of a barstool scraped the floor near him. He glanced over as a baggy-eyed, heavy-jowled Phipps, a reporter with the local paper, sat down beside him.

"Hey, Big Eddie," a man called from one of the tables. "A couple more beers over here."

"Yeah, yeah," Big Eddie grumbled.

Dougherty cast a sneering look over his shoulder at a garage mechanic in greasy coveralls sitting with a painter in splotched whites. Common laborers all of them, he thought contemptuously. Punching time clocks, letting others tell them what to do. Not him. Nobody gave him orders; he was his own boss. Hell, he owned a vineyard. He —

He remembered the paper in his pocket and felt sick. He couldn't lose that land. It was all he had left. Without it, where would he live? What would he do?

He had to stop the Rutledges from stealing it. He had to find a way to get that money. But how? Where?

Nothing had gone right for him. Nothing. Not since Becky had died. His beautiful Rebecca. Everything had gone sour after he lost her.

Tasting that sourness again, Dougherty tossed back the whiskey in his glass. As he did, his glance fell on the television screen.

"In a scene reminiscent of the assassination attempt on President

Reagan," Tom Brokaw was saying, "New York State Senator Dan
Melcher was wounded tonight and a policeman shot. Kelly Douglas
has more on this late story from New York."

A woman's image flashed on the screen. Night darkened the edges
of the picture, held at bay by the full illumination of a hospital's
emergency entrance in the background. She stood before it, a kind
of restless energy about her strong and angular features that briefly
pulled his attention.

He looked down when she started to speak. "Tom, State Senator
Dan Melcher has been rushed into surgery suffering from at least
one gunshot wound to the chest. . . ."

That voice. His head came up fast. The low pitch of it, the smooth
ring of authority in it. There could be no mistake. He knew it. He
knew that voice as well as his own. It had to be her.

But that woman's face was no longer on the screen, its image
replaced by that of a middle-aged man coming out of a black car
flashing a smile and waving at the camera, ignoring the angry shouts
from picketers outside. There was only her voice — that voice —
talking over the images.

"Since his election to the state senate two years ago, Dan Melcher
has been the center of controversy. His liberal stand on civil rights
and pro-choice issues has created loud opposition. Tonight, that
opposition took a violent turn."

The voice stopped as a woman broke from the sign-carrying
crowd. "Murderer!" she shouted and started firing.

The ensuing flurry of action was difficult to follow. An aide
grabbed the slumping senator; a policeman fell; bystanders scattered amidst shouts and screams of panic; someone grabbed the
woman, and another policeman wrestled her to the ground. The
scene was followed by a close-up of the unconscious senator, blood
spreading across the white of his dress shirt. Then it cut to a shot of
him being loaded into the ambulance.

It was back to the woman. "We have just received late word that
the patrolman who was also shot has died of his injuries. The police
have the assailant in custody. Her identity has not been released.
Charges are pending." She paused a beat, then added, "Kelly Douglas, KNBC, New York."

Dougherty frowned. She didn't look the same. The coloring was
right — the auburn hair, the dark green eyes. And that voice, he
knew he wasn't wrong about it. She had changed a lot in ten years.
She had even changed her name, taken her mother's. But her voice
hadn't changed. It was her. It had to be.

He stared at the television, blind to the patriotic commercial for Maxwell House coffee flickering across the screen. Beside him, Phipps groused to Big Eddie, "They call that journalism. You couldn't write lousy copy like that and get away with it in the newspaper business."

Big Eddie shrugged his lack of interest. "A picture's worth a thousand words."

"Some picture," Phipps scoffed. "A pretty face in front of a camera pretending to be a reporter. Take it from me, everyone in television news is overrated and overpaid."

Len Dougherty half listened to the exchange. He was confused, his thoughts jumbled. He started to lift his glass, then abruptly shoved it away and pushed off his stool. He needed to think.

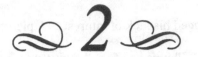

Kelly did the final standup live. She held her pose and position until the signal came that the network feed was complete. The lights were killed and she lowered the mike, dropping her calm, slightly grave on-air demeanor, a glow of triumph lighting her eyes and bringing a satisfied curve to her lips.

The producer, Brad Sommers, climbed out of the equipment-laden satellite van. Thirtyish, he was dressed in khakis and an L. L. Bean plaid shirt with short sleeves — New York country — a concession to the sultry heat of an August night in the city. Kelly was still too pumped from the adrenaline rush of covering the story to feel the stickiness in the air.

Brad gave a thumbs-up sign to Kelly and the crew. "We made network news on the West Coast." A version that was always updated with late-breaking stories to compensate for the three-hour time difference.

"We did it, guys." Flushed with the feeling of success and eager to share it, Kelly grinned at her two cohorts. "Back in Iowa where I come from, this is what we call 'walking in tall corn,'" she declared with a broad wink.

"Yeah, too bad it couldn't have been national, though." A stocky, fortyish, and balding Rory Tubbs shifted the camera off his shoulder and set it down.

"Yeah, that woman's timing was inconvenient as hell," the sound man, Larry Maklosky, mocked.

Rory flushed, realizing his innocent remark had sounded hard and insensitive to the tragic event that had left one policeman dead and a senator seriously wounded. Emotional detachment was necessary for anyone in the news business. It was his job to record events as they occurred, not react to them. That could come later.

"I didn't mean it like that," he grumbled in defense. "It's just that I've never had any of my stuff on national news before."

"You could still make tomorrow night's," Larry said with a wicked grin, always quick to needle Rory about something. Now that he had him going, he didn't let up. "All you have to do is pray the senator dies."

"Will you cut it out, for chrissake?" Rory glared the warning.

"Speaking of the senator, I'll see if there's any word from surgery yet," Kelly said, fully aware the story wasn't over.

Brad Sommers stopped her. "I'll go. You take a breather. I need to call in anyway. We should have a name on the woman by now."

Kelly didn't argue. Neither did she intend to completely let go of her high state of alertness. "Bring back some coffee. Black," she called after him.

"And a pizza," Rory added, jokingly.

Joining in, Larry cupped his hands to his mouth and shouted his order at the producer's retreating back. "I'll take a burger and fries and a chocolate shake!"

Kelly's stomach rumbled hungrily. She ignored it, something she had learned to do. In a business where the camera added ten pounds to anyone in front of it, dieting was a constant for all but a very few. Kelly wasn't one of those very few.

When she turned back, Larry shook a cigarette from his pack and offered it to her. She took it and bent close to the flame of his lighter. Tipping her head back, she blew out the smoke and lifted the heavy braid of auburn hair briefly off her neck.

"You shot some powerful footage, Rory." The warmth and admiration in her voice were genuine.

He beamed a little, then shook his head. "Man, when I think about it, I still can't believe how much I managed to get. I remember when Melcher came out, waving and grinning, I panned right to the pickets to catch their reaction. And this woman bursts out of nowhere —" Pausing, he frowned. "How did she get past the cops? Did either of you see?"

"I didn't," Kelly said with a touch of regret. "Unfortunately, I was looking the other way."

"I think the cops were concentrating too much on the guy who looked like a wrestler with an attitude," Larry offered, then glanced at the cameraman. "I saw some of the tape while they were editing it. Do you realize you even had the gun in the frame when she started shooting?"

"I thought she was carrying something, but I figured it was going to be a rotten tomato or an egg." Rory grinned. "I was excited thinking I might get a shot of a tomato splatting on Melcher's puss. But a gun . . ." He shook his head again and sighed, his expression turning serious when he lifted his gaze to Kelly. "Do you know we almost didn't get any of it? If you hadn't wanted to swing by —"

She cut in, countering, "If *you* hadn't told me about the pickets."

"If park security hadn't mentioned the pickets," Larry chimed in, adding another in the string of *if*s.

"Face it," Kelly stated wryly. "It was luck."

Rory gave her a long considering look, then smiled. "I don't know . . . I think there was some pretty sound instincts involved. Yours."

That was high praise coming from him. Kelly smiled back, moved by it, yet made uncomfortable by it, too. "I'm immune to flattery, Rory. Let's compromise and call it *lucky* instincts."

"You're right, Tubbs," Larry piped up. "It seems she has a nose for news. Guess that means we'll have to stop calling her Legs and start calling her Nose."

Kelly winced at that and complained, "What is it with you guys? Why do you always pick out nicknames that refer to some part of the body? Here it's Legs. In St. Louis, they took one look at my hair and started calling me Red."

"Very unimaginative," Larry said to Rory. "But that's St. Louis for you."

"And Legs is more imaginative, I suppose," she mocked, enjoying the exchange and the camaraderie. It kept her sharp, yet relaxed her, too.

"It's sexier." Rory grinned.

"I'll tell Donna you said that." Kelly made the threat with a straight face and only the faintest gleam in her eyes.

"Geez, don't do that," Rory protested, then started digging in his pocket. "I'd better call her while I got the chance. Rory Junior's been dealing her fits. He's cutting teeth."

He headed into the hospital. Kelly watched him dodge an arriving ambulance, and thought back to his compliment on her instincts. She wasn't sure that's what it had been. Getting some tape on the pickets had seemed merely logical.

They were already at Central Park doing a remote for the "Live at Five" report. It was part of the station's summer campaign to celebrate New York. Periodically the newscast was done partly from the studio and partly on location somewhere in New York. Previously they had used the Bronx Zoo and Shea Stadium in

Queens. This time, the site had been Central Park, with Kelly and the weatherman on hand, and the remote had gone off without a single glitch.

While they were tearing down and packing up, Rory had started chatting with one of the security officers. In passing, the guard mentioned that pickets were gathering at the Tavern on the Green restaurant in the park. He was headed there as soon as the TV people were packed up and gone.

When Kelly climbed into the station wagon to ride back to the studio, Rory relayed the information to her, treating it as a bit of interesting gossip.

Kelly suggested immediately, "Why don't we swing by since we're this close? We don't have to get to the studio right away."

If Kelly had taken the time to analyze her reasons for suggesting it, they would have been sound ones: Melcher was a controversial figure in New York politics; rumors abounded that he had his sights set on the governor's mansion; and his ultraliberal views had inflamed the state's conservative element. All of which meant State Senator Dan Melcher was an ongoing story, with the potential to become a major one in the future. Tape of the protest could be useful file footage for some later, in-depth story on the senator even if it didn't prove to be sufficiently newsworthy on its own.

As producer, Brad Sommers could have vetoed the idea, but he shrugged an indifferent "Go ahead."

Rory and Larry loaded the camera and sound gear into the station wagon and climbed in with Kelly and the driver. Taking Center Drive, they made the swing around to the Tavern on the Green restaurant.

Two dozen protesters, most carrying placards, milled in front of the building, kept away from the entrance by a mounted patrolman and two park security officers. Just as they arrived on the scene, a police cruiser pulled up and two more patrolmen stepped out to join the others.

Any hope the officers had of persuading the protesters to voluntarily end the demonstration died the instant the group saw the television crew drag their equipment from the wagon. Kelly dug a notebook, pen, and her press credentials out of the shoulder bag that served as a repository for a small clutch purse, her work notes, makeup, hair spray, and assorted paraphernalia. She spotted a patrolman conferring with a harried-looking man in formal dress near the restaurant entrance. With pad in hand, Kelly approached the pair. Neither looked particularly happy to see her.

"Hi. I'm Kelly Douglas with —"

The patrolman cut her off. "I know who you are, Miss Douglas." His expression was suitably grim but his glance was appreciative as it skimmed her face.

"What's going on?" She deliberately asked the obvious as she pocketed her press credentials and glanced back at the demonstrators.

A six-foot-two, muscled hulk of a man with a shaved head and a Fu Manchu mustache was arguing stridently with one of the officers. Rory Tubbs had his camera aimed at the confrontation, one eye tight to the viewfinder. Larry was behind him, trailing wires and a sound recorder.

"Miss Douglas, please," the tuxedoed man interposed, pulling her attention back. A nameplate on his breast pocket identified him as the assistant manager. He looked impatient, irritated, and more than a little anxious. "Don't let your cameraman take any shots of the restaurant. It can hardly matter where the banquet for the senator is being held."

She promised nothing. "Is the senator inside? I'd like to get a statement from him."

"He hasn't arrived yet." The patrolman volunteered the information, to the man's abject dismay.

Kelly seized on that immediately, aware it meant there could be an opportunity to get some footage of a face-off between the senator and the protesters. "When is he expected to arrive?"

The patrolman shrugged. "Any time."

A black Lincoln Town Car, polished to a high gleam, swung into the restaurant's drive. The assistant manager immediately tensed, his gaze fixing on the vehicle's darkly tinted windows in an unconscious attempt to penetrate the reflective glass and identify the occupants within.

Taking no chances, Kelly rushed over to alert Rory to the possible arrival of the senator. As the car pulled to a stop, he hurriedly changed position and angle to focus the camera on the Lincoln's rear passenger door.

Long seconds dragged by before the uniformed driver climbed out and moved to the rear door on the camera's side, opening it. An aide emerged first, followed closely by the senator. As usual, he wasn't accompanied by his wife, a wheelchair-bound victim of a drunk driver.

Recognizing their quarry, the protesters gave voice to their anger. The senator ignored them, his expression never losing its affable look as he paused to speak briefly to his aide. But he tugged at the cuffs of his white dress shirt, a nervous gesture Kelly had seen him make on previous occasions when something wasn't going well.

With the skill of an actor, he pretended not to notice the camera as he started forward. Flashing a confident smile, he waved. His former campaign manager and close adviser, Arthur Trent, climbed out of the car's front seat, catching Kelly's eye and nodding.

In her peripheral vision, she was aware of the forward surge by the protesters and the effort by the police to block them. She didn't see the woman slip past them — she was just suddenly there. Kelly saw the gun in her hand before she realized the sound she'd heard had been a gunshot.

The scene erupted in a flurry of frantic action — people scrambling for cover, the aide catching the falling senator, an officer reeling backward, someone struggling with the woman, police rushing to assist, and Rory maneuvering to capture it all on videotape. Kelly watched, thinking only professionally, allowing no other thoughts to intrude, yet aware all the while that they were the only camera crew on the scene.

Almost as suddenly as it began, it was over. The woman was facedown on the pavement, held there by an angry, white-faced cop hurriedly cuffing her. The aide had the senator cradled in his arms, a bloodied hand pressed to the wound in his chest.

"He's been hit!" he shouted, tears running down his cheeks. "Somebody get an ambulance!"

Kelly saw the mounted patrolman kneeling beside the downed officer, still holding the reins to his restive horse. She glanced at the blood oozing from a corner of the officer's mouth. Some part of her mind registered that it wasn't the officer she had spoken to. Rory had the camera aimed at the now sobbing woman, his fingers on the zoom.

Kelly laid a hand on his shoulder. "How much did you get?"

"All of it," he said, his concentration never breaking.

Hearing that, she raced inside to a pay phone and called the story to the news desk.

Contacted by cellular phone, the satellite van with Brad Sommers and its two-man technical crew arrived on the scene within minutes. By then, paramedics were loading the senator in an ambulance. A second one with the wounded officer on board was just pulling out, its siren screaming. The police had the immediate area sealed off and were methodically collecting the names and addresses of witnesses. Two other TV crews along with half a dozen print press, reporters and photographers, were there, adding to the confusion.

Flashing his credentials, Brad shouldered his way to them. "What's the latest?"

"I heard one of the paramedics say he didn't think the cop was going to make it," Larry answered.

"And Melcher?"

"Nobody is saying anything." Kelly had a glimpse of a paramedic holding an IV drip aloft as the stretcher carrying the senator was eased into the back of the ambulance. "We can't even get anyone to confirm he was shot."

"That blood on his shirt wasn't from a bloody nose," Rory inserted, the camera still balanced on his shoulder.

"Load up," Brad announced. "We'll follow them to the hospital. There's another crew on the way here. They can cover this end. Give me what you've got." He held out a hand for Rory's tapes. "I'll fire up the generator and edit on the way." To Kelly, he said, "Make your script a minute thirty. As soon as we get to the hospital, we'll do your standup and cut a sound track." The ambulance doors closed as Rory passed two tape cassettes to Brad. "All right, let's move it."

He sprinted for the satellite van, a marvel of high technology complete with its own power generator and small control room packed with editing and transmitting equipment. Lugging the camera and sound gear, they trailed after him and piled into the station wagon. Kelly flipped on the dome light and started scribbling on her notepad as the vehicle swung onto the road, directly behind the departing ambulance.

Subconsciously aware that what read well in print often sounded awkward when spoken, Kelly silently mouthed the words she wrote, at the same time making sure her script allowed for an introduction by the anchor. She also kept in mind that her script had to relate to the scenes in the tape without becoming a verbal description of them.

Not an easy task, especially when she had to write blind. Brad Sommers was in the satellite van, selecting portions from the cassette tapes and putting them together in a single edited piece that she hadn't viewed.

She finished the first draft, conferred briefly with Rory and Larry, then made adjustments based on some of the more dramatic pictures that had been captured on tape. She had time to do a quick polish and that was all before they reached the hospital.

While Rory and Larry set up to record her standup, Kelly slapped on some powder, blush, and lipstick. The action wasn't prompted by vanity, but rather the knowledge that the camera was notorious for washing out flesh tones. And any reporter, male or female, who looked ashen-faced didn't project the kind of image that inspired a viewer's confidence and trust.

As soon as her makeup was retouched, Kelly made a fast check with the hospital to get the latest on the senator's condition, made the necessary changes in her script, did the standup and narration for the edited tape, then drew her first truly easy breath.

She took another now, this time her brow knitting together in a small frown, that initial feeling of pride and satisfaction gone.

"I wish I could have seen the pictures Brad used," she murmured critically. "If only there had been time to review the tape."

"You did fine, Kelly," Larry assured her.

She shook her head. "I could have done better." She ran through the script in her mind, seeing a dozen ways she could have improved it — verbs she could have made stronger, more active, sentence fragments she could have used for dramatic impact, facts she could have tightened and punched up.

"It always has to be the best with you." The words were offered by Rory as an observation rather than a criticism, and one that was wholly accurate. To Kelly, the best was equivalent to success, and success symbolized approval and acceptance, two things that were vitally important to her even though that was something she couldn't admit, not even to herself.

"No wonder you're leaving us," Rory added, then paused to meet her eyes. "We're really going to miss you, you know."

Warmed by that unexpected admission from him, Kelly smiled. "You make it sound like I'm moving to some far corner of the world," she chided lightly to cover her own sudden surge of self-consciousness. "I'm only changing floors."

"Yeah, from local to network. That's like being shot into the stratosphere." He flipped his cigarette into the darkness, the glow of it making a red arc against the night shadows.

Network. It was a magic word. A goal she had strived toward ever since she graduated from college eight years ago. These last eight years had been hard ones, working sixty and eighty hours a week, making that long climb from a green television reporter at a small station in rural Iowa to being slotted to host a new magazine-style show on prime-time television. She had finally made it; she had her hands on the top rung — now all she had to do was hang on.

She felt a twinge of uneasiness at that thought, remembering the man she'd seen at the park earlier. Mentally she turned from it, forcing a lightness into her voice. "I haven't left yet, Rory," she said. "You're still going to be stuck with me for another week."

"True." He grinned.

Brad Sommers came out of the hospital at a trot. "They want you at the studio, Kelly." He waved the driver into the station wagon. "Now."

Kelly tasted disappointment. This was her story; she had broken it, and she wanted to file her reports for the eleven o'clock news from the scene. But she didn't resist when Brad Sommers took her arm and propelled her to the station wagon. With her new job at the network only days away, this was no time to risk getting labeled hard to work with and temperamental.

Minutes later, the driver let her out at the Fiftieth Street entrance to the seventy-story building that would forever be called the RCA Building by New Yorkers despite its new owner's attempts to rename it the GE Building. With her shoulder bag bumping against her hip with each quick stride, Kelly crossed the black granite lobby to the security desk.

The uniformed black guard on duty saw her coming. "Caught your special report, Miss Douglas." He opened the gate for her. "How's the senator?"

"Still in surgery." She stopped long enough to sign in.

"He's a good man. Be a shame to lose him."

"Yes."

As she swung toward the bank of elevators, someone called, "Going up?"

Kelly caught the small trace of an English accent and smiled even before she saw British-born Hugh Townsend holding an elevator for her. Slim and, as always, nattily dressed in a summer gray suit from his favorite Savile Row tailor, he had a lean and narrow face and an aristocratic fineness to his features. His neatly clipped hair was dark brown, bordering on black, with traces of silver showing up at the sides to give him an appropriately distinguished air. His manner could be aloof or charming, depending on the situation or the company. With Kelly, he invariably emphasized the charm.

"You're working late tonight, Hugh." She was never sure how to describe him — friend, mentor, adviser, or, as senior producer for the new magazine show, boss.

"Actually I planned to leave an hour ago, but I stayed to catch the latest news on the telly." He waited until she was inside the elevator, then punched the button for her floor and glanced sideways, his hazel eyes gleaming with approval. "Splendid work."

"Was it?" She still had some misgivings about that.

"It was."

The doors slid closed and the elevator started up with a slight lurch. Kelly made a mental note to get a copy of the aired report to review later in the privacy of her apartment. There she could play it over and analyze her mistakes — whether in scripting, delivery, or facial expression. It was sometimes a painful way to learn, but she had found it to be the best.

"A pity, though, that the woman didn't wait until next week to shoot the esteemed senator. What an exit that would have made for you."

"As well as great prepublicity for the new show, right?"

His look matched her wryly amused glance. "That thought did cross my mind."

"I thought so."

"Join me for a late dinner when you finish and we'll celebrate your coup with a bottle of wine. 'For wine inspires us, and fires us with courage, love and joy.' "

"You have a quote for every occasion, don't you?"

"Not *every* occasion." Hugh paused reflectively. "Perhaps we should have a Margaux tonight. The 'eighty is a charming wine."

"What? No 'forty-five Latour to celebrate?" Kelly mocked lightly.

He arched a dark brow, humor and challenge blending. "When you win me an Emmy, Kelly, that will be an occasion truly worthy of a 'forty-five Latour."

"An Emmy? You do have high ambitions, Hugh."

He met her glance, a half smile hovering around his mouth. "You surely didn't think you had a monopoly on that, did you?" The elevator stopped at her floor, the doors swishing open. "I'll have a car waiting for you downstairs."

"Dinner sounds wonderful, Hugh, but . . ." She could already hear the sounds of frantic activity coming from the newsroom. "It's going to be a wild night. When it's over, I'll want to go home and crash."

He slid a hand under the French braid, his fingers unerringly locating the tightly banded cords in her neck. "It will be hours before you wind down enough to sleep." He gave her a gentle push out of the elevator. "Dinner."

Dinner, she thought.

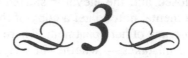

*I*t was midnight when Kelly walked out of the building onto an empty sidewalk. All the street vendors had long ago wheeled their pushcarts home, and the panhandlers had given up their search for easy marks.

The heat had eased and the traffic had thinned, leaving the streets quiet — as quiet as they ever got in Manhattan. A garbage truck lumbered along Fiftieth making its nightly rounds. A few blocks away, a siren screamed, accompanied by the deep-throated blast of a fire truck's horn.

Kelly pulled the strap of her bag higher on her shoulder, breathing in the rough night air that was New York. She spotted the lone car waiting at the curb and headed for it. When she reached it, the driver was there, holding the rear door open for her. Kelly slung her heavy shoulder bag onto the seat and slid in beside it.

Softly over the rear speakers came an old song by Hall and Oates. Mentally she tuned it out, dug in her bag and took out a bulky folder. Crammed inside were pre-interview notes and a lengthy bio on a Harvard professor-turned-author she was scheduled to interview on tomorrow night's "Live at Five" report. His weighty tome chronicling the country's economic woes was also in her bag. Kelly flipped on the reading light and searched through the sheaf of papers for the bio, as always filling what otherwise would have been idle time with work.

The car turned onto Park Avenue and joined the scattering of taxis and limousines speeding along the thoroughfare, past darkened shop windows and closed stores. Not five hours ago the street had been clogged with traffic, drivers bad-tempered from the heat and noise.

Within minutes the car arrived at an upscale address off Park Avenue. Sighing in vague irritation, Kelly cast a distracted glance at the canopied entrance to the elegantly understated French restaurant, then gathered her things and stepped from the car.

Inside it was cool and quietly pastel, precisely the sort of restaurant that would appeal to Hugh Townsend. Subtly chic without being trendy, the lighting subdued, the walls covered with pale florals, the atmosphere was one of polish, not glitz. She breathed in the scents of French cooking — burgundy, thyme, sage.

The maître d' recognized Kelly. "Good evening, Miss Douglas. Mr. Townsend has been expecting you. This way, please."

From his chair at a corner table, Hugh Townsend watched her cross the room, his attention drawn to the way she walked. There was nothing particularly sexy or flirtatious about it, yet it was the kind any man would notice. Her strides were long and graceful, the swing of her hips subtle, her head up and her eyes ahead.

Kelly Douglas had changed considerably from the first time he'd seen her. That had been on tape. Actually he'd heard her before he saw her. He'd caught the rich, mellow sound of her voice as he was passing the editing room. His curiosity and interest aroused, he had looked in.

His initial reaction to the female on the monitor had been totally negative — dark, lank hair falling straight past her shoulders, tortoiseshell glasses, strong yet rather bland features, a mannish jacket. But that voice — he had stepped into the room and listened to her speak intelligently about the plight of the homeless, becoming impatient when other people and voices took over the screen.

Gradually he had noticed the hint of red in her hair, the dark green of her eyes behind the corrective glasses, a complexion that was the delicate porcelain of a true redhead, the slim figure beneath that severely tailored suit, and the energy — the intensity — that crackled from her. He had been intrigued by the potential he saw, even if she did look like some repressed librarian.

"Who's the girl, Harry?" he had asked the editor.

"Kelly — something or other." He had reached over and checked the cassette box. "Yeah, Kelly Douglas. She's with our affiliate in St. Louis. She sends her pieces regularly. Wants to break into network, I guess." The editor had paused then and flashed Hugh a grin. "Helluva voice, eh?"

"Indeed," Hugh had murmured thoughtfully, then said, "Mind if I take the tape? I'd like to review it later."

"Be my guest." The editor had punched the eject button and handed him the cassette.

Hugh had been between projects at the time, and bored. After playing the tape several times, he had found little to fault in her journalistic skills, and he had remained captivated by her voice, its warm, calm pitch and subtly authoritative ring. But her appearance had offended his own innate sense of taste and his producer's eye.

Countless times in the past he had advised his paramour of the moment on clothes, hairstyle, makeup, to the resentment of some and the gratitude of others.

In the end, he had called and arranged for her to come to New York, ostensibly for an interview. A week later she had been in his office at NBC while a part of him had stood back and mocked him for playing the role of Henry Higgins.

Ah, but the result of his efforts had stilled the laughter. Permanently.

As Kelly neared the table, Hugh stood up and waited until she sank into the chair opposite him, her oversize shoulder bag sagging to the floor.

"What's the latest?" He resumed his seat.

"Melcher is out of surgery. In critical condition but stable." She picked up the menu and laid it aside, putting temptation out of her path. "The woman has been identified as one Delia Rose Jackson. Formerly Sister Mary Teresa and recently under psychiatric care after being arrested for trashing an abortion clinic and stabbing a nurse. No known association with the pro-life group."

"'Thou shalt not kill,'" he murmured.

"The sixth commandment." Kelly picked up her water goblet and paused, holding it in midair. "You saw the broadcast."

"No. But I would have been disappointed if you hadn't referred to it."

"I used it over a family photo of her taken in a nun's habit." She took a sip of water and lowered the glass, staring at the cubes of clear ice. "A police officer slain by a former nun. Ironic, isn't it?"

"And tragic."

"Very tragic," she said, barely containing a sigh. With an effort she lifted her head and mentally shook off the thought. Violence, tragedy, death — she dealt with such stories every day. She had learned not to let them touch her, not to let her feelings become involved. She glanced around the restaurant. "This is nice. I've not been here before." The other patrons, she noticed, seemed to be from the after-theater crowd.

"The food is superb. And the wine list —" He paused for effect, a smile curving the line of his mouth. "— is excellent."

"*The* deciding factor in your choice, no doubt." Kelly lifted her water goblet in a mock salute. Hugh Townsend had long been a wine connoisseur, a confirmed oenophile. Another irony.

"No doubt." The corners of his mouth deepened with his growing smile. "We can order now if you're hungry."

"Famished," she admitted. A juice and bagel for breakfast, a spinach salad for lunch, and three spoonfuls of yogurt before the eleven o'clock newscast to ward off the shakes had been the sum total of her food intake in the last twenty-four hours or so. Which was just about average.

Hugh signaled to their waiter, who came promptly to their table. "We'll order now."

"Very good, sir," he replied and turned to Kelly. "What would you like this evening, madam? I can highly recommend the rack of lamb. It's prepared with —"

"No, thank you." She cut him off before her resolve weakened. "I'll have a green salad, no dressing. Broiled cod with lemon only, no sauce." She ignored his pained look. "Coffee later. Decaffeinated, please."

"You will ruin the wine." Hugh arched her a look of sharp criticism, then addressed the waiter. "Bring Miss Douglas the coq au vin."

"Hugh —"

He raised a hand, cutting off her quick protest. "We are here to celebrate. You can work off the extra calories tomorrow during your morning session with Rick," he said, referring to her personal trainer.

As part of a strict regimen to keep her weight under control, Kelly went to a fitness center three times a week. In St. Louis she had run ten miles every day; in New York that was unthinkable. So Kelly routinely subjected herself to a series of grueling exercises, carried out under the supervision of her personal trainer, Rick Connors.

"The man is a sadist," she said under her breath and raised no further objection to the change in her food order. Coq au vin was, after all, only chicken cooked in wine.

For himself, Hugh ordered the duck à l'orange, then asked for the wine steward. The sommelier arrived, wearing his chain and tastevin. With half an ear, Kelly listened while the two conferred on the wine list.

Wine was an obsession with Hugh.

Three years ago when he had asked her to come to New York,

she had been eager — desperate — to make a favorable impression. Wine had proved to be the means. . . .

From the background material she had read on Hugh Townsend, his office at NBC was what Kelly had expected it to be — leather chairs, a spotless oak desk, oil paintings on the wall, a definite air of understated elegance. The grainy photographs of him, however, had not done the man justice. They had captured his sharp features but missed the patrician fineness of them, just as they had failed to register the charming arrogance of his smile and the warm gleam of his eyes.

"Welcome to New York, Miss Douglas." He came around the desk to shake hands.

Kelly was nervous, and equally determined not to let it show. "Thank you, Mr. Townsend. It is truly a pleasure to be here." She paused a beat, then reached in the small shopping bag she carried and removed the boxed gift. "This is forward of me, perhaps, but I grew up in Iowa. We have this custom of always bringing a little something to our host."

An eyebrow shot up. "A gift?"

"A way of thanking you for the interest you've shown in my work," Kelly replied.

He waved her to a seat. "May I open it now?" he asked, his curiosity plainly piqued.

"Please." She sank onto the leather chair and forced herself to appear relaxed.

There was no careless tearing of the wrapping paper and encircling ribbon. Instead he used a knife-sharp letter opener to slice through the ribbon and securing tape, freeing the box from the tissue. She watched while he opened it and lifted out a wine bottle. When she saw his hand glide over the bottle in a near caress, she allowed herself one deep, sweet, long breath.

His glance ran to her, sharp with question and interest. "This is an historic wine."

"I know." Confident now, Kelly settled back in the chair. "The 'seventy-three Stag's Leap cabernet sauvignon was the first California wine to outscore Haut-Brion and Mouton-Rothschild in a blind tasting held in Paris in 1976. Many, though, consider the 'seventy-three Rutledge Estate cabernet to be superior to Stag's Leap, but it was unfortunately not entered in the competition."

Thoughtfully he set the bottle on his desk and cocked his head. "How did you know I enjoyed fine wine?"

Kelly smiled. "I did my homework."

"Obviously," he replied and waited for a further answer.

"One of your biographies mentioned you were a member of a distinguished wine society," she explained. "I took the chance that you were not one of those total wine snobs who turns his nose up at our premier California wines."

"You took quite a gamble, Miss Douglas." He negligently leaned a hip against the desk and folded his arms, regarding her with frank interest.

"You took a gamble on me, Mr. Townsend," she countered.

"Perhaps we shall both be winners," he said. "Tell me, how do you know so much about the Stag's Leap wine? More homework?"

"In a way. I was born in Napa Valley." It had been years — not since the day she left the valley had she admitted any connection to California. She had created a new past for herself, one that held none of the embarrassment, pain, and humiliation of her real one. But this time her place of birth could be a definite asset.

"Really? For some reason, I thought you were born and raised in Iowa." Hugh glanced at his desk top, clear of all papers, as if to recheck her résumé.

"Few people grow up in the same community where they were born. Moving from place to place seems to be an American trait. In my case, the move was to Iowa." Kelly thought she had handled that very effectively, without actually lying. "Years ago, when I was in high school, I became curious about my birthplace and wrote an article about the wine country of Napa Valley for the paper. I think you'll admit, wine — the making of it and the drinking of it — has a certain cachet that fascinates everyone."

"Indeed," he agreed. "I would be curious to read that article of yours."

"I'll dig out my scrapbooks and send you a copy," she lied. She didn't have the article, and even if she had, she wouldn't have sent it to him. "But I warn you, the writing is very amateurish. It was done back when I had aspirations of becoming a print journalist."

"That was before you discovered television, of course."

"Of course."

"What are your aspirations now?"

"My goal is to become a national correspondent by the time I'm thirty," Kelly replied.

"How old are you now?"

"Twenty-seven."

"You still could make it —" Nodding, he straightened from the desk and came around it to face her, his arms still folded in front of him. "*If* you throw out those glasses, do something with your hair, and trade that mannish business suit for something more stylish. Your schoolmarm look may play well in St. Louis, but it will never make it on network."

Kelly stiffened, stung by his sudden and blunt criticism. She curled her fingertips into the chair's leather arms to keep her hands from flying defensively to her tortoiseshell glasses and the big black — sophisticated, she thought — bow that held her long hair together at the nape of her neck.

She had always known she wasn't pretty. At best, she was attractive in a plain sort of way. She had worked hard to achieve this trim and neat, studious appearance. It hurt to have him be so censorious of it. It hurt more than he could possibly know.

But hadn't she endured a lifetime of ridicule and snickering looks? The sounds of children in the schoolyard laughing and singing that horrible chant — "Fatty, Fatty, two-by-four, can't get through the kitchen door" — would be forever in her memory. But she didn't burst into tears and run anymore. Kelly had learned not to reveal she was hurt by something someone said.

Instead, Kelly brought her hands together, steepling her fingers and regarding Hugh Townsend coolly over the top of them. "My appearance has nothing to do with my competency as a journalist."

He looked amused. "I beg to differ with you, Miss Douglas. Television is a visual medium. Appearance is everything. Therefore, it is important how you look."

She desperately wanted to lash out at him, but she maintained an outward calm. "I am well aware that I am no beauty queen."

"If you were, I probably wouldn't be talking to you now. A person's looks should never distract, or attract, a viewer's attention from the story."

"This is sexist." Kelly attacked out of pure self-defense.

"Hardly." He laughed, a soft, dry sound all the more cutting for its brevity. "You have either forgotten or you are too young to remember the great debate that went on at Black Rock a few years ago over whether Dan Rather should wear a suit and tie or a sweater."

"Black Rock?" She seized on the irrelevant in an attempt to divert the flow of the conversation.

"That's what we call the CBS Building."

"I see."

"I assure you, Miss Douglas, in this business men get called on their looks the same as women. Should he grow a mustache or shave it? Let his hair go gray or dye it? Should the tie be plain, striped, or paisley? There is always the problem of fleeing hairlines — should he wear a hairpiece or have implants? In all cases, the question becomes, Does it distract the viewer?" He gestured to her. "The glasses, the hair, the severe line of your clothes distract."

She wanted to argue, to point out that Sally Jessy Raphaël wore glasses. Even NBC's Bryant Gumble occasionally slipped on a pair of reading glasses. Sophia Loren wore glasses, as did Woody Allen, Steven Spielberg, and a dozen other personalities.

But she raised none of those points. Instead she simply said, "But viewers remember me."

"A good journalist would want them to remember the story," he replied, and Kelly found herself cringing inwardly from the gently administered verbal slap. "There happens to be an opening for a reporter at our affiliate station here in New York," Hugh continued. "I've set up an interview for you tomorrow. In the meantime, I have arranged for an optometrist to fit you with contact lenses this morning. From there you will go to the stylist — Sigmund is one of the best in Manhattan. When Sigmund is finished with you, we'll meet at Saks and pick out more appropriate attire."

"What is this?" Kelly broke in.

He merely smiled and said, "Consider it an assignment. A camera crew will be along to record the events. This evening you will have an opportunity to write your story, edit the tape, and put it all together. Tomorrow you can take the finished story with you on the interview as a demonstration of your journalistic skill." He paused, his smile deepening. "Well, Miss Douglas?"

She was being challenged. Kelly didn't like it; she didn't like any of it. But she didn't see where she had a choice. She had to accept.

"What time is the appointment with the optometrist?"

"Thirty minutes from now. I have a car waiting downstairs for you."

Less than two hours later, Kelly walked out of the optometrist's office wearing a pair of extended-wear contact lenses that could be safely left in around the clock. After a four-hour session with Sigmund, her hair was three inches shorter, leaving it slightly longer than shoulder length; a body wave had added fullness and shine to her hair, bringing out its natural, deep red lights; and her makeup had been thrown out in favor of a warmer palette containing brown and gold eye shadows, peach-toned blushes and lipsticks, and light beige foundation. At Saks, her pin-striped charcoal suit was replaced by a silk and linen piqué jacket worn over an apricot silk dress with a matching suede sash.

When she saw her reflection in the boutique's full-length mirror, Kelly stared at the woman before her. She hadn't suddenly become a raving beauty. But to her the change was stunning. Her mahogany hair fell in full, thick waves about her face, a face that didn't look nearly so plain. The lines of the jacket and dress were still tailored, but softly so, the material loosely draping her figure. And the colors were . . . flattering.

"You were right," she told Hugh.

"Rare is the woman who can admit that to a man," he observed dryly. To which she laughed and executed a slow pirouette in front of the mirror. "Are you comfortable with your new image?"

"Yes." And strangely enough, she was.

The story proved easy to write, and the tape even easier to edit. The interview went smoothly. Perfectly, Kelly thought. She was right. One week later she was offered the job. She gave the station in St. Louis two weeks' notice and started packing.

That had been the beginning of her friendship with Hugh Townsend. She had come to trust his judgment and his instincts. Through him, she had met the right people and made the right contacts. Vital in a city like New York and in an industry as competitive as television.

It was the second time in her life she had had a male friend, someone to share her dreams with, someone to talk to — even if she had never been able to bring herself to confide to him the pain of her past.

The sommelier returned to the table with the bottle of wine Hugh has chosen to accompany their meal. Many times Kelly had observed the wine-tasting ritual, but she never ceased to watch, always both amused and fascinated by the rite.

First the wine steward presented the bottle, label to the front, for Hugh's inspection. At Hugh's confirming nod that the wine was as he had ordered, the bottle was uncorked with a subtle bit of flourish.

A small amount was poured in Hugh's wineglass, a snow white serviette wrapped around the bottle neck to absorb any stray drop. Kelly watched as Hugh picked up the glass by its base, a forefinger curled under it and a thumb on top, the mark of a true expert and a technique that Kelly hadn't mastered. He held the glass against the white of the tablecloth, assessing the depth of the wine's ruby red color.

Satisfied, he lifted the glass and swirled the wine with a cunning flick of the wrist, watching it ride up and seep down the sides of the glass, judging its viscosity — legs. Raising the glass, he thrust his aquiline nose into the glass and inhaled the wine's aroma — bouquet. Then he tasted it, slowly, rolling it in his mouth and letting it glide over the surface of his tongue into his throat. Finally he set his glass down, nodding his approval to the sommelier.

"Very good."

The steward bowed at his pronouncement. "Shall I let it breathe and serve it later?"

Hugh shook his head. "Pour it now. It will open up in the glass."

"As you wish." He filled both glasses and left the bottle on the table, withdrawing with another retreating bow.

Hugh fingered the base of his goblet and quoted softly, "'And when I depart from the earth to appear before my beloved Lord to account for my sins, which have been scarlet, I shall say to Him: "I cannot remember the name of the village; I do not even recollect the name of the girl, but the wine, my God, was Chambertin!"' Hilaire Belloc," he added, crediting the source.

"That is not very flattering, Hugh," Kelly chided.

Rousing himself, he smiled. "Then I will offer another. 'What though youth gave love and roses, age still leaves us friends and wine.' Thomas Moore, I believe."

"Much better," Kelly declared. "Although I still say you have memorized every reference to wine in *Bartlett's*."

He laid a hand across his heart in a mock oath. "I shall never tell."

"I didn't think you would." She glanced at the bottle. "A Burgundy. What happened to the Bordeaux? An 'eighty Margaux, wasn't it?"

"Very astute." His dark head dipped in brief acknowledgment. "You have not only an eye, but an ear, for detail. I had thought a Margaux, but I decided a Chambertin would better complement the roast duck."

"Of course." Kelly smiled, then sighed, suddenly feeling weary.

"Tired?"

She nodded. "It's been a long day. I had forgotten the pressure, the stress, and the exhilaration there is in the field when you're covering a breaking story. Basically I've spent the last two years as a newsreader and interviewer, doing the odd special series on rape or drugs or AIDS." She remembered the sheaf of work notes and the book, weighting her shoulder bag. "I really should have gone straight home tonight. I have an interview tomorrow with an economics professor who has written a book that I still have to prepare for. Plus one with a heart-and-lung specialist on Melcher's condition."

"I am glad you mentioned interviews. I meant to tell you Robert Mondavi will be attending the wine auction next week."

"That's wonderful." The wine auction, held every July to benefit charity, was a pet project of Hugh's. His efforts for this year's event had been directed at persuading as many as possible of the world's most renowned vintners to attend. Few names in California wine carried the élan of Robert Mondavi.

"More than that, Mondavi has agreed to appear on Friday's 'Live at Five' report to promote the auction on Saturday."

"Really. Maybe I'll get assigned to interview him," she said, not really caring.

"You will," Hugh informed her. "I've already arranged it."

"Have you?"

"Yes. He has also agreed to come to the private reception Friday evening at my place. You haven't forgotten about the party, have you?"

"I have it on my calendar. Written in red."

"I expect you to come."

"With the list of luminaries you have coming, I wouldn't miss it. Besides, Friday's 'Live at Five' will be my last newscast for the station. I'll be ready to kick up my heels a bit."

"And let your hair down as well?" His glance flicked to the glossy coil of her hair, a few tendrils escaping to curl softly about her face and neck. "That is a combination I would like to see. You work too much and play too little, Kelly."

"Probably." Smiling, she lifted a shoulder, shrugging off his observation. "But what can I do? It's the old Iowa work ethic coming through, make hay while the sun shines and all that," Kelly joked, then added, "Besides who has time to play in this business?"

Her day seldom varied. She was up by seven to catch the three networks' morning shows and the CNN coverage on the four television sets in her living room, and to scan the morning editions of the *New York Times,* the *Wall Street Journal,* the *Washington Post*, and the *Daily News,* all of which were delivered to her door. Three times a week she was at the fitness center by ten for a torture session with her personal trainer, followed by a much-needed hour with the masseuse.

By two in the afternoon, she was in her office at the station, handling any phone calls or correspondence and preparing for a three o'clock meeting with the producers, editors, director, writers, their ranking assistants, and her co-anchor on the newscast to go over the day's stories, the lineup for the show, and the length of the reports. Then she returned to her desk to write her copy, then back for a final meeting before airtime, the five o'clock newscast. The process was repeated all over again for the news at eleven. Rarely did she return to her Gramercy Park apartment before midnight.

Sandwiched in between all that were business luncheons with her agent, special assignments that took her out of the studio, as well as various political, social, or media functions the station wanted her to attend.

She had a woman come in once a week to clean her apartment, but there were always clothes to drop off or pick up at the cleaners, hand-washing to do, groceries to pick up, monthly bills to write, dishes to wash, trash to take out, and a myriad of other tasks.

Her weekends were invariably filled with the things she had planned to do during the week and hadn't found time for. Any free hours she managed to squeeze out of her schedule, she usually spent trying to raise money and public awareness for neglected and abused children, the one thing outside her work she was passionate about.

Except for an occasional evening with Hugh, her social life was virtually nonexistent. A fact that didn't bother her very much.

Once, a few months ago, she had walked into the studio and caught the crew in the midst of a discussion about sexual habits. Sex and sports seemed to be the favorite topics of every crew she'd worked with.

"Hey, Kelly. Come on, tell us yours," the light man, Andy Grabowski, had urged, to a chorus of hooted agreement from the others.

If their hope had been to make her blush, she had disappointed them. Instead Kelly had thrown them a frown of mock reproval and said, "Are you kidding? My only sexual habit is abstinence."

They had laughed, but she had meant it.

"You need to schedule some playtime for yourself, Kelly," Hugh stated.

"Speaks the man who scheduled a meeting bright and early on my first Monday morning I've had free in months."

"We have a show to produce, stories to line out, future subjects to be considered."

"I know." She wasn't objecting. "Sometimes it doesn't seem real that I'm actually going to do 'People and Places.' I honestly thought Linda James would get it."

"As did a great many people."

"With cause." The waiter arrived with their entrées. Kelly withdrew her hands from the table, giving him room to set the plate in front of her. "When she signed on as the West Coast correspondent for NBC, I heard they planned to develop a prime-time newsmagazine show around her."

"Plans change." Hugh nodded to the waiter as the man retreated.

"Obviously."

Hugh lifted his glass in a toast. "To your exclusive newsbreaking story."

Kelly raised her wineglass, making sure to hold it by the stem as wine etiquette demanded. "And to the show 'People and Places.'"

They touched glasses, then sipped. As always, Hugh savored his a little more, then nodded approvingly. "It has softened, mellowed perfectly."

"Shall I offend you totally by saying it's very nice?" Kelly grinned at him wickedly.

"Please." He feigned a shudder. "It is big and racy, with marvelous balance and a long finish. Never, but never, call it nice."

"I stand corrected," she said, still grinning. After a bite of wine-roasted chicken, Kelly returned to their previous subject. "I don't know what favor you called in or whose arm you twisted to get me on the show, Hugh, but thanks."

"I did nothing more than put your name on the table. Your brief stint as guest host on the 'Today' show, when Katie Couric was off on maternity leave, did the rest." He lifted his wineglass and eyed her over its rim. "You do realize that by the end of the third show, the ratings had gone up almost a half point. And the credit for that certainly didn't belong to the guests on the show. The lineup was deplorable."

"It was," she agreed with a slight roll of her eyes in remembrance. "It's funny, but I hoped my exposure on the 'Today' show might land me a position as a national correspondent. But a prime-time magazine show — never, even though I knew yours was in development." Kelly lowered her fork. "Seriously, Hugh, why did they pick me when Linda James has more experience and more national exposure?"

"Careful," he chided. "Your insecurity is showing."

But he knew few people in this business who weren't a mass of insecurities. In Kelly's case, however, she had an inferiority complex a mile wide. He doubted that anyone else had seen it but him. To the world Kelly projected an image of easy calm, an image totally at odds with the intense, organized, ambitious woman she was. A woman who rarely slept more than six hours a night and lived on the run. A woman hungry for recognition, desperate for approval, and emotionally starved. But she hid that well, under about three feet of steel.

She laughed, the sound coming from low in her throat, and lifted her wineglass, wagging it briefly. "Then be kind and stroke my ego a little."

"Very well." He liked those flashes of total honesty. "The format of our show is basically one of entertainment — interesting people, interesting places. Linda's reputation for asking the so-called tough question actually goes against her. She lacks your warmth, your ability to put people at ease. You achieve the same results of getting them to talk, but without grilling them. And, you are a new face. Which is precisely what the powers-that-be decided they wanted."

"I won't disappoint them." It was almost a vow.

Hugh concealed a smile and covertly studied her. *Wholesome* was an adjective he would never use to describe her. Her features, taken together or separately, had a strong, earthy quality that was non-threatening. She was not the girl-next-door. More like a young Mother Nature with the red of the sun in her hair and the green of the grass in her eyes. The more Hugh thought about it, the more he liked the analogy.

"I had an idea for the show that I wanted to run by you before Monday's meeting." Kelly speared a green bean from its bed of mixed vegetables. "A profile on Harry Connick, Jr., the singer who does those old Cole Porter songs and ones from the Big Band era. He's becoming quite popular. . . ."

He listened to her expound on the idea, paying more attention to her voice than her words. More than once Hugh had fantasized about what it would be like to have Kelly whispering in his ear.

During the first few months he'd known her, he had taken her out with every intention of ultimately taking her to bed. When he hadn't met with early success, he hadn't minded. Being British, he knew the chase was often more exciting than the kill.

One night he had made his move. Kelly had stopped him with a simple and well-placed "No," and pulled back to the outer edge of his arms.

"As much as I like you, Hugh, I don't want to become intimately involved with you. Lovers I can get. Friends are rare. Besides, an affair would be too tacky, don't you agree?"

With any other woman, Hugh would have dismissed the words as a token protest, made so that he would talk and kiss her into agreement to prove how much he wanted her.

Not Kelly. The determined look in her eyes, the firm lift of her chin, a dozen other things in her body language informed him that she meant every word. He laughed and released her, then lit a cigarette.

"I wouldn't call it tacky, precisely." He smiled.

"A mistake certainly. We both know it isn't wise to get involved with anyone in the business. It was a mistake I made once."

"Let me guess — your lover was a cameraman," Hugh said and smiled wryly when he saw her startled look. "Nearly every female in television has a cameraman somewhere in her past. I've never understood the attraction, but obviously there is one. Care to tell good old Hugh about it?" he joked.

"There isn't much to tell. It didn't work. He thought his career was more important than mine. One day I woke up and realized I was in a destructive relationship. I broke off with him, which made things very awkward at the station."

"Where was this?"

"Iowa. A couple months later I was offered a job in St. Louis and I left. So . . ." She took a deep breath and smiled at him. "I would rather have you as a friend, Hugh."

"Friend."

They had shaken hands on it.

At the time he had thought he wouldn't be seeing her again. What would be the point if he couldn't bed her? And for a while he hadn't. Then he had begun phoning her now and again, taking a vaguely proprietorial interest in her progress, regarding her as his discovery. He admired her drive, her intelligence and determination.

Hugh also suspected that if they had had an affair, he would never have suggested Kelly for the show. Which would have been a pity because she was perfect for it.

". . . do you think of the idea?" she finished.

"Sounds like it could be interesting. Present it at the meeting."

The sommelier returned to the table to top their wineglasses. Kelly covered hers, as usual limiting herself to one glass of wine. Hugh had never known her to consume more than two. She exercised equally strict control over her food intake, he noticed, glancing at the chicken she pushed around on her plate, barely half of it gone.

There was still half left when the waiter came to clear their plates. Kelly assured him the coq au vin had been delicious.

Over coffee they talked more about the new show, bandying about various ideas. Finally Hugh called for the check and the car.

It was two in the morning when Kelly walked into her apartment, a one-bedroom that she had furnished slowly, meticulously, and, most important, personally. She paused a moment, breathing in the faint scent of lemon oil and pine that told her Audrey had been in to clean. There was no smell of stale cigarettes, no sickly sweet odor of empty whiskey bottles. She had escaped that forever.

Turning, Kelly set to work on the door's trio of locks. When her fingers touched the last, a simple sliding bolt, they lingered. She stared at its shiny brass surface, seeing it and seeing another that had been very similar to it.

Suddenly she was ten years old again, confidently — if ineptly — gripping a screwdriver in her right hand and struggling to attach the simple lock to her bedroom door. . . .

The point of the screwdriver slipped off the head of the screw, gouging a nick in the door's painted wood. She breathed in sharply at the mark it left, the breath hissing through clenched teeth. Hurriedly she fitted the screwdriver back in the slotted head and began turning the grooved handle, leaning all her weight against it to drive the brass screw into the wood.

With one ear tuned for the sound of a car in the drive, she worked frantically to get the lock fastened in place. She had to get it done before he came back. *She had to.*

Finished, she stepped back and surveyed her handiwork, not with satisfaction, but with relief. Her bedroom had become a refuge now, a place where she could go, bolt the door, and be safe. She released a long shaky breath and smiled. She was safe now. Safe from his drunken rages. . . .

Or so she had thought, Kelly remembered and closed her eyes, hearing again the pounding on her bedroom door, the rattling of the doorknob, the bellow of anger when the door wouldn't budge, then the horrifying sound of a body throwing its entire weight against the door. . . .

*   *   *

She sat all hunched up in the farthest corner of the bed, the covers pulled protectively around her as she stared at the small brass bolt, willing it to hold. Her mouth was dry, her throat tight, too tight to let a sound out, a breath out.

Again he rammed his body against the door. This time she heard the splintering sound of wood tearing and giving. She knew at once she shouldn't have done it — she shouldn't have put that lock on the door. Now he was mad and it was her fault. Another crash, and the door gave, sagging on its lower hinge. A well-placed kick and it swung drunkenly open, then clattered to the floor.

"A goddamned lock!" He advanced toward the bed, a big dark silhouette stumbling over the fallen door. "You put a goddamned lock on the door."

The slurring of his voice told her what she'd already guessed — he was drunk again. "I didn't mean to." Her hands came up to ward off the anticipated blows. "Honest, I didn't."

"You're a goddamned liar." He grabbed her wrist with one hand and swung with the other, the flat of his palm slamming into her cheek with a force that snapped her head to the side. The coppery taste of blood was in her mouth and the stench of his whiskey breath blew over her face as he hauled her up by the shoulders and shook her hard. "Don't you ever lie to me again."

"I won't." The promise was little more than a whimper.

"By God, you better not, or next time I'll take a belt to you. You hear?"

She nodded once, her eyes blurring with tears as she took care to do nothing and say nothing that might ignite his anger again.

Kelly opened her eyes and slowly slid the bolt home. It was that man at the park. He had reminded her of all this. As much as she tried to forget, the past was never more than a memory away.

A bold sparrow hopped closer, crossing the line from bright sunlight to cool shadow in its search for table crumbs. Sam Rutledge idly watched it as he sat crosswise on a wrought-iron chair, an arm draped along the back of it, one leg hooked over the other, his thick hair showing the tracks left by combing fingers. His weathered hat sat on the green-striped cushion of the chair seat next to him. Katherine occupied the one opposite him.

Lunching alfresco on the rear terrace was a Tuesday ritual — weather permitting, which it usually did in California. It was one of the few meals they shared together, even though they lived in the same house.

But the Rutledge family had never made a practice of gathering together at mealtimes, not even when Sam was growing up and his parents were alive. Everyone had always been too busy — his father in the vineyards, Katherine at the winery, his mother with her paintings. When Sam was small, his meals had been brought to the nursery; later he had eaten in the kitchen with the servants. On the rare occasions when the whole family dined together, for Sam it had been like eating with strangers.

Even now Sam had his routine, Katherine had hers. Rarely did they coincide, and rarely did either attempt to make them coincide.

The land, the vineyards, and the winery composed the only bond between them, blood the only tie, and mutual respect the only emotion. As for affection, Sam had long ago found it impossible to give what he never received.

The vines came first; people and their feelings second. It was an unwritten law on Rutledge Estate, one Sam had been raised under by his father and by Katherine.

"I think Emile will find the terms of the proposal quite equitable,"

Katherine remarked, drawing Sam's attention back to the table. "Do you have any comments on it?"

"No." A draft of the proposal was on the glass-topped table. He had glanced through it before lunch, then laid it aside. Sam didn't reach for it now. Instead he dragged his iced tea closer and ran his fingers over the wet sides of the glass. "It seems to cover all the major points. I don't see anything that's been left out."

"Then you approve?"

"What you've lined out makes good business sense," Sam replied truthfully, aware it wasn't his personal approval she was seeking. Just as she had never consulted him before making the proposal to the baron, or asked whether he was in favor of it. If she had, she would have found out he didn't like the idea at all. If he thought it would change anything, he would have told her, but Katherine didn't care what his personal feelings were toward it. Sam knew that, too.

At this point it was no more than a proposal. With his uncle in the picture, it might never be more. Aware of that, Sam saw no reason to dwell on it, especially when he had other things on his mind.

"Flying in to New York on Thursday will give us Friday to rest and prepare for our meeting with Emile on Saturday morning. That should be ample time, I think."

"It should."

The slight breeze smelled of dust and roses. He swung his glance across the sweep of lawn flanked by flower gardens Katherine had created half a century ago out of a tangle of wild vines, scrub brush, and impenetrable manzanita.

The house stood on a wide shoulder of a mountain, its rear terrace facing Napa Valley. A concrete balustrade ran along the edge of the mountain's shoulder, marking the end of the gardens and green lawn. Beyond it stretched the valley and the opposite wall of mountains, seared yellow by summer heat and a long drought.

Dust hung in the air, a constant reminder of the tinder-dry conditions. One cigarette carelessly tossed by a tourist could easily start a major fire, and at this time of year, the roads in the valley were jammed with vacationers touring the multitude of wineries.

One carelessly tossed cigarette or one well-placed match: Sam hadn't been able to rid himself of that thought. Except for that one confrontation with Len Dougherty, there had been nothing. The man had been quiet. Too damned quiet, in Sam's opinion.

"Did I tell you we will be staying at the Plaza?" Katherine poured

hot tea into a dainty porcelain cup, aromatic steam rising from it to
add its scent to the air.

Sam frowned. "Isn't the wine auction at the Waldorf?"

"Yes." She added a twist of lemon. "Which will ensure privacy
for us at the Plaza." She stirred her tea and watched the surface
swirl as if absorbed by it. "Clayton and I stayed at the Plaza," she
said almost idly. It took Sam a second to realize she was referring
to her late husband and not his cousin Clay who had been named
after their grandfather. "He had wanted to take me to Europe on
our honeymoon, but Europe was in the throes of the First World
War so we spent a month in New York instead. We had a marvelous
time."

Her expression softened, as it always did when she spoke of her
late husband, Sam's grandfather. Seeing it, Sam could almost imagine Katherine in love, yet he still found it difficult to imagine her
deferring to anyone's wants and desires except her own.

"I remember we saw Will Rogers," she mused. "He was starring
in the *Ziegfeld Follies* at the time. That was before he went to Hollywood, of course, and —"

"Excuse me, Madam," Mrs. Vargas broke in, the thick rubber
soles of her shoes silencing any sound of her approach. "Mr. Rodriguez is here to see Mr. Rutledge. He insists it's urgent."

Sam glanced past the housekeeper and saw Ramón Rodriguez
standing outside the French doors to the terrace, anxiously fingering
the hat he held in front of him, sweat running down his face. Ramón
was one of a crew of three men Sam had sent out earlier to check
and repair boundary fences.

"What is it, Ramón?" In one motion, Sam was on his feet. Something told him the quiet was over, even before Rodriguez answered.

"It is old man Dougherty. We were over by his place and he went
loco, started shooting at us." The words tumbled from him as he
gestured, using his hands and his hat. "He's got Carlos and Ed
pinned down. I got to the truck and got out of there as fast as I
could."

"Call the sheriff and get him out there." Sam flung the order at
Katherine as he grabbed his hat and headed for the door.

"Where are you going?" She tapped her cane on the flagstones.

"To Dougherty's."

"Why?" Katherine demanded. "There is nothing you can do. The
sheriff will handle it when he arrives."

Halting, Sam threw her an impatient glance. "I hired those men,

Katherine. And I sent them out there to check the fences. I am not
about to sit here while Dougherty is taking potshots at them."

She didn't agree with his reasoning or his decision; that was evident from her expression. Sam didn't waste time arguing his case.

"Call the sheriff," he repeated, and pushed through the French
doors. The wide central hall opened before him and he broke into a
run. Ramón was right behind him, the hall echoing the sound of their
footsteps beating across its marbled floor.

Out the front door and down the steps, Sam headed straight for
the estate pickup Ramón had left parked at the head of the drive.
The key was in the ignition. He climbed into the driver's side and
turned the key, stepping on the gas and gunning the engine. The door
on the passenger's side was yanked open, Ramón's stocky frame
filling it as he scrambled onto the seat. Sam waited a split second to
make sure Ramón was all the way in the truck, then popped the
clutch and peeled up the drive.

"What happened? Give me all of it this time." Barely slowing,
Sam swung the pickup onto a narrow dirt road, one of several that
crisscrossed the property, linking the vineyards, pastures, and winery together.

"I don't know. It happened so fast." Ramón struggled to arrange
his thoughts in some semblance of order. "We were checking the
fences, like you told us. When we get to the north side, we find a
section down. A fence post, it had rotted —"

"Where on the north boundary?" Sam knew every inch of Rutledge land, every dip and rise, every tree and rock on it. Dougherty's
ten acres formed a rectangular piece that butted Rutledge property
on two sides, carving a corner out of it.

"You know where the fence runs halfway down the slope, above
where Dougherty's house is? It is there, in the middle of it." Using
his hands, Ramón tried to illustrate the exact location. "When we
find the rotted post, Ed and Carlos — they stay to dig it out and
I go back to the truck to get a new one. On my way back, I
hear somebody yelling — Dougherty, I think — then *boom! boom!
boom!* — he starts shooting."

"Ed or Carlos, were they hit?" Sam pictured the spot in his mind.
It was a new vineyard, the young vines in the middle of their second
summer's growth.

"I don't think so. When I called to them, Ed shouted they were
okay." He paused and shook his head uncertainly. "The last time I
saw them they were on their bellies, making love to the ground."

Hearing that, Sam felt a rising anger. It jumped along his jawline as he increased the truck's speed, dust plumes rising like rooster tails in the vehicle's wake.

"What about Dougherty? Where was he?" He didn't even try to guess the reason Dougherty had suddenly opened fire.

"Somewhere by the house, I think. I couldn't see." Ramón lifted his shoulders in an expressive shrug.

Within minutes of leaving the house, they reached the point where the dirt road angled sharply to the right. Braking, Sam slowed the truck and pulled off the track onto the grassy shoulder. This was as close as they could get by road to the property line the estate shared with Dougherty, still one hundred yards distant. From here, they'd have to go by foot.

Beyond the road, the land rose gently to a rounded knoll, ringed with tiered rows of young vines and crowned by a high blue sky. Sam climbed out of the truck and paused briefly. With the rising terrain blocking his view of the trouble site, he strained to hear some sound that might indicate the current state of the situation. The stillness was broken only by the breeze whispering through the vines and the odd noise from the pickup's rapidly cooling engine. There were no gunshots, no shouts. Sam wasn't reassured by that.

"This way." Ramón headed across the road toward the vineyard on the other side. Sam followed.

The plowed ground between the young vines formed an aisle that circled the swell of ground. The dry earth showed tracks of previous usage, confirming that this was the route the crew had taken. Sam spotted the fence line and slowed his steps when Ramón did. The sun was at his back, its searing rays burning through the cotton of his shirt and heating his flesh.

As they neared the corner post, Sam heard the sharp crack of a rifle shot. A yelp of pain followed it as he and Ramón hit the ground.

"You aren't going to get me to fall for a fool trick like that!" The shouted statement came from Len Dougherty. Sam recognized his voice at once. "You can tell the Rutledges for me that I'm wise to their ways."

"How the hell are we supposed to tell them anything, Dougherty, if you keep shooting at us?" Ed Braiser shouted back, more anger than fear in his voice. But the appeal for reason was lost on Dougherty.

"Yeah, you'd like me to let you crawl outta there, wouldn't you?"

Crouching low and using what cover the young vines offered, Sam worked his way closer, moving past Ramón. Ed Braiser and Carlos Jones were a good fifty yards away, hugging the plowed ground next to the fence line. Carlos was closest, with Ed stretched out behind him, lying on his side and rubbing his right hand as if it pained him. A broken shovel handle lay in the next vine row, the ends of a knotted white handkerchief fluttering from the top of it. The other half of the shovel was on the ground near Ed. A surrender attempt that had obviously failed.

Satisfied that neither man appeared hurt, Sam slipped into the next row to get a better view of Dougherty's place. A narrow and rutted weed-choked lane led to the shallow valley high on the mountainside. Years of neglect had turned the once small but tidy cottage into little more than a shack. The paint had long since peeled from the boards, leaving them gray and rotted in places. The area immediately around the house resembled a junkyard of rusted and abandoned machinery parts. A jungle-thick growth covered the rest of the ten acres.

The neglect, the decay, the deterioration of the place was enough to anger Sam. Grimly he scanned the area and finally spotted Dougherty's wiry frame hunkered down behind his shiny Buick, using the hood for a gun rest. A whiskey bottle sat on the ground beside him.

"What do we do, boss?" Ramón crouched down next to him.

Sam had been mulling that same question over in his mind. Suddenly the rifle cracked again, kicking up a puff of dust directly in front of Carlos. Carlos flattened himself to the ground, covering his head with his hands.

"Dirty rotten snakes, you aren't going to crawl out of here after you tore down my fence!" Dougherty shouted. "Try that again and I'll put a bullet through you."

"That settles it." Sam's voice was lower than a murmur. After making one last thorough sweep of the area, he backed away. Any thought of waiting for the sheriff or his deputies to arrive and defuse the situation had been discarded the instant Dougherty had made his threat.

"What do you think?" Ramón joined him.

"Do you hear any sirens?"

Ramón listened a moment, then shook his head. "No."

"Neither do I." With the demands of the heavy summer traffic and the shortage of staff mandated by countywide budget cuts, there was no telling when a car might be dispatched to the scene. Whether it was two minutes or twenty, either seemed too long. Sam pressed a hand on Ramón's shoulder. "You stay here."

"Where are you going?"

"Down there." With a jerk of his head, Sam indicated Dougherty's place. "If I can, I'll create a diversion and, hopefully, distract him long enough for you to get those two out of there."

"He will shoot you." Ramón looked at him with widened eyes.

"Not if he doesn't see me." Sam was counting on that.

Staying out of sight of the shack, Sam worked his way down the slope to the fence along the west property line. There the overgrowth of grapevines and weeds in Dougherty's vineyard offered heavy cover. He ducked between the wires and slipped into the leafy tunnel of vines. With the location of the dilapidated cottage and Dougherty fixed in his mind, he made his way toward it with slow and silent stealth — something he hadn't practiced since he was a boy, when playing Indian and sneaking up on people had been his favorite pastime.

The thought crossed his mind that he wasn't a boy anymore and Dougherty wasn't a vineyard worker or one of the maids. Before he could question what the hell he was doing there, the rifle cracked again, and the thought was forgotten, pushed aside by the conviction that Dougherty had to be stopped before somebody got hurt.

Sweat trickled down his temples. Sam wiped at it and paused to get his bearings. Not a breath of breeze penetrated the thick vegetation. The hot air was stifling, pungent with the smell of thick vegetation and ripening grapes. He batted at an insect whirring near his face and pressed on, dimly conscious of heightened senses that had made the buzz of the insect sound loud.

Dougherty shouted something and his voice sounded close. Much closer than Sam had expected. With increased caution, he crept toward the tall weeds at the end of the vine row. Through the brown stalks he spotted Dougherty, half lying and half leaning across the Buick's waxed fender and hood. All of his attention was still focused on the slope, beyond the range of Sam's vision. But the rifle was clearly visible. It looked like a military carbine, an old army issue. Sam had a vague memory of once seeing Dougherty in uniform marching in a Memorial Day parade to honor the area's war dead.

Taking advantage of the cover, Sam studied the area close up. The car was parked near a corner of the house, angled away from the front steps. From the car to the vineyard, there was nothing but open ground. If he could get the house between them . . .

On that thought, Sam retreated a few yards and found an opening between the gnarled trunks of the old vines. He took off his hat and pushed it ahead of him as he wiggled through the space on his belly, closing his eyes against the slap of leaves and weeds. He cut across two more rows in the same fashion, careful to keep the rustling sounds to a minimum.

A quick check confirmed the tumbledown dwelling blocked him from Dougherty's view. Rising from his crouch, Sam moved swiftly across the weed-choked clearing to the house. Cautiously he worked his way around to the other side of it and peered around the corner. He could see the rear tires and part of the car's green top. That was all.

He edged his way along the side of the building, planting each foot with care. The sweat was running from him now, but oddly his mouth was dry. He wetted it, conscious of the pounding of his heart, nerves strained to a high pitch of alertness. He hadn't been involved in a brawl since his college days, but right now the adrenaline was pumping and he was primed for a fight.

When he reached the corner of the house, the hood of the Buick was directly in front of him. He stopped, waited a beat, then looked around the corner.

Len Dougherty hadn't changed his position. He was still propped against the hood, muttering to himself something about the Rutledges. Sam measured the distance between them. Three long, quick strides and he'd be behind him.

There was still no wail of a siren in the distance.

"For chrissake, Dougherty, will you stop shooting and let us get outta here?"

The instant Ed Braiser yelled out from the slope, Sam crossed the intervening space. Reaching out, he tapped Dougherty on the right shoulder. Startled, Dougherty pushed off the car, whirling to the right, away from Sam, and bringing the old carbine with him. Sam grabbed the barrel in one hand, spinning Dougherty the rest of the way around, and seized the rifle stock in the other. With a twisting jerk, he wrested the weapon from Dougherty's grip and used the same movement and momentum to shove the man backward. Off balance, Dougherty fell to the ground.

Automatically Sam yanked the magazine clip and ejected the bullet in the firing chamber. There was a movement in his side vision, far up the slope, as the two workers scrambled to safety. Dougherty started to rise, preparing to launch himself at Sam, his face mottled with rage.

"Do it," Sam urged, his voice low and vibrating with a barely controlled anger. "Give me an excuse to ram this rifle butt down your throat."

Dougherty had taken a couple jolts of whiskey earlier to get rid of his hangover, a little of the hair of the dog that bit him. But he was sober enough to realize he was too old to be tangling with a younger man like Rutledge. He sank back on his elbows.

"Make you feel big to knock an old man around?" he jeered.

"You may be old, Dougherty, but you stopped being a man years ago." Sam stepped back in disgust. But he was still close enough to smell the sickeningly sweet stench of whiskey.

A marked car careened up the rutted lane and swerved to a stop near the Buick, its lights flashing and its siren silent. A uniformed deputy got out of the driver's side and approached with caution, his holster flap unfastened and his hand on the butt of his gun.

"What's going on here?" His glance ran from the prone Dougherty to the carbine in Sam's hands.

"He was shooting at two of my workers." Sam passed the weapon to the deputy, keeping the muzzle pointed skyward. "I already unloaded it."

"You just can't stay out of trouble, can you, Dougherty?" The deputy shook his head at him.

Outraged, Dougherty clambered to his feet. "He's the one in trouble." He jabbed a finger in Sam's direction. "I didn't do anything wrong. A man has a right to defend his property and that's what I was doing. They were tearing down my fence and I stopped them." He turned to Sam. "This land doesn't belong to you yet. And I swear on my Becca's grave, it never will."

"You crazy fool, is that what this was about?" Sam challenged, his voice thick with anger. He flung a hand in the direction of the slope. "Those men weren't tearing down that fence. They were repairing it until you started shooting at them." He paused, his eyes narrowing. "My God, you could have hit one of them."

"Not likely," Dougherty scoffed. "I only hit what I aim at."

"You hope," Sam countered.

"You calling me a liar?" Dougherty bristled and punched a hand to his chest. "I've got a sharpshooter's medal to prove it. I could have shot them anytime I wanted to, but all I did was scare 'em and keep 'em pinned down."

"Nobody got hurt then, is that right?" The deputy looked to Sam for confirmation.

He glanced at the slope. Ramón and the other two workers had moved back into the open again. "It doesn't look like it."

The deputy hesitated. "Do you want to press charges, Mr. Rutledge?"

"What are you asking *him* for?" Dougherty demanded. "He's the one trespassing on my property."

"Don't push it, Dougherty," Sam warned, his temper again near the flash point. "Or I'll have you hauled up on assault with a deadly weapon." To the deputy he issued a clipped "You know where you can find me."

He walked away, turning a deaf ear to the empty threats Dougherty shouted after him.

Under the deputy's watchful eye, the rotten post was replaced and the wire restrung. Not until it was done did the deputy leave, taking the rifle with him and telling Dougherty he could pick it up in a few days after he'd run it through ballistics. That had tasted as bitter as the lecture he'd gotten.

When the patrol car pulled out of the yard, Len Dougherty stormed into the house, snatched up a nearly empty whiskey bottle, and sloshed some in a dirty glass, still seething from the injustice of it all. He knew exactly where the blame belonged — right at the feet of the great Madam and her high and mighty grandson. Between them, they had turned everyone in the valley against him.

He tossed down the liquor in the glass, drinking it in one big swallow and welcoming the fiery burn in his throat. Immediately he refilled the glass, emptying the bottle, and flopped down in the lumpy armchair that had doubled as his bed after he'd passed out the night before.

Cigarette butts and ash spilled over the sides of the cracked and chipped ceramic ashtray on the end table next to him. The walnut-stained wood was pockmarked with the blackened scars of old cigarette burns. Empty matchbooks, crumpled cigarette packs, and other unidentifiable bits of trash were piled around it. The only relatively clean area on the table was occupied by a cheaply framed photograph of a young, dark-haired woman, smiling shyly and anxiously from it.

Len slouched against the stained cushions and stared at the amber-brown liquor in his glass. "Thought they could tear down my fence, but I showed 'em. I showed 'em." He grunted in emphasis and took another drink of whiskey, rolling it around in his mouth before swallowing it. Then he turned his head and gazed at the picture. "I showed 'em, Becca," he repeated, very softly.

He let the empty whiskey bottle slip from his hand and tumble onto the seat cushion, wedging there against his thigh. Carefully he picked up the photograph and propped it on his lap, facing him. Grief and a vague kind of anger twisted his face.

"Why did you have to die, Becca?" he moaned. "Why did you go and leave me? You know I was never any good without you. It wasn't fair for you to die. It wasn't fair when I needed you so much."

A sob threatened to escape his throat. He swallowed it back with another gulp of whiskey. He looked at the photo again, this time with watery eyes.

"We had such dreams, Becca. Such dreams for this place." His voice was husky and soft. He sniffed noisily. "I won't let them take our land. I swear that to you, Becca. I'll find the money. I'll get it somewhere . . . somehow. Maybe . . . maybe . . ." He let the thought trail off unspoken, the fragment of an idea — a hope — spreading across his face. He returned the photograph to its former resting place and smiled. "I'll get it. You'll see."

He drank down the rest of the whiskey in his glass and pushed out of the chair. With surprising purpose in his stride, he crossed to the door and slammed it behind him as he left the house and headed straight for the car.

Half an hour later, he pulled up in front of the crumbling brick tavern and went in. The hanging fixture over the pool table threw its light on the green felt surface and left the lone player in shadow. Billiard balls cracked together as Len crossed to the bar.

"I need some change for the phone." He slapped a crumpled ten-dollar bill on the counter. "I gotta make a long-distance call."

"Does this look like a money-changing place?" Big Eddie grumbled, but he pocketed the ten and took a roll of quarters from the cash register drawer, then slid it across the counter to Len.

Tightly gripping the paper-wrapped tube of quarters, he headed back to the rest rooms and the pay phone on the wall. Once there, he hesitated and rubbed a hand across his suddenly dry mouth. Maybe he should have a drink first. Just one short shot. He immediately rejected that thought.

A dozen times he'd tried to work up the courage to make this call, and each time he'd drunk a little too much courage. Not this time. He'd promised Becca.

Still he hesitated before reaching for the receiver, and ran a hand over the stubble of his day-old beard. He wished he had shaved, cleaned up a little before making the call. It was important to make the right impression.

Why the hell was he worrying about that? It was just a damned phone call. It didn't matter how he looked.

Before he confused himself with more crazy thoughts, Dougherty snatched the receiver from its hook and punched 0 for the operator.

A woman's voice came on the line. "Thank you for using AT and T. May I help you?"

"Yeah, I want to call . . ." He had to search a minute before he remembered the name she was using. ". . . Kelly Douglas in New York."

"And the number, please?"

"I don't know the number."

"You can contact information directly by dialing area code two-one-two, five-five-five, one-two —"

"No, you get me the number," he broke in impatiently, then caught himself, and tried to summon up some of the old charm that had once worked so well for him. "You see, I'm calling from a pay phone, miss. I don't have a pen or any paper to write it on."

"That is a problem," she agreed pleasantly. "One moment and I'll get it for you."

"Thanks." He waited, chewing nervously on his lower lip, his mouth getting drier by the second. Then came the bad news — according to New York information, there was only one Kelly Douglas in the book and that number was unlisted; under no circumstances could it be given out. "But this is an emergency," he protested in agitation. "I have to get ahold of her."

"If you will state the nature of your emergency and leave a number where you can be reached, we will be happy to relay the message to the individual party so that they may contact you."

"No, that won't work. I've got to talk to her myself." He pressed a hand to his forehead, trying to think. "Look, let's try her at work instead, okay?"

"Where does Miss Douglas work?" the operator asked.

"She's a television reporter. She works for — the one with the peacock, NBC."

"Shall I make it a person-to-person call?"

"What? Oh yeah, right, person-to-person." He shifted his weight from one foot to the other and grabbed on to the metal telephone coil, the tension working on his already frayed nerves.

Soon there was a ringing sound on the other end of the line. It continued for an intolerable number of times before it was finally answered by a brisk voice. "Good afternoon, NBC."

"I have a long-distance call for Kelly Douglas, please," the operator announced.

"Kelly Douglas? One moment." There was a brief pause. "Miss Douglas does not work here."

With that, his control snapped. "That's a goddamned lie! She works there. I know she does. I just saw her on the news a couple days ago."

"I'm sorry, but —" the voice attempted to continue.

"She told you to say that, didn't she?" His fingers throttled the metal cord as his face flamed red with rage. The operator said something, but he was beyond hearing. "You put her on this phone right now! Do you hear me? I want to talk to her." He continued to shout his demands into the receiver. It was several seconds before he realized no one was listening; the phone was dead. In anger he rammed the receiver onto its hook. "She'll talk to me. By God, I'll make her talk to me," he vowed.

But first he needed a drink.

5

*T*he studio lights blazed, bathing the anchor desk and its occupants in hot light. Beyond the bright arc, the rest of the studio lay in shadows. The bulky studio cameras and their operators, the stagehands, sound technicians, makeup man, production assistants, and the studio stage manager were dimly lit shapes arrayed around the anchor set. All of them were mindful of the labyrinth of black cables on the floor, waiting to trip the unwary.

At the anchor desk, Kelly faced camera three and waited for a cue that she knew was only seconds away. Her long hair was plaited in a French braid, a few tendrils escaping to soften the look and conceal the earpiece that kept her in direct contact with the control room and the technicians on the floor. A microphone was pinned to the lapel of her smoke blue jacket, an unobtrusive adornment next to the blue-and-gold paisley scarf at her throat.

The red light on camera three came on, followed by the anticipated hand signal. "Governor Cuomo was in New York today to — " As Kelly began to read the copy on the TelePrompTer screen, strategically placed directly below the camera lens, the screen went blank. With no noticeable break in her delivery, Kelly referred to the papers in front of her, a printed copy of the TelePrompTer's script that she kept with her as a precaution against just such an eventuality. "— meet with city leaders and discuss the assistance the state might be able to provide to help the city out of its current budget crisis. John Daniels has more on that story."

Facing the camera, Kelly continued to appear perfectly composed, but over her headset she could hear the executive producer in the control room shouting for pictures and the director repeating the order, adding a few choice obscenities. She glanced down, ostensibly at her papers, but in reality at the small monitor concealed in the anchor desk. She saw only her face.

On television, three seconds of dead air could seem like an eternity. With nerves on edge, Kelly switched papers to the next story in the lineup in case this one was shifted to later in the hour. Then her face faded abruptly from the monitor, replaced by that of John Daniels standing in front of City Hall.

"All right." The stage manager's voice echoed the relief Kelly felt. "The tape runs a minute thirty, then we come back to you, Kelly, for the tag."

Kelly nodded and leaned back in her chair, letting her arms hang. She raised her voice slightly to address everyone in the studio. "If you guys wanted to make my last broadcast memorable by turning a bunch of gremlins loose, you have succeeded."

There were a few faint chuckles from behind the cameras, and Chuck, her co-anchor, grinned. "We just wanted to make sure you didn't forget the thrills of live television."

"Thanks a lot," she murmured dryly.

The first of the minor glitches had occurred minutes before they had gone on air. One of the production assistants had come up to Kelly while she was being miked by an audio technician. She informed Kelly that she wouldn't be interviewing Robert Mondavi; his flight had been delayed and he wouldn't make it to the studio in time for the broadcast.

"Then we'll be scratching that segment." In her mind, she had been thinking they could insert a short tell story on Saturday's gala wine auction.

"No. Townsend showed up with a substitute. They're in makeup now."

"Who is it?" Kelly hated to go into an interview cold, with no previous knowledge of the guest, his background, accomplishments, or the unique tidbits that might make him interesting to the viewer. There was too much risk of asking stupid questions that revealed her ignorance.

"I can't remember the name, but don't worry — we'll write up an introduction and a list of questions for you." The assurance had been barely out of her mouth when she had been called away, leaving Kelly with the uncomfortable feeling that she might have four very long and potentially awkward minutes of airtime to fill with an unknown guest.

Then three minutes into the broadcast a light had exploded, show-

ering a corner of the anchor desk with glass fragments. Shortly after
that, a fly had landed on Kelly's nose and taken an exploratory stroll
across her cheek, an unwelcome distraction made worse by the fact
that the subject of the story was the city's sanitation department.
The latest mishap had, of course, been the sudden failure of the
TelePrompTer.

It was almost enough to convince Kelly her final appearance on
the show was jinxed. Still, she joked with the crew. "No more surprises, guys. Okay?"

"Guess we can forget about surprising her with that cake," the
cameraman Rory Tubbs spoke up.

The cake and the small farewell party the crew had planned for
Kelly had been one of the worst-kept secrets in the building.

"A cake? Something sinful and rich, I hope." Kelly grinned.

"Maybe not rich, but it will definitely be sinful," Rory promised,
drawing knowing chuckles from others in the crew.

"Just what kind of cake is this?" Kelly put a hand on her hip in
mock demand.

"All right, ten seconds." The stage manager issued the warning.
Kelly saw the TelePrompTer was functioning again and quickly
checked to make sure the opening words on her papers matched the
large-print letters on the screen. They did. "Nine — eight — seven —
six — five — four — three — two . . ."

At his hand signal, she addressed the camera. "While in New
York, Governor Cuomo will also visit State Senator Dan Melcher.
The senator is still hospitalized, recovering from a gunshot wound
he suffered earlier this week. According to a hospital spokesman,
the senator's condition is listed as 'improved.' A full recovery is
expected."

The attention shifted to her co-anchor as he read the lead-in for
the next story, which would be followed by a commercial break. Off-
camera, Kelly unclipped her microphone and slipped it from under
her jacket, leaving it draped across her chair seat as she rose and
silently exited the set. After the commercial came the weather, then
Kelly's interview segment with her as yet unknown guest. She had
roughly five minutes to learn everything she could and she intended
to make full use of the time.

Sally O'Malley, one of the production assistants who regularly
accompanied show guests into the studio, met her at the edge of the
anchor set and passed two sheets of yellow paper to her.

"The intro and questions," she said in a very hushed whisper,
then motioned. "This way."

Guessing that Sally was taking her to meet the guest, Kelly followed, picking her way carefully over the cables strewn across the floor. She spotted Hugh Townsend standing near the back of the studio with two other people. Her glance fell on the slim, straight woman on Hugh's right. Her summer suit in a soft pink pastel had all the marks of a Chanel, and the stylish cut of her white hair —

My God, it was Katherine Rutledge. Kelly froze, a sense of panic surfacing with a rush. She couldn't face her. She couldn't risk being recognized. She couldn't.

But how could Katherine Rutledge possibly recognize her? She wasn't the tall, overweight girl with glasses and stringy hair that Katherine would remember. She had changed. Changed her name, her appearance, her life — everything.

Yet that failed to lessen the high tension that gripped her as Kelly approached the trio. She was too experienced, too well schooled, to let any of it show in her expression.

Hugh smiled a silent greeting at her, a faint gleam of triumph in his hazel eyes. Then, with impeccable manners, he turned to Katherine Rutledge. "Katherine, may I present Kelly Douglas. She will be doing your interview." Then he reversed it. "Kelly, this is Katherine Rutledge."

"It's an honor to have you as a guest, Mrs. Rutledge." Up close, Kelly could see she had aged little in twelve years. The eyes were still as sharp and bright as ever, and the heavy stage makeup gave a smooth look to her face, concealing any new lines time might have added.

"Miss Douglas." Katherine offered her a white-gloved hand, a regal quality to the gesture that Kelly remembered well. It was as unforgettable as her voice — like cut glass. When Kelly released her hand, Katherine used it to gracefully direct her attention to the third member of the group. "This is my grandson Sam Rutledge."

Kelly turned and looked up to a face that was strong and lean, all lines and shadows, hollows and angles. The soft, boyish look that she remembered was gone, even though she had seen him only a few times. Not surprising considering they had hardly traveled in the same circles. Sam Rutledge had belonged to the vintner set with their sleek sports cars, festive lawn parties, and the latest fashions, while she had belonged to — no, she wasn't going to remember. She refused to remember. She had left that life far behind her.

"Welcome to New York, Mr. Rutledge," she said, conscious of his eyes studying her with a detached interest. There was no recognition in his look, yet her tension went up a notch, along with her pulse rate. A reaction Kelly dismissed as purely nerves and nothing more, although it didn't explain her heightened awareness of him.

"Miss Douglas." He didn't offer to shake hands, but simply smiled. The movement of his mouth caused the hollows to deepen and the shadows to shift, with attractive results.

"Will you be joining us for the interview, Mr. Rutledge?" she asked while silently wondering how she was going to get through it.

"No." There was a small shake of his head, and another faint movement of his mouth. "I merely accompanied Katherine to the studio."

Kelly thought it odd that he referred to his grandmother by her given name, but she was too preoccupied to give it more than passing notice.

Behind her, voices rose, signaling the beginning of a commercial break. Welcoming the distraction, Kelly looked back. Two cameras pulled away from the anchor desk, the operators kicking the attached cables out of the way as they maneuvered the cameras into position before the set to the right of the anchor desk. The overhead bank of lights came on, throwing their bright glare on the two chairs angled toward each other and separated by a solid round table. A stagehand hurried onto the set and added a wine bottle and stemmed glass next to the vase, filled with an arrangement of lilies and roses.

The young production assistant nudged Kelly. "Why don't you take Mrs. Rutledge to the set and get her settled before the interview?"

"Yes." She hesitated a split second, fighting to control the nervous churning of her stomach and taking a silent vow to make this the best interview she had ever done. It was the focus she needed. "If you will follow me, Mrs. Rutledge."

At the woman's nod, Kelly took the lead, avoiding the tangle of cables as best she could.

Hugh watched them make their way to the set he called the conversation pit. A shifting movement drew his glance to Sam Rutledge.

"Your grandmother is in good hands," Hugh assured him. "Kelly is an incredible talent — with an incredible voice."

"Yes." But it wasn't her on-air voice he was thinking about, with its quietly firm tone, smooth around the edges, not crisp or officious. His mind kept turning back to the warm and friendly sound of her voice when she'd been joking with the crew during a break.

When the pair reached the set, the bulky studio cameras blocked them from view. "Let's move over there." Hugh motioned to some unidentified spot. "We'll be able to hear better and still see the monitor."

"Whatever you say." Sam followed when Hugh Townsend walked to an area to the right of the cameras but still behind them.

The angle gave Sam an unobstructed view of the set and its occupants. Katherine was already seated in the far chair, her very posture giving it the look of a throne. Kelly Douglas was still standing, tapping a finger to her headset and shaking her head that she couldn't hear. In the shadowy corner of the studio, her auburn hair had looked almost black. Under the lights, Sam noted, it caught fire.

An audio technician rushed onto the set. Kelly presented her back to him — and to Sam. He raised her jacket up to check the battery pack attached to the waistband of her skirt, giving Sam a glimpse of the ice blue silk and lace of the camisole she wore under it. He found it an interesting contrast to the tailored lines of her jacket.

Whatever adjustment the technician made, it worked. Almost immediately, she flashed him a smile. "It's loud and clear now. Thanks, Carl."

The man responded with a one-fingered salute and retreated from the set as the stage manager called out, "All right, quiet. We'll be coming out of the break in twenty seconds."

Kelly sat down and murmured something to Katherine that Sam couldn't catch. Then she was bent over the papers on her lap, her pen busy slashing and scribbling across them.

"Fifteen seconds" came the warning, followed quickly by the countdown.

Sam glanced at the monitor and idly watched faces give way to weather graphics. But his mind wandered, as always his thoughts drifting to the winery and vineyards, and the work to be done. He had postponed the thinning of Sol's Vineyard until he got back to supervise the work. The bottling of the two-year-old cabernet sauvignon was continuing, under Claude's watchful eye. The merlot was scheduled for bottling as well.

Len Dougherty wasn't a concern, at least for the time being. Before they'd left for New York, the sheriff had called to tell them he had been arrested by the St. Helena police. He had pleaded guilty to a drunk-and-disorderly charge. Currently Dougherty was in the city jail, serving a four-day sentence.

Belatedly Sam noticed a shot of Kelly Douglas on the monitor. A set of graphics flashed on the screen, promoting the gala wine auction, listing the time, the location, the ticket prices, and the charity that would receive the proceeds.

Privately he wished they could have their meeting with Baron Fougère, skip the auction, and fly home. But he also recognized this might be the last major function Katherine attended. God knows she had devoted her entire life, every bit of her energy, to Rutledge Estate, its vineyards and its wines, to the exclusion of nearly everything else. She deserved to bask in the glory her wines had achieved.

And Sam had no doubt the auction would prove to be a triumph for Rutledge Estate wines. Katherine had donated a case of the '73 cabernet sauvignon Rutledge Estate Reserve, a vintage that every wine expert had rated as a classic wine, the highest accolade a wine could receive. And it was a vintage that now could be found only in the cellars of private collectors. The last time a single bottle of the '73 vintage had been offered at auction, seven years ago, it had sold for five hundred dollars, a phenomenal sum for a California wine. The price for an entire case could end up being in the tens of thousands.

To call that a triumph might be an understatement, Sam conceded.

Beside him, Hugh Townsend murmured, "Brilliant. Absolutely brilliant."

Sam turned, glancing at him, a slight frown creasing his forehead. Townsend stood, one arm folded in front of him, propping an elbow while he rubbed fingers across his mouth in a thoughtful pose.

Catching Sam's questioning look, he flicked a finger toward the set. "She threw out most of the introduction and wrote her own. It's superb," he murmured from behind his hand.

Only then did Sam give his attention to the words Kelly Douglas was saying.

". . . truly can be considered a legend. During Prohibition, while others were replacing their vineyards with orchards, she kept her winery going by making sacramental wines. At the same time, she replanted her vineyards with the finest vinifera cuttings, personally selected and imported from France, always firm in the belief that the great experiment of Prohibition would one day end. A belief that history has proved correct. Ask any connoisseur of California wines about Rutledge Estate, and they will speak, with a trace of awe, about 'Madam's' wine." Kelly paused and smiled at Katherine. "I said it to you earlier, but I must repeat myself, because it is truly an honor to have you with us, Madam Rutledge."

"Thank you, but the pleasure is mine." Katherine inclined her head briefly, charm radiating from her expression to become part of her inherent dignity.

"Curiosity. The term 'Madam' — how did that come about?"

"It began years ago." She dismissed the exact number with a lift of her hand. "When I first came to Rutledge Estate as a bride, the servants referred to me as 'the young madam,' to differentiate, I'm sure, from my husband's mother, who was still living at the time. Then later, when I returned from France after my husband had died, I was accompanied by Girard Broussard and his young grandson, Claude. Despite the existence of Prohibition in America at the time, Girard had agreed to become the wine master at Rutledge Estate. A post his grandson, Claude, now occupies. Being French, both Girard and Claude addressed me as Madam. It grew from that."

Kelly was aware that Katherine had been accompanied by her two young sons, Jonathon and Gilbert, the cuttings for the vineyard, and the coffin with her husband's remains inside on her return from France, but she chose not to mention it.

Instead she observed, "I know it's rare for you to leave Napa Valley these days. Is it merely coincidence that both you and Baron Fougère are attending this year's gala auction in New York, or is there truth to the rumors that you are vying with your son Gilbert's winery, The Cloisters, to form a joint venture with the baron's Château Noir firm in Napa Valley?"

Katherine smiled pleasantly. "With the presence of so many great châteaux, such as Pétrus, Lafite-Rothschild, Moët and Chandon, already in the valley, there are always rumors. However, if you are asking me whether I shall be seeing the baron while I'm in New York, then the answer is yes. Our families have been friends for many years."

Kelly gave her full marks for so deftly evading the question. Age had not lessened either the sharpness or the quickness of her mind. With less than a minute left, there wasn't time to pursue it.

"It can't be easy for any mother to compete with her son in the same business, whether it's the making of fine wines or anything else. I'm sure the rivalry between you and your son Gilbert is no different."

Katherine tilted her head to one side and smiled at Kelly with a wide-eyed look. "But the wines of Rutledge Estate have no rivals, Kelly."

Instinctively Kelly knew that was the perfect note to end the interview on. She turned to the camera. "As I'm sure those who attend tomorrow evening's gala auction will attest. Katherine Rutledge of California's renowned Rutledge Estate, thank you for being with us. It has been a rare treat for everyone."

The interview had been flawless, and Kelly knew it. That certainty offered some consolation to nerves that were raw from the strain of it.

As soon as they cut to a commercial break, Kelly excused herself and went back to her chair at the anchor desk, leaving Katherine in the capable hands of the hovering Sally O'Malley.

The last remaining minutes of the broadcast were a blur. Kelly didn't remember any of it. She knew she made some appropriate remark when her co-anchor announced to the viewers that she was leaving, moving on to bigger and better things, and plugged her new prime-time show for the network. But, for the life of her, she couldn't have repeated it.

While the credits rolled over a shot of the anchor desk, she remained in her chair, smiling and nodding, pretending she was actually listening to the crosschat of the broadcast team. The instant the lights were killed, Kelly wanted to throw her papers in the air in relief. But she wasn't capable of such an emotional display in public, especially when she didn't want anyone to know what an ordeal the interview had been for her.

She ditched the microphone and headset with more haste than usual, angry and scared after her encounter with Katherine Rutledge. Scared because twice she had caught herself starting to slouch in the chair, as if somehow that would make her appear less tall, and wanting to avoid eye contact, as if people wouldn't look at her if she didn't look at them. She hated that. She hated being reminded so forcibly of her past. It had nothing to do with who and what she was now. She'd put the past far, far behind her, and she wanted to keep it there.

Without the hot television lights on, the cool of the air conditioner could be felt. Kelly breathed it in, noticing for the first time that the regular studio lights were on. She took a step away from the anchor desk and stiffened.

Hugh hadn't left after the interview was over. He was by the door, waiting for her. Katherine Rutledge and her grandson were with him. Kelly wanted to scream at them to leave. Of course, she couldn't — and didn't.

Instead, she scraped together the remnants of her composure and rebuilt it, layer upon layer, before she walked over to join them.

"I thought you had left already," Kelly managed to keep any hint of accusation from her voice.

"Katherine wanted to stay and compliment you on your knowledge of the wine industry — and the history of Rutledge Estate,"

Hugh explained, smiling almost smugly. "I confess, I failed to inform her before the interview that you were born in Napa Valley."

"Really?" Katherine studied her with new interest.

"I'm afraid that implies I was also raised in Napa Valley," Kelly inserted quickly. "I do admit that I have long been fascinated by my place of birth. As for my knowledge of wine, Hugh has a habit of instructing anyone in his company about the finer points of wine and wine making, whether they want to learn or not."

"You must be an apt pupil." The remark came from Sam Rutledge.

She turned slightly toward him. "Thank you." Despite her inner turmoil, Kelly met his eyes straight on, and felt again the unnerving impact of his presence and the ensuing tug of attraction. If he had been anyone other than Sam Rutledge, she might have explored the latter, tested the strength of it to see if it went beyond the physical. As it was, Kelly had no choice but to try to ignore it.

"Kelly is more than an apt pupil," Hugh interposed. "She is NBC's new rising star. In fact, as of this moment, she is officially on the network's payroll as host of a prime-time magazine-style show."

"Congratulations." Sam held out his hand and waited for her to accept it.

"Thank you." She let her hand rest in his, but only briefly.

Kelly Douglas was an attractive woman, something he had noticed before, just as he had noticed the lacy feminine garment she wore beneath that tailored jacket. But it was the wariness behind her facade of composure that aroused his curiosity. And his interest.

"We mustn't keep you, Miss Douglas," Katherine remarked, to Kelly's relief. "I merely wanted to compliment you on the interview. We shall look forward to seeing you again sometime in the future."

"You will," Hugh said. "Kelly will be at the reception tonight."

"I may be late, Hugh," Kelly warned. "The crew has a cake for me, and probably a few other surprises as well."

"Late or not, I'll expect you there. Consider it an order from your new boss."

"Yes." She smiled stiffly, unable to think of a single way out of it.

"Until tonight, Miss Douglas," Sam murmured when they took their leave from her.

6

*T*he cab swung up to the curb on Fifth Avenue and stopped in front of the entrance to Trump Tower. Kelly paid the fare, adding a tip, and stepped out into the warm summer night. She paused, her glance lifting to the marble-and-glass showplace that soared sixty-eight stories into the air.

She fought off the last-minute qualms. She had dressed carefully for the party, telling herself it was important that she make the right impression, given her new status as host of a network show, and Hugh's formidable guest list. That was a lie. The smart, sophisticated clothes gave her confidence. Who could feel vulnerable in a Calvin Klein original?

The swing coat was antique gold satin, full cut with dolman sleeves and a stand-up collar. She wore it over a short dress of dark gold lace that was both eye-catching and chicly simple. Two-inch heels in a softer, subtler shade of gold and a waterfall of gold-mounted white stones at her ears provided the finishing touches of invulnerability.

Thus armored, Kelly entered the tower lobby, its walls and floors swathed in apricot-colored marble. A cascading fountain immediately drowned out all sounds of the city. Security directed her to the bank of private elevators that led to the exclusive apartments stacked above the shopping atrium on the building's lower floors. The ride to the sixtieth floor was, fortunately, a swift one.

Outside Hugh's apartment, which was really two redesigned into one, Kelly could hear the muted sounds of the party, already in progress. She took a deep, steadying breath and rang the bell.

Within seconds the door was opened by a jacketed member of the staff Hugh had hired for the occasion. Recognition registered quickly in his glance. "Good evening, Miss Douglas." He swung the door wider and stepped back to admit her.

"Good evening." Kelly surrendered her coat to him, slipping the chain to her narrow evening bag onto her shoulder before gravitating to the focus of the party noise.

She paused inside the living room that stretched some forty-two feet long. Glass walled the length of one entire side, the sheer drapes pulled back to show off the city's nocturnal glitter. There was no doubt the apartment was pure New York, modern in design and spirit, an island of serenity and order yet never denying the energy of the city beyond the glass.

Though the apartment was far from serene at the moment, Kelly thought as she scanned the living room where the majority of the guests were gathered, some sitting, more standing, clusters forming and breaking to reform again in a new blend. It was an artful mix of society and celebrity, politicians and power brokers, the wealthy and the well-connected, and — of course — the vintners, elevated by the wine mystique to the status of demigods in certain circles, such as this one.

A white-jacketed waiter presented a tray of smoked salmon and spinach canapés to her. Kelly refused politely and he moved on. A second later, Hugh spotted her and came over, brushing her cheek with a kiss.

"You are late," he said into her hair. She wore it down, thick and full about her face, tumbling in stylized disarray about her shoulders.

"Which is better than never," she reminded him.

"Probably. How was the farewell party and the cake?"

"The cake was good, but the male stripper who popped out of it was better." Kelly smiled, pretending there hadn't been moments when her face was redder than her hair. "The guys on the crew insisted he was a wide receiver on waiver from the New York Jets, but they couldn't fool me. One look and I knew he wasn't."

"How did you determine that?" Hugh turned a curious and amused look on her.

"It was easy," she insisted. "I may not know much about football, but I know a tight end when I see one."

He laughed, then caught the eye of a passing waiter and summoned him over. "Something to drink?"

"No wine?" She saw not a single stemmed glass on the tray.

Hugh raised an eyebrow at her question. "With this group?

Hardly. No matter what wine I might have chosen, I would offend nearly everyone here. And I definitely didn't want to exhaust my cellar by turning this into a wine-tasting affair. Mixed drinks were the only safe and practical alternative."

"And very politic."

"Very," he confirmed with his usual attractive arrogance.

"Sparkling water with a lime twist," she told the waiter. "Whatever brand you have will be fine." He bowed and left. "So tell me," she said as she leaned closer to Hugh, lowering her voice and sweeping the guests with another searching glance, on guard against the moment when she encountered Katherine Rutledge and her grandson again, "who is here that I should know and don't?"

He smiled almost smugly and perused the group. "This gathering could be fodder for an Agatha Christie novel — were the dear lady still alive." His side glance touched her. "This little soiree of mine has lured not only Katherine Rutledge and Baron Fougère here, but also Gil Rutledge. The plot, as they say, thickens."

"Assuming it doesn't blow up in your face."

"What an interesting thought," he replied. "Too bad they are being so very civilized about it."

"You are hopeless, Hugh." But she laughed softly all the same.

"I know." The waiter returned with Kelly's drink. Hugh neatly plucked it from the tray and handed it to her. "Do you know Gil Rutledge?"

"I know *of* him." Which was true. "Where is he?"

"Over there." Hugh nodded discreetly at a silver-haired man chatting with two other guests off to the side. "Come, I'll introduce you."

With a hand at her elbow he steered her through the gathering toward Gil Rutledge. If Kelly hadn't known he was Katherine's son, she wasn't sure she would have seen the resemblance. But it was there — in the mane of silver hair, and in his features, which were classically handsome, as hers were classically beautiful. Kelly knew Gil had to be somewhere in his sixties, but, like his mother, the years rested lightly on his shoulders. And he had Katherine's blue eyes as well, eyes that could probably turn icy hot with displeasure as easily as they could radiate warmth and charm.

But the dissimilarities were more obvious. He didn't possess Katherine's dignity, her hint of reserve, or that aura of supreme authority. Gil Rutledge was more outgoing; he had dash, a subtle hint of flamboyance, and an abundance of charm. It flashed through his smile, through his face, when he observed their approach.

Unable to resist, Kelly smiled back, understanding thoroughly why Gil Rutledge's reputation as a marketing genius exceeded that as a vintner.

He gave Hugh no opportunity to introduce them as he reached for her hand. "Miss Douglas." The instant she gave him her hand, he carried it to his lips, the gesture absolutely natural, with no trace of affectation. "I had the enormous pleasure of seeing you on television earlier this evening."

"You are very kind, Mr. Rutledge." Kelly briefly wondered what his reaction to her interview with Katherine had been, but it was hardly polite to ask.

"And *you* are too modest," Gil chided lightly, continuing to hold her hand, now engulfing her long fingers with both hands. "And the name is Gil."

"Kelly." She returned the courtesy.

"Kelly." He smiled. "Obviously I'm not the only one who recognized your talent, or the network wouldn't have snapped you up for their new show."

"Much of that I owe to Hugh."

"Don't believe her," Hugh inserted.

"I don't," he replied and half turned, one hand dropping away to direct her attention to the man on his left. "Kelly, I want you to meet my son, Clay."

The sheer force of Gil's personality had prevented Kelly from noticing the man at his side. Movie-star handsome was her initial impression of Clay Rutledge, from the top of his dark blond hair to the tips of his highly polished Italian shoes. He had a deep California tan, lazy blue eyes — bedroom eyes — and a mouth that could only be described as sensual. There was no doubt he had his father's charm, but there was a different quality to it, less expansive and more intimate.

"Mr. Rutledge." Smiling faintly, Kelly offered her hand to him after his father released it.

"Clay. I insist." He took it, but he didn't carry it to his lips as his father had done. He simply held it, the pressure of his fingers warm, more personal.

"Clay." She saw the way his glance skimmed her face. And the frank appreciation in his eyes.

There was a time, not that long ago, when she would have been flattered by his attention, when her head might have been turned by his smile, his look, or his touch. Working in television, especially in New York, she had been exposed to too many politicians, too many

celebrities and bureaucrats who would flirt and flatter, use any
means to get what they wanted. She was much wiser to such things
now, and she deftly withdrew her hand.

"Congratulations on your new show," Clay offered. "Now that
I've met you, I will definitely make a point to watch it."

To Clay, every woman he met was a challenge. They were an
obsession with him, or rather, the conquest of them was. When he
had first observed the approach of this slim, statuesque woman,
noticed the reddish highlights that gleamed from her silky hair, the
hunting instincts had risen, and he had tensed like a thoroughbred
at the starting line.

"I hope you do watch," she replied easily. "The more viewers,
the higher the ratings. And the more chance the show has of being
a success."

"I have the feeling it will be a huge success." He smiled faintly,
as if there was something known only to him.

"Certainly everyone involved will be working toward that end."
She acknowledged his remark with another smile.

He recognized the reserve in her eyes and her smile. Yet it was
the intensity beneath all that bland composure, the hint of strength
that intrigued him. He made a few more comments, idly and decep-
tively probing, trying to draw her out, always searching for some
opening through her pride, her vanity, her career, or her romantic
notions, and always watching for the signs that would tell him the
best approach.

Clay never expected to succeed on the first encounter, always
operating on the assumption there would be others at some later
point. When Hugh Townsend took Kelly's arm, asking for them to
be excused so she could meet some of his other guests, Clay didn't
offer any protest, not even a polite one.

Instead he watched her walk away, mentally assessing the few
things he'd learned about her. "She's a sharp, very intelligent
woman."

Beside him, his father made a sound in his throat, disputing that,
and raised the glass of Chivas and water to his mouth, muttering
behind it, "Katherine handled her easily enough." He was still
seething from Katherine's remark that the wines of Rutledge Estate
had no rivals.

"Speaking of Madam, where is she?"

"Over there. Holding court," Gil Rutledge added with a definite
undertone of sarcasm as he tipped the rim of his glass, indicating
the woman across the room.

Clay turned slightly, following the line of his father's vision, and easily located his grandmother. She stood near the room's center, her hands lightly clasped in front of her, her chin elevated a degree or two while she addressed the small group plainly hanging on her every word.

Most women as they grew older weighted themselves down with magnificent jewels to distract the eye from their telltale wrinkles. Not Katherine. Other than the South Sea pearls at her ears and the diamonds in her wedding rings, she wore none.

Nor was she overdressed, as were some at the party Clay could mention. A floral scarf in soft shades of aqua, rose, and amethyst draped her throat and trailed down her back in long, diaphanous folds, like a train. Her dress was in the same floral chiffon, falling in a slender column to a handkerchief hem, the points nearly brushing the floor. The effect was pure elegance.

Privately Clay saluted her. But only privately.

"You can bet she thinks she has the deal with the baron in her pocket," Gil muttered.

"Doesn't she?" Clay countered dryly.

"Not after I've met with him, she won't." He took a sip of the Scotch, then lowered his glass, his expression grim and determined. "All I have to do is open his eyes to a few facts."

"Such as?"

"There's already a glut of overpriced prestige wines on the market. A market, I might add, that is already depressed. To successfully launch a new one will require aggressive marketing, and an experienced sales force. We have everything in place: the organization, the facilities, and the experience. She doesn't; her operation, her volume, is too small. Not only that, she's ninety years old. She can't live much longer. And without her, there is no Rutledge Estate."

"You're forgetting Sam."

He scoffed at that. "He's as spineless as his father. Katherine — and only Katherine — runs Rutledge Estate, and she runs it her way. She doesn't tolerate any interference, any arguments, or any ideas except her own. That company is family owned in name only. As I learned years ago," he declared bitterly, his fingers tightening around his glass.

"I know." Clay nodded absently. He'd heard it all before.

"All he had to do was buy grapes from other vineyards, but she wouldn't let him. Rutledge wine would only be made from Rutledge grapes." He remembered her words as vividly as if they had been

uttered yesterday. "We were losing all those sales, all that profit that
we were supposed to be sharing, but she wouldn't listen to me. Not
even when I suggested bottling the wine under a different label.
Other wineries do it all the time, but she wouldn't. Not Katherine."

Gil paused, the memories rushing back, and the anger with them.
"Dear God, there was one year when it rained constantly before the
grapes were ready to pick. She sold off every bit of them rather than
risk making a wine that might have been inferior. One entire vintage
gone. And Jonathon agreed with her. He always agreed with her."

He glared across the room at her. It made him sick with disgust
to see the way people fawned over her. She was a cold, heartless
bitch.

Lies. Her whole life was one lie on top of another. To her, family
meant cheap labor. And that nonsense of hers that she had kept the
winery going during Prohibition by making sacramental wines was
another invention. As for that false image she projected of a woman
faithful to her husband's dreams *and* his memory — did she think
he'd forgotten the sight of her with her lipstick all smeared and her
blouse unfastened, exposing her breasts? Or the way she had bent
down to him, gripping his arms, her eyes blazing: "You must never
say anything about this, Gil. Not to anyone. Not ever. Do you hear
me?"

He nodded stiffly, jerkily, just as he had done then, those same
hot feelings of shock and betrayal sweeping through him. He hadn't
said a word. And he hadn't forgotten.

"I see Sam standing over there by himself," Clay remarked idly.
"I think I'll go say hello to my dear cousin."

"Right," his father replied gruffly and lifted his glass again.

Sam stood next to a gilded Louis Quinze console table, one hip leaning against a corner of its marble top. His jacket was unbuttoned, a
hand buried in a side pocket of his trousers, negligently holding the
jacket open.

He noticed Clay slowly but steadily moving in his direction and
took another sip of the beer he'd been nursing most of the evening.
It was stale and warm, but he continued to hold it, his glance flicking
to Clay with disinterest when he reached him. They had never been
close, or even friendly. Sam didn't pretend it was otherwise.

"I saw you were alone and thought you might want some company," Clay said in greeting, his mouth curving in a smile.

It was a smile that could charm and capture a woman without

effort, Sam knew. And he also knew that his cousin had all the scruples of a tomcat.

"You thought wrong," he said and let his gaze drift over the room. He caught a flash of gold and focused on it.

It was Kelly Douglas. He'd seen her when she first arrived at the party. She had been impossible to miss in that dress of gold-filigree lace. It would catch any man's eye the way it softly molded her small breasts and hinted at the slenderness of her waistline, then stopped short a little below midthigh, celebrating the length of her long, shapely legs.

"An unusual woman," Clay remarked, following the direction of his gaze.

Sam threw him a glance, his mouth slanting in a dry smile. "Don't tell me you struck out with her," he taunted, having witnessed the meeting between Kelly and his cousin from across the room.

Clay gave him an amused look. "I haven't even stepped up to bat yet." He studied him for another long second. "Are you still upset over that little incident with your wife? Sorry — Adrienne is your ex-wife now, isn't she?"

His marriage to Adrienne Ballard had ceased to exist, in everything but name, six months after the wedding, long before he had surprised her with Clay in what could be euphemistically described as a compromising position. But the incident had certainly done nothing to promote any feeling of closeness to his cousin.

"You haven't changed a bit, Clay." Sam set the pilsner glass on the marbled table next to a trio of equestrian figurines of Kangxi porcelain. "You have such class. Such low class."

Clay just laughed. Sam held his gaze for a long second, then moved off. He preferred to choose his own company.

Hugh shifted closer to Kelly and murmured near her ear, "Now for the third member of our triangle — Baron Fougère. Mention his library at Château Noir and he'll be a fan forever."

Kelly smiled to herself. This was hardly the first time Hugh had coached her, feeding her pertinent tidbits of information before introducing her to some important personage. Not only did such coaching give the illusion that she had personal knowledge of the individual, creating a favorable impression, but it also provided a topic of conversation so that neither party had to resort to such mundane subjects as weather.

When she was presented to the baron, her first reaction was a

vague disappointment. Emile Gerard Chrétien Fougère did not
match her image of a French aristocrat. He had all the accoutre-
ments of one — the signet ring; hand-tailored evening dress; shoes
of the finest leather; manicured nails, lightly buffed. But it stopped
there. In his fifties, her own height, on the stocky side with thinning
hair, he had the staid and solid, inwardly absorbed look of an aca-
deme. Kelly realized Hugh's reference to the baron's library should
have been her clue.

"It is a pleasure to meet you, Mademoiselle Douglas." He greeted
her with a preoccupied courtesy, the line of his mouth curving without managing to break his sober face. Kelly wondered how many
had mistaken his distracted air for aloofness.

"The honor is mine, Baron Fougère," she insisted, then added,
"and New York's."

He nodded with a trace of vagueness, then, almost belatedly,
remembered the woman at his side. "Forgive me, my wife, Baroness
Natalie Eugenie Magdalene Fougère. Mademoiselle Douglas. And
you know our host, Monsieur Townsend."

Kelly turned toward his wife, a slim, petite woman, easily twenty
years younger than her husband. "I'm very happy to meet you,
Baroness Fougère."

"Natalie, please." Her smile was bright and quick, like her eyes.
Her hair lay darkly on top of her head, exposing small and dainty
ears with diamond-and-ruby pendants. A love of color was obvious
in her gown of metallic silk chiffon in a swirl of rainbow hues.
"We are in America. It is not the place for titles. May I call you
Kelly?"

"Please." It was impossible not to like her. And impossible not to
see the stark contrast of natures in husband and wife.

"Your city is a most fascinating place," she told Kelly. "It must
be very exciting to live here."

"At times," she admitted. "Is this your first visit to New York?"

"I have been here twice before, but there is so much to see and
do, I could never tire of it," Natalie Fougère declared, unaware that
the baron's attention had already wandered. But Kelly was.

"Nearly everyone feels that way — New York may tire you, but
you never tire of it," Kelly replied, and the baroness laughed in
delighted agreement, the sound like musical notes on a scale, all
light and airy. The baron glanced at her in his grave, absentminded
way, having heard none of the exchange.

"That is an excellent — how do you say? — bon mot, Kelly."

"Merely an observation from one who lives here," she corrected, then turned to include the baron. "I'm told, Baron Fougère, that you have an outstanding library at Château Noir."

His eyes lit up at the mention of it, his expression becoming almost animated. "It is true the collection holds many fine and rare first editions. But the credit is not mine. They are books acquired by my family over the years. Over the centuries. The library is a source of great enjoyment to me."

He went on at length, referring to works by some of the world's greatest writers and philosophers. A few of the names and titles Kelly remembered from her college days, enough that she was able to respond with some display of intelligence.

"You must come to Château Noir so that I may show you the treasures of its library," the baron stated in a tone that made it sound like a command.

Before Kelly had a chance to respond, Gil Rutledge walked up and laid a friendly hand on the baron's shoulder. "Emile," he said in greeting. "I see you have met the very charming and attractive Miss Douglas."

"Indeed I have."

Gil flashed a smile at Kelly. "Did the baron tell you that he was still in short pants the first time we met?"

Kelly tried, and failed, to imagine this scholarly-looking man before her as a very young boy. "No, he didn't mention that."

"It was back in 'forty-five," Gil recalled. "The war in Europe was over and the first atomic bomb had been dropped on Japan only the day before. I was a young second lieutenant, stationed in France at the time. I had a month's leave coming and Emile's grandfather graciously invited me to spend it at Château Noir."

"The 'forty-five Château Noir," Hugh murmured almost reverently. "That is a truly noble wine."

"I am proud to say I was there for the birth of it," Gil declared. "Even as it fermented, one could sense the future greatness of it. Several years later when the wine was released, Emile's grandfather very generously sent a case to me. A memento of my visit to Château Noir, he called it. I still have a few bottles left. I assure you they are reserved for very special celebrations." He turned to Emile. "Perhaps we will have an occasion to open one in the near future, Emile."

"Perhaps," he replied and added nothing more.

Clay Rutledge observed the initial meeting between the baron and Kelly Douglas. His attention centered on her in absent appraisal and he continued to stand by the gilded console table. The faint thinning of his lips was the only outward sign that he was still smarting from the cut Sam had made in parting.

When his father joined them, Clay's glance drifted to him. There was nothing his father wouldn't do to steal this deal from Katherine. Years ago Clay had learned that his father lived for only one thing— besting Katherine in the wine business. For as long as Clay could remember, she had dominated their lives, both before and after she had thrown his father out of the company and his young family out of the house. He had come to share his father's hatred of her.

The baron's wife laughed at something Kelly said, drawing his glance. Clay studied her in quiet speculation, watching her smile fade, replaced by a look of polite interest as her husband took over the conversation. She was the baron's second wife. Considerably younger than Fougère, she needed brightness and drama in her life and, Clay suspected from previous meetings, yearned for an ardent kind of affection her husband was far too sedate to show.

He thought of the merger his father wanted so desperately. It was a thing that could be attacked on two fronts. While his father worked the business angle with the baron, he would use his persuasions on the baron's wife.

Clay waited until Kelly and Townsend had moved on to another cluster of guests, then wandered over to join the baron and his father. After an exchange of greetings, he chatted with the baron a full minute or more about the wine auction and the vertical selection of Bordeaux vintages donated by Château Noir. Then, with a slight turn of his head, he glanced at Natalie Fougère, giving her a faint smile, a nod, and nothing more.

The baron divided a blank glance between them, then roused himself as if suddenly reminded of his manners. "You have met, *non?*" he inquired of his wife.

"Yes." She smiled slightly. "On two or three occasions."

"This makes the third, I believe," Clay inserted smoothly.

"We have attended many social functions. It is difficult to remember," the baron offered in excuse.

"I understand." Clay nodded.

Gil said something to the baron, claiming his attention. Clay moved to the side, as if to avoid intruding on their conversation, and held Natalie's gaze, returning its veiled inspection. There, in the hollow of her throat, he saw the rapid beat of her pulse and knew he had stirred her. Instinct and experience told him the best method of approach: dark and serious, saying more with his tone than his words.

"Are you enjoying your stay in New York?" he asked.

"It is an exciting city. Do you not find it so?" She continued to watch him, her expression composed to show a mild interest in the conversation — and him.

"If you are lonely and bored, it makes very little difference where you are." Clay kept himself perfectly still, everything about him showing the intensity of restraint — his stance, his voice, his look.

"I would think a man would find many enjoyable diversions here," she replied, almost casually.

"Perhaps I wish for things that can't be." He looked directly into her eyes. "As you do, I think."

Her eyes widened slightly. For an instant she was completely engrossed with him, her control slipping briefly to let a warmth and a hunger show before she recovered.

"Many would wish for the things I have, Monsieur Rutledge."

"Of course," he said, and turned back to his father and the baron without pressing her further. He had aroused her interest. For now that was enough. Tomorrow he knew the baron had a meeting with Katherine. And he also knew the baron never took his young wife to such business appointments. Which meant she would be left to her own devices. Or to his.

Kelly slipped into the softly lit library. After more than an hour of circulating among the guests, smiling and chatting, she needed a break. She had never been comfortable at large social gatherings like this one. At least, not as a guest.

She crossed to the window with its view of the Empire State Building, and the more distant twin towers of the World Trade Center. She opened her gold evening bag and took out a cigarette, lighting it.

"Haven't you heard? Smoking can be hazardous to your health."

With a faint start, she turned to face Sam Rutledge, her pulse skittering in reaction, all her nerves swimming to the surface. He lounged in a taupe-and-white-striped chair, the lamp beside it unlit. She noticed the faint curve of his lips and the tanned skin taut across his facial bones.

Snapping her bag closed, she blew the smoke at the ceiling. "So are eggs, prime rib, sticky doughnuts, and walking along city streets after dark." With effort, she managed an easy smile.

"You left out alcohol." He swirled the beer in his pilsner glass.

"If you listen to all the health experts, the list is endless."

"True." He rose from the chair and wandered over to stand by the window, his body angled toward her.

She wished he had remained in the chair. She was tall, but he was taller. She was usually eye-level with most men, but with him, she had to look up. She didn't like that. She felt a hum of tension and fought it.

He leaned a shoulder against the glass and glanced back at the open doorway and the throng of well-dressed guests beyond it. The din of their collective voices filtered into the room. He brought his gaze back to her. The metallic threads woven through the gold lace of her dress shimmered in the room's subdued lighting. It caused him to wonder if she wore more silk beneath it, or simply nothing at all.

"I take it you felt the need for a little quiet, too," he said and took a sip of beer.

She smiled and nodded, something automatic in both responses, as if they were programmed. "It's been a long day for me."

"I imagine it has."

"For you, too, I suppose," she added. She looked relaxed, at ease, but there was a guarded look to her eyes when she glanced at him, giving Sam one more thing to wonder about. "Did you fly in today?"

"Yesterday. Which gave Katherine a chance to rest a little before all the activities started."

He had calm eyes, Kelly thought. Dark and calm with a kind of quiet strength that would draw a woman. She had the impression he would defend what was his, protect it from harm.

Annoyed, she looked away. She had learned to fight for herself long ago. She didn't need anyone to look after her. She could take care of herself with no help from anyone.

"Didn't your wife come with you?"

"I don't have a wife."

Kelly gave him a half-startled look. "I thought I read somewhere that you were married."

"Past tense. We're divorced."

"I never know what to say when people tell me that." She toyed with her cigarette. "Whether I should be sympathetic and say I'm sorry, or rejoice with them and be glad."

"Be glad." He smiled faintly. "I am."

"All right. I'm glad for you."

"Thanks."

"Katherine seems to be enjoying herself." Kelly had a brief glimpse of the Rutledge family matriarch through a break in the string of guests clustered around her. "She's had an audience surrounding her all evening." Which thankfully had meant Kelly had needed to do no more than catch her eye, smile and nod from the fringes, and any social obligation was satisfied.

"Katherine enjoys any opportunity to talk about the wine trade. Which is hardly surprising, I guess. To the whole Rutledge family, life is a cabernet." His mouth slanted in a wryly cynical line.

Kelly smiled at his play on words, and then eyeing him curiously, she felt compelled to point out: "You're a Rutledge."

His grin became more pronounced, as did the gleam of amusement in his eye. "Katherine would tell you that I'm one of those big, strong, slow-growing cabernets, with a little too much tannin yet. She tends to describe people as wines, regarding both as living things with individual characteristics. In your case —" He paused, his look turning thoughtful as he studied her, his gaze a little too direct, and a lot too personal. "I think she would have some difficulty figuring you out. You're definitely a dry wine rather than a sweet. Probably a white variety —"

"I hope not," Kelly interrupted with deliberate lightness. "They don't have a very long life."

"Some do, depending on the variety and the vintage."

"That wouldn't be so bad then." She tapped her cigarette on a crystal ashtray, knocking off the buildup of gray ash. "I hope Katherine wasn't offended by any of the questions I asked during the interview."

"If she was, you would have known it already," Sam assured her, conscious that she had deliberately swung the focus of the conversation away from herself. "I have the feeling she probably found your questions challenging, and Katherine likes challenges. Any vintner does. If they don't, they'd better get out of the business."

"Obviously that has to mean you like them, too."

"I do." And he was looking at one now. "How long did you live in Napa Valley before your family moved away?"

"Not long." She let out the smoke slowly, stalling. "Iowa is a great place to grow up, though. The air is fresh. No smog, no pollution. Everybody knows everybody, and there's always something going on — Friday-night football games at the high school, home-

coming parades, hayrides, Christmas programs at the church, sled-
ding parties, Memorial Day parades, summer softball games, county
fairs, detasseling crews walking the corn rows —"

"Did you detassel corn?" he broke in curiously.

"By that, are you implying that you think I was tall enough?" She
raised an eyebrow in light challenge.

"Actually I was trying to picture you in blue jeans and a plaid
shirt, your hair in pigtails and a straw hat on your head." His gaze
skimmed her face. "With your fair skin, you must have wound up
with a ton of freckles."

"No." But she noticed he had some, although very faint beneath
his sun-bronzed tan. They should have given him a boyish look, but
his face was too rugged. "I looked like a boiled lobster instead."

"Then you did detassel corn."

Little escaped him — she needed to remember that. "Just one
summer. After that, I got a job at a low-budget, low-frequency radio
station, first as a receptionist and general dogsbody. Within a couple
months the station manager had me subbing for the disc jockeys
whenever one of them didn't show up. It wasn't long before I got a
slot of my own."

"With your voice, I'm not surprised."

"It helped. And it also helped that I could double as an engineer,
newscaster, weatherperson, and interviewer. Even program director
and salesperson, if I had to."

"I suppose doing the news on radio is when you decided you
wanted to get into the television side."

"Not really." Kelly saw that he wasn't drinking his beer, merely
holding the glass, swirling it occasionally and letting the beer ride
up the sides. "It was a very small radio station," she reminded him.
"Doing the news consisted of tearing the latest sheet from the wire
and reading whatever was there. We called it rip 'n' read. At the
time I wanted to get into print journalism, become a newspaper
reporter. It wasn't until my second year of college that I became
interested in the television side. I worked as an intern for one of the
local television stations for credits. Then, right before I graduated,
they offered me a job as a reporter. I accepted." She lifted one
shoulder in a light shrug. "The rest, I guess you would say, is
history."

She had spoken easily and naturally about her early work in radio,
but Sam had noticed the subtle changes that had occurred the instant
she mentioned television: the added warmth in her voice, the soft-

ening around the lips, and the quickening light in her eyes. Television was a medium Kelly Douglas loved, even if she didn't express it with words. Just as he had never found the words to explain the challenge and contentment he found working in the vineyards and winery.

"Your family must be very proud of you."

"I don't have any." Kelly ground her cigarette out in the ashtray and instantly regretted it. Now she had nothing to occupy her hands. "My mother died when I was eight, and I had just graduated from high school when I lost my father. There wasn't anyone else, no brothers, no sisters, no one."

"It must have been rough for you."

"Life always seems rough — until you consider the alternative."

"True," he conceded, a smile briefly lifting the corners of his mouth. Then he tipped his head to one side. "What kind of work did your father do?"

"Anything, everything. As they say in Iowa, he would work wherever he was hitched."

Sam nodded absently as a hint of a frown touched his expression. "I just realized you said you were born in Napa Valley, but you never said what part. Was it St. Helena, Rutherford, Napa, Calistoga Springs?"

When he started naming off the towns in the valley, Kelly knew she had to stop him. She crossed her arms and cocked her head, giving him an amused look.

"What is this? Am I being interviewed or something?" she chided. "If you're trying to find out how old I am, the answer is twenty-nine. I'm five-foot-eight, one hundred and twenty-five pounds, auburn hair and green eyes, single. I attended the University of Iowa, graduated fifteenth in my class. I like earth colors, Calvin Klein clothes, Cole Porter music — especially when it's sung by Sinatra. I like Yoplait yogurt better than Dannon, and German chocolate cake, but I can't stand devil's food. I'd rather drink Evian water than Perrier. I have an occasional glass of wine, but never drink so-called hard liquor. I smoke, though I'm trying to cut back. There, have I left anything out?"

"No hobbies?" His eyes glinted with something between admiration and amusement.

"You are relentless," Kelly declared, stunned that her factual recitation hadn't brought an end to the probing, personal questions.

"Curious," Sam corrected, his mouth curving in a crooked smile.

"It's obvious that you are a very private person. And as expert as any politician at dodging questions." He straightened from the window glass. "No offense intended."

"None taken." But she was shaken that he had so easily recognized her evasive answers for what they were.

"Good." He continued to regard her steadily. "I imagine privacy is important to someone in the public eye the way you are."

"It is."

His smile widened a little. "So what are your hobbies? You still haven't told me."

Bothered by the way he was looking at her — and the way she was reacting — Kelly hesitated an instant. "I don't know whether this qualifies as a hobby, but I like to restore and refinish old furniture, take something that's scarred and battered, strip it down to bare wood, then sand away all its scratches and gouges, give it a fresh coat of stain, and make it look all shiny and new again." As she warmed to the subject, she gradually lost that initial self-conscious quality. "It started out as a way to fill the unfurnished apartment I rented when I moved to St. Louis. Now it's something I just enjoy doing. In fact, I'm in the middle of restoring a gorgeous old turtle-top center table I found at a thrift shop just a few blocks from where I live in Gramercy Park. It's made out of mahogany. So far, I have managed to strip off the old paint and stain it, but it needs two or three coats of wax yet. Hand-rubbed, of course."

"Of course." His answering smile was quick and warm, a look of understanding in his eyes that Kelly hadn't expected. It drew her, even as she recognized the danger of it, and the attraction she felt.

"What can I say? Doing it gives me a lot of pleasure and satisfaction." She tried to sound offhand, without success.

"That's obvious." He paused and reached out to take her right hand, turning it palm up as the fingers of his other hand tactilely examined its smoothness. "It's also obvious that you wear gloves while you're doing all this stripping and sanding and staining."

The caressing brush of his fingers took her breath and sent little tingles rushing up her arm and down her spine. No man's touch had ever made her feel breathless before. It wasn't fair that it should belong to Sam Rutledge. And it wasn't fair that she saw the same awareness flickering in his eyes.

"As a matter of fact, I do wear gloves." Kelly drew her hand free and tried bodily to pull back from this trembling edge of tension.

"Funny," he murmured.

"What is?" She slipped a hand onto her evening bag, clutching it a little tighter than necessary while searching through her mind for some casual way to end this conversation.

"I like old things, too. Only in my case, it's planes."

"Planes," Kelly blurted in surprise. "You fly?"

He nodded. "When I can get away, which isn't often, unfortunately. I own a vintage Cub." Seeing her blank look, Sam explained. "That's an old, two-seater biplane, with open cockpit."

"A biplane. Like the kind Snoopy flies when he's out looking for the Red Baron in his Sopwith Camel?" she asked, referring to the character from the "Peanuts" cartoon strip, unable to keep a smile from breaking across her face.

Sam grinned back. "My little Cub is nowhere near as old as the Sopwith, but there are similarities. Mine was built about forty years ago, designed for aerobatics. It was in pretty bad shape when I bought it. It took me almost two years, working in my spare time, to get it back in flying condition."

"It must have been quite a thrill the first time you took her up." Remembering the way she felt each time she viewed a piece of furniture she had restored, Kelly could readily imagine the immense feeling of pride and satisfaction Sam must have known.

"It was," he agreed.

She studied him thoughtfully. "Flying isn't a sport I would have associated with you. If you had asked, I probably would have picked racquetball or tennis or polo." All choices that were physically and mentally demanding, and suitable for someone from the vintner set. "I suppose there is a great sense of freedom when you are up there in your plane."

He nodded in agreement. "Freedom, power. But more than that, a sense of total control. That's something you learn to savor when you work with the land, always at the mercy of Mother Nature's whims."

"I guess it is." A burst of laughter came from the living room. Kelly glanced at the doorway. "Someone's having fun."

"Sounds like it."

She saw her opening and took it. "I think it's time I slipped back and rejoined the others."

"Katherine is probably wondering where I am. Maybe it's time we both went back."

It wasn't the kind of remark that required a verbal response. Turning, Kelly started toward the door, uncomfortably aware that Sam was directly behind her. The instant she set foot in the living room, she gave him an over-the-shoulder smile and parting nod, and headed toward the closest cluster of guests.

Hugh intercepted her before she reached them. "Kelly. I was beginning to think you had already left."

"Truthfully I was on my way to look for you, to let you know I'd be leaving soon." Very soon.

"Considering the full day you've put in, I expected that." His eyes were gentle with understanding. She could have hugged him. "I'll call you a cab. At this hour it might be hard to find one."

"There's no need for a cab." Sam Rutledge was still there. He hadn't moved off as she'd expected, as she had hoped. "We have a car waiting outside. I can give Miss Douglas a lift home."

"Thank you, but it really isn't necessary," Kelly insisted, turning to him.

"If it isn't a necessity, then try considering it a pleasure," he suggested smoothly.

"Take his advice," Hugh said. "The last time I took a taxi, it reeked from the last drunk who had ridden in it."

"But if Katherine should decide to leave —" Kelly began.

"Why would I decide to leave?" Katherine Rutledge joined them, showing not the slightest trace of fatigue. "To go where?"

"Back to the Plaza," Sam replied.

"Why would I want to do that? No one else is leaving," she reasoned calmly.

"Miss Douglas is," he explained. "And I offered to take her in our car, but she was concerned that you might want to leave before I got back."

"That was very thoughtful of you, Miss Douglas, but you need not trouble yourself over that. I am enjoying myself too much to leave anytime soon. I insist that Jonathon take you home."

"Jonathon?" Kelly frowned. "Don't you mean Sam?"

"Did I say Jonathon?" Momentarily nonplussed, Katherine dismissed the mistake with a careless wave of her hand. "Naturally I meant Sam. He will take you."

Without choice in the matter, Kelly thanked her, collected her coat, and left, with Sam at her side. Exiting the building's air-conditioned cool, they stepped out into the steamy summer night. Sam scanned the handful of cars ranged along the curb outside and gestured to one.

"Our car is over here." He lifted a hand to the driver, who hurried to open the rear passenger door.

Kelly slid onto the seat and arranged the folds of her satin coat around her. Any hope that she'd make the ride alone died when Sam folded his length onto the seat next to her. She gave the driver her address and settled back.

"You didn't need to come too." She had to say it, if nothing else just to release some of the tension inside.

"Probably not," he agreed easily enough. "But I wanted to make sure you got home safely. As you pointed out earlier, city streets can be dangerous after dark."

"Hazardous," she corrected. It was an ingrained habit for any quote to be accurate.

"Hazardous." He conceded the point.

Kelly leaned back, suddenly wanting to relax and refusing to let his presence stop her. She released a long, cleansing breath and closed her eyes, the corners of her mouth turning up for the briefest of instants.

"I admit this is better," she said. "The taxis in New York are not exactly the cleanest or the most comfortable vehicles to ride in."

"Or the safest."

She glanced sideways, meeting his half smile. "True."

The car sped in and out of the pools of light cast by the street lamps. Sam was silent a moment, watching the play of light and shadow, light and shadow on her face. She was attractive in both, her features strong, the lines clean, her hair like fire one minute and midnight the next.

"Will you be at the wine auction tomorrow evening?"

"No." Her head moved against the seat back in a slight negative gesture. "I'm anchoring the weekend edition of the nightly news tomorrow night. It's part of the network's campaign to give me more national exposure. From now on, I'll be sitting in once a month until the new show airs in midseason, after all the bowl games are over."

"You'll be busy."

"Very. Especially when we actually go into production and start taping segments. Hugh can be a slave driver."

"Have you known him long?" Sam found himself wondering about their relationship. Not that he cared.

"We've been friends for over two years."

Friends. The casual way she used the word gave him no reason to suspect there was anything more than that between them.

The car slowed and came to a stop in front of the turn-of-the-century red brick building that housed Kelly's apartment. The driver stepped out and opened Kelly's door. As she climbed out, she heard the slam of the opposite car door. Her gaze tracked Sam's dark shape moving toward her.

Suddenly it hit her. A Rutledge had brought her home. A Rutledge was walking her to the front door. She felt the delicious irony of it, a sense of triumph — and the heady feeling of power that accompanied both.

He signaled the driver to wait and cupped his hand under her elbow, guiding her up the short flight of steps to the building's arched entrance. A pair of old cast-iron coach lanterns lighted the entry. The door key was in her hand. She surrendered it to him when he reached for it. He held it, making no move to insert it in the security lock.

"Thanks for the ride home," she said, unable to keep the secretly pleased smile from curving her lips.

"Maybe we'll see each other again sometime."

"Maybe." She doubted it.

Sam didn't think it was likely either. He unlocked the door and opened it for her. Halfway through the doorway, she paused and turned back for the key, one hand moving to hold the door open. He gave it to her.

Then, on impulse, Sam slid his fingers into her hair, cupping the back of her head as he lowered his mouth to hers. She went still at the contact, but her lips were soft beneath his. He explored that softness and the warm curves, felt them heat and move against his with returning pressure.

He drew her closer, wanting to discover more, to taste more. She was all lace and soft scent and long limbs, strong and pliant, warm and willing. A kiss wasn't enough. He wanted to wrap himself in her, lose himself in her. Even as he felt the need build, Sam drew back from it. He had met, made love to, and married his ex-wife in a sexual haze. He wasn't about to become lost in another.

"Good night, Kelly." Sam stepped away from her carefully, like a man retreating from the edge of a very sheer cliff.

"Good night." She avoided his eyes, turning and pulling the door closed behind her.

Listening to the solid click of the night lock, Kelly felt none of that earlier sense of power. She felt shaken and vulnerable, forcibly reminded of too many half-forgotten needs that were suddenly impossible to deny. It scared her.

❦ 7 ❧

*F*rom his post by the antique clock, the centerpiece of the Waldorf's richly tinted lobby, Clay Rutledge saw the baroness the instant she stepped from the elevator. She wore a large-brimmed hat of red straw and a swingy summer dress of white silk, lightly splashed with irregular dots of red, royal blue, and green. The look was both saucy and sophisticated, very chic and very French, and very easy to spot in a crowd.

She hesitated briefly, then turned and made her way toward the hotel's Park Avenue entrance. Clay waited several beats, then followed at an unhurried pace.

Her slim heels clicked across the floor's patterned mosaic, then down the short flight of steps to the revolving door at street level. She pushed through it, then paused again. A doorman came into view.

Clay lingered at the top of the steps and observed the exchange between the two, watching as the doorman pointed to the right, obviously giving directions. Clay smiled when he saw the city guidebook Natalie Fougère held against her narrow red clutch purse. Smiling her thanks, she moved off in the direction the doorman had indicated. Again he waited until she was out of sight before following.

Outside he saw her again as she crossed the street and walked along East Fiftieth, heading toward Fifth Avenue. If it had been any other woman, Clay would have suspected she was on her way to explore the exclusive shops on Fifth Avenue. But the guidebook she carried and the inquiring turn of her head, which suggested an eagerness to discover the many sights and sounds of the city, negated that thought. Clay strolled after her, trying to anticipate her destination.

Perhaps the plaza at Rockefeller Center. Or the Museum of Modern Art.

All the while he continued his appraisal of her. After last night, there was no doubt in his mind that she was a lonely woman with unspent emotions, ready for the excitement of an illicit affair.

A moment later she surprised him when she turned onto Fifth Avenue. He quickened his steps, reaching the corner as she climbed the steps to St. Patrick's Cathedral. Maintaining a careful distance, Clay entered the ornate stone-and-white-marble structure.

A few worshipers sat in the gleaming pews while others, tourists mainly, wandered about the sanctuary, admiring the stained-glass windows and the religious statuary, conversing in hushed murmurs. From the back of the church, Clay scanned the scattering of people and finally spied the distinctive red straw hat the baroness wore. She was at one of the alcoves surrounding the nave. He watched as she lit a candle and knelt to pray, the gleam of a rosary in her hand.

He watched her thoughtfully for a moment, then withdrew, crossing to the opposite side of the avenue. While he waited for her to come out, he made a few minor revisions in his original assessment of Natalie Fougère: she was not the type to casually flirt with a man for the diversion; no doubt she truly cared for her husband, wanting to please him and struggling against the unhappiness she felt in her marriage. None of which changed the fact she was lonely and ripe for an affair. It meant only a slight altering of his approach.

Clay faced one of the most photographed views in New York: the white gleam of the cathedral's Gothic spires against the black glass of the Olympic Tower rising behind it; but his gaze was fixed on the bronze doors. When Natalie Fougère walked out of them, luck and Saturday were on his side — there was no traffic on the street.

He reached the opposite side of the crosswalk as she came off the last step. He showed surprise and pleasure at seeing her, before quickly veiling the latter.

"Baroness. Good morning."

"Good morning, Monsieur Rutledge."

She had dark brown eyes, the rich color of bittersweet chocolate. He noticed the glow that came and went quickly in their depths, reflecting his own look of repressed pleasure. Just as closely he observed the slight change around her lips. It was these small, barely discernible shifts in a woman's expression, the differing sounds of a woman's voice, little gestures, or sentences left unfinished that told him the things he needed to know. Just as her expression told him now that his sudden appearance had had an effect on her.

He glanced past her, toward the cathedral entrance. "Where is Emile? Isn't he with you?" he asked as if he didn't know.

"He had a meeting to attend."

He brought his glance back to her face, examining it. With her he would play the man of honor, fighting the strong attraction he felt and displaying that emotional restraint in his every look, his every gesture, his every word.

He smiled with politeness. "Then, may I walk you back to the hotel?"

"Thank you, but . . . I thought I would view some of the sights of New York." A little self-consciously she indicated the guidebook in her hand.

"Alone?" Clay gave her a look of alarmed concern, then masked it with a smile. "Let me show you New York. The experience is much more enjoyable when it's shared."

She hesitated, her eyes rushing over his face. "I have no wish to inconvenience you."

"It would be a pleasure, Baroness."

"Natalie, please."

He caught the faint movement of teeth sinking into her lower lip, a signal that she questioned the wisdom of inviting a further familiarity.

Clay inclined his head with a courteous reserve that promised he wouldn't take advantage of it. "Only if you will call me Clay."

"As you wish," she acknowledged with equal reserve.

"We are very close to the plaza of Rockefeller Center," he said, raising a hand to indicate the direction.

He walked at her side, taking deliberate care not to touch her or let their shoulders brush, even accidentally. They strolled down Channel Gardens and stopped at the stone parapet to gaze at the lower plaza with its open-air café and golden statue of the fire-stealing hero of Greek mythology, Prometheus, agleam in the mist of dancing water jets. Other than mentioning points of interest, Clay said little; her comments were equally restrained.

"Where next?" he asked, then suggested, as a lark, "The Empire State Building, perhaps. No true tourist could ever come to New York without visiting it."

"Is it far?"

"Too far to walk. We'll take a taxi." He hailed a passing cab, then held the door for her before sliding in after her, carefully keeping his distance.

He read nothing into either her silence during the short ride or her previous brevity. His glance strayed to her frequently and he let her catch him looking at her. She was, he decided, a beautiful, elegant woman, her dark hair pulled away from her face and neck, its fullness hidden beneath the crown of her hat. In his mind, he likened her to an instrument of many strings, waiting for a master's touch.

The cab stopped at the Thirty-fourth Street entrance to the Art Deco skyscraper that filmdom and King Kong had long ago immortalized. Inside the marbled lobby, Clay purchased tickets for the observation deck and escorted Natalie onto the high-speed elevator crowded with tourists. It shot them to the eightieth floor, where they switched to another elevator that would take them the rest of the way. Even with the press of bodies and mingling odors, he could smell the subtle sexiness of her perfume.

He waited for the elevator to empty, then guided her out, past the souvenir stands to the heavy door leading onto the deck. Natalie laughed at the slap of the wind and grabbed at her hat, holding it on her head as she crossed to the wall. Clay walked over to stand beside her, gazing with mild interest at the architectural potpourri of glass-and-steel towers, venerable brownstones, and Gothic churches that was Manhattan.

With a reckless disregard for height, Natalie peered over the observation glass. "The taxis, they look like bright yellow marigolds."

She stepped back and lifted her face to take in the far-sweeping view. He studied her rapt expression of wonder, the delicate curve of her long neck, and the silk of her dress, molded to her shapely figure by the wind.

"Magnificent, isn't it?" He pretended an interest in the view of the island of Manhattan, the Hudson River, the specks of sailboats on the Sound. "So high above everything. Isolated from the hustle of the city below. One could almost believe we are the only two people in the world," he mused with feigned idleness. "Of course, two people can make the biggest world of all — when they are the right two people." On that, he turned to look directly at her.

Whether deliberately or not, she misread his meaning. "You are missing your wife."

"My children, perhaps," he offered, then shrugged, glancing away. "It's no secret my wife and I have little in common anymore, except our love of the children," he lied smoothly. "She is content with her flowers and her painting, while I . . ." He stopped, scowling darkly. "Why am I telling you this?"

"Perhaps you knew I would understand."

Her dark eyes were a mute testimony to the loneliness of her own marriage when he turned back. He held her gaze for a significant moment without making any response.

"Have you ever taken a carriage ride through Central Park?"

She seemed momentarily thrown by his question. "No."

"Neither have I." He smiled an invitation. "Shall we?"

She hesitated not at all, a smile lighting her whole face. "Yes."

Twenty minutes later they were sitting in the backseat of a carriage traveling through Central Park. Beyond idle comments on sights they passed, they spoke little, but Clay saw by the small smile on her lips that she was comfortable with the silence.

As they rode by the eighteen-acre lake within the park, Natalie sat forward. "Do you see the rowboats?" she asked and continued to gaze at the sunlight glinting on the water's glass-smooth surface. "How beautiful it looks on the water."

"I think we should find out if it is," Clay announced and instructed the driver to drop them off near the boat-rental site.

When they pushed away from the dock, Natalie sat at the bow. The red straw hat was in her hand, exposing the sleekly coiled knot atop her head. She gripped the sides of the boat and leaned back, tilting her face to the sun.

Beautiful, Clay thought again as he stroked the oars, propelling the boat through the water with slow, languid pulls. His sports jacket was folded neatly on the seat beside him; the cuffs of his shirt were rolled back.

"This is wonderful." She dipped a hand in the sun-warmed water and watched the drops fall from the tips of her fingers. "You were right, Clay." She looked at him with a wistful quality. "It is better when it is shared."

"Yes," he said, then stayed silent for several strokes of the oars, continuing to hold her gaze. "I shouldn't say this, Natalie, but you are a very lovely woman." His voice was full of tightly suppressed intensity.

For a moment, there was such a tightness in her throat she couldn't speak. Many times — too many times in recent months — she had looked at Emile and longed for him to notice her again, to see her as the beautiful, desirable woman he had claimed she was before their marriage. There were even times when that longing had been a physical ache.

She knew it was wrong to find so much pleasure in another man's compliment, but she did. She was too starved to care where the nourishment for her soul came from.

But she said, slowly and carefully, "It is rather nice to be noticed, Clay."

"Forgive me," he murmured.

"For what?" she chided, needing to make light of his words. "For being kind?"

"It wasn't kind. You are a very lovely woman. A man would have to be blind not to notice that."

Sometimes she thought her husband was blind. Blind to her needs.

When Clay fell silent, she did nothing to encourage further conversation and tried to turn her mind instead to the serenity of the lake and the blue of the sky overhead. But she found it impossible not to notice the way the sunlight glinted off the dusky gold of his hair, the play of muscle beneath his shirt, and the easy strength of his arms.

What a fool his wife was, Natalie thought, not to appreciate this man. Did his wife not know how lucky she was to have such a sensitive, caring husband, a man so attuned to her that he could anticipate a whim and indulge it even before it was voiced?

Like renting this rowboat to glide across the lake, just the two of them, New York's tall buildings nothing more than a vague intrusion on the skyline beyond the trees. She watched his hands pulling on the oars, the flexing muscles in his arms. His hands would be warm and sure in the caress of a woman, seeking to please, to arouse, to satisfy. And his kisses would be moist and heated, swift to ravish.

Conscious of the quickening strike of her heartbeat, Natalie looked away. It was not wise to indulge in idle fantasies, even harmless ones.

Too soon, it seemed to Natalie, the hour was up and the rowboat had to be returned. Clay helped her from the boat, his grip firm and subtly strong. But he didn't release her once she was on the dock. He stood behind her, a steadying hand still on her waist and the other on her arm, below the cap sleeve of her dress.

"I was wrong," he murmured, ever so softly. "Even a blind man would notice you — the headiness of your scent, the music of your voice, the satin of your skin. . . ."

One finger, and one finger only, traced the curve of her arm before he drew his hand away. She breathed in, and found it difficult to breathe out.

For a moment, she imagined swaying back against him and feeling the solidness of his body along her length, the warmth of his arms folding around her, the sensation of his lips exploring her neck. Before the thought could become an impulse, he stepped back, releasing her, and the moment was gone. But not the memory of it.

"There is a fairly good restaurant not far from here," Clay said. "If you feel hungry, we could go there for lunch."

She looked at her watch for the first time since she'd left the hotel. "It is late." She discovered this with a twinge of guilt, aware that she had been enjoying his company too much to notice the passage of hours. "I must return to the hotel. I promised Emile I would meet him for lunch at one. It is nearly that now."

"Of course." Clay nodded, but she caught the flicker of regret in his expression, and understood it because she felt the same.

During the cab ride back to the hotel, Clay bided his time, occasionally filling the silence with banalities and waiting until they were a block from the hotel before saying, "I don't know if your husband discusses business with you, but my father and he are talking about forming a partnership to build a winery in California. Both sides bring a lot to the table. The Cloisters not only makes award-winning wines, but we also have a sales base, market skills, and an organization that can't be equaled. As for Château Noir, I hardly need to tell you about it."

He was careful to keep his tone casual. He glanced at her and smiled, observing that she listened with mild interest. "Naturally a partnership will, of necessity, mean frequent trips across the Atlantic by both parties." Clay paused, letting the smile fade and his gaze become intent on her face. "I find I'm looking forward to that a great deal."

The taxi pulled up at the Park Avenue entrance. She had no chance to respond directly as the doorman swung the rear passenger door open on her side. But Clay had already gotten all the response he wanted when her gaze had first clung to him, then moved abruptly away.

He paid the fare and followed Natalie out of the cab. On the sidewalk, she turned to him. "Thank you for the tour of New York. It was most enjoyable." She was careful not to use his name, and that very care was telling.

"It was my pleasure." His smile was properly polite as he again showed her a demeanor of severe restraint. "My regards to your husband."

Clay deliberately didn't mention the gala auction tonight, aware she would be there, and equally aware that she knew he would be attending it as well.

With a small, polite smile, she moved away from him and entered the hotel. He lingered outside and stared thoughtfully after her, considering whether he would speak to her at all that evening or merely let their eyes meet, keeping the room between them.

Either method would be effective, depending on how soon his father planned to meet with the baron again after this weekend. Clay needed to find that out before he settled on his approach. After all, timing was critical in such things.

He wandered into the hotel, pleased with his morning's work and certain the evening's event would prove to be most interesting.

A hush gripped the black-tie-only crowd in the Waldorf's palatial Grand Ballroom as the price on the case of Rutledge Estate '73 cabernet sauvignon Private Reserve continued to rise in spirited bidding. Sam sat next to Katherine, one leg crossed, a hand resting lightly on his thigh and the other arm lying across it in a pose of calm nonchalance.

Katherine appeared equally composed and unmoved by the bidding that had already taken the price well above the anticipated figure. But the tension was there, as noticeable to Sam as the avid glow in her eyes.

When the gavel came down, the winning bid was a history-making sixty-five thousand dollars, the most ever paid for any lot of wine made in the United States. There was an instant of silence in the room as the significance of the final bid registered.

Katherine's pose of dignified calm never changed, but out of the corner of his eye, Sam caught the subtle shift in her expression. A cat with telltale traces of rich cream on its whiskers couldn't have looked more satisfied.

Someone started to applaud. A few chairs away, Hugh Townsend stood up and turned to direct his applause to Katherine. As others came to their feet, Sam rose to add his tribute to theirs. Katherine acknowledged the ovation with a slow and graceful nod of her head. But the applause didn't stop until she was escorted to the front.

She waved aside the microphone that was offered to her, her voice in its pure tones lifting to address the gathering. "Thank you. Thank you all." She paused briefly, waiting for silence to fall, then continued. "My late husband, Clayton Rutledge, was long an admirer of Thomas Jefferson, one of America's first Renaissance men and a connoisseur of fine wines. Like Jefferson, Clayton believed that one day America would make wines that were the equal of the great châteaux of Europe. It was his dream that the wines of Rutledge Estate would be among them, a dream I have carried on alone these many years. Tonight you have bestowed a great honor on the house of Rutledge Estate. And a very worthy cause will receive the benefit of it. Clayton would be very proud of that, as I am. Thank you."

More applause broke out when she finished. As several of the guests pressed forward to extend their personal congratulations, the auctioneer wisely announced a short break in the proceedings while they prepared for the next lot.

Sam wasn't surprised to see Baron Fougère and his wife among the first to approach Katherine. In a business where image and prestige were all-important, that of Rutledge Estate had risen sharply. The baron was impressed and it showed in his deferential manner, a stark contrast to the brusque, slightly overbearing attitude he'd displayed at this morning's meeting. It had irritated Sam a few times, but Katherine had dealt with him smoothly, and a partnership between them seemed to be only a matter of time. At least, in Katherine's opinion. Sam, on the other hand, knew his uncle was still fighting to stay in the race.

And there stood Gil, all charm and smile as he faced Katherine. "A stunning price, Katherine. Congratulations." He sounded exactly like a son, happy for her, but something told Sam that the bright gleam in his uncle's eye came from jealousy rather than pride.

"Thank you, Gil." As usual, she was gracious yet reserved with her estranged son. "I am certain your lot will acquit itself very well when it's offered. The Cloisters 'eighty-seven cabernet is quite good for a young wine."

Gil stiffened slightly at the condescending compliment. "Perhaps one day you will agree to submit your 'eighty-seven vintage in a blind tasting with mine, and we'll see which one comes out on top."

Katherine drew her head back. "I would never do that to you, Gil."

Color stained Gil's cheeks. Katherine had not only parried his challenge but delivered a killing thrust in the process. She had sounded sincere in her desire not to engage in a head-on confrontation with her son, and thus spare him the humiliation of losing to her, but Sam didn't even try to guess whether that was really her motivation.

Gil managed to choke back his anger and force a smile. "No one wins all the time, Katherine. Not even you." With commendable aplomb, he moved off, toward the bar.

Sam joined her. "I don't think that was very wise."

"Perhaps not, but it was necessary," she replied coolly, then beamed a smile at Hugh Townsend. "Mr. Townsend, you are the one to blame for this embarrassment of attention."

"Richly deserved attention, Madam." He took her hand and bowed over it. "'Like the best wine that goeth down sweetly,' if the auction ended at this moment, it would be a huge success — thanks to you."

She didn't dispute his extravagant claim, nor did she acknowledge it. Instead, she asked, "Is your young friend Miss Douglas here this evening? I remembered a Zachary Douglas owns a vineyard in the valley's Carneros district and I wondered if she might be related to him."

"I don't think Kelly has any relatives in California. I'm sorry you won't have the opportunity to ask her. She had a broadcast to do tonight." He glanced at his watch. "In fact, she's probably still at the studio, wrapping things up before heading home."

"Six days a week. I hadn't realized she had such a grueling schedule," Katherine remarked, an eyebrow arching in faint surprise.

"The glamour of television," Hugh replied dryly.

"I do hope all that glamour doesn't extend to Sunday," Katherine responded, matching the dryness of his humor and tone. "Everyone needs an opportunity to rest."

In Sam's opinion, that was a strange remark coming from her. He'd never known her to have time for anything but the vineyards and winery. True, she had slowed down some in recent years. But rest still wasn't a word he could associate with her.

After chatting a few more minutes, Townsend excused himself and moved on. Sam let his gaze scan the throng of guests — elegant people in elegant clothes having elegant conversations. He had been raised in this environment, moving as freely through it as he did the vineyards. But tonight he was bored, and edgy.

He spotted Gil near the bar, talking with the baron and his wife. Clay was with him. As usual, the whole of Clay's attention was directed at Natalie Fougère. Sam watched, his mouth twisting in a smile. Last night Clay had made a play for Kelly Douglas; tonight he was using his wiles on the baroness, with more success, judging by the pleased glow in her expression.

"What do women see in him?" Sam didn't realize he had voiced the question until Katherine answered.

"What they want to see." The hint of bitterness, of anger in her voice, the impression that she was speaking from experience, drew his glance. "A man who could end the loneliness, someone to fill the emptiness of their existence with all the richness of those feelings for which the human spirit was created. When the color goes out of a woman's life and the romance shrivels, she hungers to be important to someone again. Hungry, she dreams." Her gaze was fixed on the couple across the room, but Sam wasn't sure it was the baroness and Clay she was seeing. "When a man comes along and pays attention to her, feeding that hunger, she believes — because she wants to believe, because she wants her dream to be real. She refuses to consider that his only desire may be to take advantage of her, that to him it is a cheap thing, because that would destroy her dream."

Katherine gave him a half-startled look, then her expression smoothed, leaving only a glint of bitterness in her eyes. "My mother was such a woman," she said briskly. "After my father's death, she went from man to man. Long ago I lost count of how many step-fathers I had and how many lovers she took. Men like your cousin prey on such women. They are chameleons, changing color to be what the woman dreams. Ultimately, the delusion on both sides becomes the only thing that is real."

Never in his life, not even when he was a boy, had there ever been a whisper of talk in the valley that Katherine had been seen in public in the company of another man after the death of her husband. On the contrary, the locals had marveled over the fact she hadn't.

Yet, for a brief moment there, Sam had almost been convinced that she had been secretly involved with some man, one who had used her and left her with the bitterness of regret. Obviously he'd been wrong. Her knowledge of men like Clay could just as easily come from her mother, as she'd said. Still, he had never looked at her as a woman before. She had always been Katherine, too strong and self-sufficient to ever need anyone. But had she wanted someone?

He almost asked, then caught himself. What the hell did he care? Suddenly impatient, whether with himself or Katherine he didn't know, Sam swung a glance over the crowded room, that restless, edgy feeling returning with a rush.

"I'm going out for some air before they resume the auction," he told Katherine and headed for the nearest exit. Someone laughed, a soft, musical sound, but Sam didn't bother to identify the source of it.

"Mr. Rutledge," Natalie greeted Clay in the softest of voices.

He nodded to her, not smiling, but letting his gaze travel warmly over her face. Her glance fell beneath it, then came back to him, a soft glow radiating from the depths of her eyes.

Clay waited until his father had engaged the baron in conversation before saying to her, "This morning, after I left you, I thought I had only imagined how beautiful you are. I didn't."

She smiled suddenly, brilliantly, then cast a quick glance at her husband, but he was too engrossed in his discussion to notice. Deliberately, it seemed to Clay, she let her smile blossom into soft laughter and placed a hand on the baron's arm.

"Emile, you should know this handsome gentleman has paid me the most extravagant compliment," she declared and flashed Clay a flirtatious look.

Clay wasn't fooled. He heard the silent cry within her words that pleaded for her husband to look at her. But when Emile glanced at her in his faintly surprised, courteous manner, he didn't see what she so desperately wanted him to see — that she was a beautiful woman who would soon sour for lack of being wanted.

Instead Emile patted her hand, as one would a child's, and gave her an absent smile. *"Naturellement."*

There was not a flicker of jealousy or concern in his expression. The fool took her completely for granted. Clay gave Natalie credit for covering her hurt well. No doubt she'd had considerable experience at being ignored. Which was so much the better for him.

"May I bring you a drink?" Clay offered. "A glass of champagne, perhaps?"

"Yes, thank you." Natalie watched Clay as he made his way to the bar.

In the last two days, she had overheard comments made by other women about Clay Rutledge, comments that suggested he was something of a philanderer who had caused his wife no small amount of grief. Perhaps it was true; she didn't know. Even if it was, she found it difficult to feel sorry for his wife. At moments like this, she thought she would prefer a husband who possessed an excess of passion over one who was scarcely aware of her much of the time.

In truth, she envied Clay's wife. More damning than that, she wasn't shocked by the discovery.

Still, she turned back to her husband and tried to give her attention to his conversation with Clay's father.

". . . a remarkable woman," Emile concluded.

"Katherine is a very remarkable woman," Gil Rutledge asserted, then lifted his shoulders. "But what will Rutledge Estate be when she leaves this life? A shadow of its former self, I'm afraid."

Emile frowned. "But her grandson . . . ."

"Sam?" An eyebrow lifted sharply, amusement in the look. "Sam is a good man. But this is a highly competitive business. You have to be more than good to succeed in it." He paused, and shrugged again. "But I'm sure you have considered that."

"But of course." Yet Emile's troubled look led Natalie to suspect that perhaps he hadn't considered whatever it was Gil Rutledge had meant by his remark.

There was a pounding of the gavel, signaling the auction was about to resume. People were filtering back to their seats as Clay returned with her glass of champagne. She thanked him and let Emile guide her back to their chairs.

With the chair previously occupied by Sam vacant beside her, Katherine sat alone. A quiet settled over the ballroom as the next wine lot was presented. She listened idly while the imperial-size bottle from a rare vintage of a famed first-growth château in Bordeaux was praised in familiar wine language, called "intensely flavored and chewy, with a wonderful interplay of currant, oak, and berry flavors, and anise, bay leaf, and cedar notes sneaking in on the long, complex finish; intense and concentrated but gentle, with tannins smoothing to a velvety texture."

All were words and phrases she had often used in the past herself. It was the language of the business after all, although personally Katherine tended to think of wine in human terms, aware of the many parallels that could be drawn between wine and people.

Just as brothers and sisters born to the same parents can differ in physical appearance, personality, and ability, so it was with vintages of wine. Each year, wine was made from grapes picked from the same vines as the previous year, yet each possessed differing characteristics and qualities. One might be handsome and charming, rich in color and clarity, possessing a heady bouquet, yet taste false in the mouth.

Even as she thought that, Katherine found herself looking at the burnished gold head of her grandson Clay, seated only a few rows away. Gil was beside him, his head slightly turned to murmur some comment. Seeing him, she remembered the hostility, the animosity that had been in his eyes when he had congratulated her earlier — rather like a wine that showed a promise of greatness in the barrel only to turn hard and bitter with age.

Silently Katherine gazed at him and felt a mother's ache for a child who had grown to hate her. How had it happened? Where had she gone wrong with him? Had it begun that long-ago night? No, she didn't accept that. Granted there were times in his youth when he had looked at her with eyes that said *I know what you did,* but there were more times, many more times, when those bright, intelligent eyes of her youngest son had danced with laughter and mischief.

Perhaps the seed of his hatred had been planted that night, but nothing can grow unless it is fed and watered. What had provided the nourishment for it? What had turned him against her? Had it begun with Jonathon? With the bitter rivalry that had developed between Gil and his older brother?

As boys they had done their share of fighting and bickering, but no more than usual. Without question there had been occasions when Gil resented that Jonathon was allowed to do certain things because he was older. Naturally the two vied for her attention; that was to be expected in any family. If she spent more time with Jonathon than Gil, it was only because Jonathon took such a genuine interest in the vineyards and winery that demanded so much of her time. And in those days, Gil had found it boring. It wasn't until Gil came home after the war . . .

Yes, Katherine thought, it wasn't until after the war that the real trouble started for all of them, but especially for Gil and Jonathon. During those years he was away, it had been just herself and Jonathon. Suddenly Gil was back, fresh from two years in France, where he had tasted the great Bordeaux and visited many famed wineries, Château Noir among them. He had come home full of enthusiasm and ideas for the family business.

Looking back, Katherine saw how difficult it must have been for Jonathon to suddenly have his younger brother thrusting himself onto the scene. But it had been equally difficult for Gil, at times feeling like an outsider. No doubt it was what had made Gil so sensitive anytime she rejected one of his ideas.

Her sons had always been completely opposite in personality and temperament. Jonathon was quiet, something of a loner, while Gil was outgoing and gregarious; Jonathon was slow to anger and Gil was hot-tempered; Jonathon was conservative in his thinking, the type to examine things carefully before taking a step, and Gil wanted everything *now.*

Katherine had hoped that ultimately they would complement each other — one holding the other back and one pulling the other up, achieving a balance. Instead they had clashed.

True, that first year, even the first two, they had tried to work together. But it hadn't been long before business disagreements began to escalate into personal quarrels.

Both had been young, in their twenties. She had thought they would grow out of it and took steps to give them separate but equal responsibilities, placing Jonathon in charge of the vineyards and winery, and Gil in charge of sales and marketing, which entailed considerable travel.

But that hadn't worked either and the arguments continued. Over the years, the issues had been many and varied: Gil felt they should buy new equipment to modernize the winery, streamline production, and cut down on costs; Jonathon reminded him that the winery was his responsibility and there was no reason to buy new equipment when there was nothing wrong with what they had. Jonathon thought Gil was spending too much money on the road, using the entertainment of buyers as an excuse to dine at expensive restaurants; Gil argued that he couldn't take buyers out to some bistro and expect them to buy quality Rutledge Estate wines from him. Gil wanted to get into the table-wine market by producing a sweet wine under another label, insisting that's where the money was; Jonathon refused to even consider it, declaring that Rutledge Estate made only quality wines, never vin ordinaire.

And Katherine always found herself caught in the middle of these arguments. No matter what her reason or whose side she took, the other felt wronged by her. One was always accusing the other of trying to turn her against him. Toward the last, the estate had turned into a battleground, with even the workers taking sides in the undeclared war between Gil and Jonathon.

Yet Katherine had continued to hope that the two would settle their differences right up to the last, violent argument. She had been in Claude's small office, talking on the telephone to someone, a salesman or some state official, she no longer remembered. She had left the door to the winery partially ajar, giving her a clear view when Jonathon had stormed into the winery, with Gil close by, continuing an argument that had obviously begun elsewhere. . . .

"Dammit, Jon." Gil grabbed him by the arm, forcing him to stop. Jon swung around to face him, angry in a deadly quiet way. "Stop being so damned righteous and at least look at this proposal." Gil slapped at the papers in his hand, his own face red with anger. "Figures don't lie."

"No, but liars figure."

"Are you calling me a liar now?" Gil shouted in outrage. "Fine!"

He threw the papers in Jon's face. "*You* get the numbers and *you* put them together. The bottom line will still be the same. Buying that old winery down the road and the two hundred acres that go with it is the smartest damned move we could make. Why the hell are you so afraid of growing and expanding?"

"And why can't you be satisfied with what you've got?" Jonathon hurled back. "Nothing is ever good enough for you, is it? Look at you in your Italian shoes, your silk tie and two-hundred-dollar suits. It's always more, more, more. More wine, more money, more clothes, more trips."

"What the hell is wrong with wanting more?" Gil snapped. "Why don't you just admit you can't handle running two wineries?"

"I could handle it." Jon bristled, his hands sliding up to his waist in a challenging stance. "But I'll be damned if I will just to satisfy your greed."

"I am sick to death of being told how greedy I am. And I am sick to death of you going to Katherine with your tales about me, trying to undermine me."

"Tales? I'm not the one padding my expense account, siphoning off money from the company. That's you." Jon jabbed a finger at Gil. "Her precious baby boy."

"You bastard," Gil spat, swinging a fist even as he added, "you've accused me of being a thief for the last time!"

From Claude's desk, Katherine watched in horror as the blow struck Jon on the chin, catching him flat-footed and sending him staggering backward. He shook his head and raised a hand to his chin, then lunged at Gil with an inarticulate roar.

She hung up on the caller and hurried out from behind the desk. By the time she reached the door, Jonathon was swinging at Gil with both fists. Jonathon was bigger and heavier, but Gil was quicker. Jonathon swung a right and Gil went under it, hooking a left into Jonathon's stomach, then driving a right into the same spot. Jonathon grunted and half doubled over. Gil smashed a fist into his mouth, splitting his lip and splattering blood.

"Stop it. Stop it, both of you!" Katherine pulled at Gil, trying to separate the two, but he continued to pummel Jonathon with his fists.

Not until two other workers in the winery came running up to grab Gil from behind was the fight stopped. By then, Jonathon was on the floor, dazed and badly shaken, one eye half closed, bleeding profusely from the cut on his lip. Katherine knelt down beside him and tried to stem the flow of blood.

"Two grown men fighting like a pair of little boys," she murmured angrily. "I am thoroughly ashamed of both of you."

Gil shook off the restraining arms, breathing heavily. "He started it."

Katherine threw him an icy look. "We will discuss this later, after we get your brother to the house."

"Let them." Gil gestured at the workers. "I wouldn't lift a hand to help him if he was dying." He turned and walked away.

Katherine knew then the situation couldn't be allowed to continue. Steps had to be taken. Drastic ones.

Once she got Jonathon to the house and his injuries tended, Katherine summoned Gil to the library. When he walked in, she looked at the bruised swelling along his jaw and remembered Jonathon's battered face.

"If you have called me here to listen to another of your lectures about working together, give it to your eldest son," Gil announced, a banked anger in his eyes. "I am tired of being stabbed in the back by him. I may have swung the first punch, but he deserved everything he got."

He would have continued, but Katherine held up a hand. "I am not interested in hearing the provocation, and there will be no lectures." On the desk before her were the papers that Gil had attempted to show to Jonathon, a little dirty and crumpled from being ground into the winery floor during the fight. "After that disgusting brawl between you and your brother, it has become obvious to me that both of you cannot continue to work here."

"It's about time you realized that," Gil declared. "Give Jonathon one of the vineyards and let him grow his damned grapes. That's all he cares about anyway. I can run the winery." He saw the papers on her desk and recognized them. "We can buy the old Schmidt place down the road, the one he refused to even look at, and double our production. In five years, I can make Rutledge Estate a name everyone will know."

"I am quite certain you could. You have a remarkable business sense, Gil, and a gift for marketing." Both of which had led Katherine to the decision she had reached. "In fact, that is the very reason I believe you will do quite well on your own."

"You're throwing me out?" His outrage was instant.

"You must admit, Gil, you have never fully shared my vision of Rutledge Estate."

"Don't you mean yours and Jonathon's?"

Katherine ignored his jeer and continued. "Numerous times over the years, you have chafed under the policies I have set for this winery. You have long held your own ideas and beliefs. A small winery of your own will provide you with the opportunity to put them into practice. To help you get started, I will purchase your interest in Rutledge Estate."

"To help me get started? What you really mean is you're buying me off. Throwing money at me to assuage your conscience before you boot me out the door!"

"I am attempting to be fair."

"Fair? Is that what you call it?" he challenged angrily. "It's always been Jonathon with you. You never could stand having me around."

"That is not true."

"Do you honestly expect me to believe you when I know how you lie? Your whole life is one big lie. And I know it. You can't stand that, can you? You can't stand that I know what really happened that night."

"That has nothing to do with this."

"Doesn't it? You have never wanted me around because I'm a constant reminder of what you did — what you concealed. Do you think I don't know that, that I haven't always known it?"

"You are wrong."

But Katherine had never been able to convince him of that. Not then and not later. When he had walked out of the library that day, he had left hating her. Once she had believed that as his winery grew and became successful, he might finally recognize that leaving Rutledge Estate had been best for everyone. But that hadn't happened, and she no longer believed it would.

Sam pushed through the revolving doors and stepped out into the hot night air. He paused and looked up at the buildings that blocked out most of the sky. There was no glitter of stars high above, and the steamy air smelled of exhaust and yesterday's garbage.

The doorman came over to him. "Cab, sir?"

"No thanks."

He unbuttoned his jacket and started walking. By the time he reached the traffic light on the corner, the sweltering temperature had him shedding the jacket and slinging it over his shoulder.

Ignoring the red light, Sam crossed the street and strolled down a shadowed side street past an old brownstone. He had no destination in mind. When he heard the driving beat of an old rock-and-roll song, he wandered toward it.

A three-piece band entertained the patrons at the outdoor café on the lower plaza of Rockefeller Center. Tourists had gathered around the upper level to watch. The band struck up an old Fats Domino number and Sam drifted over to the corner and paused there.

A woman came out of the building across the street, a heavy shoulder tote slung over her arm. The way she moved, fluidly with just a hint of hip, Sam knew at once it was Kelly Douglas. It was those long legs.

"Yes, it's me and I'm in love again," the vocalist in the lower plaza sang, a microphone amplifying his voice. "Had no loving since . . ."

Suddenly Sam was angry with himself. He could have walked in any damned direction from the hotel, why the hell had he come this way? He'd already been burned once, and he had no intention of going near a fire again.

Yet he stood and watched while she climbed in the backseat of the car parked at the curb. He thought she glanced in his direction, but he couldn't be sure. He told himself it didn't matter anyway. He was leaving this concrete island tomorrow and flying back to California. That would be the end of it.

8

The production offices for the new magazine show "People and Places" had none of the newsroom's underlying thread of urgency, none of its moments of near frenzy with stories breaking and airtime approaching. Here, voices seldom snapped, orders were seldom barked, even the ring of the telephones sounded somehow civilized, Kelly thought as she walked down the hall to her office.

After three days she still hadn't adjusted to the easier tempo that didn't demand a finished product at day's end. The pressure and the tension were still there, but it was a different kind, more subtle.

"Kelly. Hey, Kelly."

She halted at the sound of her name and backtracked two steps to the open doorway she had just passed. When she looked in, DeeDee Sullivan was halfway around her cluttered desk. She was dressed in her usual attire of baggy slacks and an equally baggy polo shirt. A pair of glasses rested on top of her head, the earpieces buried in the sides of her short brown hair, already liberally streaked with gray at thirty-six.

"You're back early." DeeDee glanced at the big, leather-banded Timex on her wrist, her Texas origins revealed the instant she opened her mouth. "I figured you would be digging into your plastic chicken about now. How did the speech go?"

"The speech went fine, and the luncheon was sold out. Which means the coffers for the child-abuse program are a little richer," Kelly replied, then smiled. "And the plastic chicken came first, then the speech."

"The film on the children, what was the response to it?" DeeDee had produced it, donating her time and persuading others to do the same.

"Sorry, I slipped out when they started to show it. I had too many things I needed to get done back here to stay and watch it." In truth, Kelly hadn't been able to face the scenes of bruised and battered children, their frightened eyes and haunted looks, just as she'd never been able to work directly with them. The feelings of rage were always too great. But that wasn't something she discussed with anyone. "What do you need?"

DeeDee gave her a big smile and a thumbs-up sign. "I just got off the phone with John Travis's press agent. Lunch tomorrow, Russian Tea Room, one o'clock with the man himself."

Kelly brightened, hope springing. "Does this mean he's agreed to let us do a profile on him?"

"Officially they won't commit yet. They claim they want Travis to meet you first, see how you get along. It's part of the game they like to play. As far as I'm concerned, honey, we can break out the tequila and the tacos — we got him."

"I hope you're right," Kelly murmured, too cautious by nature to share DeeDee's exuberant optimism.

"I know I am," she insisted and leaned back against the door-jamb, pulling her glasses from atop her head and wagging them in a release of energy. "My God, do you know what this means, Kelly? This guy is hotter than a Mexican jalapeño. His new movie has been breaking box-office records everywhere and it's only in its second week of release. More than that, his role has 'Oscar' written all over it. Have you seen the film yet?"

Kelly nodded. "I went to a private screening a few weeks ago."

"So did I." DeeDee leaned forward and her look became intent, determined. "If we slot this profile in the first show, it will air about the same time the Academy Award nominations come out. Think what that will do for our ratings. It's just the kind of kickoff we need."

"I agree, but I still can't help thinking about his costar. Has any-one been able to find out whether there's any truth in those rumors that she won't be doing any more films?"

"Who can separate the truth from all the Hollywood hype that's surrounded that movie?" DeeDee lifted one bony shoulder in a shrug.

"To me, if it's true, it would make a terrific story for the show. I mean, why on earth would Kit Masters give up her career when she was on the verge of stardom? It doesn't make sense." Kelly frowned, then sighed. "Unfortunately, Hugh doesn't think it's a compelling story at all."

"He's right, you know. The public isn't going to care why she turned her back on the American dream. Why should they? It's practically unpatriotic. They're just going to shrug and figure that she needs her head examined. They definitely won't turn the show on to find out. Viewers want to see stories on people like John Travis who have been knocked down and pulled themselves back up to the top."

"What's this about John Travis?"

Turning, Kelly found herself face to face with Linda James, the network's West Coast correspondent and her former rival for the position as host on the new show. She gave Kelly a cool smile and made no effort to conceal the glitter of animosity in her blue eyes, a glitter that was as chilling as the ice blue suit she wore.

"Hello, Linda." She kept her voice level, forcibly reminded that, deservedly or not, she had made an enemy out of this woman when she'd landed the job of host of the show.

"Well, well, well, if it isn't the network's West Coast correspondent Linda James." DeeDee Sullivan folded her arms and kicked back against the doorjamb. "What brings you all the way out here to our corner of the world?"

"Business. I was just in chatting with Hugh. I wanted him to know that I was disappointed I wouldn't have the opportunity to work with him, but naturally I wished him the best." She paused fractionally. "As I do you, Kelly. It's a little late, I know, but congratulations."

"Thanks." Kelly accepted the hand Linda offered. "To be honest, right up to the minute they offered me the job, I thought I would be the one congratulating you."

"Really?" Linda raised an eyebrow, as golden as her hair. "As close as you and Hugh are?"

"Yes, really," Kelly replied firmly, inwardly bristling at the innuendo of favoritism.

Linda James reserved comment on that and idly glanced down at her hands before again lifting her gaze to level it at Kelly. "Actually, after Hugh explained the format of the show, and the focus of it, I realized that it doesn't have sufficient challenge to appeal to me. I prefer doing stories that have more meat to them and less fluff. But I'm sure a light treatment will be much more suitable for you."

"It's very reassuring to know I have your support, Linda." Deliberately Kelly matched the saccharine sincerity in the woman's voice.

Linda's lips thinned briefly, then smoothed out into another fake smile. "When I walked up, the two of you were discussing John

Travis. By chance, were you hoping to arrange an interview with him for the show?"

DeeDee spoke up. "Kelly is having lunch with him tomorrow."

"How nice." She almost purred the words. "John T. and I are old friends. He's in such demand now that he's become very selective about what shows he'll do. I'll put in a word for you." She smiled at both of them. "Luck to you all," she said and walked off toward the elevator lobby.

"I have the feeling the only luck she's wishing us is bad," Kelly murmured.

"She'll put in a word with Travis all right." DeeDee echoed the sentiment. "A word to queer the interview. She definitely doesn't like you, Kelly."

"I'm taking that as a compliment."

"Smart thinking." DeeDee grinned briefly, then sobered. "And you'd be smarter yet to watch out for her. The dangerous snakes are the ones that don't rattle before they strike."

"I fully intend to stay out of reach. We didn't have many snakes in Iowa, but we had plenty of skunks. They don't give you much warning either."

DeeDee glanced down the hall and frowned before turning back to Kelly. "Do you know what bothers the hell out of me?"

"What?"

"That people who meet Linda James might believe that all women in television are like her." She pushed away from the door frame, her shoulders moving in a theatrical shudder that had Kelly laughing. "Don't forget — lunch tomorrow."

"I'll have Sue mark it on my calendar," Kelly promised, referring to her assistant. With a parting wave, she set off down the hall to her own office.

But Sue Hodges wasn't at her desk when Kelly walked into the anteroom outside her office. The day's mail and phone messages lay in a stack on a corner of the desk. Kelly picked them up and carried them with her into the small private office that overlooked the plaza.

She sifted through the phone messages first. Finding none that required her immediate attention, Kelly turned to the mail and gave most of the letters little more than a skimming glance until she reached a handwritten note from Katherine Rutledge, graciously thanking her for the interview and expressing admiration for her work.

Even as she read it, it wasn't her meeting with Katherine that came to mind, but rather that moment outside the building Saturday night when she'd looked across the street and saw a lone man standing on the corner. For a split second, she had thought it was Sam Rutledge. Which was ridiculous, of course, considering he'd been blocks away at the wine auction.

More ridiculous was the disappointment she'd felt when she had realized it wasn't him. She should have felt relieved — she *was* relieved.

The phone on her desk rang. Kelly glanced at the blinking line, then at the connecting door to the anteroom. When the call wasn't intercepted after the second ring, she knew Sue wasn't back yet. She laid Katherine's note aside and picked up the receiver, pushing the button to the blinking line.

"Kelly Douglas." Automatically she reached for a pen and notepad.

The long-distance operator announced, "I have a person-to-person call for Miss Kelly Douglas."

"This is she."

"Go ahead, sir." There was a faint click that signaled the operator had left the line.

"Lizzie-girl, is that you?" The voice, the hated nickname that had never been used with affection, only with a taunting edge, had Kelly stiffening in her chair, shock sweeping through her in angry waves. "Lizzie-girl, it's me —"

She cut him off. "I know who it is." Instantly she regretted that admission, furious with herself for not feigning ignorance. It was too late now. "What do you want?"

"I saw you on television the other night, giving the news. First time I saw you, I thought my ears were playing tricks on me."

"Don't you mean the whiskey?" she snapped.

"You always did have a sassy mouth."

"What do you want? Why did you call?" But she knew the answer, and bitterly said, "Let me guess — you want money, right?"

"It's the Rutledges. The great Madam herself. She's trying to take my land away. I got a little behind in my payments; now she won't give me a break. She's demanding that I've got to pay all of it, or she's taking the land back. The house, the vineyards, everything. I can't let that happen. You've got to help me. You've done pretty good for yourself, got a big job on television, making lotsa money. Thirty-five thousand wouldn't be much to you."

"No." Her answer was quick and final.

"You've got to help me. I've got no one else. Dammit, you owe me!"

"I owe you nothing!" The anger that had been just below the surface broke through. It trembled through her voice and her body. "Nothing, do you hear?"

"Lizzie-girl, you're not thinking —"

But she didn't want to listen to him anymore; she'd heard enough. "Don't ever, ever try to get hold of me again."

"You don't mean that!"

Kelly slammed the phone down, cutting off his protest, then pressed her hands to her face, covering it while she fought through the shock, the anger, the memories. She hated him. After all this time, she had hoped he was dead. She had wanted him to be.

She pushed her hands into her hair and dug her fingers into her scalp. Fear came, just as it always had, right after the anger and defiance.

"My God, what have I done?" Kelly swung out of her chair to cross to the window and stare blindly out. She hugged her arms across her stomach, trying to stop its nauseous churning as the panic set in.

She should have sent him the money. She had the thirty-five thousand. She had saved religiously ever since she'd started working in television, squirreling away every penny she could. With the accumulation of interest, she had almost fifty thousand invested in ultra-safe, ultrasecure treasury bonds. Why hadn't she simply given him the money and shut him up?

It was blackmail, she knew that. And it wouldn't stop at thirty-five thousand. She rested her forehead against the glass pane and closed her eyes. It would be just like before, he'd take every penny she made. She had been able to keep only what she could hide from him.

No, she had been right not to give him any money. She tried to reassure herself with that.

But what if he talked? What if he started telling people about her? What if —

"Stop it. Just stop it." Kelly caught herself up sharply and gave herself a hard mental shake. She tilted her head back and stared at the ceiling, blinking at the tears that tried to form in her eyes. "Now think, what if he told the world? What is the worst that could happen?"

The answer was easy. Hugh, DeeDee, everyone on the production staff, everyone at the network would know the truth about her — how she had lived, how she was raised, every humiliating detail about her life and her family. While they might admire her for the success she'd made of herself in spite of it, more than that, they would feel sorry for her, and she hated pity. She hated it!

But she'd endured it before and survived; she could do it again. The world wouldn't come to an end; she wouldn't lose her job, her career. Whatever happened, she would make it. She was good at surviving. She'd had to be.

"Kelly?"

Her name was spoken a second time before she heard it and turned. Hugh stood inside her office, one hand still holding the door open. He was frowning at her. Kelly saw that, yet it didn't really register.

"DeeDee just told me about your luncheon date tomorrow with John Travis. . . ." He cocked his head, the frown deepening, his eyes narrowing. "Kelly, are you all right?"

She nodded once, and seized on the sudden pounding in her head as an excuse for her momentary abstraction. "I have a headache, that's all."

"Let me guess how you got it," he murmured and Kelly went cold for one split second, thinking that he'd overheard the phone call and knew everything. "Linda James. DeeDee mentioned she cornered the two of you in the hall and flexed her claws a little. Ignore it, Kelly. Ignore her."

Linda James. Her encounter with the woman seemed so long ago Kelly had forgotten all about it. But she could hardly admit that without inviting more questions.

"I will." She nodded again.

His gaze narrowed on her. "Are you sure you're all right? You look pale."

She looked at him. Should she tell him the truth now, before he found out some other way? This was the perfect opening, the perfect opportunity to confess it all. But what if nothing happened? Wouldn't it be better to wait and see?

When he took a step toward her, Kelly immediately moved back to her desk, putting a barrier between them. She felt too fragile, ready to shatter at the slightest touch.

"Pale skin goes with having red hair." Seeking to change the subject, she picked up the note from her desk. "I had a card in today's mail from Katherine Rutledge, thanking me for the interview."

"Exactly the sort of thing one would expect from Katherine."

Hugh took the card from her hand and idly scanned its contents. "She comes from an era when such courtesies were strictly observed."

"My thought, too," Kelly murmured to keep the conversation safely on track.

"Interesting you should receive this." He idly tapped the card against his fingers. "These last few days I have been mulling over an idea to —" He broke off the sentence and frowned. "Have you taken anything for that headache of yours?"

"No. I was going to ask Sue if she had any aspirin when she got back," she lied, then remembered. "I also need to have her mark down the luncheon with Travis, and pull all the research we have on him. I want to know more about his life and career than he does before I meet him tomorrow."

"You have a full afternoon ahead of you," Hugh observed and laid the handwritten note on top of her stack of mail. "We'll chat about my idea another time."

"Sounds good." Kelly managed a smile as he moved toward the door. She picked up her phone messages and pretended to look through them until the sound of his footsteps faded. She stared at the phone, wondering what she was going to do if he called again.

Slowly, mechanically, Len Dougherty returned the receiver to its hook and stared at the pay phone. She wasn't going to give him the money, that was as clear to him as the hatred in her voice. Dear God, what was he going to do?

Stone-cold sober, without a single drop to drink for the last six days, he staggered down the twisting alleyway, past a handful of shopping boutiques, the tucked-away entrance to the Hotel St. Helena, and emerged on Main Street. Traffic clogged both lanes, Lincolns and Mercedeses bumper to bumper with campers and farm trucks, creating a steady hum of idling engines. Overhead, the flag atop the hotel's cupola snapped and crackled in the strong breeze.

Dougherty saw and heard none of it. He felt sick inside, sick and frightened. He bumped into a heavyset man in yellow Bermuda shorts and a Hawaiian floral shirt without ever seeing him.

"Watch where you're going."

But the sharp complaint didn't register either. Any second he thought his knees were going to buckle. He clutched at the solid support of an old iron lamppost, one of the antique electrolaires that lighted Main Street. He stood there, swaying in shock.

He had been so certain she would come through with the money.

So certain . . . He passed a hand in front of his eyes, wanting it all
to be a bad dream. But it wasn't.

He was going to lose the land. He'd promised Becca he wouldn't.
He'd promised her.

His breath started to come in little sobs as he slumped against the
post. There was nothing he could do, no one else he could turn to,
no one who would give him that much money. Without it, the Rutledges would take his land away.

"They're gonna win." Whispering, he looked up to the sky, mind-
less of the disgusted stares from passersby. "I can't stop 'em, Becca.
I've got no one else to go to, no one who'll stand up to the
Rutledges. . . ."

His voice trailed off as he stared at the high, blue sky, a thought
slowly forming in his mind, forming and growing. The Rutledges.
Maybe he hadn't lost yet. He had to try. Becca would want him
to try.

9

*O*ver the next few days each ring of the telephone became Kelly's own personal sword of Damocles. Every time she mentally braced herself for the worst. Over and over again she had rehearsed what she would say, how she would react, the words she would use to deflect the pity.

So far, nothing.

Kelly sat at the walnut conference table amid the producers and writers on the show's staff, all of them gathered there for the regular Monday-morning meeting. She doodled absently on her notepad, making little squares and rectangles, connecting them with straight lines. It was too soon to draw an easy breath. But at least she felt fully prepared now, ready to handle whatever came.

When Hugh began to talk, she looked up in a show of interest, only half listening to his words, too distracted to really concentrate until she caught the phrase "wine country of Napa Valley."

"What?" She broke in, drawing a frown from Hugh and amused glances from the rest. "Sorry, I wasn't listening," Kelly admitted, half convinced her mind was playing tricks on her. "What was it you just said?"

He glanced at the others, an eyebrow arching as he quoted from the Bible, "'They are drunken, but not with wine.'" When Hugh focused on Kelly, his look was faintly impatient, but he repeated himself. "I have decided we will do a feature on the wine country of Napa Valley. DeeDee will produce it. I spoke with Katherine Rutledge over the weekend and she has agreed to be interviewed. Believe me, it would be impossible to find a better subject than Katherine Rutledge. She exemplifies the area's past, its present, and quite possibly, its future direction." He paused, his attention again coming back to Kelly. "By the way, Kelly, she specifically asked me to give you her regards. I had the feeling that she is genuinely looking forward to seeing you again."

No! Kelly screamed the word in her head. Napa Valley was the last place she wanted to go. But when she opened her mouth, she managed to voice her objection very calmly and very reasonably. "Do you really think it's wise to do a story on wine, given the growing antidrinking sentiment in the country and the tougher drunk-driving laws?"

"A good point, but I think it's very wise, very topical, and very rich in scenery and mystique. More than that, I think the risk of offending anyone is very small, especially when you remember that Katherine Rutledge lived through the years of Prohibition. The subject has to be addressed."

She felt trapped, and stalled. "How soon do you plan to put this on schedule?"

"In two weeks."

"Two weeks? That's impossible," Kelly protested instantly. "There isn't enough preparation time."

Hugh's eyebrow shot up, his look both puzzled and amused. "This from a woman who had less than ten minutes to prepare before doing a live interview with Katherine nearly two weeks ago? And superbly, I might add," Hugh challenged, then continued without a break. "Logistically it works out perfectly. While you, Kelly, are wrapping up the segment on Harry Connick, Junior, DeeDee and her crew can fly out to California, shoot the color footage on the grape harvest, and select the locations for the interview portion. Then Kelly can fly out, do the interview, and go directly from there to Aspen for the feature story on John Travis."

He flashed Kelly a smile of silent congratulations on the latter. The day after her luncheon with Travis, his press agent had called, agreeing to the interview. If there had been any attempt on the part of Linda James to sabotage it, it had obviously failed.

"Two stories from one transcontinental flight," DeeDee observed. "The boys in budget will love you."

"Exactly my thought. By the way, DeeDee, the grapes at Rutledge Estate won't be ready to pick for two or three more weeks. Therefore, you'll have to scout around for other vineyards in the valley that are being harvested. I promise you will find many. Different varieties of grapes mature at different times."

"Why not wait to shoot the harvest at Rutledge Estate?" Kelly argued, seeing it, at least, as a means to stall for time.

"That was my first thought, but Katherine was adamantly

opposed to it. She insisted they were much too busy during crush, and a television crew would be much too disruptive. We do it at her convenience or not at all."

Kelly was strongly in favor of the latter, but she knew better than to say that. She couldn't without giving a reason, and how could she do that when this panic she felt was without reason? There was no hope at all of talking Hugh out of doing this story, not now that he had his mind set on it. She had only one way out of this — convince Hugh that it wasn't necessary for her to go.

"Considering how important this interview with John Travis is," Kelly began, sliding her fingers down her pen and flipping it end over end in a small show of agitation, "I think it would be best if I concentrated my efforts on it. DeeDee can do the wine story without me, the interviews and everything. Later I can do the lead-in and narration and the whole piece can be edited together."

It was something that was done all the time, giving viewers the impression that the person had actually conducted the interview when, in fact, it had been done by the producer of the segment. More than that, the show had three stories currently being shot in just that way.

"Every piece we do is important, Kelly." Hugh fixed his gaze on her, his look both puzzled and faintly irritated. "One may pull the viewers in, but the rest have to be equally good to keep them from switching to another program."

"I know that, but —"

"You will do the interview," he stated. "There is a definite chemistry between you and Katherine. It may not be there with DeeDee. In any case, I have no intention of finding out." He paused a beat, his study of her narrowing. "You surprise me, Kelly. You have always professed to have an interest in the place where you were born. Here's your chance to go to Napa Valley, at the network's expense, yet you're coming up with reasons not to go."

She was trapped, trapped by her own lies and fabrications. "It isn't that I don't want to go," she lied again. "This show — the success of it — is far more important to me than going to Napa Valley. I thought it was best, I still think it's best, to have my energies directed toward the interview with Travis."

"That is for me to decide. Not you." It was Hugh Townsend the show's executive producer talking. Not her friend and onetime mentor.

He had listened to her arguments and rejected them. His tone of voice made it clear that he considered the matter closed. If she continued to press it, she would be challenging his authority and putting both her personal and professional relationship with him at risk. She wasn't willing to do that; she couldn't afford to do it.

"As you say, you're the boss, Hugh." She lifted her shoulders in a shrug of concession, and privately tried to rationalize away as childish the dread that she felt.

Granted, the valley held only unpleasant memories for her, memories she preferred to forget. She'd go there, do the interview, and leave. With luck, she'd encounter very few ghosts. And only she would know when she did.

Brave words. It bothered her that they rang so hollow in her mind.

In the coolness of the great pillared building that was the winery of Rutledge Estate, Claude Broussard moved along the alleyway between the huge stainless-steel tanks. They stood empty now, but in a month's time, perhaps less, they would seethe with the juice and skins of this year's grape harvest. All must be in readiness for that time.

A worker emerged from one of the tanks, momentarily blocking the alleyway. Claude paused, searching the pointy features of this new worker, a wiry man with glasses and a swiftly fleeing hairline. He tried without success to recall the man's name.

The man gave a small start of surprise when he saw Claude standing there. He threw him a jerky nod, his glance bouncing away from him as he pushed his glasses back onto the bridge of his nose and turned to drag his hose to the next tank.

His suspicions aroused, Claude challenged, "This one is clean?"

"Yup." The man's head bobbed in a quick and nervous affirmation. "Shiny as brand-new."

The man was too new and his words rang too false. Claude grunted his doubt and crouched down to peer inside. The interior walls gleamed as if in confirmation. But Claude trusted his instinct more than his eyes.

In the next minute, he performed a seemingly impossible feat as he squeezed his broad shoulders and big torso through the small hole near the base of the tank. Once inside he made a closer inspection. When he had finished, he wedged himself back through the opening with the ease of experience, then stood, holding himself stiffly to contain the rage within.

"Have you a wife?" He glowered at the worker.

"Yes." The man nodded, his eyes blinking rapidly behind the lenses of his glasses.

"Would you have a child of yours born in there?" Claude thrust a rigid finger in the direction of the tank.

"In there?" The worker frowned, his mouth staying open, bewildered and uncertain.

"You would not because this tank is not clean." The instant the words were out, his control snapped and he bellowed, "Do you think a great wine can be born in a place that is not clean? It cannot! Go!" With a slash of a big hand, he waved the worker toward the door. "Leave this place. I will have no slacker in my winery."

"But if it isn't clean enough, I'll do it again. You can't just fire me without giving me another chance."

"Would my wine have had another chance if I had not found this? No. You shall not have one here. Seek it in the employ of some other winery." When the worker remained rooted to the floor, Claude took a step toward him, his big hands balling into gnarled fists. "Go. Collect your things and go."

"But . . ." The worker paused and glanced past him. "Mr. Rutledge, I —"

"If Claude says you're through at Rutledge Estate, you're through, Johnson." Sam Rutledge walked up to stand next to the cellar master.

"But it isn't fair."

Sam smiled without humor and replied, "What is?"

Red-faced with anger, the man threw down the hose and stalked off, grumbling under his breath.

"Achhh." Claude made a sound as if ridding his mouth of a bad taste. "I regret I did not take the hose and use it on him. Wine will have no future if it is plagued by careless workers such as that one. It is vital that wine has its beginnings in clean vessels if it is to start its life well. That imbecile thought only of finishing his task quickly."

"He's gone." Sam laid a hand on a sloped shoulder, feeling the vibrations of the old man's lingering wrath. "I'll round up Gino and have him clean the tanks."

"All of them," Claude added with a quick glare. "When he has finished, I shall inspect them."

"I'll be sure he knows that." Sam gave his shoulder a final pat and walked off.

Claude watched him. But it was several minutes before his temper cooled sufficiently to allow him to consider the worker Sam had chosen to clean the tanks. Claude nodded his grizzled head in approval. The choice was a sound one. Gino D'Allesandro could be trusted to do a thorough job. Still, he would inspect the tanks. One could not be too careful.

"Claude."

Turning, Claude saw Katherine coming toward him, a grimness about her lips and a snap of anger in her eyes. This was not the time of day she came to the winery.

"Madam." He frowned. "What is wrong?"

"Have you seen Sam? I was told he was here with you." Her glance searched the area, then came impatiently back to him.

"He left only minutes ago. He is to get Gino to clean the tanks. Is there trouble, Madam?"

"Indeed, there is trouble, and it is all the doing of my son."

"Gilbert," Claude said, giving his name the French pronunciation.

"Yes, Gil." The grimness in her expression increased. "I spoke with Baron Fougère this morning. It seems Gil has been talking to him at some length, and casting doubts."

"Doubts?"

"About Sam. His ability to lead Rutledge Estate, or any other winery. The very thing I have long questioned."

"Sam is a good man," Claude stated, firm in his belief. "He cares strongly for the vines, for the land."

She released a breath of disgust. "It is the only thing he feels strongly about. Sometimes . . ." Her voice dropped. "Sometimes I wish he were more like Gil, that he had some of his aggression. But he lacks ambition. He is too soft, too content. He would never fight to hold Rutledge Estate."

Claude gently disagreed with that. "I think he would never start a fight, Madam, but he would finish one."

Her look was full of skepticism, but she didn't argue the point. Instead her hand tightened on the cane and her head came up, her chin lifting to a determined angle. "I must know that the future of Rutledge Estate is secure. This business arrangement with the baron can give me that. Nothing and no one must prevent that from happening. Certainly not Gil." With that, she turned. "I must find Sam."

Claude nodded in understanding. As she moved away from him, he noted the pride in her carriage. As a boy he had thought she must be a princess from some royal house. To him she had been the most beautiful woman he had ever seen. While he had grown gnarled and old with the passing years, his face creased with as many lines as those that ringed a tree stump, she had kept much of her beauty. Just as she had kept the slimness of her youth.

Her hair had been black then, with all the shine of the onyx ring his patron, the baron, wore. It had been cut short then, too, in the new fashion of those years that followed the end of the Great War. The one they now called the First World War.

He had been a mere boy of eleven the first time he had seen Madam, in the château's garden with his mistress, the baroness, and another man with hair as yellow as the sun. Though he hadn't known it at the time, the man was her husband, Clayton Rutledge.

Laughter had been a rare thing to be heard coming from the château in those days. But it had been the sound of hers, so musical and so clear, that had drawn him to the château for a closer look at the guests who had arrived that day. . . .

A May breeze brought to him the mixed scent of lavender and roses as Claude crouched behind a trellis of roses and peered through the latticework into the garden. Beyond it rose the brooding magnificence of the château. Its collection of soaring towers and turrets built of huge, age-blackened stones jutted into the polished sky.

He took no more notice of it than he did the green web of vineyards that stretched behind him, in full leaf nearly all the way to the back of the Gironde. He had eyes for nothing except the young woman with the baroness. Her coloring was vivid, her skin as white as chalk, her hair as black as ink, her lips red like the wine in the *chai*, and her eyes bluer than the sky and sparkling with laughter.

The man spoke English. Claude thought his accent might be American, though he didn't know, for he understood none of the words. But the woman spoke French. Beautifully.

How long he hid there, looking and listening, he didn't know. He felt the tingling begin in his legs from being forced too long in one cramped position. Yet he didn't want to leave, not even when she strolled along the path of carefully raked gravel toward his hiding place.

When she turned to call to the baroness, Claude recognized the threat of discovery. He intended to slip away, to steal along the trellis of climbing roses until he was safely out of sight. But his big feet failed him, tripping him up and sending him crashing into the thorny roses.

Claude scrambled up as quickly as he could, but it was too late. There she stood, her blue eyes traveling over him in frank curiosity.

"And who are you?" she asked.

Claude faced her squarely and pulled himself up to his full height, which for his age of eleven was considerable. "I am called Claude

Henri Broussard." He darted a quick glance at the baroness, fearing
a reprimand, but she seemed more amused than angry. Suddenly, he
desperately wanted to have stature in the eyes of this beautiful
woman, and he added, very importantly, "My *grand-père* is the
maître de chai here at Château Noir."

"He is." She looked suitably impressed. "And your father?"

His glance fell as he fought a tightness in his throat. "He is dead,
Madam. Killed in the war."

The baroness inserted, very softly, "He was gassed in the
trenches. A fever took his *maman* soon afterward. He lives with his
grand-père now."

"I am sorry, Claude." The beautiful madam looked at him with
gentle eyes. "My father died when I was young like you. It was a
very painful time for me. Sometimes it still hurts when I think of
him."

He felt his heart swell that she would tell him this, that she would
understand what made his voice gruff. "When I am a man," Claude
told her, "I shall one day be *maître de chai*. My *grand-père* is teaching me all the things I must know."

"Then you must know a great deal about the vineyards." She
clasped her hands in front of her, her gloves white as pearls against
the pale pink of her dress.

Claude attempted one of the august nods his *grand-père* so often
gave. "I know about the vineyards and the winery. My *grand-père*
often consults with me in the tasting of the wines."

He had stretched the truth a bit with that one, but he had been
asked to taste the young wines on several occasions. And each time
his grandfather had sought his opinion. Perhaps not his opinion, but
he had been questioned on what he tasted and instructed in the
things to look for.

"How fortunate that I have met someone so knowledgeable as
you. My husband and I will be spending several weeks here. Perhaps your grandfather will allow you to be our guide, show us
through the vineyards and the winery."

There was such a swelling of pride in his chest, Claude thought
he would burst. "I will ask him." He bobbed his head quickly to
both the madam and the baroness, then tore off toward the *chai,* the
long, low, imposing building where the wine was stored in giant barrels until it had matured enough to be bottled. The place where he
knew he would find his *grand-père*.

Permission was not immediately given. His *grand-père* seemed to
doubt that the request was a serious one, and said he must check

first with the baron. It wasn't until later that evening that his *grand-père* told Claude to present himself at the château promptly at ten the following morning.

Dressed in his cleanest shirt and best pants, his unruly hair slicked to his head with water, Claude arrived at the château precisely at ten. He was excited and nervous. He wasn't sure which made him more nervous: his glimpse of the gilt-and-marble grandeur of the great *galerie* when the door opened; or the sight of the baron, slim and handsome in his tweed country jacket and fair-isle sweater, and the realization that he intended to accompany them.

But it was the beautiful madam who had his heart and his attention. Though he had thought it impossible, she looked even more beautiful today in a pale blue dress that made her hair appear blacker and her eyes darker than the rare and rich blue of the marble on the floor of the *galerie*.

It was difficult to tear his eyes from her, especially when she smiled at him and inquired after his health. Reddening, Claude mumbled a reply and turned to the baron, his *patron*.

"I thought to begin in the vineyards, if that is satisfactory with you," Claude said.

The baron withheld comment and deferred to his guests, leaving the choice to them. The madam spoke briefly to her husband in their language, then said to Claude, "Great wines have their beginnings in the vineyard. It is the place for us to begin, too."

That morning the vineyard seemed to know it had important guests and put on its brightest emerald dress for the occasion. Long ago his *grand-père* had taught Claude how to distinguish the variety of a vinifera vine by the shape of its leaves. Eager to show off his knowledge, he stepped quickly into the meter-wide space between the vine rows.

"This is the youngest of our vineyards. It has been planted to the cabernet sauvignon," he began. "You can tell this by —"

But the madam wasn't listening. She had bent to scoop up a handful of the turned soil between the rows, and now held out her gloved hand to her husband, showing him rough soil cupped in her palm. Although Claude couldn't understand what she said to him, he caught the marveling tone in her voice.

Finally she said to him in French, "We had not expected to find the soil so poor."

He thought she was being critical and sought to explain. "It is true the soil is poor for the growing of other crops, but it is the best for the growing of wine grapes. It is as my *grand-père* says — the water drains quickly from it and the vine roots must grow deep to find the moisture and nutrients they need. It is very important they should have deep roots. It is the way they stay strong and healthy when there is too little rain here, or too much. It is also important for the vines to bask in the sun from morning all the way to night." With a sweep of his arm, he indicated the whole vineyard, located to receive full sun all day long.

"I see that." She let her glance run over the vineyard, then brought it immediately back to the coarse soil in her palm. She stirred it with the tip of a gloved finger. "The land we own in America is rough and gravelly like this."

She seemed to find this significant, so Claude nodded. But it was the word *America* that he seized on, seeing it as another opportunity to impart his knowledge to her.

"You have heard of the phylloxera, *non?*" He referred to the tiny, louselike insect that attacked the roots, ultimately killing the vine plant.

In his grandfather's youth, the phylloxera plague had ravaged the continent, destroying two and a half million acres of French vineyards alone, eventually reaching all the way to Australia. The deadly invader had come to them from America, but Claude didn't want to offend the madam by mentioning that.

She started to shake her head in denial, then her husband said something. They conversed briefly. "My husband tells me that his grandfather lost his vineyards on our land to this plague. He replanted many of them, but not all."

"Did he tell you the way it was done so the phylloxera would not attack the roots of the new plants and kill them as well?"

"No," she admitted.

His mouth curved in silent pleasure that he could be the one to tell her. "It was discovered the phylloxera did not attack the roots of certain American grapevines. Cuttings were taken from our vinifera plants and grafted onto the American roots. A great many people believed this meant fine wines could no longer be made from these grapes that gained their nourishment from American roots. But my *grand-père*," Claude said proudly, "he did not agree with such talk. He said the vines would know the soil was French even if the sap that brought the taste of it to them traveled through American roots." He paused and echoed the words his *grand-père* had spoken so often. "It is all in the earth, Madam. Great wines can be made only from great grapes, and the earth gives the grapes their greatness. Of course, they also need the correct weather and care," he said, adding the other two items in the essential trinity. "God provides the weather and we provide the care." Claude made it sound as if he were personally responsible for the latter.

She didn't dispute him. "I have no doubt you give the vines very good care."

Swelling a bit at her praise of him, he continued the tour of the vineyard. He pointed out the distinctive shape of the cabernet sauvignon's leaf, showed her a flower cluster and the tiny grapes that were forming in places, and explained that these vines were enjoying their fifth summer of growth and that this year promised to be the first one in which the grapes would have the potential to produce a great wine.

Claude searched his mind for every scrap of knowledge his *grand-père* had taught him about the vines. Occasionally the *patron* inserted a comment, although for the most part, he allowed Claude to do all the telling.

Too soon the sun crested and began its downward arc, time for the midday meal and the tour to end. With reluctance, Claude faced the madam and prepared to take his leave of her.

She smiled at him. "Thank you, Claude, for a very informative tour. Perhaps tomorrow, if you are free, you can take us through the winery."

He hesitated and glanced at his *patron*, wishing he would be the one to tell the madam. But the baron merely looked at him with a knowing eye and waited for Claude to speak.

He felt awkward, not at all certain how to bring up the subject, and worried that he would upset her. "Forgive me, Madam," he began anxiously. "But the fragrance you wear. It is very lovely," he inserted hastily. "But, my *grand-père,* he is very strict. He allows no strong scents, no perfumed hair creams to be worn, nothing that might taint the young wines." He saw the flush of color come into her cheeks and immediately dropped his gaze, mumbling, "I am deeply sorry, Madam. Were it not for that, I should be happy to show you the winery."

"Does your *grand-père* have any objections to the clean smell of soap?"

He lifted his head, hardly daring to hope. "*Non.*"

"Tomorrow, I promise, my husband and I will smell of nothing else." Her voice was cool, but her look was kind. "Will that do?"

"*Oui,* Madam." Claude beamed back at her. "It will please my *grand-père* very much that you understand. Many times he has told me the wine must always come first; people and their feelings, second."

She seemed to consider his words carefully for several long moments, then nodded to him and took her husband's arm to start toward the château. Claude backed away, then turned and raced to the small cottage on the property that he shared with his *grand-père*.

Claude was much too excited to eat and his stew grew cold while he told his *grand-père* of all that had happened, and everything the madam had said. It mattered little that his *grand-père* shared neither his excitement nor enthusiasm.

The next morning, he again presented himself at the château. This time Claude took his same group to the old stone winery. Progress was much slower on this day. The madam's husband had many questions, necessitating the translation of both the questions and their answers. Fortunately his *grand-père* was on hand to respond to the more technical ones.

After the midday meal the tour was resumed at the *chai* to sample some of the young wines. The temperature inside was cool, the thick walls maintaining a constant of fifty-five degrees. Claude stood by while his *grand-père* climbed a short ladder to reach the top of one of the large oak barrels lying on its side. Using a wooden mallet, he knocked the bung from its hole and thrust a long tube of glass, called a wine thief by some, into the barrel. He closed the top of the tube with his horny thumb and extracted a tall column of purple wine. With a deftness that came from a half century of practice, his *grand-père* released a precise measure into each glass.

For a moment Claude was afraid his *grand-père* would not prepare a glass for him. Just as he started to shift uneasily, his *grand-père* offered one to him, treating him as a grown man — just as the madam did.

With glasses in hand, the baron took over and went through the tasting process step by step in his faulty, heavily accented English that Claude couldn't follow. Instead he copied his *grand-père*, as he always had.

First Claude studied the color of the wine. It was a shade of purple more red than blue, which indicated its youth. Cupping his hands around the glass, he warmed the wine to the optimum temperature and moved the glass in a vigorous, circular motion to agitate the wine and release its vapors. He stuck his nose in the glass and breathed them.

This was the wine's bouquet, which consisted of a variety of odors. He was pleased when the madam detected so many separate smells — oak, definitely cedar, a fruitiness that reminded her of black currants more than grapes, and a trace of violets. Even his *grand-père* appeared to be impressed that she had such a sensitive nose.

Finally Claude took a sip of the wine, drawing it into his mouth in a thin stream, stroking it with his tongue, then using his tongue to push it into every crevice of his mouth, chewing it the way a taster did, the way his grandfather had taught him. It was strong and hard, yet without the balance it needed, Claude thought.

At this point, his *grand-père* had always had him spit out the wine. But nothing had been provided into which he could spit it. Claude looked around uncertainly, then swallowed it in a noisy gulp. The taste of it stayed in his mouth a long time. His *grand-père* would have said it had a long finish, he thought, remembering the correct term.

Both the madam and her husband took their time in tasting the wine in their glasses. Afterward, she briefly placed her fingers against her lips, then lowered them.

"It is strong," she told the baron. "It made my mouth pucker a little."

"That is the tannin you taste," the *patron* explained. "It is what gives the wine a long life. Yet there cannot be too much or it will taste bitter, like tea that has steeped too long."

"I can see that." The madam nodded, then translated the baron's remarks to her husband.

In the days and weeks that followed, Claude saw the madam frequently. She and her husband were always somewhere about, looking at this, asking questions about that, curious about everything around them. Sometimes Claude accompanied them; at others, he could only watch while he performed some task his grandfather had given him.

But he learned much about the madam, most of it from his conversations with her and the rest from other workers on the property. In America, she lived in a place called California where inferior American wines had once been made, before that country passed an absurd law that forbade the making and selling of wine, or any alcoholic beverage.

She had become friends with the baroness some years ago when they both had attended the same school in Switzerland. According to gossip from the house servants, she had brought her two young sons to France with her; the youngest was called Gilbert, and the oldest had an English name Claude found difficult to pronounce: Jonathon. He had never seen them. He was told the madam had brought along a woman to look after them and see to their needs.

Also he learned that both the madam and her husband believed the day would soon come when it would be legal again in their country to make wine. When it did, they would make wine from grapes grown on their own California land that would rival the best wines from the great châteaux of France. An impossibility, of course, their soil was not French. Yet Claude secretly hoped the beautiful madam would fulfill her dream.

Still, as much as he had learned about them, as much as he adored the madam, he doubted he would ever understand these Americans. They were very different from the guests who usually stayed at the château. They were definitely very different from his *patron,* the baron.

The *patron* would regularly inspect the vineyards, examine the vines for disease, the grapes for ripeness. Just as often, he came to the *chai* and consulted with Claude's *grand-père* on the wines aging in the barrels and bottles, checking their progress. But for the *patron* to associate with the workers, to be at their side hour after hour, to learn their work, to do it himself — it was unthinkable!

Yet the madam's husband did it almost as a matter of course. As vintage drew near and the time came for the old leaves to be snipped away to let more sun reach the ripening grapes, he was in the vineyards with the workers, watching what they did, finding out why they selected certain leaves over others, then copying them.

His French was so bad, his sentences interspliced with English, that most times the madam was with him. Claude thought she took as much interest in the work as her ruddy-faced husband.

Even though he didn't know what to make of her husband, like the rest of the workers Claude grew to like him. Not as much as the madam, of course. She was special; her husband was unusual. He wanted to do everything, know everything.

On the dawn of the morning when the first grapes were to be picked, her husband arrived at the vineyard in shirtsleeves. He collected a basket and a knife with a curved blade from the foreman and went to his assigned row. More astonishing than that, he worked as long as the other pickers did.

The next day, instead of going to the vineyards, he went to the winery and learned how the grapes were stemmed and crushed. The madam stayed with him the whole time, conveying his endless questions to Claude's *grand-père* and relating the answers.

Day after day it went on like that. Many times Claude's *grand-père* grumbled that the man was a nuisance, a plague to him. But Claude had seen the glint of approval, of respect, in the eye of his *grand-père* and he had heard the patience in his voice when he explained something, frequently in lengthy detail, to Monsieur Rutledge.

Yes, his *grand-père* liked this man. And he liked the madam, too, though he never said so.

When crush was over and the vineyards donned their red and gold coats of autumn, Claude expected the couple to leave. Yet they stayed, although a few times, they did, as they had on occasions during the summer, climb into their touring car and motor off to Paris or to visit another winery in the Médoc. Why? Claude didn't know. There was none that made better wines than Château Noir. Some were as good, perhaps, but none was better.

That winter they were on hand for the first pruning. What a sight it was to see the tall monsieur bent almost double as he worked, cutting away the unproductive wood from the vine. At the end of the day he showed the madam the blisters on his hand, with some pride in them, and both laughed.

With the approach of spring, both went to the vineyards for the second pruning, the green pruning, the critical one both in timing and extent. Albert Girardin, the château's horticulturist, took them from plant to plant, and taught them to imagine the bare cane fully grown. From that mind picture, the plant was pruned so the branches and leaves matched the root area.

Albert later told Claude's *grand-père* that he wished the other workers learned as quickly as these Americans. He also admitted, with some embarrassment, that the madam showed a remarkable affinity for the vine, unusual in a woman. Claude was very proud of that.

That summer was a joyous time. There were many guests at the château, many parties. Sometimes at night, when he was sure his *grand-père* was asleep, Claude would sneak out of the cottage and slip through the moon-silvered vineyards to the château, aglow with elegance from dozens of windows.

Lively music from within filled the night air; jazz, they called it. The guests would be assembled in the grand salon, the men resplendent in their black tailcoats, worn open over double-breasted white waistcoats and sharply creased black trousers, their hair gleaming with brilliantine. And the ladies in their slim gowns, shimmering with beaded fringe and trailing satin ribbons and chiffon scarves, ropes of pearls hanging from their necks to below the waist. How beautiful they all looked, how sophisticated with their long cigarette holders and crystal glasses of champagne. Always, always Claude was relieved when he located the madam among the guests, and saw again that none were as beautiful as she. Only then did he sneak back to his cottage and his bed.

Autumn came, with no hint of the tragedy it was to bring. On a crisp September morning, the monsieur drove away from the château. He waved to Claude and shouted that he was off to select cuttings to take home to America with them. The madam was not with him. Their youngest son, Gilbert, was ill with a fever; a doctor was coming to treat him.

How unfortunate to be unwell on such a glorious day, Claude thought, looking at the mist sparkling on the Gironde. Somewhere a lark trilled a greeting to the rising sun, its golden light glinting on the dew-wet leaves in the vineyard and casting deep shadows between the rows. The air smelled good, fresh. It was indeed a glorious day.

It wasn't until late that afternoon when Claude returned from school that he learned the terrible news — the American monsieur had been killed in a motoring accident. He had swerved to avoid a horse-drawn cart and lost control of his vehicle. It had careened off the road and overturned, killing the monsieur instantly.

A pall hung over the estate that not even the bright sun could penetrate. That evening, when the day's work was done, the workers gathered, men, women, and children collecting in small groups, tongues clicking at the tragedy of it, heads shaking, everyone remembering. . . .

"The monsieur, he must have been traveling too fast. He was always in a hurry, wanting to know everything, wanting to know it immediately." "*Oui*, the monsieur and his endless questions." "The poor madam, how she must be grieving. She went with him everywhere." "*Oui*, they were always together . . . until today." "If she had gone with him, their children would have lost both their parents. It was the will of God that her youngest should be sick this day of all days." "The malady is not a serious one. Already the fever has come down."

Claude stood among them, listening. He was too big to cry. But he wanted to, for her, his beautiful madam. Who would look after her now? Who would protect her and keep her from harm?

A private Mass was held the following day for the American monsieur Clayton Rutledge. The families of every worker assembled at the pebbled courtyard of the château's front entrance and waited for the madam to return. Shawls covered the women's heads, their clothes as somber as the gray skies above. Like the other men, Claude wore a black arm band around his sleeve as a symbol of mourning.

He saw the cars pass through the iron gates and make the long, and slow, return trip down the white graveled drive to the château. When they stopped in front of the. assemblage, he respectfully removed his cap.

The *patron* himself assisted the madam from the car. She was draped in black — shoes, dress, gloves, veil, and cloche hat. She paused when she saw the workers who had gathered. She took a tighter grip on the hand of her oldest son, a boy of eight or nine in short pants, his hair a lighter shade of yellow than his father's. He looked confused, and frightened. The youngest, it was said, was still in bed but greatly improved.

Claude passed over the young boy to dwell on his beautiful madam. When she stepped forward to face the large crowd, she didn't bow her head, but lifted it higher. Her shoulders were not curved in grief but squared and proud. Yet, through the veil, Claude could see the shine of wet cheeks, and his heart went out to his poor, brave madam.

When she spoke, her voice never wavered, never broke, but reached out to them clear and pure. "You do my husband a great honor by coming here today. The days he spent with you, learning from you, were among the happiest of his life. I thank you for that. In the days and years ahead, when I remember these times, I promise I will remember the happiness we knew, not the grief, for I have memories I shall treasure always. And when you think of my husband, I hope you will remember him with fondness, as I shall remember all of you."

Then she went around and shook each hand, save for Claude's. Soon she would be leaving and he could not bear that. He slipped away, unnoticed, and hid in the vineyard. There, among the vines and the purple-black grapes, he let the tears stream down his cheeks and his broad shoulders shake with silent sobs.

Every morning for a week, Claude woke up with a sick feeling of dread that this would be the day she would leave. But the week passed and she was still there, though he had not seen her venture from the château once in all that time.

He kicked a rock in front of him, walked dully after it, and used the scuffed toe of his shoe to send it flying again toward the winery, lifting his head only to look at the black spires of the château rising, above the wall of poplars. It was the eve of vintage, yet Claude felt none of the excitement he'd experienced at previous harvests.

He saw his *grand-père* outside the winery, talking with the *patron*, not a particularly noteworthy event for this time of year. He slowed his steps even more. His *grand-père* would not welcome an interruption now, and the evening meal, prepared by the wife of Albert the horticulturist, would stay warm on the cooking range back at the cottage.

Thinking of the madam in seclusion at the château, Claude stared at the baron and idly shoved the dry, pebbly soil around with his toe. The baron looked stern, and a little sad. He seemed to be the one doing all the talking; Claude's *grand-père* responded with little more than an occasional curt nod. This was not a normal exchange, Claude thought, and looked more closely at his *grand-père*. How rigid he held himself, and his face — it was stiff with anger.

This was a curious thing. His *grand-père* was frequently impatient, frequently irritated, but angry? Claude could not recall that.

His *grand-père* made a stiff bow to the baron and walked off. He came straight toward Claude and walked past him without a word, without a glance. Tears. Were those tears he had seen in the eyes of his *grand-père?* For a moment, Claude was too stunned by the sight to move. Then he ran after him, to make certain his own eyes hadn't deceived him.

When he caught up with him, one single tear laid a wet track down his *grand-père*'s craggy cheek. "*Grand-père*. What is wrong? What has happened?"

But he received no answer as his *grand-père* opened the door to the cottage and gave it a violent push, sending it banging into the wall. It swung back toward Claude. He caught it and slipped inside, closing the door behind him. His *grand-père* stood at the trestle table in the kitchen, his hands braced on the top of it, his head bowed.

"*Grand-père*." Claude took a cautious step toward him, then stopped.

His *grand-père* pushed off the table and stalked to the small window, looking out with a scowl on his face. "As of today, I am no longer *maître de chai*." His voice was low and gruff, thick with outrage. "André Paschal is to take my place."

Claude stared at him. This was not possible. "Wh-what?"

"The *patron*" — he almost sneered the word — "says I am too old. That for the good of the wine it is time for me to step aside. Too old!" He slammed his open palm on the worktable that held the washbasin, and Claude jumped at the explosive sound it made. "My father was *maître de chai* when he was eighty. I have many more good years left in me. But *he* cannot see that." He swung around and shook his finger at Claude. "This would not happen if the old *patron* were still alive."

The old *patron* had died before Claude was born. He had never known any *patron* but the baron he now served. He stared at his *grand-père*, wide-eyed, struggling to take this all in, to figure out what it meant.

"What will happen?"

His hand dropped to his side and he again stood stiffly facing the window. "I am to be pensioned off. For my years of service, I have been given a cottage and three acres of vineyards —" He paused and started to tremble. "— in the fifth-growth district! I, Girard Stephen Louis Broussard, who was born in the Médoc, in the first-growth district." He bellowed the words and punched a fist against his chest in emphasis. "*I,* who have spent a half century of years making the finest of wines, I am now relegated to spending my final years making vin ordinaire. Not because I have lost the knowledge, the skill, or the experience to make a premier Bordeaux. *Non,* it is because the *patron* thinks I am too old."

His *grand-père* fell silent and they both stood motionless for a long time, thinking their own thoughts. For Claude, this was the only place he had ever known, the only home he had ever had. Soon he would be leaving it, just as the madam would. He had thought he would grow to manhood at Château Noir, that one day he would be *maître de chai*, that he would make wines in which he could take pride. Now . . . now, he didn't know what would become of him, of them.

At last his *grand-père* turned from the window, a sound of disgust coming from his throat. "The food grows dry. Let us eat."

He dished the food from the warming pots, slapping it onto the plates. They sat down at the table and each went through the motions of eating, but most of the food had to be scraped from their plates when they were done.

Later that evening, after the sun went down, Claude sat at the table, his schoolbook open in front of him, a lamp burning beside it. His *grand-père* sat in the dark by the fire, its flickering light playing over his face, giving it the look of old leather, all cracked and dry. Hands that had known the purple grape stains of fifty years of harvests dangled limply from the ends of the chair's wooden armrests. Tonight he looked old, old and broken in spirit. Claude wanted to say something to him, but he didn't know the words. Finally he turned back to the blurring print on the pages of his schoolbook.

There was a knock at the door. Claude started to scramble from his chair, but his *grand-père* waved him back to his schoolwork and went to answer it himself.

It was the madam! Claude gaped when she walked through the doorway. With a snap of fingers and an impatient wave of a hand, his *grand-père* sent Claude scurrying to light more lamps and chase the night's heavy shadows from the room. He was embarrassed by the humbleness of their kitchen and common room, recognizing the poorness of the wall's whitewashed plaster after having glimpsed the silk-covered walls in the château.

When his *grand-père* pulled out a wooden chair for the madam, Claude raced to get a clean cloth to cover it. But when he came back with one that he had found in his mother's trunk of things, Madam was already seated, speaking quietly to his *grand-père.* Claude stood just beyond the pool of light from the lamp and stared, still unable to believe the madam was here in his cottage.

She wore the black of mourning, but no veil screened her face. It was composed and pale, without a trace of rouge on her cheeks or red on her lips. Yet she was beautiful. And her eyes, their look fixed intently on his *grand-père,* they seemed to burn. Not with anger or temper. It was something different, a kind of power perhaps.

Her words drifted to him. Claude stepped closer to catch all of them.

". . . the dream my husband and I shared to one day make wines as fine as any in France. I am going to fulfill that dream, but I cannot do it alone. I shall require help. I need your help, Monsieur Broussard."

"Mine?"

"Yes. I will require your assistance to help me select strong, healthy cuttings. I will need you, and your grandson" — she glanced briefly at Claude — "to come to California with me to help plant the vines and take care of them. Until the day comes when Prohibition is repealed, you will be able to make wines only for the church and medicinal uses. We — I have a permit that allows that," she inserted, then continued. "In the meantime, it will take several years for the vines to grow and mature to the stage where they produce grapes with the potential to make a fine wine. Will you do this, Monsieur Broussard? Will you go to America with me and become my *maître de chai?*"

Claude waited for his *grand-père* to speak, afraid to hope, afraid to breathe. For a long time his *grand-père* was silent, then he nodded and lifted his head.

"I have heard much about America and the bad wine you make," he said and Claude nearly moaned aloud at the trace of contempt in the voice of his *grand-père*. "Perhaps you need a Frenchman to show you the way to make a good one."

A small smile lifted the corners of Madam's mouth. "Then you will go with me?"

"I will."

Claude could have whooped for joy, but he contained his excitement until the madam had departed. His grandfather closed the door, then turned to Claude and winked.

"Too old, eh?"

"We are going to America. We are going to America!" Claude threw himself at his *grand-père* and hugged him fiercely.

There was much to be done, cuttings to be purchased, arrangements to be made, belongings to be packed, passage to be booked. It was late winter before they sailed from Bordeaux.

Claude stood among the shiny fermentation tanks, no longer the husky young boy he had been when he first arrived at Rutledge Estate, but an old man, as weathered and lined as his *grand-père* had been.

How odd that he should remember the place of his birth so vividly after all these years. The jutting towers and spires of the château, its blackened walls, a lark spiraling toward the sun, the chirrup of the grasshoppers, the vineyards along the banks of the Gironde, the taste of the stew made by Albert's wife, the scent of lavender and roses from the formal garden at the château, the music, the beaded dresses — what had brought the memories back so sharply to him? Had it been the madam's reference to the new baron? Or the mention of her youngest son, Gilbert?

Did it matter? It was all so long ago. This was his home now, his true home. He looked about him, a contented smile cracking his face. He knew every inch of this old building, every corner and every crevice, every sound and every smell. He knew its every secret, and kept them.

He had a small stone house on the property, where he slept. But this winery was his home, this was where he spent his waking hours, where he ate his meals, where he made wines every bit as fine as those from Château Noir.

Wine. He must prepare his home to receive this year's vintage. Time. Where did it go? It seemed to pass so quickly now, he thought, and hurried off to check the new cooperage.

*　　*　　*

The low building a short distance from the brick winery had once been a stable for the draft horses that had pulled the wagons and plows on the estate. Twenty years ago it had been converted into offices, the stall doors bricked halfway up, the openings framed in, and windows installed. The stall partitions had been knocked down and sturdier ones erected to divide the building into comfortably sized rooms. Oak flooring covered the old concrete.

An ancient live oak stood outside, its great limbs arched over it to keep the building in shade most of the day. Sam passed beneath it and entered the former stable.

Gaylene Westmore, a buxom brunette who acted as receptionist, secretary, mail clerk, file clerk, and general do-everything, was on the phone. Without a break in her conversation, she picked up a sheaf of messages from her desk and handed them to him, tapping the top one. It was from a distributor in the Northwest pleading for five cases of the '86 Reserve cabernet. Sam doubted they could send him more than one but he'd check the inventory on his computer.

He heard the clack of a computer and headed down the old stable corridor to the accounting section. He stopped in long enough to give Johnson's time card to Andy Halsted and let him know Claude had fired Johnson.

"We'll have to document this, Sam. List the cause and circumstances."

"Leave the necessary form on my desk. I'll fill it out and sign it," Sam told him, fully aware that Claude didn't do forms, certainly never in any timely fashion.

Retracing his steps, Sam headed down the corridor to his own office at the opposite end of the building. The stable's old, hand-hewn beams had been left exposed, giving the room a slightly rustic look. A scarred and battered mahogany desk sat by the window.

Sam had run across it seven years ago when Katherine had sent him up to the attic to bring down the Christmas decorations. He'd dragged it downstairs, along with an old tintype of his great-great-grandfather George Simpson Rutledge, the first Rutledge to own the estate, seated behind this very desk.

When Katherine realized he intended to put it in his office, she'd taken one look at the desk and said, "You are going to have it refinished."

"As soon as I can get around to it," he had replied.

Of course he hadn't. He liked the scratches and gouges, the ink stains and cigar burns; they gave the desk character. The old tintype held a prominent place in the bookcase on the wall behind the desk, tucked between volumes on viticulture and enology while sharing space with an old spectrophotometer, a broken wine thief, and some calibrated glass tubes.

The scratchy horsehair sofa along the opposite wall was another of Sam's attic finds. A more uncomfortable piece of furniture had never been made. It was reserved for salesmen he didn't like and wanted to get rid of quickly. A pair of wing chairs, covered in burgundy leather and studded with brass, faced the desk, castoffs from the library at the main house. The walls were painted a soft green, picking up the colors in the siskel rug that stretched over most of the oak floor. Their bareness was covered by a collection of rare Audubon prints and botanical drawings of vinifera vines.

Sam crossed to the desk and hooked his hat on a modern sculpture that supposedly depicted Bacchus, the Roman god of wine. A stack of completed questionnaires and government forms occupied the center spot on his desk, awaiting his signature. The state and county ag reports and the questionnaire from the wine association he skimmed before affixing his signature and the date at the bottom. The monthly report for the Bureau of Alcohol, Tobacco, and Firearms, giving the amount of wine in cask and storage, the amount of bonded wine, and the amount Rutledge Estate paid taxes on, Sam took with him as he rolled his chair over to the computer terminal to verify the figures listed.

Satisfied with their accuracy, he rolled back to the desk. As he reached for his pen to sign the report, Katherine walked in. He raised an eyebrow in mild surprise.

"At last I have caught up with you," she stated in a cool tone that implied censure. "I have been through half the winery looking for you."

It was rare for Katherine ever to seek him out. "What's wrong?" He motioned toward a wing chair, inviting her to take a seat, but she ignored the gesture and continued to stand.

"Gil has invited the baron and his wife to spend some time in Napa Valley. Emile has accepted." Her words were clipped. "He feels he owes Gil the courtesy of inspecting his facilities and operation. While he is here, he naturally plans to spend some time at Rutledge Estate as well."

"When is he coming?" Sam went ahead and signed the report.

"In two weeks."

He lifted his head, frowning slightly. "Then he must intend to stay through crush."

"Obviously." She walked to the window by the horsehair sofa and looked out the panes at the view of the old brick winery, both hands resting atop the carved head of her cane. "You do realize that Emile will be specifically looking you over. Gil has planted doubts that you have the ability to run a large winery on your own."

"He would have missed a good opening if he hadn't," Sam replied dryly. "The whole valley knows you run Rutledge Estate. All the major decisions come from you. My role here is simply to carry them out."

She turned her head to cast him one of her cool, challenging stares. "I expect you to remove those doubts while Emile is here."

Amused, Sam rocked back in his chair. "How do you propose I do that, Katherine, when I have never been able to convince you of my ability?"

Startled by his frankness, Katherine stiffened. Her own lack of faith in him was something she had never discussed with him. Nor did she intend to address it now.

"That is not the issue here," she insisted.

"But it is," Sam countered. "If you truly believed I could run the winery on my own, you never would have contacted the baron in the first place, would you?"

"I have never questioned your dedication to your work. As a manager, you are more than adequate."

"That's called being damned by faint praise, Katherine." His smile was hard and cool.

Irritated that he should persist on this topic, Katherine retorted, "By nature, you are much too easygoing."

"Easygoing." He steepled his fingers in a pose of mock thoughtfulness. "I suppose I was too easy on Dougherty when I took his rifle from him and didn't ram it down his throat after he shot at my men. And last year when you were laid up after your fall, I filed suit against Rutcliff Winery in Sonoma and got an injunction to stop them from distributing wine they had bottled under a label that was all but identical to ours. You were upset when I dropped the suit after they agreed to make substantial changes in their label design. You wanted to continue the litigation, force them to pay damages, make an example of them to other wineries. In my opinion, there was no need to get involved in a costly legal battle."

"It would have been money well spent. You were too lenient."

"So you said at the time."

"I was right."

Anger darkened his eyes, an occurrence so rare that it immediately captured her full attention. For an instant Katherine thought her grandson was going to come out of his chair. Unconsciously she held her breath and waited for the show of fire. But it didn't come. Instead the fire was banked as he rocked forward and picked up his phone messages.

"Your way is the only right way, isn't it, Katherine?" His cynical tone held the smallest trace of sarcasm.

"My way is the only right way for Rutledge Estate." Disappointed in him again, she let it show. "Weakness can never be permitted."

His head came up. "Don't mistake good judgment for weakness, Katherine," he warned. "The poor soil and rough landscape of Rutledge Estate is a harsh environment, exposed to the full heat of the sun and an almost constant wind. It produces grapes that look small, maybe even puny. But all of them have developed the thick skins they need to survive in this climate."

"I am fully aware of that, Jonathon."

"Sam," he corrected, breaking off their near-argument, regarding it as futile. "Better not make that mistake around the baron or he'll think your mind is slipping."

"I want this merger." It was a flat, hard statement.

"And Gil is going to do his damnedest to take it away from you," Sam reminded her. "It's a personal thing with him."

A silence ran for several seconds before Katherine responded. "There is that personal aspect on his part, but he also needs it for financial reasons. All of his vineyards are infected with that new strain of phylloxera." She spoke slowly, her voice full of thought. Sam was reminded of a computer sifting through all the data and compiling an answer. "Over the next four years, every single acre will have to be replanted, which will require an enormous influx of cash."

"I assumed he got into the futures market to finance that."

"True." Her lips curved in the smallest of smiles. "But how much better it would be to have outside capital contributing to a large share of that cost. I wonder if Emile is aware of his situation," she mused. "Perhaps I should mention it to him . . . just in passing, of course."

"Of course," he mocked. "Just out of curiosity, where is the baron staying while he's here?"

"Gil offered him the use of his guest house, but Emile has reserved a suite at Auberge du Soleil. Neutral ground," she explained and turned from the window, a confident tilt to her head. "I must arrange to have a party to welcome the baron to the valley, perhaps while the television crew is here."

"What television crew?" Sam frowned.

"I planned to tell you tomorrow at lunch. I talked to Hugh Town-send last week. He wants to do a story on California wines and feature Rutledge Estate."

"And you agreed?"

"I wouldn't want Emile to have the impression that Gil is the only one who can generate publicity. We can do it as well, and it will be national in scope. Perhaps even international," she added with a graceful lift of a shoulder. "Certainly it will be much more effective in elevating the name of Rutledge Estate than a lot of photographs and articles in trade publications and wine magazines. I understand that the crew will be here for several days. Who knows? Perhaps we shall have a major announcement to give them while they are here." She started toward the door. "Lunch at one tomorrow."

Privately Sam wondered whether Kelly Douglas would be among the crew. But he didn't ask. Instead, he nodded and confirmed, "Tomorrow."

Alone, he stared at the door Katherine closed behind her. He wasn't sure why the memory of his meeting with Kelly Douglas in New York had stuck so fast in his mind. Maybe it was the contrast between the calm, smooth sound of her voice and the tension and restless energy he sensed vibrating from her. Maybe it was the strength and intelligence in her features. Or maybe it was the wariness he had sometimes seen in her eyes, a wariness that indicated she was somehow vulnerable despite the strength she showed.

Or maybe it was nothing more than the heat of that damned kiss.

Shaking off his wandering thoughts, Sam concentrated on the phone messages before him.

10

Rain pattered against the window in Kelly's office and ran in sheets down the panes. Ten stories below, New York still rushed, bumped, and shoved its way through another day, taxis splashing through the streets, horns blaring in impatience, people scurrying along the sidewalks beneath umbrellas, folded newspapers, or bravely facing the rain bareheaded. The pace, the energy of the city never slackened.

Kelly turned from her contemplation of the scene below and glanced at her desk. Idly she ran a hand over the edge of its walnut surface. The desk was one Kelly had discovered at a garage sale in St. Louis shortly before she moved to New York. Used as a worktable by its previous owner, it had been in sad shape, its top mottled with dents and black stains, several of its drawer pulls missing, its sides scratched and gouged, and one leg cracked. The moving company men had looked at her with raised eyebrows when they learned she wanted it shipped with the rest of her furniture.

Today eyebrows arched in silent admiration. All trace of its numerous scars and blemishes was gone. A damp cloth and a warm iron had eliminated the dents; colored wood filler had fixed the cracked leg and mended the scratches; two applications of wood bleach had removed even the worst discolorations; a coat of walnut stain had brought out the wood's rich grain; and three coats of wax had given it a glow of deep luster.

Feeling the smoothness of the polished surface, Kelly thought of the hours she had spent rubbing the clear paste wax over every inch of the newly stained wood. Even now the smell of beeswax lingered, overpowered by the stronger fragrance of roses and violets that sprang from a lemonade pitcher of Pickard china. The pitcher was one of her finds at the flea market on Sixth Avenue and Twenty-sixth Street, along with a cast-iron black hare, once used as a door-stop, that now adorned her desk. Posters of paintings by Monet and O'Keeffe gave color to walls.

Her glance fell on the thick folder in the middle of her desk, a folder that Research had dropped off a few minutes ago, containing all the information and articles they had been able to gather on Katherine Rutledge and Rutledge Estate. In truth it wasn't as thick as she had expected it to be.

Kelly opened the folder and leafed through the contents, laying aside for the time being an eight-page typed summary of the information within. The rest was mainly copies of magazine articles, newspaper clippings, pages excerpted from books on the local history of wine making, and photographs, both old and new.

All of it was in chronological order, beginning with George Simpson Rutledge, who had made his fortune in the import-export business during San Francisco's gold-rush days. In 1879 he purchased the five-hundred-acre rancho that was to become Rutledge Estate. Like many other wealthy San Franciscans of his day, he built a summer home in the valley that, according to the flowery language of the time, was "every bit as grand as any European duchy." In the same article, mention was made that in addition to raising cattle, sheep, and horses, he intended to plant several of his acres to vineyards and follow the lead of others in the valley "in the making of wine from grapes."

A later article on the destructive effects of phylloxera in the valley included a line that read: "All fifty acres of vineyard owned by George Simpson Rutledge of San Francisco have been ravaged by this terrible plague. Mr. Rutledge states he will replant if a remedy can be found."

There was an obituary notice on the death of his wife in the last year of the century. Another short article followed that one, only months later, stating that Mr. Rutledge had turned his San Francisco company over to his eldest son and had moved permanently to his home in the valley.

A grainy newspaper photograph showed damage suffered in the valley from the great quake that devastated San Francisco. The caption under it identified the rubble as the stone sheepshead on the property of George Rutledge. "Bricks were shaken loose from the chimneys of the main residence and the winery suffered minor damage. Mr. Rutledge feels fortunate the destruction was not worse."

At his death, in 1910, there was a lengthy article chronicling the accomplishments of his life. The last paragraph stated that he was survived by two sons, a daughter, and four grandchildren. None of them were named.

That was followed by a 1917 article on the wedding of Clayton Rutledge and Katherine Leslie Fairchild. The reporter went on at length, describing the gowns worn by the bride and her attendants, the lavish reception, the refreshments served, and the wedding presents. "The groom's parents gifted the happy couple with the family summer home in Napa Valley." Later the same year, a society column mentioned that the Clayton Rutledges had decided to live permanently in their Napa Valley home and "pursue the life of a gentleman farmer."

An article on the proposed Prohibition legislation that threatened the burgeoning wine industry in the valley included a quote from Clayton Rutledge stating that he felt certain the making of wine would be exempted. Then came a clipping, dated after Prohibition had gone into effect, that mentioned the Rutledge Estate winery had been granted a permit to make sacramental wines as well as some for medicinal uses. The next article contained news of his death, six years later, in a motoring accident near Bordeaux, France. He was survived by his wife, Katherine, and two young sons, Jonathon, age eight, and Gilbert, age six.

Kelly sighed. So far there was nothing here that she hadn't already known. She started to skip ahead to more recent articles. Then her glance fell on the headline of the next article.

FREAK ACCIDENT KILLS MANAGER
AT RUTLEDGE ESTATE

The body of Evan Dougherty was found early this morning in the cellar of the Rutledge Estate winery by a worker. Authorities surmise that a wine keg rolled from its rack and fell on the victim, crushing his skull. The county coroner believes the death occurred the previous evening. Other workers at the estate confirmed that Dougherty frequently made night checks of the winery. There were no witnesses to the accident.

It is indeed a tragedy for Dougherty's young wife, who is anticipating the birth of their first child.

Kelly stared at the clipping, surprised it was even included, although it did show that the researchers had been relentless in their quest for any information relating to the Rutledges. She glanced through the following sheets. The bulk of them were write-ups on awards won by the wines of Rutledge Estate in the ensuing years, and the acclaim given various vintages by wine critics. The few magazine pieces on Katherine Rutledge contained no new information.

As the door to her office swung open, Kelly glanced up. Hugh paused in the opening. "Am I interrupting?"

"You are. But no interruption has ever been more welcome." She closed the folder and tapped it on her desk top, straightening the sheets inside. "I have just been doing some very dull reading."

"On what?" He walked in, leaving the door standing open.

"The Rutledge family. There isn't much." She slipped the folder in a desk drawer. "Katherine has given very few interviews and there's almost nothing on the estrangement with her youngest son. Obviously there has been more gossip than articles written about it." Kelly paused and smiled. "Sorry, you came in here for something. What was it?"

"Just to let you know there has been a slight change in the schedule," he said. "One I think you will like. The interview with John Travis has been pushed back two days due to a conflict in commitments that he has. Which means you will have two free days to spend in Napa when you wrap up with Katherine. It will be less expensive to hold you over there than to fly everyone back to New York, then turn around and fly to Aspen the next day."

"Make those two days in San Francisco and you have a deal," Kelly countered as the phone rang and her assistant picked it up in the outer office. "We'll be that much closer to the airport."

"No problem." Hugh shrugged.

Sue stepped into the doorway and rapped lightly on the frame to catch Kelly's attention. "You have a call on line one, Kelly," she told her. "It's a man, but he wouldn't give me his name. Do you want it or should I tell him you're busy?"

For a long moment, Kelly didn't say anything, struck by this flat feeling of inevitability. Somehow, she had known all along he would call again now that he knew where she was, how to reach her.

Hugh moved toward the door. "If you are free around three this afternoon, come by my office. I should have a demo on the proposed theme music for the show."

She managed a nod, then reached for the phone. "I'll take the call, Sue." Kelly picked up the receiver and waited, her finger poised above the blinking light. "Close the door, please."

As it swung shut, she pressed the button. "Kelly Douglas speaking. Who is this?" she asked calmly. The worst had already happened; there was nothing left to dread.

"Miss Douglas, hello. This is Steve Gray with the United Gold Exchange. I'm calling to give you a rare opportunity to take advantage of a tremendous offer."

With the first words, she wavered between laughter and anger. She chose a middle ground and broke in. "Steve, I am so glad you called. This is such a coincidence. This morning at our story meeting we were talking about doing an exposé about the false claims made by telemarketing companies."

There was a click and the line went dead. Kelly leaned back in her chair with immense satisfaction, and a belated feeling of relief that she had been wrong.

A hot wind blew through the open window of the green-and-white Buick as it roared down the Silverado Trail, its muffler dragging, striking sparks on the pavement. The deep green of well-tended grapevines stretched off to the right in neat, symmetrical lines. Len Dougherty couldn't help noticing them and comparing them to his own, which still had a wild, jungle look despite the hard week he'd spent, working from dawn to dusk, trimming and thinning to give some order without damaging too much of the crop.

Just ahead tall columns of poplar trees lined the short drive that led to the collection of monastic-style buildings housing the winery, tasting rooms, sales area, and offices of The Cloisters. Len drove past the entrance and continued down the road another mile to a private road that wound up the steep side of a mountain. He turned onto it.

Lofty stands of eucalyptus trees, redwoods, and oaks hugged both sides of the narrow road, their limbs arching over it to form a leafy green canopy. The rocky ground at their feet was a tangle of parched grass, poison oak, and tough, crimson-stalked manzanita.

As he neared the crest of the spiny ridge, he came to a set of ornate iron gates and slowed the car to a stop. The trailing dust swirled in the open windows and instantly began to settle in the still, hot air. He slapped it off the sleeves of his best suit — his only suit, a navy pinstripe he'd bought to wear to Becca's funeral.

The gates stood open. Dougherty debated whether to drive on through. At most it was probably another quarter mile to the house. He climbed out of the car and slammed the door, slipping the ignition key into his pocket. He started walking and the sweat started rolling. Cursing under his breath, he held his arms away from his sides. He didn't want to show up at the door with wet circles of sweat staining his underarms.

A short distance past the gate, the dirt road gave way to a paved drive of aggregate concrete, edged with red paving brick on each side. He followed it around a curve and spotted the stuccoed walls and tiled roof of the guest house, tucked in the side of the ridge slope. Lush green grass surrounded the rock garden and mock waterfall at the rear of it.

The drive widened and made a looping circle around a marble fountain, ringed with bright flowers. At the apex of the circle sat the main house, low and sprawling, its red tiled roof baking in the afternoon sun.

Dougherty stopped and pulled a handkerchief from his hip pocket, mopped the sweat from his face and ran it around the neck of his collar, then stuffed it back in his pocket. As he started toward the house, he had a glimpse of the tall fence surrounding the tennis court off to his left, and more green lawn and flowers.

"The whole place takes up more than my ten acres," he murmured with envy.

It was almost enough to make him want to turn around, but it was also enough to keep him walking all the way to the front door. There, he hesitated again and licked his lips, trying not to think how good a shot of icy-cold whiskey would taste right now. Before he lost his courage, Dougherty punched the doorbell and tried to peer through the lens-thick panes of glass that checkered the door from top to bottom. But they distorted the view. He had the impression of a dark shape moving toward the door seconds before it opened.

A Mexican dressed in the black suit of a servant gave him a quick once-over, followed by a cool stare. "How may I help you, señor?"

"I'm here to see Mr. Rutledge," he said quickly, nervously.

Again the dark eyes examined him with skepticism. "Is he expecting you?"

Dougherty was saved from answering by a woman's voice calling from some room in the house. "Who is it, Luis? If it's Clay, tell him his father is at the croquet court."

"The croquet court. Is that over there?" Dougherty jerked his thumb in the direction of the tennis court.

"No, señor. It is around the house on the lower lawn," the Mexican replied, none too certain he should be telling him.

"Thanks." Dougherty immediately set off to find it.

He rounded the corner of the house and dragged the handkerchief from his pocket again to wipe the sweat from his neck and brow. He ducked through a wisteria arbor and felt the breeze. He wished he could take his jacket off and enjoy it, but he needed to look businesslike. After all, it was a business proposition he was going to put to Rutledge.

As the ridge fell away from the house, he saw a swimming pool off to his left, complete with a bathhouse and cabana, lounge chairs and umbrellaed tables. He heard a cracking sound that reminded him of billiard balls breaking.

Then he spotted the familiar figure of Gil Rutledge, dressed in white shirt, shorts, socks and shoes, a white visor shading his eyes and blending with the gray of his hair. He was on a flat stretch of lawn, terraced into the side of the ridge. He stood slightly bent at the waist, with his legs apart and a long-handled wooden mallet between them. He aimed the end of it at a red ball and knocked it through a wire arch sticking out of the grass.

Dougherty picked his way down the steep incline to the lower lawn. When Gil Rutledge heard him, he looked up and gave him a cool stare, just as challenging as his mother's. It made Dougherty bristle, but this was no time to be losing his temper.

"Afternoon, Mr. Rutledge."

"Good afternoon." The response was anything but friendly.

"You probably don't remember me. I'm Len Dougherty." He kept his smile broad and confident.

"Dougherty." His eyes narrowed, then slowly opened again. "Yes, you were an assistant winemaker at Rutledge Estate once. I seem to recall you were fired for drinking on the job."

"Just a little something to ward off the cold," Dougherty replied, instantly defensive. Again he caught himself and said, more calmly, "You know how it is sometimes."

Rutledge bent over the red ball again and measured the angle to the next wire arch. "If it's a job you want, go to the winery and fill out an application."

"I didn't come about a job, though I could use one," he admitted in an afterthought.

Rutledge swung the mallet between his legs and struck the ball, sending it rolling through the neatly clipped grass straight at the arch. It stopped an inch short of it. Rutledge glared at it for an instant, then walked after it.

Dougherty tagged behind him. "I have a business proposition for you."

Rutledge threw him a glance as he assumed the same stance over the ball. "Not interested." He gave the ball a light rap with the mallet. It rolled through the arch and stopped inches beyond it.

"I think you will be interested in this one." Dougherty wished Rutledge would quit knocking that damned wooden ball around. "At least you will be if you're as interested in getting back at your mother as I think you are."

Rutledge had started to hit the ball again, aiming toward a pair of twin arches with a stake at the end. He straightened at the reference to his mother. "Katherine?"

"Got your attention, didn't I?" Dougherty grinned.

"What does Katherine have to do with your business proposition?"

"It's like this." He paused a second to get it lined out in his head. "You see, I own ten acres of land that butts up to Rutledge Estate on the north. Ten prime acres of the best vineyard land around. At least, I own it now, providing I can figure out a way to keep her from stealing it from me. That's where you come in."

"How can she steal it from you if you own it, as you claim you do?"

"I own it, all right, but I also owe her thirty-five thousand, and she has my vineyard for collateral. If I don't come up with the money by the end of October, she gets it. We both know it's worth a lot more than thirty-five thousand. Why, prime vineyard land is selling for forty, fifty, maybe even a hundred thousand dollars an acre."

"There's your answer — sell it."

"Who will make an offer when she has the right to match any legitimate one I get?" Dougherty countered. "Besides, if I sold it, then I wouldn't have a place to live, I wouldn't have anything."

"What are you suggesting?"

"That you loan me the thirty-five thousand so I can pay her. I can pay you back so much every year when I sell my grapes, and you have the land for security. You can't lose."

Rutledge smiled and again bent over his ball. "I am not a banker. I'm in the business of making wine, not loaning money." He swung the mallet. It hit the ball with a solid whack, and the ball streaked across the grass, coming to a stop in front of the arches, in a direct line with the stake at the end of them. "You have your problems with Katherine, and I have mine." He walked after the ball.

Dougherty stood a minute, then hurried after him. "But you both want to work a deal with that French baron." He saw the sharp look Rutledge shot him. "Everybody knows about it. This valley is just one big grapevine. Rumors travel fast on it."

"If you know that, then you must know that currently all my efforts are concentrated on achieving that goal." He stood over the ball and gave Dougherty a long considering look. "If I'm successful,

I might be in a position to help you. But the money wouldn't be a loan. There has to be something in the deal for me."

"What do you mean?" Dougherty was suddenly wary.

"The thirty-five thousand would give me a long-term lease on your land for a modest annual sum. Naturally you would still be allowed to live there." The more Gil thought about the idea, the more attractive it seemed.

Katherine wouldn't like it if he had control of Dougherty's vineyard. He knew that land. It was prime grape-growing soil. Dougherty hadn't lied about that. How sweet it would be to use the berries from that vineyard for the new wine to be made under his cooperative deal with the baron. That would gall Katherine as much as losing out to him.

He smiled, gloating a little in anticipation of her reaction, and knocked the ball through the arches. It hit the stake and bounced back.

"When will you know about your deal with the baron?" Dougherty asked as Gil scooped up the ball, measured a mallet's length from the stake, and set the ball down at precisely that distance.

"Soon, I expect. The baron is arriving today. In fact, he should be here." He took aim and knocked the ball back through the double arches.

"It has to be soon," Dougherty warned, hurrying after him, the change jingling in his pocket when Gil walked to the ball. "I need that money by the end of October. If I can't get it from you, I'll have to offer this deal to some other vintner."

"Don't do it." It was a threat, not a suggestion.

"Oh yeah?" He made a weak attempt to challenge him, but he couldn't hold his eyes. "How can you stop me?"

"Easy." Gil again stood over his scarlet croquet ball. "I'll simply start spreading the rumor that Rutledge Estate used that land years ago as a dump for all its toxic chemicals and insecticides, that every inch of it is contaminated. Nobody will touch it. Nobody will even buy your grapes."

"It isn't true."

"Of course it isn't. But will they believe you — or me?" The lay of the ball gave him a difficult angle on the next arch. His brow furrowed in concentration as he studied the situation.

Dougherty angrily swung a hand at the landscaped ridge with its guest house, tennis court, pool, expansive lawns, and the sprawling grandeur of the main house. "Thirty-five thousand is nothing to you. You probably spend that much every month just keeping up this place. Why does this deal have to hinge on your agreement with the baron?"

Three years ago, before the first of his vineyards was found to be infected with phylloxera, thirty-five thousand would have seemed little more than pocket change to Gil. Now he was faced with a staged replanting of every vineyard within the next four years — at a cost that could run as high as seventy thousand dollars an acre, with a minimum of four years before the vines produced fruit suitable for wine making. The total cost would run in the millions. In the meantime, production would go down, the cash flow would decrease, and the cash drain would increase.

The bankers were nervous, watching over his shoulder, looking at every penny he spent. To them, thirty-five thousand dollars for leased land was not a good deal. They would undoubtedly go through the roof if he even suggested it.

In their eyes, his deal with the baron was another story altogether. They were strongly in favor of it once he had explained the proposed terms to them. In fact, they had practically salivated when they learned of the baron's financial strength and the cash he would be contributing. But until it happened, they weren't about to loosen the strings.

Gil positioned the mallet between his legs and took several practice swings at the ball. "Paying you the thirty-five thousand hinges on my deal with the baron because I have no need of your land without it."

"But this is one beautiful chance to thumb your nose at Katherine," Dougherty reminded him.

It was, but financially his hands were tied. "There will be others." He took aim on the arch and swung the mallet. The head struck the ball with a solid *thwack*. Gil straightened and watched the ball roll straight and true across the green. "Those are my conditions."

"But I have to have that money before the end of October, otherwise —"

"You have nothing to worry about," Gil broke in. "The deal with the baron is all but struck. Katherine is not going to win this one. I will do whatever I have to do to make certain of that. Trust me."

Dougherty hesitated and chewed at his lip. "If you're sure I guess that's good enough. If there's anything I can do, any way I can help . . ."

"I'll let you know if there is." He turned, catching a glimpse in his side vision of Clay coming down the fieldstone steps to the pool level. The baron had arrived. Gil shouldered his mallet and glanced pointedly at Dougherty. "Good day."

The man's glance fell under the weight of his. Dougherty nodded, then took off across the lawn, slipping once climbing the grassy slope. He reached the top and ran a finger around the neck of his shirt, then headed off again toward the driveway in front of the house.

Gil watched him with contempt, certain the man wouldn't stop until he'd reached the nearest bar or the nearest bottle. Clay joined him.

"Who was that?"

"Len Dougherty."

"That drunk who owns the small vineyard next to Katherine's," Clay recalled and shook his head in amusement. "I saw an old Buick parked near the front gates and wondered who it belonged to. It must have been his. What did he want?"

"He had a business proposition for me."

Clay looked at his father, expecting to see a smile that reflected his own amusement, but his expression was sober. "What kind of business proposition could he offer that would interest you?"

"A tempting one." Gil swung the mallet off his shoulder and cast a brief smile in Clay's direction. "Did you get the baron settled in?"

Clay nodded. "I passed on your dinner invitation for tonight, but he's tired from the flight and plans to dine in. We're to meet him for breakfast in the morning, then go from there to the winery."

"Sounds good." He walked over to the ball.

Clay strolled after him. "Did you receive an invitation to the party Katherine is throwing for the baron next week?"

"Yes." His father smiled broadly, assuming his shooting stance.

"So did I. And I thought she was determined that neither of us — especially you — would ever darken her door again," he remarked drolly.

"I intend to darken her entire life." He lightly rapped the ball through the wicket.

"Yes," Clay mused faintly in agreement, watching his father set up for his next shot. He was a master at croquet, a game that required the putting skills of golf, the ball positioning of billiards, and all the wiles of chess. "It may interest you to know, I believe the baroness is solidly in our corner."

"You talked to her?"

"Briefly. While the baron was checking in." It had been simple

enough, innocent enough, to have a few moments alone with Natalie
Fougère while her husband was otherwise occupied.

After Clay unlocked the trunk, he left the porter to unload the luggage and went inside the poshly simple resort Auberge du Soleil, the
Inn of the Sun. The baron stood at the small registration desk, looking haggard from the long flight. His wife was wandering toward the
glass doors to the terrace and the beckoning view beyond them.
Clay stopped at the desk long enough to make certain there was no
difficulty with the reservation, then followed Natalie outside.

She stood with her arms apart, her hands resting on the wooden
rail, her face lifted to the afternoon sun. He heard her sigh as he
walked up beside her.

"You must be tired after your flight," he said, adopting his previous restrained manner with her.

She glanced at him and shook her head, her dark hair coiled
sleekly in a simple twist. "*Non.* I had a very long and very wonderful sleep on the airplane. Emile, he has never been able to sleep
during a flight."

She turned back to the view the terrace commanded of the patch-
work of vineyards spread over the valley floor, punctuated with
modern windmills to ward off frosts. The rugged Mayacamas Mountains formed a dark wall not four miles distant.

"This is lovely," she said. "It reminds me a bit of Provence. Perhaps it is the palms and the olive trees that give it such a Mediter-
ranean look."

"I knew that would be your impression of the valley." He gave
her a long, meaningful look. They were in full view of the baron.
Clay didn't care. If anything, it added a little spice to the game.
"Odd, isn't it? how I could know what you think, what you feel.
Sometimes, it's as if I've known you all my life." Then he glanced
away. "Foolish, isn't it?"

"*Non.*" She touched his arm, the pressure very light.

He looked down at her fingers. "I'm glad you came, Natalie."

"So am I."

"I thought you might not. I thought you might stay in France."

"And miss the opportunity to see your valley of which I have
heard so much?" She kept her tone light, but he caught the emotional edge in her voice and moved confidently forward with his
plan.

"You shouldn't have come." He tightened his jaw and frowned at
the view.

"But —"

"Forgive me, Natalie, but it is damned hard for me." He pushed the words out, low and rough.

"What is?"

With a shift of his head, he caught her glance and held it. "To see a woman. To know that she's your kind of woman, dreaming the same dreams, laughing at the same things, feeling the same desires. To lie awake at night . . ."

"Clay," she whispered in protest, but her eyes were full of him and her lips were parted.

"Tell me you don't feel the same and I swear I will never mention it again."

"I cannot," she admitted and smiled at him, her dark eyes full of longing. Then, with the calm of a woman who had reached her decision, she looked down the slope at the hillside olive grove. "I like to take walks in the evening. Doesn't it look peaceful among the olive trees, the little stream flowing?"

"I have admired the setting many times myself. It would be beautiful in the moonlight." That simply, the rendezvous was arranged. Nothing more needed to be said by the time Emile joined them.

The sun sank behind the western range of mountains, leaving streaks of scarlet and magenta in the sky and bathing the land in coppery hues. Natalie stood at the deep-set window of the sitting room and watched the sinking light, achingly conscious of the dead silence in the room.

Emile sat in the bright yellow chair, his feet propped on a matching ottoman, his reading glasses perched precariously near the end of his nose, his hands holding open a book. The riffle of a page had been the only sound from him she'd heard since dinner. As usual, he wasn't even aware she was in the room.

Beyond the room's private terrace, the tops of the olive trees angled down the hill slope. Natalie kept her vigil, waiting until the shadows under them had deepened and the evening star glittered in the twilight sky.

Moving away from the window, she crossed the tiled floor and turned on the lamp next to her husband's chair. He glanced up without really seeing her and grunted his thanks. Once again, he was engrossed in his book, some philosophical treatise that she knew she would find quite boring.

"I am going for a walk, Emile," she told him.

Distracted, he looked up and frowned. "It is dark."

"It will be cool. It was much too hot to explore the grounds when we arrived this afternoon," she explained as she walked to the door. "I have the key. There is no need for you to wait up for me if you become tired." She glanced back and saw he was already absorbed in his reading.

She stepped out of the suite into the gentle warmth of the night air and quietly closed the door behind her. She saw no one in the parking area outside the row of *maisons,* and took the narrow dirt path that wound around the terra-cotta building and across the parched grass to the olive grove.

The lights from the resort above winked at her through the branches, branches that shielded her from sight. She wandered among the trees, not hurrying as she slowly made her way toward the quietly trickling stream.

A boulder, dark and gray, jutted from the tall grass next to the streambed. Automatically Natalie brushed the dust from the top of it and sat down. Over her shoulder, she could see the rising moon, a silver disk joining the dusting of stars in the sky.

Somewhere off to her left, she heard the sound of a car door closing. On the other side of the stream, the ground ran up a sheltering hill covered with more trees. She listened and heard nothing for the longest time. But she knew it was Clay. She knew he had come, just as she knew he was there now struggling with his own sense of honor, his own sense of what was right.

For herself, she had no such questions, only a strong feeling of destiny that it had been meant for her to meet him, that it had all been marked out to happen long ago despite her marriage. She felt no guilt at being here, no sense of shame or regret, only a great contentment that brought a kind of thrill.

A rock tumbled down the slope, its passage followed by the sound of rustling grass. Vaguely she could make out the tall shape of him moving through the trees. Then he was there, stepping across the rivulet of gleaming water to join her as she rose to her feet.

"Natalie." He stopped, his face in shadows. "I almost didn't come tonight."

"Then why did you?"

"Because you asked me."

"You could have stayed away."

"No." He shook his head. "You know I couldn't stay away."

"No more than I could."

When he took the last step, eliminating the distance between them, she went into his arms and his mouth came down, taking hers in a kiss that was rough and needing. She gave it back eagerly. This was the fire and the glory that had been missing in her life for so long. So very, very long.

He ripped his lips away and dragged them across her cheek and into her hair. With her arms around him, holding him close, she felt the molding pressure of his hands, curving her to fit against him.

"Being with you tonight won't be enough." His breath, his lips teased her ear. "Emile and my father, they have to come to an agreement. I have to be able to see you again." He rubbed his mouth over the sensitive cord in her neck, sending delicious chills dancing over her skin. "If Emile chooses to work with Katherine instead —" He broke off the thought and shuddered, his arms tightening around her.

"I think he will not," she murmured in assurance, running her fingers through the crisp silk of his hair in a loving stroke. "He does not share the madam's passion for wine. To him, it is a business. That is why, I think, he favors your father."

He pulled back, framing her face in his hands while his gaze bored into her. "It has to be that way, Natalie." The things he felt were hot enough, real enough at this moment, to show in his face. "It has to be for us to see each other — to be together."

"I know." With her fingertips, she traced the angle of his jaw and the outline of his lips. "Love me, Clay. I need you to love me." She arched up to meet his mouth, letting his kiss spin her away.

The next morning, across the breakfast table, Clay discreetly studied her, paying scant attention to the conversation between his father and the baron. She was radiant, her eyes glowing each time she shyly met his glance. There was no doubt in his mind — she had the look of a woman in love. He marveled that her husband hadn't noticed the change in her. The man was obviously a fool when it came to women, but most men were.

Watching her butter a croissant, he considered again how easy it had been. Much easier than he'd expected. She was now their strongest ally. He started planning when he would meet her again, what he would say, what he would do.

~11~

*T*he Ford Taurus sped along Highway 29, its headlight beams slicing through the gathering darkness. Their light flashed off the giant eucalyptus trees that flanked the road, standing like ghostly sentinels in the night. The twin range of coastal mountains that ran the valley's thirty-odd miles of length to form its narrow corridor were little more than looming black shapes against a star-sprinkled sky.

DeeDee Sullivan sat behind the wheel of the rental car, a pair of sunglasses relegated to a perch atop her short-cropped hair. Kelly was beside her, her glance continually straying to the darkened landscape beyond the passenger window. She found it ironic that it had been nighttime when she'd left the valley twelve years ago and it was nighttime when she was returning, breaking the vow she had made never to come back.

"Considering the way our luck's been running, I'm not surprised your flight was delayed more than an hour." DeeDee flipped to low beams when she saw the oncoming car. "I hoped it would change when you got here. But if that's any indication, it isn't."

"I take it you've had some problems."

A scattering of yard lights gave Kelly glimpses of vineyards sleeping in the moonlight. Here, on the flat floor of the valley's southern end, the land was planted predominantly to chardonnay, Riesling, the white varieties of wine grapes that benefited from the cool of the sea fogs that rolled off San Pablo Bay in the summer and spread thick, white mist up the valley, leaving the occasional hillock isolated in sunshine.

"Problems." DeeDee pushed out a short laugh. "So far, it's been nothing but. We've been here two whole days, three counting today, and we don't have one usable tape. One whole day's work — great shots of the grapes being picked, Mexican laborers with faces that told a story all their own, workers running to empty their baskets of grapes in the truck at the end of the row, the foreman keeping a running tally on the number for each worker, the trucks rumbling down the highway mounded with grapes, the men at the wineries with grape-juice stains running halfway up their arms, the grapes tumbling through the stemming machines, the juice seething and foaming in vats, the workers at the end of the day against the most spectacular sunset you have ever seen — all of it." Both hands left the wheel as she dramatically flung them in the air. "All of it ruined!"

"How?" Kelly asked, trying to ignore the images that flashed through her mind, memories of harvests she had seen, triggered by DeeDee's word pictures. "What happened?"

"There was something wrong with the camera." She sighed in disgust. "There were light streaks through every tape. What makes me so furious is that Steve wanted to review the tapes from the winery on the monitor in the van, but I didn't want to take the time. I wanted to get out to the vineyards and get the scenes with the grape pickers while we still had some morning light that would give us some shadow effects. What would it have taken? Ten, twenty minutes to look at the tapes? We could have found the problem then. As it was, we didn't discover it until that night. Steve drove into San Francisco yesterday to get the camera fixed. Some lens part had gone bad, and he had to wait for a new one to be flown in. He got back today just before I left to pick you up at the airport."

"But it's working now." Just ahead, Kelly spied a familiar old building that had once housed a roadside general store. Almost twenty years ago it had become the Oakville Grocery and a highway landmark. She had gone in it many times just to look at the strange items they had — truffles, quail eggs, tins of caviar, and French pâtés.

She remembered the aroma of French bread, freshly baked, workers hot and sweaty from the vineyards shouldering their way to the deli counter for a sandwich and cold beer, tourists in shorts with cameras around their necks standing in line with women in heels and silk dresses, Mercedeses and dusty winery trucks parked side by side in front.

"It's working," DeeDee confirmed, the tone of her voice grim. "It's a damned good thing we have two extra days here. We're going to need them."

"It sounds like it." Off to the left, landscape lights illuminated the entrance to the Mondavi winery. Kelly found it difficult to concentrate on what DeeDee was saying as she recognized more places, remembered more things. Yet she needed to keep the conversation going; she needed the distraction of it. "Have you been out to Rutledge Estate yet?"

DeeDee nodded. "Yesterday. I stopped to let Mrs. Rutledge know we were here." Mrs. Rutledge — the name sounded wrong to Kelly. She was Madam or Katherine Rutledge, names that echoed the force of her personality. "She showed me around her garden. A great setting for part of the interview, by the way." She paused and shot Kelly a smile, one eyebrow arching. "I'll have you know she *informed* me that it would be convenient for us to come tomorrow afternoon at one-thirty. Thank God, she agreed to let us come early the following morning, otherwise who knows how long it would have taken to get the various sequences with her at the house, the winery, the vineyards, and the gardens all shot."

"A day and a half will be plenty for the interview segment," Kelly said. "As it is, this is going to be a difficult story to edit down. Katherine talks in quotable material."

"Judging from the brief time I spent with her, you're probably right. I'd love to do a full-length documentary on her. I wonder if I could talk Hugh into letting me edit two versions," she mused. "A short one for the show, and a longer one —" She broke off the sentence and shrugged. "Oh, well, it's nice to dream."

"Isn't it?" Kelly murmured as they passed the hamlet of Rutherford, which was little more than a collection of buildings at a crossroads.

"You'll be glad to know you can sleep in tomorrow morning. The rest of us are getting up before dawn. I found a vineyard where they'll be picking grapes tomorrow. I want to get some footage of the workers among the vines at first light. We'll be back around noon to have lunch and pick you up. You'll love this place where we're staying. It's a great little bed-and-breakfast. Margerie, the gal that owns it, is a real gem. She fixes cold lunches for us and everything. Wait until you taste her French toast," DeeDee declared. "She uses Grand Marnier in the batter."

When they reached the outskirts of St. Helena, DeeDee slowed the car to turn off onto one of the side streets. "I meant to tell you, we've been invited to a big bash at Rutledge Estate to honor Baron Fougère. We have permission to tape part of the festivities on the condition that once everyone sits down to dinner, the camera is put away." She glanced at Kelly. "You've met the baron. What do you think about doing a short interview with him, getting his reactions to Napa Valley, Rutledge Estate, et cetera?"

"We could," she agreed without enthusiasm. "But he's a bit pedantic. In a way, I'd hate to interview him and find out it was too dull to include in the story."

"Good point." Minutes later DeeDee pulled into the driveway of a Victorian-style house, shaded by towering oaks and elms. "Here we are," she announced, shifting the car into park. "We kept the best room for you."

The bed was a marvelous old four-poster with a feather mattress and antique quilt, soft and pale from numerous washings. The chair facing the mahogany secretariat was Chippendale. A brightly patterned chintz fabric covered the sofa in front of the fireplace. The adjoining private bath had an old swan-shaped tub with claw feet. A ruffled shower curtain hung from the oval ring suspended above it.

Kelly set her luggage on the floor and walked over to the doors that opened onto a private veranda. The long brass handles felt cool and smooth beneath her fingers. She pulled the doors apart and stepped into the night.

Roses climbed the trellis that walled off one side of the veranda, their fragrance scenting the warm air. The branches of the oak trees arched high, framing the view of the moon-silvered vineyard beyond the house lawn. To the east, the not-so-high mountains of the Vacas range cut a black and jagged silhouette against the night sky. She stared at the small pinpoints of light scattered along its slopes.

This particular view was not familiar to her, but the scene was. She gazed at the section of mountains she had once known so well, unconsciously scanning the darkly shadowed slopes for her favorite lookout place beneath a twisted oak, thinking of the hours she'd spent there, sometimes with a book, sometimes just dreaming, sometimes crying for herself, nursing her hurts, sometimes staring at the western Mayacamas Mountains lushly forested with great stands of redwoods, so different from the drier Vacas range studded with oak, pine, and madrona trees, and sometimes just observing the change of seasons in the valley below.

Winter with the dormant vines strung out like grotesquely twisted dark skeletons, sometimes white with hoarfrost or blurred by chilly winter rains. Rains that turned the hills green and the vineyards bright yellow with masses of wild mustard.

The fresh breezes of spring, the riot of flowers, the greening of the vines with, every day, more and more color showing until they reached the full leaf of summer and the heat came, parching the hillsides a tawny shade of yellow, and the vineyards were plowed, stripped of all weeds, while the grapes ripened.

The initial frenzy of autumn when migrant workers made their way down row after row, stripping the vines of their sweet grapes, and the air smelled of fermenting juices. The leaves changing color, painting the valley with vibrant scarlets and golds, then dropping and the pruners moving in, trimming the vines to the shape of the winter skeletons. The haze of wood smoke in the air from burning fires.

Season after season, the land had changed, but the misery in her own life hadn't.

She was back. And every instinct told her to run — now — while she still had the chance.

The soft-footed Han Li, the resident chef at Rutledge Estate and a fifth-generation Chinese-American, brought a pot of dark and rich, European-style coffee to the terrace and set the tray on the glass-topped table within Katherine's reach. "Would the madam care for anything else? A fresh pastry with her coffee, perhaps?" he suggested.

She glanced at the baron. He refused with a small shake of his head. "I think not, Han Li. Thank you," she told him as she lifted the two demitasse cups from the tray.

Giving her a slight bow, he withdrew as silently as he had come. She filled both cups with the steaming coffee, passed one to Emile, then returned the pot to its tray.

"I am glad you were able to come this morning, Emile." She spoke in French, aware he was more comfortable conversing in his own language. "I know Gil has kept you very busy these last few days."

"He has had much to show me." His air of reserve had increased from their last meeting in New York, proof of Gil's success in undermining her position. "He has a most interesting marketing strategy and sales campaign for his winery. Your son is a very innovative businessman."

"He is. His success in this business speaks to that." She took considerable pride in Gil's accomplishments, a fact that would surprise many in the valley — and her son most of all. "Just as important to me is that the quality of his better wines has improved with each vintage, with minor exceptions. Of course, the entire region has made great strides in the last decade. It is perceived as quality. Ask any distributor and he will tell you that any bottle of wine bearing a label that lists Napa Valley as its origin sells." Katherine took a small sip of her coffee. "That is remarkable when one considers that of all the wines made in California, Napa Valley contributes less than five percent to that total. Within a few years, even that percentage will decrease."

"For what reason?" Emile frowned.

"The new type of phylloxera." She lowered her cup to its saucer. "It has been estimated that as much as seventy-five percent of the vineyards here in the valley will have to be torn up and replanted. Unfortunately, as recently as two years ago, a few winegrowers were still grafting their cuttings to the AXR one rootstock, which is not resistant to this new strain." It was a hybrid rootstock, a cross between a vinifera vine called amaron and the American rupestris.

"But this is foolish," Emile protested. "In France, we have long known this was not a good rootstock. It is true it is easy to grow, but it is too vigorous."

"I recall your grandfather was just as adamantly opposed to it over sixty years ago. Thankfully, I took his advice. Not a single vine on Rutledge Estate has to be replaced." She made a slight moue of regret. "Poor Gil is not so fortunate. He is faced with replanting all his vineyards, but I am sure he has told you that."

Emile made a valiant attempt to mask his ignorance with a shrug. "But of course."

She caught the sound of approaching footsteps and glanced at the French doors opening onto the terrace as Sam walked through them. The timing couldn't have been more perfect.

"Ah, here is Sam," Katherine announced, automatically switching to English. "I have arranged for him to give you a brief tour of our vineyards and winery. It will give the two of you an opportunity to become better acquainted."

"Assuming you have the time, Baron." Sam inserted the qualification, and walked around the table to shake hands when the baron stood. Inwardly he chafed at this role of tour guide that had been forced on him, fully aware that Katherine wanted him to impress the baron with his knowledge of the wine business.

"I will make the time," the baron stated.

After the baron had finished his coffee, he left with Sam in the Jeep. Sam drove first to the hillside vineyard they called Sol's Vineyard. He showed him the drip irrigation that had been installed during the second year of the drought to sustain the vines, and the runty grapes that were responsible for as much as seventy percent of the wine they bottled as Reserve, their best. The baron asked a few questions about the rootstocks and the phylloxera problem in California vineyards, but showed little interest in the vineyard itself.

Claude waited for them at the entrance to the old brick winery. Sam made the introductions, then explained, "Claude is originally from Château Noir. His grandfather was *maître de chai* there."

"That was many years ago," Claude inserted, his grizzled head tilted at a proud angle, "in the days when your *grand-père* was the *patron*."

"Your *grand-père* was Girard Broussard, *non*?" The baron studied him with a thoughtful and curious gaze.

"He was." Claude nodded crisply.

The baron responded with a nod that was idly contemplative. "The name of your *grand-père* is greatly revered at Château Noir." Claude's big chest puffed out a little more at these words of praise for his grandfather. "You have been at Rutledge Estate a long time?"

"I sailed on the ship that brought the madam to America after the death of her husband. I was thirteen years of age, not yet a man. I helped the madam plant the new vines and make the first wine from their grapes."

The entire exchange was conducted in French. Sam understood only snatches of it. The same was true when Claude took the baron through the winery. Sam doubted that Katherine had anticipated this would happen. Personally he found that more than a little amusing.

"A remarkable man, your Monsieur Broussard," the baron commented as they left the winery and crossed the dusty yard to the winery offices.

"He is the best," Sam stated. "If he has an equal in the valley, it would be André Tchelistcheff. The man is in his eighties, he may be ninety by now, but he continues to work as a private consultant for several wineries in the valley."

"I have heard of him, of course." The baron nodded.

No one who spent any time in Napa Valley could fail to hear the name André Tchelistcheff. He was as much a legend as Katherine; like Claude Broussard, he was a winemaker who had never owned his own winery.

The paper side of Rutledge Estate proved to be of more interest to the baron than either the vineyards or the winery had been. He examined sales figures, production reports, and cost sheets, asking many and varied questions. An hour passed before Sam ushered him into his office at the rear of the converted stables.

Gaylene, the secretary-receptionist, brought them coffee, American style. Between sips, they discussed the weather, the ongoing drought in California and its effects on the valley. At last, the baron set his empty cup on the desk and leaned back in the wing chair.

"Tell me, what are your feelings on this proposed collaboration between Rutledge Estate and Château Noir? I cannot recall that you have mentioned them," he said.

There was a sideways movement of his head that passed for an indifferent shake as Sam leaned back in his own chair. "My personal feelings don't enter into it. This is a decision that has to be made by you and Katherine."

"But it is your opinion I am seeking," he persisted.

Sam tried again to evade the question. "Obviously it has its merits."

"That is hardly an answer."

"Perhaps not." Sam dipped his head, conceding the point. "But it's the most diplomatic one I can give."

The baron seized on that immediately. "Then you are not in favor of this?"

Sam rocked back in his chair, his mouth slanting in a wry, tight line. "You are determined to put me in an awkward position."

"*Non.* I am determined to learn your opinion."

"In that case," Sam said as he shrugged, "to be perfectly honest, I find the whole thing too one-sided for my taste."

The baron frowned. "I do not understand. How is it one-sided? The proposed terms are quite equitable."

"Equal on the surface, maybe. But if this deal is struck, you are the one who gains. We will lose too much."

"How is it that you will lose?" His hands and shoulders lifted in a shrugging gesture of confusion. "Explain this to me."

"This is Rutledge land, Baron. Every year we pick Rutledge grapes and make them into Rutledge wine. All that changes the minute you and Katherine reach an agreement. In the future, when a great wine is made here on the estate — one superior to any from the great châteaux in France, including yours — Château Noir will share in the credit and the glory." Sam paused a beat. "To put it mildly, I don't like that idea. If the roles were reversed and it was Château Noir that stood to lose its identity, I don't think you would either."

A look of satisfaction spread across the baron's face as he settled back in his chair and continued his thoughtful study of Sam. "Then if the decision were yours to make?"

"If it were mine to make," Sam said, smiling, "I would never have contacted you in the first place."

"Have you expressed these feelings to Katherine?"

"No. And she has never asked."

"I can understand that," the baron replied with a slow and thoughtful nod, then glanced at his watch. It was nearly one. "The hour, I had not realized it was so late. I promised my wife I would return in time to have lunch with her. There has been little time for us to spend together on this trip."

"I'll take you back." Sam rose from his chair.

After he dropped the baron off at his resort hotel, Sam returned to the estate and drove straight to the house to check in with Katherine. When he swung into the circle drive, he saw a light blue rental car, then the van, its side doors pushed open to reveal lighting and camera equipment. The television crew had arrived.

His first impulse was to drive away, but it was his second impulse that took Sam out of the Jeep and into the house.

Sunlight came through the panes of the French doors at the opposite end of the marbled entry hall, backlighting the group standing in front of them. Katherine's petite shape was among them, but it was the tall, slender form of Kelly Douglas that Sam sought out first.

With deliberately unhurried strides, he walked toward the group, the sound of his footsteps intruding on their conversation. He observed that unguarded moment when Kelly turned and saw him, the recognition shining in her eyes and the smile of pleasure softening her lips. Why was it that he only had to look at her to feel all churned up and hungry?

Stopping, he addressed his first words to Katherine. "I saw the baron safely back to his hotel." Then he turned. "Hello, Kelly." He felt the quickening tension, almost like a hum in the air between them.

"Sam. It's good to see you again." Her expression was warm and polite, nothing more, as she took his hand. Her defenses were now up and solidly in place. Why?

"Welcome to Rutledge Estate." He was conscious of the firm grip of her fingers and the quick loosening of them as she pulled her hand away. He wondered if she had felt the same warm jolt when their palms met.

"Thank you," she said and proceeded to introduce him to the rest of the television crew.

At the conclusion of it, his attention came back to her. She wore her hair pulled back in a French braid that was both simple and sophisticated, the sunshine coming through the terrace doors touching off the deep red lights in it.

"Didn't Hugh come with you?" he asked.

"He wanted to," Kelly replied. "But he couldn't get away."

"He did give us his list of not-to-be-missed restaurants in the valley," the other woman in the group, the producer, DeeDee Sullivan, inserted with a faint drawl. "Too bad he didn't schedule us enough time to go to them."

There was the soft squelch of thick rubber-soled shoes on the marble that signaled the approach of the housekeeper, Mrs. Vargas. "Excuse me, Madam, but you have a phone call," she informed Katherine, as always her appearance stern and stiff in her starched black uniform. "It seems the caterer has some difficulty he needs to discuss with you."

Katherine nodded, a little curtly, then said, "Sam, would you show Kelly and Miss Sullivan through the house while I take this call?"

"Yes, we want to shoot some at-home scenes with Mrs. Rutledge," DeeDee Sullivan explained. "Maybe take the viewer on a mini-tour of the house. Subtly, of course."

"Of course." Sam returned her droll smile as Katherine left them to take the phone call.

"We'll go ahead and set up out on the terrace," the cameraman said. "We should be ready to go by the time you're through."

"Sounds good." DeeDee nodded, then waved a hand forward. "Lead the way," she told Sam.

Obligingly he set off. Kelly followed with barely contained eagerness. When she was growing up, she had thought this house was the grandest that had ever been built.

There were parlors with curvy old Louis Quinze sofas and fragile porcelain. Ming vases, Foo dogs, Lalique crystal, and Limoges pottery. Walls were done in soft mellow colors, offset by rich woods and Impressionist paintings.

Behind two heavy carved doors, there was a walnut-paneled library lined floor to ceiling with books, everything from fiction to nonfiction, classics to children's stories. Faded Persian rugs were scattered over the floor, and an ancient vinestock, twisted and bare, hung on the wall above the fireplace mantel like a piece of sculpture.

The formal dining room was enormous, dominated by heavy mahogany servers and sideboards, all bearing the distinct lines of Louis Seize. Overhead, a three-tiered chandelier of Waterford crystal rained its light on the long table and tapestried chairs.

The south wing held a garden room, filled with tropical greenery and furnished with a mix of ornately carved, hand-painted furniture and wrought-iron pieces finished in pewter and aged iron.

There was a music room, complete with an ebony grand piano, a new stereo with compact disc player, and an ancient Victrola. An airy morning room that looked onto the terrace was filled with vases brimming with fresh autumn flowers, and a fireplace with a pickled-pine finish.

Down the hall, up the marble staircase, there were guest rooms furnished with four-posters or beds with intricately carved head-boards, fringed ottomans, and Oriental chests, arranged in an order that was spare and stylish.

Kelly had stopped counting rooms by the time Sam led them to the second floor's south wing. He pushed open a door on the right and stepped back to let them enter. As DeeDee started to walk in, Steve, the cameraman, called to her from below.

"I'll catch up with you later," she said and hurried off to see what he wanted.

Hesitating only briefly, Kelly walked in. It was a corner room, empty of any furnishings, the parquet flooring scarred and dull. Tall windows filled two sides of the room. Sunlight poured through them, flooding the room with light. The air smelled different, stale and dusty, tainted with something else Kelly couldn't identify.

Her curiosity aroused, she turned back to Sam. "What is this room?"

He stood in the doorway, one shoulder propped against the frame. "My mother used it as her studio, although she preferred to call it her 'atelier.'" The dryness in his voice bordered on amusement.

"That's right, your mother was an artist," Kelly remembered, able to identify at last the trace scents of turpentine and artist's oils that lingered in the air. "She worked in oils, didn't she?"

"Among other mediums. At one time or another she tried them all." His gaze wandered over the room. "She went from wanting to be the female Dali, to the female Wyeth, to the female Warhol, and never stuck with any one style long enough to master it. When the muse struck her, she would stay in this room for hours on end, sometimes days on end."

His thoughts had turned back to that time. Kelly could hear it in his voice, see it in his expression. "You must have spent a lot of time in here watching her paint when you were growing up," she guessed.

His gaze came back to her, his expression hardening. "I wasn't allowed in here."

She was stunned by his answer, the total absence of emotion in his voice — and the sudden realization that he stood in the doorway, not crossing the threshold of the room he had been forbidden to enter as a child.

"And your father?" she asked softly, thinking of all the times she had longed to live in this house, to be a Rutledge.

"The vineyards kept him busy. The vineyards, and arguing with my uncle."

"What about you?"

A shoulder lifted in an offhanded shrug. "My parents made sure I had qualified nannies to look after me until I was old enough to take care of myself."

My parents made sure I had nannies. The words chilled her, shattering the illusions she had about life in this house. Trying to hold on to them, Kelly said, "But you had Katherine — you had your grandmother."

His mouth twisted in a smile that mocked. "Katherine is hardly the type you'd cast as the ideal grandmother, always ready with a few kind words and a plate of homemade chocolate chip cookies." He pushed away from the door, his eyes on her, and Kelly sensed immediately that Sam regretted this brief glimpse he had given her of his childhood. "Ready to move on?"

Kelly well understood that he wanted neither pity nor sympathy from her, and offered none. "Of course." She left the empty room and followed him down the hall.

There were more rooms, guest suites, a game room. When they reached the end of the hall, only one door was left to open. Sam reached for the brass knob. "This is my room."

Her reaction to that was quick and strong — she didn't want to see it; she didn't want to know any more about him. "There's no need for me to go in. We won't be using it for any of our shots," she told him, then went on, without giving him a chance to respond. "They're probably ready for me outside. Is there a bathroom close to the terrace? I need to add makeup for the camera."

"Fairly close." He moved away from the door.

They retraced their steps to the marble staircase and followed it down to the entry hall. After Kelly had retrieved her bulging canvas shoulder bag, Sam directed her to a powder room on the first floor.

When she came out ten minutes later with her face powdered and her eye makeup, blush, and lipstick subtly intensified, he was gone. It was just as well, she told herself. She was already nervous about this interview. About being here. She didn't need an audience watching her, not even an audience of one. Especially when that one was Sam Rutledge.

$\mathcal{L}$ 12 $\mathcal{L}$

A lamp cast a pool of light over the bright yellow chair the baron occupied. Night shadows darkened the rest of the suite's sitting room. The wood-louvered shutters at the windows stood open, letting in the evening air. A breeze whipped through them, heady with the scent of olive trees and fermenting grapes as it riffled the gilt-edged pages of the book Emile held. It was a minor distraction, succeeding only in shifting his grip to hold the pages down, never rousing him from his absorption in the material before him.

Not until he had finished his apportioned chapter of Bergson's *L'Evolution créatice* did he lower the book. He removed his reading glasses and thoughtfully considered the passages he had just read. Several more minutes passed before he reached for the silver bookmark, designed in the shape of the family crest, that lay on the table by the lamp. He held it a moment, then slipped it between the pages and closed the book, absently recalling that Natalie had given him the silver marker for his birthday two years ago — or had it been three?

He started to ask her, then realized she wasn't there. She had gone out for a walk; it had become almost a nightly routine since they had arrived.

Laying aside his book he rose from the chair and wandered over to the tall doors, standing open to the private terrace. Darkness had closed around the resort, turning the olive trees along the hillside into indistinct black shapes. A check of his watch confirmed it was late. He rubbed his eyes and considered retiring for the evening, then decided he would wait until Natalie returned, certain it would be soon.

Emile went back to his chair and opened the book again. But, as the minutes passed and the hour grew later, the tome of philosophy failed to hold his interest. His mind kept turning to Natalie, paying her more attention than he had in months. Soon the book lay unnoticed on his lap.

When he heard the turn of the key in the lock, followed by the click of the metal latch, he lifted the book and pretended to be reading it. Light suddenly filled the corners of the sitting room, chasing off the shadows.

"I thought you would be in bed." She paused briefly when she saw him still in his chair.

But it was the tone of her voice that caught him, the easy strength of it, the light lilt to it. He put the book aside to study her as she came the rest of the way into the room. There was color in her cheeks and a brightness in her dark eyes. The smile she gave him was almost radiant. Emile could not remember when he had last seen so much happiness in her expression.

"You must have walked a long way this evening."

"Out of the black shadows of doubt all the way to the bright moonlight of promise."

Emile frowned. "I am not familiar with that quotation. In which book did you find it?"

"It was a very big book." Her voice seemed to tease him. "Much too big to hold on your lap." She smiled at his confusion. "It was the sky. The sky at night."

"I had not realized you had this fascination with nature," he reflected. "Perhaps the works of this American writer Thoreau would interest you. I have one or two of his books in our library at the château. I must remember to locate one for you when we return." Yet the more he observed the glow in her eyes, the spirit she displayed, the more he thought this was not the answer. "Perhaps I should walk with you some night, though it would not be wise to venture too far. This country is full of rattlesnakes. Gilbert tells me they are about mostly at night, though they frequently crawl into the grapevines searching for the eggs birds have laid."

She gave him a surprised look. "You spoke with Gilbert today? You never mentioned this at dinner."

"Not today, no. He told me of this several days ago. You would be wise to keep to well-traveled paths on your walks, Natalie," he advised.

He was bothered by the way she smiled at him, showing the tolerance of a daughter to her overly cautious father. Was that how she looked at him? Her next remark seemed to confirm his fear.

"It is late, Emile. You should be in bed," she said, as if to an old man needing his sleep.

But when he finally went to bed, he lay awake for a long time, mulling over the little changes in her attitude, her manner, trying to find the cause for them. Stray thoughts came to him. Almost harshly he pushed them aside. But they came back to trouble him.

The trail was wide and smooth, shaded by towering live oaks, madronas, and the odd eucalyptus tree, the rough ground beneath them cleared of undergrowth. Here and there shafts of morning sunlight broke through the leafy canopy and dappled the dusty earth at Katherine's feet.

Mounted on a tripod several yards away, the camera captured on tape the almost mystical effect of the sunbeams breaking around her. Steve Gibbons kept one eye pressed to the viewfinder, the tension in his body indicating the excitement of the shot he was getting. The sound man, Rick Meers, was crouched at his feet, listening intently to the voices coming over his headset while he constantly checked the levels.

Kelly stood out of frame, letting the camera focus solely on Katherine while they talked. "Tell me about this trail we're on, Katherine."

Like a veteran performer, Katherine repeated the explanation she had given earlier when she had first showed it to them. "This trail is actually an old bridle path that runs from the main house to the winery. Once I traveled it four to six times a day. For many years, it was much easier to check the vineyards and the work being done around the estate from horseback. Frequently I was in the saddle by dawn and rarely out of it until after sunset." She paused and smiled. "For my sixty-fifth birthday, my son Jonathon bought me a golf cart and persuaded me to put my gray hunter out to pasture. But, once, the two of us could have traveled this path blindfolded."

Several beats of silence followed her concluding remark. Then DeeDee said briskly, "That's it. Stop tape. We've got it. And it's perfect." The short, clipped sentences were indicative of the excitement she struggled to suppress in her voice. But Kelly had worked with her long enough to pick it up. "Let's head to the winery. Great job," she told Katherine, almost as an afterthought. "We'll take that wonderful photo of you on your horse watching the workers in the vineyards and edit it into this sequence. It's a terrific picture. My God, with your jodhpurs and riding crop, you look like Barbara Stanwyck on that horse. Didn't she, Kelly?"

"A very young Barbara Stanwyck," Kelly inserted as the three
of them set off down the bridle path toward the winery.

"Does it matter? That woman always seemed ageless to me."

"In any case, I take your original statement as a compliment,"
Katherine declared with typical graciousness.

"This is actually a shortcut to the winery, isn't it?" Kelly asked,
mentally visualizing the layout of the house and winery and the location of the path between them.

"It is much shorter, yes," Katherine replied as they rounded a
bend in the trail and the brick winery rose before them.

Seeing it, Kelly felt the tension thread through her nerves. Mentally she braced herself against the private memories she had of the
place. She couldn't think about them. She had to block them from
her mind.

A man came out of the winery, dressed in khakis and a tan work
shirt and wearing a beat-up old felt hat. It was a full second before
Kelly realized it was Sam Rutledge. He drew up when he saw
them.

"Good morning." The greeting was directed to all of them, but
his glance went to Kelly. She felt the instant and strong tug of
attraction.

"I like the hat," she said, letting it pull her in.

His mouth quirked in a half smile. "You need something to keep
the sun off you when you're out in the vineyards all day." Steve and
Rick joined them, lugging their equipment. "Still at it, I see," Sam
observed.

"They want to film a portion of the interview in our aging cellars," Katherine explained.

"Are you kidding?" DeeDee declared, raising her eyebrows high.
"How could we *not* include cellars that were dug out of the hillside
by Chinese laborers over a century ago? That would be like doing a
story on Texas and not mentioning the Alamo."

"They are a unique feature of Rutledge Estate," Sam conceded.

"Bud's bringing the van around," Steve Gibbons told DeeDee.
Bud Rasmussen was technically a lighting assistant, but he filled
multiple roles, ranging from electrician to makeup artist when necessary. "All our lighting equipment's in the van. I figured we would
probably need more light in there to get the right look and effect. Do
you want to point us in the right direction and we'll start heading
that way?"

"Good thinking." DeeDee nodded, then looked around. "Where
are the cellars from here?"

"On the other side of the winery." Kelly automatically supplied the answer. "It will be quicker to cut through than go around the building."

"True," Katherine agreed. "Although I think it would be best if I showed you the way."

"I'll go with you," DeeDee said. "Why don't you stick around, Kelly, and wait for Bud."

"All right." As they walked off, Kelly was conscious of being left alone with Sam. She turned, discovering how close he was, and felt something rush along her skin, something race through her blood. Automatically she stepped back. "You left yesterday before I had a chance to thank you for the tour of the house."

He cocked his head at her, a puzzled look in his eyes as the sun's slanting rays sculpted his facial bones in high relief. "How did you know how to get to the cellars from here?"

Panic froze her for a moment. Like any strong emotion, it sharpened her senses. She could smell the dust in the air, the aroma of fermenting juices, and the clean scent of soap emanating from his skin. The tinny taste of fear was on her tongue. She ignored all of it to toss him an artificially careless smile; her mind, thankfully, had not stopped functioning.

"Our research department is without equal. If I had asked, they probably could have gotten me blueprints on the winery and the house, instead of just a simple layout on Rutledge Estate. Believe me, we came prepared."

"I guess you did." He nodded, accepting her explanation, and Kelly drew an easy breath. The van pulled into the yard, stirring up more dust. "Looks like your man has arrived. I won't keep you. I've got work to do myself." He made a move to leave, then his gaze came back to her. "Will you be at the party for the baron tomorrow night?"

Kelly nodded. "All of us will be."

"See you then." He sent her a quick smile and walked off toward a parked Jeep.

The way he'd looked at her, with a warm light in his eyes, it had made her feel good. Yet she didn't want to feel this attraction to him. It was too potent. In its way, too dangerous. Briskly she started for the van to link up with Bud Rasmussen.

"Hi." He clambered out of the van, short and pudgy like the can of beer that had given him his nickname. "Where is everybody?"

Before Kelly could answer, shouts came from the winery, the

words indistinct but the tone of anger unmistakable. She swung around to face the thickly timbered door.

"What in the world," Bud murmured as DeeDee came charging out of the building with Steve and Rick right on her heels. They headed straight for the van. Even before they reached it, Kelly saw that DeeDee's face was fire red.

"What happened?" Kelly frowned. "We heard yelling."

"We just caught holy hell, that's what happened," she snapped, embarrassment beginning to give way to anger. "Katherine was about to introduce us to this old winemaker when he suddenly turned into a raging bull, bellowing at us to get out, that our cologne would ruin his wine. I thought — oh, God, here he comes." DeeDee dropped her voice the instant she saw the stocky old man come out of the winery with Katherine at his side.

He hurried to them, his leathered face drawn in contrite lines. "Forgive me. My temper is a terrible thing. I should not have shouted so."

Katherine broke in, "I have explained to Claude the fault was mine. I failed to advise you not to use any strong colognes today. While it is unlikely, there is always the chance the wines may absorb some of its fragrance. Therefore, we have a strict rule against it."

"Naturally," DeeDee murmured, only slightly mollified by the apology and explanation.

"You understand," Claude inserted anxiously. "It is not that I do not wish for you to visit the cellars. It would be my greatest pleasure to show you our treasures, to give you a taste of them. Please."

Kelly interrupted him. "Please don't apologize, Monsieur Broussard. You had cause to be upset. We understand that. Honestly, we do."

"But that does not excuse my anger," he said, his grizzled head bowing with abject regret.

"Come." Katherine took charge. "You can shower at the house. I will have Han Li prepare coffee and some of his delicious pastries, and we will forget this unfortunate incident took place at all."

That night, in the bed-and-breakfast's dainty front parlor, they were all able to laugh about it while they reviewed the tape they had eventually shot in the cellar. From her perch, curled up at one end of the Victorian sofa, Kelly watched the television screen as Claude Broussard used a wooden mallet to knock the plug, called a bung, from its hole atop a wine barrel.

"That guy is a real character." DeeDee sat cross-legged on the floor in front of the set. "A snaggle-toothed grizzly one second, and a cuddly teddy bear the next. I didn't think I was going to like him, but I swear I do."

"Except when he roars, right?" Steve gave her a good-natured shove in the back before hooking a leg over the sofa's armrest and sitting back on it.

"I have the feeling he's like my father," DeeDee replied. "His roar is much worse than his bite." Kelly tended to agree, though she didn't say so. She was too intent on the scene on the television screen.

They had chosen a spot in the underground cellars where two tunnels intersected, the camera angle showing both stretching back. Wine barrels of French oak, stacked three high, lined both sides of each limestone tunnel. Lights were mounted at regular intervals along the arching walls of the man-made caves, but they threw as much shadow as they did light. She stood in the foreground with Katherine and Claude Broussard, talking and sampling the wine Claude had extracted from the barrel with his wine thief.

But it wasn't her own performance, good or bad, that held Kelly's attention. It was the cellar caves — the coolness of them, the earthy smell of them, and the memories of all the times she had roamed them as a young girl, slipping into them when no one was looking to escape the heat of a summer day, hiding in the deep shadows to avoid discovery when a worker happened by, thinking about all the people who had worked in these tunnels in the last century, imagining their ghosts still walking those underground corridors. She had been fascinated by the caves, their rich history, their heady smells, their eerie yet soothing silences. For a time they had been a refuge for her from her own stormy world.

Just as the darkness of night had later become her refuge, ready to conceal her and hide her from his unreasoning wrath. The way it had that one night when she had been sitting in the kitchen. She had turned the radio up to catch the lyrics to a new song. She hadn't heard the front door open. She hadn't known he was there until he spoke from the doorway to the kitchen.

"There you are sitting on your fat ass again." He said it loudly, saying each word carefully the way he always did when he'd been drinking.

The chair clattered backward as she hurriedly pushed out of it and swung around to face him, every nerve screaming with alertness. "I didn't hear you come in." Wary of him and his uncertain temper, she made sure the chair was between them, and wished it were the table.

"I'm surprised you could hear yourself think with that radio blaring like that." He waved a hand at the radio sitting on top of the refrigerator. "Turn that damned thing down. Better yet, turn it off."

Welcoming the excuse to put more distance between them, she ran to the refrigerator and reached up, switching off the radio. In the sudden silence, she heard the scrape of chair legs on the linoleum floor behind her, followed by the heavy plop of his body on the chair seat.

"How come you don't have supper on the table?"

She wanted to tell him that it had been ready two hours ago, but she bit back the words, unwilling to antagonize him.

"It's in the oven. I kept it warm for you." She grabbed a pot holder off the top of the stove and lowered the oven door.

Reaching inside, she gripped the plate of food on the middle rack using the pot holder and lifted it out. When she turned back to the table, she avoided looking at him. She didn't want to see the meanness in his face.

"Here you are." Leaning across a chair, she slid the plate onto the table in front of him, then drew back, out of reach. "I'll get you some silverware."

She hadn't taken more than a step toward the silverware drawer when he said in disgust, "You call this dried-out slop food?"

Out of the corner of her eye, she caught the swing of his arm as he swept the plate off the table. Peas flew, a grilled hamburger patty tumbling through them. Only the macaroni and cheese stuck to the plate when it crashed to the floor and broke, scattering pieces and chunks of sticky macaroni.

For an instant, she stared at the mess on the floor and fought to swallow back a sob of frustration. She wanted to walk out of the house and leave it for him to clean up. But she knew he wouldn't do it. It would still be there in the morning, all dried and crusted to the floor.

Skirting his chair, she went around the table and bent down to start picking up pieces of the broken plate. "I can scramble some eggs for you or heat up a can of chili," she offered, then sucked in a sharp breath, dropping the first large fragment of ironstone plate still hot from the oven.

"Chili or eggs," he complained as she bit at her burned finger, closing her eyes against the threatening tears. "Is that all we got in this house to eat? What did you do with all that money I gave you for groceries? Spend it on candy bars?"

She sprang to her feet. "You only gave me twenty dollars."

"So?" he challenged. "Where's the food?"

"Twenty dollars doesn't buy much," she protested in an emotion-choked voice, and immediately swung away to drag the wastepaper basket closer to the mess.

"I am not stupid," he declared as she snatched paper napkins from the plastic holder on the table and bent down to begin cleaning up the floor again. "Twenty dollars buys more than eggs and a can of chili."

"Not much more," she muttered under her breath, thinking of all the nonedible items on her list, like toilet paper and toothpaste.

"What did you say?" His voice was low and threatening.

She froze for a split second, then answered, "I said I could fix you some pancakes."

"And burn them like you did the last time? No thanks." Abruptly he shoved the chair back from the table. Instantly she drew back, cringing away from him. But he wasn't coming toward her; he was walking over to the kitchen cupboards.

When she saw him opening a door and rummaging through the contents on the top shelf, she knew exactly what he was looking for — the bottle of whiskey she'd found earlier and emptied into the drain. In a panic, she bowed her head and concentrated on scooping up the mess, using both hands and sandwiching chunks of food and fragments of pottery between the paper napkins.

"Okay, what the hell happened to the bottle of whiskey I had up here?" His voice cracked over her like a whip. She stiffened under it.

"Bottle of whiskey." She tried to strike an innocent note as she kept her eyes on the floor. She'd gotten up the worst of the spill; it would take a mop to clean up the rest. She dumped the nearly shredded paper napkins in the wastebasket and stood up, brushing at her knees. "Are you sure?"

"You're damned right I'm sure. I put it up there myself." His eyes suddenly narrowed on her. "You've been snooping around in there, haven't you? All right, what did you do with it?"

"Nothing. I didn't even know it was there," she lied, and hurried on to conceal it. "But I did find an empty bottle next to your chair in the living room earlier tonight. It's here in the wastebasket some-where. Maybe you forgot you drank it already."

"I didn't forget anything. I'm not stupid like you. That bottle was up there, and it was practically full," he declared, repeatedly jabbing a finger at the cupboard's top shelf.

"If you say so, I guess it was." She feigned an idle shrug and walked over to the sink. "Since you can't find it, why don't I put on some coffee."

She picked up the electric percolator and held it under the faucet, turning on the cold-water tap. He slammed the flat of his hand on the Formica countertop. She jumped sideways, startled by the explosive sound.

"Don't you lie to me, dammit! I want to know what you did with that bottle."

She tried to laugh off his demand, but the sound came out nervous and thready. "I told you I don't know anything about it. I'm not lying." She turned off the water and set the filled percolator on the counter. "Honest, I'm not." She knew somehow she had to get him off this subject. "I have an idea," she said brightly and headed toward the stove as she spoke. "Why don't I fix you a fried-egg sandwich with cheese on it? Remember, you always said I make the best ones you ever tasted."

"I don't want any egg sandwich with cheese." Heavy footsteps punctuated his words. "And I don't want any damned coffee!"

Hearing the slosh of water in the percolator, she turned back. Too late she saw his arm uncock in an arcing, backhanded swing directly at her, his fingers clutching the coffeepot's handle. She ducked and instinctually threw up her hands to protect her face and head.

The heavy pot rammed into her left forearm. Something snapped audibly. Blinding pain shot up her arm, ripping a scream from her throat. She staggered backward into the counter next to the stove, then her legs gave out, her knees buckling as she sank to the floor. The jarring stop unleashed more pain until her head seemed to roar with it.

"My arm," she moaned and tried to cradle the injured limb. "You broke my arm."

"Too bad I didn't break your goddamned neck."

The jeering voice was close. She opened her eyes and saw him standing there, his face all twisted and cold.

"Come on, get up, you disgusting slut."

She shook her head, afraid if she moved too much, she would throw up.

"Get up or you'll get more of the same, slut." The threat wasn't an idle one; she realized that the instant she saw him draw his leg back to kick her.

She couldn't take any more pain. She couldn't.

She lashed out with her foot, catching him squarely in the ankle. Off balance, he fell against the kitchen table, howling in pain. There was a crash and clatter of chairs falling. There he was, all tangled up in them, a steady stream of obscenities pouring from him.

This was her chance, possibly her only chance to escape. Cushioning her broken arm against her body as best she could, she managed to get to her feet. She crossed the kitchen to the back door and staggered outside into the blackness of night.

Unconsciously Kelly rubbed the forearm that had been broken that long-ago night. It had been morning before he had sobered enough to take her to the hospital to have it set. She shuddered when she recalled the long hours of pain she had shared with the warm night.

With an effort, Kelly dragged her thoughts out of the past and focused on the taped interview. The past didn't matter, only the present.

Katherine had just finished speaking when DeeDee's voice came from off camera. "One of your workers was killed by a freak accident. Would you tell us about that, Katherine?"

It wasn't unusual for a producer to interrupt a taped interview to ask a question of her own, but her choice of questions had taken Kelly by surprise. At the time, she had been too startled to catch Katherine's reaction. Now, watching the tape, she had time to observe it.

She went still at the question, then sent a glacial look in DeeDee's direction. "That happened long ago. Almost sixty years now."

"But he was killed here in the cellars," DeeDee persisted. "Did it happen near here?"

"Not far," Katherine admitted, her expression still composed in stiff lines. "It was a very tragic thing for all of us."

"What happened?"

"No one knows. A barrel was found not far from his body. There was blood on it. The sheriff believed it came loose from the rack and fell, killing him instantly. As you said, it was a freak accident."

DeeDee sighed audibly when she heard Katherine's response to her questions again. "I think we can count on editing all of that out, Kelly. No wonder you didn't ask her about that clipping on the accident Research dug up. I hoped there might be an interesting story behind it. Ah, well." She sighed again and rose up on her knees, pushing a button on the VCR and fast-forwarding through the cutaway shots.

No comment seemed to be expected from Kelly, so she made

none. DeeDee released the button, letting the tape resume normal play on a shot of Katherine in the bright sunlight, the vineyard in the background stretching away from her like dark green corduroy.

Kelly heard her own voice say, "You were a woman in a business that was dominated by men. You were a woman in business at a time when a woman's place was in the home. Yet you built Rutledge Estate. How? The obstacles had to be monumental."

Even before she heard Katherine's answer, she felt the flesh raising on her arms. "There are always obstacles to everything," Katherine replied. "You must either go around them, over them, or through them. If the desire is strong enough, you will always find a way to attain what you want. However, if it is no more than an idle wish without the willingness to strive, to work, to sacrifice to achieve it, then you will only find excuses why you cannot."

Katherine couldn't possibly have known it, but she had once spoken almost the exact same words to Kelly when she was an overly plump adolescent with glasses and stringy hair. She hadn't forgotten them, not once in all these years.

Yet, hearing them again, Kelly had the feeling she had come full circle — from the past to the present, and from the present back into the past again.

Bright sunlight flashed on the collection of gray buildings of The Cloisters. The structures housing the winery and offices were designed with a monastic simplicity that gave them an imposing look of severe grandeur. Len Dougherty stood in the shade of the main office and gazed at the paycheck in his hand. Old Gil Rutledge had hired him to be a security guard and keep the tourists from straying into areas of the winery where they weren't allowed. His wages didn't amount to much considering the horde of tourists that went through The Cloisters every day, at five bucks a head.

Dougherty folded the check neatly in half and planned on what he might do with it. Maybe buy some new clothes, or pay his back phone bill and get his number reconnected. He definitely wanted to get a big bouquet of flowers to put on Becca's grave. She had always liked flowers.

As he slipped the check in his shirt pocket, he heard the powerful purr of a Mercedes engine. Looking up, he saw the sleek blue-gray car Gil Rutledge always drove whip into the paved parking lot.

"I wonder what his hurry is?" Dougherty watched the Mercedes skid to an abrupt halt in the reserved stall.

Gil Rutledge charged out of the driver's side and gave the door an angry push, slamming it behind him. Dougherty took one look at his face and knew the man was livid. But he didn't stride into the office as Dougherty expected. He struck out across the lot, straight for the crimson Ferrari parked two spaces away.

It was the first time Dougherty noticed Rutledge's son had come outside the building. Rutledge intercepted him, stopping him from climbing into the low-slung sports car.

Something was wrong. Dougherty could smell it. Worse than that, he had an uneasy feeling it had something to do with Rutledge's deal with the baron. If it did, he had a right to know. He left the building's shade and hurried over to see what it was about.

". . . he called me not thirty minutes ago." Rutledge's voice was low with fury. "Why the hell didn't you tell me things were going sour? You're the one who claimed you knew what was being said behind closed doors."

"But," Clay Rutledge said with a stunned look, "it's impossible. I played tennis with Natalie this morning. According to her, everything was fine."

"The hell it was!" Gil exploded, then broke off when he saw Dougherty hovering near the hood of the sports car. "What do you want?" He glared.

"This is about the baron, isn't it?" Dougherty guessed. "Your deal with him fell through, didn't it? She beat you out of it."

"That remains to be seen," he said curtly.

"What about my money? I need it."

"I'll tell the baron that. I'm sure it'll make a difference to him." His voice was riddled with sarcasm. In the next breath, he waved Dougherty away. "Go on, get out of here."

Dougherty hesitated a moment, then took off, making a beeline for the Buick he'd left parked in the shade. Gil watched long enough to make certain he was leaving, then turned back to Clay.

"Dammit, I had that man in the palm of my hand. I know I did." Gil closed his fingers over his open palm and shook it in emphasis.

"What made him change his mind? Did he say?" Clay continued to frown in disbelief.

"No. When I asked, he would only say it was a business decision. It was impossible to press for a more specific answer over the phone."

"I think I'll go over there. Maybe Natalie can tell me what this is all about." Clay reached for the Ferrari's door handle.

"Don't bother. They've checked out," Gil informed him tightly. "I just came from there myself."

"Checked out?"

"Yes." Gil smiled with cold anger. "The baron asked the desk clerk to forward his mail, messages, everything to Rutledge Estate."

Clay's shoulders sagged. "You're joking."

"Hardly." He exhaled the word in a disgusted breath. "Only one person is doing any laughing right now, and that is Katherine. But I promise you, it won't be for long."

"What about the party tonight?" Clay remembered. "You won't go now, will you?"

His mouth curved again in a smile. "I wouldn't miss it for the world."

"You're serious," he said, realizing.

"You're damned right I am. And I want you there, too." He jabbed a finger in Clay's direction. "Get his wife aside. Katherine has poisoned the baron's mind. Find out how. Got that?"

"Right."

"I want this deal, Clay. And I'm going to get it. One way or another." He stalked off.

Clay stood beside his car for a long moment, his initial shock slowly turning to anger. This was all Katherine's fault. She had made his life miserable for as long as he could remember. God, he hated that woman.

13

*F*rosted lights were strung over the terrace, forming a latticelike canopy that cast a soft glow over the entire area. Below, there was the gleam of china and crystal on white linen, the series of long tables arranged in a horseshoe design to accommodate the fifty-odd guests at the party.

Torchères blazed at strategic intervals in the garden, their flames dancing to the strains of Mozart that the string quartet played. Background music to the friendly chatter of voices. The atmosphere was California casual, Napa Valley style. The warm September night dictated the dress: lightweight sports jackets and open collars for men; dresses of chiffon, crepe de chine, and ethnically embroidered gauzes for women. The satins, taffetas, and lamé were left at home, along with the diamonds, rubies, and emeralds, leaving a predominance of pearls, silver chokers, and gold jewelry for adornment.

With the camera balanced on his shoulder, Steve Gibbons wandered through the throng of guests, capturing vignettes of the party scene. Kelly trailed after him, on hand to do the occasional interview and identify to DeeDee anyone of importance she recognized.

The vast majority of the guests were vintners and their spouses, with a noted wine critic, a world-renowned chef, two reporters for the trade, and the occasional celebrity or two thrown in for variety. The spice, in Kelly's opinion, was being supplied by the presence of Gil Rutledge and his son, Clay. It made for an interesting scene, all the players on stage at one time — Katherine, Baron Fougère, Gil.

When Steve stopped to get a shot of a laughing group, Kelly let her gaze stray back to Gil Rutledge. He looked relaxed, completely at ease in his surroundings, the charm turned on full force as he indulged in the predinner socializing of cheek kissing, glad-handing, and wine chatting.

Kelly wondered what kind of comments they might get from Gil about Katherine. She turned to mention the thought to DeeDee — and found Sam Rutledge at her elbow. She struggled to ignore the quick frisson of response to his nearness.

"Hello." Kelly smiled. The last time she'd seen him, Sam had been part of the informal receiving line, made up of himself, Katherine, the baron, and his wife, welcoming the arriving guests. "All finished meeting and greeting guests?"

"Unless someone decides to crash the party, the last of the guests has arrived." Sam made another brief survey of her. The chamois-soft texture of the sand-washed silk she wore seemed to invite the stroke of his hand, the rich aquamarine color of it intensified the green of her eyes. Her auburn hair was piled atop her head, a few wisps escaping. Sam idly wondered how many pins held it in place.

"You don't really think anyone would crash the party, do you?" She sounded more amused by the unlikeliness of it than the likeliness.

He shrugged. "You never know."

Sam could think of one — Len Dougherty. Although his foreman, Ramón Rodriguez, had mentioned to him just this morning that Dougherty was a security guard at The Cloisters. Sober, Dougherty wasn't a problem. It was only when he drank that he caused trouble.

Yet it was curious that of all the wineries in the valley, Dougherty was working for The Cloisters. Sam wondered if Gil knew Dougherty was on his payroll or if it was purely chance. He cast a speculating glance in Gil's direction and took a sip of the iced Calistoga water in his glass.

"Have you taken your plane up lately?" Kelly asked.

His gaze came back to her, regret pulling at his half smile. "I've been too busy these last couple weeks to do any flying." He seemed pleased that she had remembered his interest in planes. "I thought I might slip away for a couple hours on Sunday and put the Cub through her paces. I have a vacant passenger seat, and the view of Napa Valley from the air is a sight that shouldn't be missed."

"I'll have to take your word for it," she replied with a quick smile and a shake of her head. "I went to an air show back in Iowa once. There were a couple of those small little biplanes in the show, very similar, I suspect, to the kind you have. They used them in an old-time barnstorming act, complete with wing walkers, mock dogfights, and smoke tails trailing behind them. I remember watching those little planes, spinning and diving, skimming over the tops of cornfields *upside down*. I have a fairly strong stomach, but I

don't think it could take all those rolls and dives and loop-the-
loops."

"What if I promise to keep the wings straight and level the
whole time?" His tone was teasing but his look was serious. Dis-
turbingly so.

Kelly found herself wanting to accept his promise and his invitation. That was impossible, of course. She was leaving tomorrow.
She didn't know why she didn't tell him that; instead, she said,
"Maybe another time I'll take you up on that," and instantly shifted
the subject. "I remember the pilots of those other planes wearing
goggles when they flew. Do you?"

She also remembered the local band playing over and over again
"Those Magnificent Men in Their Flying Machines." At the time,
she had been amused by the choice of songs. Now, looking at Sam,
it seemed totally appropriate.

"In an open cockpit, goggles are virtually a necessity." In the next
beat, a glint of amusement appeared in his eyes. "Sometimes I even
don a long white silk scarf like the aces in World War One wore."

"You do?" She wasn't sure whether to believe him or not.

He nodded. "I do when I'm feeling nostalgic — or want to cut a
dashing figure for a particularly attractive passenger."

"Female, of course."

"Of course." Sam grinned.

"I imagine you've taken a great many female passengers up in
your plane," Kelly said, and felt an immediate, sharp twist of dislike
for all of them.

"Actually I haven't. In fact —" He paused, his gaze searching her
eyes. "— you are the first one I've ever asked."

She didn't want to know that. Somehow it just made everything
seem worse. Yet she managed a smile and a fairly even response.
"In that case, I feel very honored."

"I hope so." A waiter walked purposefully among the party
guests, carrying a silver triangle and striking it at intervals. "I think
that's our cue for dinner," Sam remarked.

"And our cue to pack away our camera. Excuse me." She moved
off to rejoin her crew. She was safer with them.

Entwining silver grape leaves held the place cards in front of each
table setting. Kelly found the one with her name and sat down,
relieved to discover DeeDee on her right. Making social small talk
with strangers was not her forte.

"Beautiful," DeeDee murmured and nodded at the centerpiece

before them, identical to others scattered along the tables. The silver epergne held cascading clusters of grapes, purple-black clusters of cabernet sauvignon contrasting sharply with golden-green bunches of pinot chardonnay.

"It is." Kelly glanced at the arrangement. "Hugh would certainly approve of it. He deplores the use of floral centerpieces at dinner parties. According to him, the fragrance of the flowers not only interferes with the flavor of the food, but it also affects the taste of the wine that's served."

"That sounds like Hugh."

Kelly nodded and idly scanned the seated guests, pausing for a moment on Sam. He sat next to Katherine at the head of the tables' horseshoe arrangement. The baron was on her right, and his wife next to him. Yet Sam was the only one Kelly noticed.

The sun had bronzed his skin and bleached his hair the color of light caramel. His brown eyes were only a shade darker. Even now, seated at the table, chatting with the woman next to him, there was an aura of calm about him that drew her, the pull of it as strong as the attraction she felt. Suddenly, more than anything, she wanted to get out of here, leave this party, this place, this valley.

Tomorrow. She could run tomorrow.

A waiter blocked her view as he leaned between her chair and DeeDee's and poured a pale golden wine into DeeDee's glass. Then he was on Kelly's left, filling her glass, his actions repeated by a cadre of black-jacketed waiters serving the guests.

A hush settled over the tables when Katherine stood. She waited until she had the full attention of everyone, then began to speak. "I have invited you here tonight to welcome a special guest to our valley. For the last two centuries, the Fougère family has made great wines at their château in the Médoc. Wines we have all enjoyed despite the taste of envy they left on our tongues." Her comment drew smiles and a few chuckles. "Baron Emile Fougère has continued his family's proud tradition of making fine Bordeaux wines." She picked up her wineglass and turned toward him, raising it in a toast. "To Baron Fougère. May this be the first of many visits he makes to our valley."

Murmurs of agreement swept the tables as everyone stood and lifted their glasses to him before sipping the crisp chardonnay. He rose and stood stiffly before them, then motioned them into their seats.

"It is the time, I think," he said with a quick glance at Katherine, "when it should be known that two wine families — Fougère of

France and Rutledge of California — have agreed to link together
and make one great wine from the grapes of Napa Valley." There
was a collective breath drawn at his announcement. The baron
raised his glass. "To Fougère and Rutledge."

Judging from Gil Rutledge's expression and the ease with which
he lifted his glass, Kelly didn't think the news was any surprise to
him. Oddly enough, the only involved party who seemed to be
caught off guard by the announcement was Sam. Had he not known
about it? Or simply not expected the announcement to be made
tonight? Kelly couldn't tell, his frown passed too quickly and the
smile came too readily as he responded to the congratulations from
the blonde beside him. She took a thoughtful sip of her wine as the
baron sat back down.

"What name will you give your wine?" a reporter with a respected
wine magazine asked. "Have you decided, Baron?"

"It will be Fougère-Rutledge," he replied.

Smiling, Katherine immediately spoke up. "Or Rutledge-
Fougère."

"I think you'd better wait to print that, Ed," Gil Rutledge
declared in a joking voice, "until you find out who actually comes
out on top."

Clay laughed with the rest at his father's comment, but unlike
them, he knew his father wasn't referring to the wine label but to
the deal itself. To their knowledge, nothing was down in ink yet.
Until it was, the battle wasn't over.

A waiter set his appetizer in front of him, fresh scallops in a
lemon-coriander vinaigrette, and Clay tried again to catch Natalie's
eye at the head table. It had been impossible to have a private word
with her before dinner. Too many people had been around to over-
hear. But the look of anguish that had been in her dark eyes when
she'd greeted him had reassured Clay that her husband's decision
had come as a total surprise to her.

Yet it worried him that she hadn't so much as glanced in his direction. Surely she had noticed where he was sitting.

But the appetizer plates were cleared away and the medallions of
lamb with an olive-anchovy sauce and fried artichokes were served
before her gaze sought him out and clung for several seconds, a
desperation in her eyes.

All his tension dissolved as confidence surged through him. She
would slip away from the party to meet him. She would do anything
he asked. The stupid woman loved him.

A little smugly, Clay ate his lamb and deliberately left his glass of cabernet sauvignon untouched. It was a Rutledge Estate Private Reserve, Madam's wine. It would be as galling as swill, as far as he was concerned. But he drained the last drop of the sweet and icy Château d'Yquem, the crème de la crème of dessert wines, that accompanied the dinner's final course.

After dinner, the party shifted to the gardens where a five-piece band played swing music, taking the place of the string quartet. When Clay spotted Natalie standing slightly apart from her husband, he knew he had his chance.

He strolled over and stood barely a foot away, facing the band and pretending to listen to the music. "Natalie, I have to talk to you. Don't look," he whispered in warning when she started to turn. "Just listen. On the other side of the house, there's a trail that leads into the trees. Meet me there."

"I cannot," she whispered back. "Not tonight."

"It has to be tonight," he told her. "It may be our only chance." He heard her draw another breath of protest and said quickly, "If you love me, you'll be there."

The line was disgustingly old, but it never failed to work. Women were so easily manipulated by their emotions. Smiling to himself, Clay moved off before she could make any response.

A smile edged the corners of Katherine's mouth as she scanned her guests. The announcement at dinner had everyone talking, instilling a sense of excitement in the air. She glanced sideways at Emile.

"We have created a stir," she murmured. "Many expected an announcement, but very few thought it would come this soon."

"I suspect your grandson was not entirely pleased to hear it. You have cause to have such faith in him."

"Oh?" Katherine gave the sound a mildly curious note.

"I confess I questioned his ability for a time. I thought his nature was too placid, that he lacked your firm hand in running the winery. It is obvious to me now that I was wrong."

"What changed your mind?" She studied him with new interest, piqued by the certainty in his voice.

"A comment he made to me the other day," Emile replied and Katherine waited for him to elucidate. "He expressed his dislike that a Fougère would share the credit for a great wine made by a Rutledge. He had no care whether he offended me or not." He gave a thoughtful nod. "He is not a man to back down from what he believes. That cannot be said for many men."

Katherine had no reply. Anger had been her first reaction when

Emile had revealed Sam's comment. On its heels came a rush of
questions and doubts, along with a growing sense of uneasiness.
Had she misjudged Sam all along?

She thought back to her conversation with Sam a few days ago
regarding Emile's impending visit, remembering Sam's unexpected
boldness in bringing up her own lack of faith in his ability. At the
time she had considered it childish, a totally inappropriate subject
for discussion. But had it been?

And there was that shooting incident with Dougherty when Sam
had rejected her recommendation to let the sheriff handle it and had
gone there himself. She had viewed his actions then as motivated by
a foolish sense of male pride, a need to prove his masculinity in the
face of danger. Could it have been that he went out of loyalty, out
of responsibility to his men?

And that suit against the Sonoma winery last winter; she had been
angered by the weakness he had shown in reaching such a quick
settlement and dropping the suit. The minute she learned of it, she
had rescinded the power of attorney she had given him after she had
been injured by the fall. In her eyes, he had displayed no stomach
for a fight. And yet . . . he had saved them from a lengthy legal
battle that would have been costly and time-consuming.

If she looked back further into past years, would she find similar
incidents, actions of Sam's that she had misconstrued? Age hadn't
dimmed her vision. But had it narrowed her mind? Suddenly Katherine was confused, uncertain.

"Do you hear that song, Katherine?" Emile murmured. "Natalie
and I danced to it the night I proposed. I think I will find her and
see if she would like to dance to it again."

She responded with a nod, hearing his voice but nothing of what
he said. She didn't even notice when he walked away.

Kelly could have hugged Steve when he came over and asked her to
dance to a slow song, rescuing her from a garrulous vintner who had
been bending her ear for the last twenty minutes, telling her the
story of his very dull life, naturally with the hope she would want
to interview him for her television show.

"I'd love to." Kelly grabbed Steve's hand and sent a forced smile
at her boring partner. "Excuse us."

"Come back when you're through. I've got more," the man called
after her.

She waved an ambiguous reply and followed Steve onto the portable dance floor on the grassy lawn in front of the vine-draped

bandstand. Steve gave her a swing into his arms and started walking her around the floor.

"Great party, isn't it?" He grinned at her in absolute sincerity.

"Great." She smiled wanly, certain she was the only one who wasn't having a wonderful time. DeeDee was over there laughing it up with a pair of transplanted Texans. Rick was talking woofers with a fading rock star who had become a little too respectable. As for Steve, she suspected he could have a good time at a cemetery.

"I like this song, don't you?" Steve said and started singing the lyrics in her ear. Luckily he had a good voice.

As they started around the dance floor a third time, Sam stepped up and tapped Steve on the shoulder, his eyes on Kelly. "May I cut in?"

"Why not?" Steve shrugged.

In the next moment her hand lay on Sam's shoulder, her other caught firmly in the grip of his fingers. Their steps matched, although Kelly didn't notice. Never in her life could she remember being so totally aware of one person. Worse, she felt like the awkward, tongue-tied teenager she had once been.

"You didn't mind my cutting in, did you?" His voice was a pleasant rumble. She could feel the vibration of it through his shoulder.

"No." She continued to stare over his shoulder, watching the other couples moving around the dance floor.

She couldn't completely relax in his arms, though she tried. But his body was close, and the pressure of his hand at her back possessive. She remembered the time he had kissed her, the needs he had aroused, that he still aroused. Just for an instant Kelly let herself wonder what it would be like to have Sam make love to her, to know the caress of his hands, and experience that rush of pleasure and release. But that would never happen; she couldn't allow it.

"You're very quiet," he said at last.

"It's been a long day." Kelly grabbed at the first excuse and directed a quick smile at him. "I'm afraid the food and the wine added the finishing touches."

The grooves that framed his mouth deepened. "In other words, 'Show me the way to go home. I'm tired and I want to go to bed.'"

She laughed and added the next line, "'Had a little drink about an hour ago and it went right to my head.'" But when she looked at Sam, it was more than the wine that was going to her head. She broke off the contact and murmured, "Now I know I'm tired."

"The others in your crew don't look like they're ready to call it a night yet."

Kelly spotted Steve squiring somebody's wife around the floor, and smiled. "I have the feeling they're ready to party all night."

"If you want to leave before they do, I'll take you home."

"Don't tempt me," she warned lightly. "Or I just might take you up on that offer."

"In that case what would you say if I told you I'd bring the car around right after this dance?"

Kelly hesitated only an instant. "I'd say yes."

"Good. Consider it done." His smile was impossible to resist.

With his head lifted, Emile moved among the guests, nodding to a few in his unconsciously aloof way and scanning the rest, searching for Natalie. By chance, he turned and saw her walking alone in the formal gardens. He immediately changed course.

"Natalie. Do you hear this music?" He spoke before he reached her. Startled, she whirled about, her crimson skirt fanning out like a flame. "We danced to this the night of our engagement. I have forgotten the name of it. I knew you would recall."

She looked pale, stricken, uncertain as her fingers touched the pearls at her throat in a nervous gesture. "I . . . I have forgotten, too."

"Shall we dance to it again?" he asked in his grave way.

There was a small, negative movement of her head. "It is almost over, I think. Perhaps another time." She nearly managed a smile.

Emile caught the faint tremor in her voice and looked at her with an intensity that was uncommon to him. "Is something wrong? You seem pale."

"No. I have a headache." Her hand fluttered in dismissal of it. "The party, the noise, the music, it has made my head pound. That is all. I thought to come out here among the roses. It is quiet, a lovely respite."

"Shall I have a waiter bring you something for your pain?"

"I have taken something already. Please do not concern yourself. I will be better soon. I am sure of it. You must return to your guests," she said anxiously. "They have come to see you. You must not neglect them."

"Very well." But he was disturbed by her manner, her agitation. He considered it thoroughly as he rejoined the party, more deeply troubled than he chose to admit to himself. But it was the reason he kept the rose garden — and Natalie — in view.

*   *   *

Katherine stopped a waiter. "When you see my grandson, tell him I want to talk to him."

"Yes, Madam." With a nod, he moved off.

"What's the matter, Katherine?" came Gil's taunting voice. "Has Sam done something to disappoint you again?"

She made a slow pivot to face him. He stood off to one side, a brandy glass in his hand, an amused smile on his lips, and a loathing in his eyes.

"Fortunately Sam is not like you," she replied, regarding her son coolly.

Hot color darkened his face and a vein stood out in his neck as he glared back at her. He took a quick swallow of brandy and made a visible attempt to control his temper. "Your party tonight is guaranteed to be the talk of the valley. But nothing is signed yet, is it? I plan to have a little talk with the baron tonight. Who knows? This could turn out to be the laugh of the valley."

"I am in no mood to trade clever remarks with you tonight, Gil," Katherine said, openly impatient with him. "For you, it was always personal, and it was never that. The jealousy that raged between you and your brother was destructive. Like the phylloxera that is killing your vineyards, it eats away at the roots and, in time, the vine itself dies. I could not allow it to continue. I had hoped that once you were on your own, you would see that. I was wrong." She felt suddenly weary and sad — and old. "Jonathon is dead and you are still infected."

"Is that how you justify throwing me out?" he demanded in a low and angry voice.

"You poor, angry old man," she murmured and walked away, this time using the support of her cane.

Avoiding the guests, she headed for the terrace where the tables had been separated, some removed entirely and the rest left for those guests who preferred to sit and gossip. There were few of them. Lost in thought, Katherine almost didn't see Sam as he strode across the fieldstones toward the terrace doors.

"Sam. Sam, I want to talk to you," she called out and quickened her steps.

He stopped, throwing her a half-irritated glance. "I'm taking Kelly Douglas back to the Darnell place. I'll be back in a half hour or so."

"It will not hurt her to wait a few minutes." Her response was sharp. Somehow her own temper had grown short. "Come inside."

Her arbitrary tone stung and Sam stiffened under it. A muscle leaped along the line of his clenched jaw as he opened a terrace door for her and followed her inside. He stopped within the marbled entry hall and faced her, unconsciously assuming a combative stance.

"What is it that can't wait?"

"I spoke to Emile —"

"And the two of you have reached an agreement. I know. I heard the announcement at dinner." Sam didn't try to temper the hardness in his voice, the memory of it cutting through him again. "You could have mentioned it to me before you told the world, Katherine. I think I deserved that much from you."

"I had every intention of telling you. Emile and I had agreed that an announcement would not —" She stopped and impatiently waved off the rest of the sentence. "That is not what I wish to discuss with you. Emile told me a few minutes ago that you resent the idea of a Rutledge wine carrying the Fougère name. Is this true?"

"It is." He started to leave it at that, then changed his mind. "Frankly, Katherine, I don't understand why the hell you don't. From the time I was a little boy I heard you say over and over again that one day the name of Rutledge Estate would be spoken in the same breath with Pétrus, Mouton-Rothschild, and Margaux. You devoted your whole life to that. The vines, the grapes, the wine — nothing else mattered to you. Now it's over. Gone." He looked at her and shook his head. "There is no Rutledge Estate anymore, not after tonight. Only Fougère-Rutledge, or Rutledge-Fougère. But no Rutledge Estate."

"And that matters to you." She wore a strange expression as she searched his face.

A short, bitter laugh escaped him. "My God, Katherine, I'm a Rutledge. We all have wine in our veins, not blood." He turned and walked off, leaving her standing in the hall.

When Kelly came out of the house, she expected to see Sam's Jeep parked in the circular drive. But he was standing next to a Jaguar convertible, painted an English racing green. Reaching down, he opened the passenger door for her.

"Now this looks like the car a successful vintner would drive," she said in a half-jesting voice.

"I bring it out whenever I want to impress someone." He waited until she was seated and her skirt was out of the way, then pushed the door shut.

"I'm impressed," Kelly assured him as he walked around to the driver's side.

"Good." He opened his door, keys in hand. "If you want, I can put the top up."

She shook her head. "It's a beautiful night. Leave it down." The wind and noise would mean less conversation during the ride; Kelly preferred that.

Once away from the house and its shine of lights, Kelly saw the stars were out and a half-moon rode high in the night sky. There was little traffic on Silverado Trail. The sports car zipped along it, handling its curves effortlessly. The wind tunneled in the car's open sides, bringing the muffled roar of the engine and the smells of the valley. She turned her face into the rush of air and let it blow over her, not thinking, not feeling.

Soon, the car slowed and Sam turned off the highway onto a side road that would take them into the outskirts of St. Helena. The last two miles went fast. Kelly almost regretted it when he pulled into the driveway and stopped, switching off the engine and the lights.

"That didn't take long." He turned in the seat to face her, laying an arm along the back of it.

"Not long at all." She unfastened her seat belt and started to reach for the door handle to make her escape. "Thanks for the ride. I —" She caught the faint sound of music drifting across the still night air and paused to listen, trapped by the familiar sound of it, the memories of all other times she'd heard it. "Spanish guitars," she murmured.

Sam lifted his head to listen for an instant. "Some migrant workers must be camped nearby."

"I guess," she agreed softly, still intent on the intricate play of notes.

"How much longer will you be staying?" He hadn't meant to ask that.

"I leave tomorrow morning."

"Tomorrow?" His brow furrowed in surprise. "I thought you were going to be here a few more days yet."

"The others are. They have more scenes of the valley they need to get. The migrant workers in the vineyards, the trucks mounded with grapes on the highways, the activity at the wineries during crush — that sort of thing, but they don't need me for that," she explained. "My job is done."

"I guess this is good-bye then." Sam brought a hand to her face, skimming the wisps of dark hair back with his fingers, then fitting his hand to the slope of her neck, stroking the line of her jaw with his thumb.

"I guess it is." Her voice was a little breathy, not as steady as she wanted it to be with his eyes on her.

She saw the change in them, the deepening of them, the darkening. Emotion swarmed through her, stirring up again all those needs. She raised a hand to his wrist, telling herself she didn't want this, but that was a lie. She did.

Still Kelly murmured, "I have to pack yet. I should go in." But she didn't pull away from him.

"You should," he agreed and leaned closer, his free hand sliding up her throat to frame her face.

Beneath his thumb, he could feel the fast thud of her pulse, a match to his own. It, and her stillness, were the only encouragement he needed.

Gently Sam rubbed his lips across hers, creating a moist, delectable friction. It warmed him; it warmed her as her mouth moved against his in tentative answer. He wanted more and took it, pulling her closer, his fingers in her hair, plucking pins and dragging down barriers better kept up.

Sam didn't know when her lips had parted, when their tongues had come into play, but he knew she tasted fresh and clean, like rainwater. He knew he could drink and never get enough. But the need was there to try, hot like the night, like the distant throbbing notes of a Spanish guitar — like the demanding pressure of her mouth against his. Yet, at the core of all that heat, he sensed he would find peace.

Drawing back, Kelly let her head dip down to avoid his searching glance while she fought through a storm of useless longings. She was leaving in the morning. Nothing would come of this; nothing could.

She breathed in deeply, inhaling all the warm, earthy scents she identified with him. She had slid her hands inside his jacket. She left them there a moment to steady herself, feeling muscle and sinew, the hard strength of him. It gave her the resolve she needed.

"Good-bye, Sam." She got out of the car and walked swiftly to the house.

Sam watched her, not moving until the front door shut behind her. Then he opened his closed hand and looked at the pins lying in his palm. There were five pins. He curled his fingers around them again, then slipped them in his pocket and started the sports car, the growl of the engine drowning out the distant sound of a lonely guitar.

*   *   *

Katherine continued to stand at the window, watching the circular drive long after the Jaguar's red taillights had disappeared. The party and her duties as hostess were forgotten as her mind went over and over her conversation with her grandson. The fire was gone from her eyes and her shoulders drooped as she leaned heavily on her cane, looking like what she was — a confused old woman.

"What have I done?" she murmured of the night.

Something moved in the shadows near the drive. She watched it with a certain vagueness, slow to recognize a man's shape, and slower still to realize it was Emile.

What was he doing out there alone? Why wasn't he with their guests? Her frown deepened when she saw him swing onto the old bridle path and disappear into the tunnel of trees.

She had to talk to him. But Katherine stood at the window for another long minute while the thought gained sufficient strength to propel her into action. With her cane tapping the floor in sharp accompaniment to her steps, she left the front salon and crossed the marbled hall to the mahogany door.

Outside, Katherine cut across the driveway and the narrow stretch of lawn between the drive and the wide trail. The instant she ventured beyond the reach of the glow from the house lights, her eyes failed her. She had long known that she had difficulty seeing at night. Now the darkness seemed impenetrable, and she stopped, surrounded by it, black shadows blending together to form a solid wall.

Katherine hesitated, then started to turn back to the house. But she had to talk to Emile; the need had become imperative, something she refused to postpone. Hadn't she told Kelly Douglas that she knew this old bridle path well enough to travel it blindfolded? It had been true when she said it, and it was still true. Guided by instinct, memory, and her cane, Katherine moved slowly and cautiously forward.

Gradually the sounds of the party on the terrace faded and the hush of the wooded trail closed around her. Twice Katherine thought she heard voices ahead of her, and stopped to listen. Each time she was forced to conclude it was the whisper of the night breeze through the leafy branches overhead.

A rock rolled from underfoot. She lost her balance and nearly fell, but the cane saved her, steadied her. She pressed a hand to her wildly thumping heart.

"You stupid old woman," she whispered to herself. "Wandering about in the dark without a flashlight, you deserve to fall and break your neck."

But she pushed on, although with considerably more care. The trail seemed much longer than it had in the light of day. She began to worry that she had somehow strayed off it. Katherine stopped more often to peer ahead, expecting to see the blackness broken by the gleam of the security lights in the winery yard.

Suddenly, there they were, winking at her through the branches. She drew a breath of relief, no longer concerned that she had lost her way. Only then did she pause to wonder why Emile had gone to the winery, and how he had known about this old bridle path. She mentally shrugged off the questions; she would have answers to them soon enough.

She moved on, confident of her destination now, the security lights serving as beacons to guide her. Several yards farther on, Katherine heard voices somewhere ahead of her.

"Emile?" she called in a questioning voice. There was instant silence. Katherine frowned, certain she hadn't imagined them. "Who is it? Who is there?" she demanded, and received no answer.

There was a rustle of movement off the trail, but she saw nothing, only more blackness. Quietly she moved forward, listening intently for any other sound, an uneasiness growing.

At last she reached the light-bathed clearing of the winery yard. She scanned it without seeing any sign of Emile. Deciding he had gone into the winery itself, she headed toward the big timbered doors and blocked out the thought of her own ghosts.

A muffled curse came from the shadows at the building's far corner. She saw the black shape of a man crouching low.

"Emile? Is that you?" she called out, taking a step toward him. The figure straightened abruptly, the head jerking up, his face clearly visible in the wash of the security light. Startled, Katherine stopped, demanding instantly, "What are you doing here?"

At the sound of her voice, he dropped the object in his hand and bolted, running into the darkness behind the building, the swift beat of his footsteps breaking the stillness.

What had he dropped? She started forward, then noticed the large black shape on the ground, nearly hidden by the building's deep shadows. It looked like . . . Katherine raised a hand to her throat.

Dear God, it looked like a body.

Inwardly Katherine reeled from the sight, and the images flashing through her mind, even as she pushed herself forward. It was a man, lying facedown, unconscious. She sank down and touched a black-jacketed shoulder. It moved limply under the pressure of her hand.

"Emile." She choked off the cry in her throat.

He wasn't unconscious. He was dead.

Katherine knew it even before she searched for a pulse. She looked up. Instantly she was gripped by something much worse than déjà vu.

14

*T*he pounding continued, loud and insistent. Kelly buried her head under a pillow and tried to block it out. It didn't work. She groaned a sleepy protest before catching a muffled voice calling her name. She threw the pillow off and groggily lifted her head, pushing the hair out of her face. Her contacts were sticking. She blinked to clear them and cast a bleary eye at the window and the pearl gray light of dawn coming through it.

"Kelly. For God's sake, wake up!" The pounding came again at her door, rattling the solidness of it against the frame.

Kelly recognized DeeDee's voice and called an answer, her voice husky with sleep. "I'm coming."

She crawled out of bed and grabbed her silk robe from the foot of it, slipping it on as she crossed to the door, frowning in irritation. She hated waking up like this. She unlocked the door and opened it. DeeDee burst into the room.

"Hurry up and get dressed," she said to Kelly. "We don't have much time. The baron was killed last night."

"What?" Instantly awake, Kelly again pushed her hair back.

"You heard me, the baron was killed, as in 'murdered.'" She walked over to the suitcase Kelly had packed the night before and began pulling out clothes. "A suspect has been arrested. The guys are down at the jail now. I talked to Hugh and he wants us to cover it." She tossed a peach silk camisole trimmed with lace onto the bed, along with a pair of matching panties.

"When did it happen? Where? How? Why?" This was no time for modesty, and Kelly stripped off her robe and nightie, leaving them lying where they fell, and tugged on her underclothes.

"Last night. Not long after you left the party." DeeDee pulled an oatmeal skirt and a gold blouse out of the suitcase and piled them on the bed. "Katherine found his body down by the winery. He'd been hit over the head with a quote blunt instrument unquote. As for the *why,* you'll have to ask whoever did it." She dragged a pair of panty hose out of the lingerie bag and tossed them to Kelly, then dropped a pair of beige heels by her feet. "A satellite van's on its way from the Bay Area. I'll get us some coffee and meet you in the car." She was out the door, her long skirt whirling, the same one she'd had on the night before the party.

In five minutes flat, Kelly was dressed. She ran down the stairs to the front door, her hair loose and flying, her heavy canvas bag slung over one shoulder, weighted down with makeup, brushes, combs, and hairspray.

DeeDee was in the car, the engine running, when Kelly slid into the passenger seat. "Fill me in on the rest." She balanced a mirror on her lap and began putting on her makeup, something she had learned to do quickly and expertly. "What was the baron doing at the winery?"

"Either no one knows or no one's telling." She reversed out of the driveway and headed up the street.

"Katherine has to know," Kelly reasoned as she patted a matte powder over her foundation and blush. "You said she found him, which means she had to know he would be at the winery. It couldn't be a coincidence they both went there."

"Good point. But Katherine's not talking to anyone but the police. I think she saw it. One of the officers on the scene all but admitted she's the one who ID'd the guy they've arrested."

"Who is he?" She traced the outline of her lips with a coral pencil, added lipstick, then went to work on her eyes.

"They haven't released his name yet."

"Until he's formally charged, they probably won't. It wasn't someone from the party?" She stroked the mascara wand over her lashes, darkening their brown color.

"No. The police questioned everyone before they let them leave. I got the impression it was definitely not one of the guests they arrested."

"It's the motive that puzzles me." With nimble fingers, Kelly twisted her long strands of hair into a French braid. "Why would anyone want to kill Baron Fougère?"

"Maybe it was a simple mugging that went bad," DeeDee suggested with an idle shrug of her shoulders.

"Robbery." Kelly considered that without much enthusiasm.

"Why not? There's an abundance of poor migrant workers in the valley right now."

"I know." But her instinct was to discount that.

There was no more time for conversation as DeeDee pulled up at the city hall building that also housed the police station and jail. Kelly counted at least three other television crews milling around on the sidewalk. According to the logos on the vehicles parked at the curb, they were all from the Bay Area.

Kelly spotted Steve and Rick off to one side and made her way over to them. DeeDee was right behind her. "Anything new?" she asked, a notebook and pen in hand.

"In a way," Steve replied and gave a nod of his head at something.

Kelly turned as Linda James left her crew and came striding over, hostility in every line of her body. "What are you doing here?" she snapped. "I cover the West Coast."

"We're doing a feature on Rutledge Estate, where the murder happened." She didn't even try to sound conciliatory. It was too early in the morning and she had yet to have her first cigarette or more than a sip of coffee.

"Stick to your feature. I'll do the reporting on this story," Linda informed her.

"You do your job and leave us alone to do ours," Kelly retorted.

Linda raked her with a scathing glance. "You can do it . . . . for as long as it lasts." She pivoted on her heel and walked off.

"The bitch," DeeDee muttered.

Kelly silently echoed the thought as she glanced at the Jeep pulling up to the curb. Sam climbed out, spotted all the media, and hesitated. No one else seemed to notice him. Kelly excused herself and walked over to him. He looked tired and drawn, like a man who hadn't slept all night, the shadow of a beard darkening his tanned, hollow-cheeked face.

"I should have known you'd be here." There was something grim and hard in his expression, the strain of a long night showing in the faint irritability in his voice.

"How's Katherine?" she asked.

"Fine."

"And the baroness?"

"Don't pump me for information, Kelly," he warned, making it clear he was in no mood to deal with more questions from the press. She could well imagine the way they had swarmed over Rutledge Estate when word of the baron's murder had gone out.

"I was concerned, Sam," she said quietly.

His straight glance explored her face. Then he nodded, a small, tired sigh escaping from him. "The doctor has her under sedation.

She took it pretty hard." He paused, then added grimly, "This shouldn't have happened."

She heard the self-blame in his voice and laid a hand on his arm, the first time she had initiated contact between them. "Even if you had been there, Sam, there was nothing you could have done to prevent any of this."

He started to say something, then stopped and looked at her, a wariness back in his eyes, aimed as much at her profession as it was at her. Still, it hurt. She wanted Sam to trust her. She didn't know why it was suddenly important.

Finally he said, "Maybe I could have. And maybe not."

A tan car drove up and parked in a space reserved for official vehicles only. A man in a dark suit and tie stepped out, then reached back in the car to drag out a briefcase. His arrival triggered a mass rush of reporters straight to him.

"Who's that?" Kelly stared curiously. As the man straightened, the light from the rising sun glinted on the wire rims of his glasses. A lock of brown hair fell across his forehead. He pushed it back and turned to face the oncoming reporters before she could see more of his face.

"Zelinski, the county prosecutor," Sam replied.

Kelly shot him a startled look, then just as quickly swung her glance back to the attorney. Zelinski. He couldn't possibly be Ollie Zelinski, could he? Ollie had been her best friend — her only friend — while she was growing up. He had talked about going to law school.

Her legs carried her over for a closer look, without any conscious direction from her. She wasn't even aware that Sam came along with her. She had eyes only for the tall, slim man in the suit and tie.

She finally saw his face. It was Ollie, tall and gangly Ollie, his Adam's apple still bobbing up and down in his throat when he talked, the corrective lenses in his glasses still thick, magnifying his hazel eyes, making them look even bigger, rounder. Ollie the Owl, the other kids had called him.

What a pair they had been — Ollie the Owl and Lizzie the Lump. She almost smiled at the memory of the two of them, one fat and one thin, objects of ridicule by their classmates, banding together out of self-defense and becoming fast friends as a result.

Now look at the two of them, Kelly thought, Ollie was a county prosecutor and she would soon have her own show on national television. She felt proud — for both of them.

Ollie certainly seemed to be handling the impromptu press conference well. Microphones were thrust in his face; questions came at him from all sides; some he fielded, the rest he ignored. She stopped thinking about the past and began to listen to his firm, baritone voice.

". . . been charged with murder."

"Have you talked to him?" a reporter in the back shouted. "Has he said why he killed the baron?"

"Any discussion of motive at this point in our investigation would be sheer speculation," Ollie replied. "And to answer your first question, no, I haven't personally spoken with him." His glance swept over the faces of the news media, touching briefly on Kelly as he anticipated more questions.

Linda James fired the next one. "Does he have any family?"

"He —" Ollie stopped, his glance racing back to Kelly, a sudden and warm glow lighting his eyes. He recognized her. She hadn't expected that, although who else had known her so well? Abruptly he glanced down, breaking the contact. When he lifted his head, his gaze sought her again, this time with a pained look in his eyes. She had a sudden, sick feeling in the pit of her stomach. "He has a daughter. She left the area years ago. To my knowledge, he has no other relatives."

Somewhere behind them, a man's voice complained loudly. "Quit pushing me. I'm going."

"There he is," a reporter cried, drowning out the small, protesting sound Kelly made in her throat.

Only Sam was close enough to hear it. He glanced at her as all eyes centered on the gray-haired prisoner being escorted by three officers to a police cruiser. Sam's gaze narrowed on her ashen face, her eyes wide with shock.

The others flocked toward the prisoner, his wrists handcuffed behind his back. But Kelly remained frozen in place and stared, unable to move, to run.

Linda James aggressively pushed her way to the front of the media mob and shoved her microphone past the flanking officers. "What's your reaction to the murder charge, Mr. Dougherty?"

"I didn't do it. I'm innocent, do you hear?" Len Dougherty shouted the answer to all of them as he balked under the hands that propelled him toward the wailing cruiser. "It's all a frame. They're trying to hang something on me that I didn't do. I've never killed anyone and anybody who says I did is a liar."

"Can you prove that, Mr. Dougherty?" Linda James challenged.

"I . . ." His voice trailed off. For an instant he looked like a sick, scared old man. He recovered his anger and bravado when he saw Sam. "Those Rutledges aren't going to let me. They want my land and they're hanging this murder charge on me to get it. It's a lie. I'm no killer." He saw Kelly and craned his head to keep her in sight. "You tell them, Lizzie-girl. They'll listen to you. You tell 'em your old man isn't a murderer. You know I'm innocent, Lizzie-girl. You know."

The rest of his words were cut off as the escorting officers forced him into the rear seat of the cruiser. By then heads were swiveling to discover who and where this "Lizzie-girl" was. Kelly was the only female in the immediate vicinity.

"He was talking to you, wasn't he, Kelly?" Linda James stated with a faintly pleased look. "You are Leonard Dougherty's daughter, aren't you?"

For a long second, Kelly said nothing, conscious of DeeDee's disbelieving stare and Sam's narrowed eyes. But she knew there was no escape from the truth, not now that Linda James had caught the scent of it. No more lies could hide it, no more pretense could make it easier. The reality of it had to be faced.

"Yes." She sounded numb; she felt that way, too. There was no more dread, no more anger or resentment, just a leaden feeling of inevitability.

Suddenly she was bombarded with questions, voices hammering at her from all sides. A forest of microphones sprang up in front of her. Camera lenses were trained on her. There was a bitter irony in the memory of all the times she had been part of the encircling horde of press, and now she was the center of it.

"How long since you've seen your father?"

"Do you think he's guilty?"

"What's it like to have your own father charged with murder?"

She shook her head at all the questions, avoiding eye contact with any of the reporters. "I have nothing more to say," she insisted and tried to walk away, but they followed her.

No matter which way she turned, someone was there with a mike or a camera, a notebook or tape recorder. Surrounded, jostled from all sides, Kelly tried to push her way through, but they were two and three deep.

Suddenly an arm gripped her shoulders and a body shielded her left side, an arm thrusting out to force a path through them, and Sam's voice demanded, "Move back. Let us through."

Ollie joined him, flanking Kelly on the right. Together they hustled her through the corps of press straight to Sam's Jeep. Sam split off and Ollie helped Kelly into the passenger seat.

"Get her out of here, Sam," Ollie said, then gave her hand a quick squeeze. "I'm sorry," he murmured to her, then turned to block off the trailing reporters.

Sam drove off. Kelly didn't know where he was taking her. More than that, she didn't care. She stared sightlessly ahead while the wind blew in the Jeep's open sides, stinging her face. She didn't feel it. She didn't feel anything. Not yet.

Somewhere along a twisting road that wound into the Mayacamas range, Sam pulled the Jeep onto a graveled lay-by next to a stream of softly chuckling water, bordered by tall trees, dripping moss. He switched off the engine and let the silence settle around them. Kelly sat motionless, her expression blank, her fingers tightly laced.

When Sam thought of Len Dougherty, the kind of father he must have been — always drunk, always in trouble — he wanted to swear, loudly, viciously. His own parents had been nothing to brag about, forgetting all about him half the time, never bothering to come to his ball games or teacher conferences. But he'd never been ashamed of them. He could hate Dougherty for that alone.

Why in hell had he let security get lax? Dougherty shouldn't have gotten within a hundred feet of the winery. Dougherty had been too quiet for too long. He should have recognized that, but he'd let too many other things crowd Dougherty from his mind. And Kelly had definitely been one of them.

"Where did they take him?" Kelly broke the silence.

Sam took a deep breath before answering, wishing there was a way he could spare her, protect her. That was impossible. "To the county jail in Napa."

She nodded as if they were talking about the weather. He looked for signs of shock, but her eyes were clear and bright, the color was back in her face. She had her emotions firmly under control. It was part of that strength he'd sensed in her, and he knew she'd need all of it before this was over.

"What are you going to do?" he asked, thinking she looked beautiful sitting there. Beautiful and alone.

One shoulder lifted in a semblance of a shrug. "I can't run away. I can't pretend none of this happened. Not this time." A cardinal flitted among the branches of a redwood tree, a flash of scarlet against dark green. "He made my life a kind of hell. Now he's doing it again."

"You aren't responsible for his actions." Sam's eyes were dark and caring in their study of her.

"No, I'm not." But she would suffer from them, just as she

always had. It wasn't fair or right, but that's the way it would be. Kelly had grown up knowing what it was like to be judged, to be made to feel worthless because of her father. "I'm responsible only for my own behavior. Still . . ." She left the thought unfinished as some of the old anger and resentment threatened to surface. "What happened last night?"

How many times in the past had she asked a similar question? How many times had she needed to determine the circumstances surrounding her father's latest brush with the law? So many times that she thought it had ceased to bother her. This time was different; this time the charge was murder.

"There isn't much I can tell you," Sam admitted. "Katherine saw Emile take the old bridle path that leads to the winery. She wanted to talk to him, so she went after him. Her night vision has become very poor over the years and she's old. I'm sure it took her longer to reach the winery than it did for Emile. The security lights at the winery were on. She heard some noise and saw Dougherty bending over Emile's body. When he saw her, he dropped the mallet in his hand and ran."

"He ran." The braid felt hot and heavy on her neck. "He wouldn't have run if he wasn't guilty, I suppose."

Kelly absently rubbed her forearm, the left one that her father had broken in drunken anger. She remembered other occasions when he'd hit her, bruising her face or blackening an eye. She knew he was more than capable of violence. If he had killed someone in a fight, she would have believed that readily. But murder. The word sounded like an obscenity. Even though she hated him, Kelly didn't want to believe he was capable of that.

"What now, Kelly?"

She took a deep breath and let it out, fighting the anger she felt, keeping it inside. "Go back to town, I guess. Back to Darnell's."

"They'll be waiting for you."

"My fellow members of the press, you mean?" she said a little bitterly then looked around at the sylvan setting. "As peaceful as this is, I can't stay here forever. Sooner or later I'll have to face them. After that, I'll just take it moment by moment. But I needed this time." She met his gaze. "Thank you for that, Sam."

"It isn't necessary." He turned the key in the ignition switch.

The noise of the engine and the wind tunneling in the Jeep's open sides made further conversation difficult. They drove back to town in heavy silence.

15

DeeDee pounced on Kelly the minute she walked through the door. "Where have you been? Hugh has called half a dozen times for you already. The man is having a hissy fit wanting to know what's going on. What *is* going on, Kelly?"

"You were there. My father has been accused of murdering Baron Fougère." The sharpness in her voice was inadvertent, a reflection of the need she felt to be doubly on guard. It proved effective in silencing DeeDee.

Kelly walked past DeeDee straight to the phone in the dainty Victorian parlor and dialed the number to Hugh's private line, mentally bracing herself. He answered on the second ring, his voice very clipped, and very British.

"Hello, Hugh. It's Kelly." She made an effort to project a calmness and gripped the telephone cord tightly, twining her fingers through its coils.

There was a full second of thick silence before he spoke in a voice much too quiet and much too controlled. "Kelly, how good of you to call. You do realize your name is making headlines on every wire service in the country."

"I thought it might be." The professional side of her recognized what a sensational story this made — a wealthy French baron murdered at a famed wine estate by the father of a television-news personality. It was the kind of story that could make someone's career.

"You thought, did you?" He was struggling to keep his anger in check, but it came through with a quiet force. "Then perhaps you would be good enough to explain what this is about? Is this man your father? I recall, distinctly, that you told me he was dead."

"At the time, a lie was easier to tell than the truth." But she doubted he would understand that.

"Kelly, Kelly, Kelly," Hugh murmured in soft but angry censure. "The publicity on this has just begun. There are a great many people in this building who are not — pleased, shall we say, by what they are seeing and hearing. Is he guilty?"

"Probably. I don't know." Her head started to pound. She rubbed at her temple.

There was a sigh of regret, of resignation. "Under the circumstances, it will be best if you take a leave of absence from the show."

"No." Her protest was instant and strident.

"That is not a suggestion, Kelly."

"But I need to work, Hugh. I'll go crazy if —"

"Then pray some disaster occurs to push this story off the front page," he snapped, then he added stiffly, "I'll do everything I can, but . . ."

He was already considering replacing her. Kelly could hear it in his voice. If that happened, she would be finished; her career would be over. She had devoted her life to it; it was the center of her existence. The people she worked with — the camera crews, the producers, the writers, the show staff — they were her family, her friends. And Hugh — she had expected him to be upset, even angry, but she had been certain he would stand behind her, certain he would mount a campaign on her behalf to remind the world the sins of her father were not hers. Instead he was ready to turn his back on her. With this leave of absence, he was already distancing himself and the show from her.

A horrible tightness squeezed at her throat and her chest. Even after all this time she still wasn't immune to the pain of betrayal and rejection.

Dimly she heard Hugh's voice. "Kelly, I said, Is DeeDee there?"

She half turned to confirm that DeeDee was standing in the parlor's arched entrance, listening. "Yes."

"I need to talk to her. Be sure to give her all your notes and materials on John Travis. She'll need it to interview him. And, Kelly, you would be wise to drop out of sight. Linda James is out for blood on this one."

Kelly held out the phone to DeeDee. "He wants to talk to you."

When DeeDee took it, Kelly immediately climbed the mahogany stairs to the room she'd left with such haste mere hours ago. She slung her shoulder bag on the unmade bed and crossed to the window.

There, in the vineyards beyond the live oaks, she could see the stooped shapes of migratory workers stripping the vines of their grapes. The morning was new, but the day was long and they paced

themselves, conserving energy to be expended later. Had it been
one of them playing the guitar last night? she wondered. It seemed
an eternity ago, something she had dreamed along with the heat of
Sam's kiss.

She closed her eyes against this sudden, aching need to be held
and comforted, to know the warmth of strong arms around her and
to draw on that strength. She was so tired of facing everything alone.
But hadn't it always been that way since her mother died? Hadn't
she learned she couldn't depend on anyone but herself? She felt the
sting of tears and opened her eyes wide. Crying never changed anything; she'd learned that, too.

There was a light rap on her door, followed by DeeDee's voice
saying, "Kelly, it's me. Can I come in?"

Kelly shook off the remnants of self-pity and gathered up her
defenses, squaring her shoulders as she swung away from the window. "It's unlocked." At the click of the latch, she walked to her
suitcase and dragged out the thick folders on John Travis. "Hugh
asked me to give you these."

DeeDee hesitated, then took them from her. "I'm sorry about
this, Kelly. Hugh's concerned about the show. A lot of jobs are riding
on it."

"What's one job compared to many? I can't fault the logic of that.
But this is my job. My career."

"He only wants you to take a leave of absence, Kelly. This whole
thing could blow over in a couple of days and you'll be back to work.
You haven't lost your job."

"And I'm not going to," she vowed as she began to rearrange the
clothes in her suitcase.

"This has to be hell for you." There was pity in DeeDee's gaze.
Kelly hated that. "What are you going to do?"

She lifted her shoulders in a telling shrug. "I don't know. Hugh
wants me to disappear for a while."

"Are you?"

It was a tempting thought. Only God knew how tempting it was.
"Most of my life I've been hiding, lying, pretending. What has it
gotten me?" Yet she felt trapped, restless, her nerves jagged and
raw.

"If you stay, it better not be here. Right now everyone thinks
you've gone to visit your father in jail." By *everyone*, it was understood she meant members of the various news media sent to cover
the baron's murder. "Once they find out differently, they'll be
camped outside."

Kelly had already considered that. "I'll need the car."

DeeDee shifted the folders to the crook of one arm and dug in her pocket for the car keys. "Where are you going?"

"I don't know yet," Kelly admitted. "Right now I need to think." She curled her fingers around the keys, aware she held freedom in her hand. But was it freedom?

The wind whipped at the pale brown ends of Sam's hair, bringing with it the sharp smell of fermenting grapes mixed with a faint tang of sea air as it blew in through the Jeep's open sides. The iron gates that marked the main entrance to Rutledge Estate were closed, barring reporters and camera crews from entry. Sam turned off onto an unmarked side lane before he ever reached it.

Bone-weary from lack of sleep, Sam headed straight to the house. He left the Jeep parked outside and walked in the front door. The staircase was off to his left, making its grand sweep to the second floor. He angled toward it, intent on a shower and a few hours' sleep.

When he was halfway to the steps, the housekeeper, Mrs. Vargas, stopped him. "Madam is in the morning room. She requested that you meet her there when you returned."

Tired and irritable, he started to snap a reply, then dragged in a deep breath and said, "Tell her I'll be there *after* I shower and change."

He went up the stairs and down the hall to his room. He kept his mind blank as he walked into the adjoining bath and flipped on the shower. Water gushed from the shower head, ice-cold at first then gradually warming.

Without wasting motion, Sam stripped off his clothes and tossed them in a heap on the mosaic-tiled floor. He tested the temperature of the water. It was hot and he stepped beneath the spray, swinging the glass door shut behind him. He stood beneath the pulsing jets of water, letting them beat the tiredness from his muscles, the water sluicing over his broad shoulders, down his back and chest to reach onto his narrow hips and strong legs.

Water pelted the tiled sides of the shower stall; the hiss of it surrounded him like the billowing steam. Cupping a bar of soap in his hands, Sam rubbed it over his arms and chest, working up a lather that the coursing water immediately washed away, leaving his tanned skin slick and glistening.

As he ran his hands over his body, Sam caught himself thinking of Kelly and the way she'd reacted when she learned it was her

father who had been arrested for killing the baron, the initial shock
that had drained the color from her face, leaving her looking
exposed and vulnerable, the way her hands had balled into fists as
she fought to control her emotions and face the onslaught of reporters. That had been much more appealing, in its way sexier, than
hysteria or sobbing flight.

Swearing softly, he lifted his face to the spray and closed his eyes,
trying to shut her out of his mind, but he only succeeded in conjuring
up the image of her sitting beside him in the Jeep, all that magnificent hair plaited in that damnable braid. He scraped his fingers
through his hair, pushing the wet strands off his face. That braid had
been like knowing she wore a woman's lacy things under those tailored clothes.

He stood motionless beneath the pulsing jets, his mind caught on
that erotic thought. He tried to tell himself that he'd slept alone for
so long that any woman could stir him. God knows out there in the
Jeep he had wanted to take her in his arms, hold her, comfort her.

But he hadn't. He hadn't because it wouldn't have stopped there.
It wouldn't have stopped with a kiss either, and sex wasn't what she
had needed from him then.

He hadn't because he had never felt so damned protective toward
another human in his life, even to the extent of protecting her from
himself. It was a new emotion for him and Sam wasn't sure he liked
it, but that didn't lessen the feeling.

Ten minutes later Sam walked into the morning room, dressed in
khakis and a chambray shirt, his face clean-shaven and smooth, his
hair still damp from the shower. Katherine sat at the breakfast table
looking fresh and rested, every strand of white hair perfectly in
place. Only the faint shadows below her eyes indicated that she had
been deprived of any sleep the night before.

"Good morning." Sam walked to the sideboard, ignored the silver
coffee service and filled a glass with freshly squeezed orange juice.
"How's Natalie?" He pulled out a chair and sat down.

With her lips curving in faint amusement, Katherine took a sip of
her coffee. "Clay called an hour ago to make the same inquiry." She
lowered her cup. "She is still in bed. Mrs. Vargas took a tray up to
her earlier, but she refused it. I suspect Natalie will spend most of
the day in her room."

Whether from guilt or grief, Katherine chose not to speculate.
Just as she had chosen not to speculate to the police when they had
asked her why Emile had left the party and gone to the winery last

night. But she had her suspicions. And fears. Both would be kept totally to herself.

"Emile's death has naturally nullified all agreements we made. Perhaps that is best. Our wines will continue to carry only the Rutledge Estate name," Katherine stated. "There is a sad irony that something good can come from such a terrible tragedy."

"A very sad irony." He drank down a swallow of juice and stared into the glass, his expression closed.

If only he had let her know how strongly he felt about Rutledge Estate, she thought. If he had, she would never have gone to Emile, he would not have come to Rutledge Estate, there would have been no party, and Emile would still be alive. That was the real tragedy of all this. But there was nothing to be gained by dwelling on it, and Katherine turned her mind back to the present concerns.

"Did the police indicate how soon they would be taking down their barriers?" she asked. "They have combed the area thoroughly. Surely by now they have collected all their evidence and have taken all the necessary pictures of the scene."

"I wasn't able to talk to anyone. There was a mob of reporters at the police station when I arrived," he explained, then paused a beat. "They transferred Dougherty to the county jail."

"Yes, I heard on the radio that he was officially charged with murder."

He cocked his head toward her. "Then you must have heard about Kelly, too."

Katherine nodded. "The report made much of the fact Dougherty was her father."

"She's one tough, gutsy lady." He swirled the juice in his glass and watched it ride up the sides. "It's hard to believe she's his daughter."

"Guts," she mused as if testing the word that sounded so strange coming from her. "That describes Evan Dougherty, her grandfather, very well. Her intelligence and determination probably came from him as well. The green eyes, the red hair — perhaps I should have seen the resemblance, though it hardly matters."

"No, it doesn't." He didn't give a damn who her parents were, but he remembered her wariness around him. Her father hated anyone connected to Rutledge Estate. Did Kelly see him as her enemy, too? Dammit, he wanted her to trust him.

"Did I mention the weather forecast calls for showers to move into our area in the next day or two?" Katherine said.

"That's the last thing we need right now," Sam muttered in frustration.

"Unfortunately they are calling for a seventy percent chance."

He sighed heavily at that. "I'll get the crews out this morning and start checking the vineyards to make sure there's plenty of room for air to circulate around the grape clusters. That should help some."

"I quite agree, Jonathon. Sam," she said, catching her mistake and correcting it at once. "Mold can form so quickly on wet grapes after a rain, especially if the rain is followed by hot days."

Aware of that and the crop loss that mold would cause, Sam pushed his chair back from the table. "I'd better call Murphy and arrange to have his helicopters on priority standby."

"Helicopters," Katherine repeated sharply. "What possible use would we have for them?"

"After the rain stops, Mother Nature might not send us strong enough winds to dry the grapes. I plan on using the helicopters to give her a helping hand."

"Really, Sam," she murmured in disapproval. "I know you have always had an interest in aircraft. No doubt it is a diverting hobby for you, but the vineyards are no place to indulge your hobbies."

"This has nothing to do with my interest in flying, Katherine."

"Please do not insult my intelligence." She gave him a cold, angry look. "If it was not for your interest in flying, this foolish notion would never have occurred to you."

"There is nothing foolish about it." Sam fought to keep his voice level. "On the contrary, it is both logical and practical. The rotating blades of helicopters hovering over a vineyard act like a giant fan blowing air directly onto the plants. I admit there has been limited use of them in situations like this, but when they have been employed, they have proven to be fairly effective, especially when the leaves around the grape clusters have been cut back."

"Perhaps." But her expression showed she was unconvinced. "But we have never used them before and I see no reason to begin now."

"I do." Sam rose from his chair and walked over to the telephone.

"What are you doing?" Katherine demanded when he picked up the receiver.

"Calling Murphy." He began punching out the numbers on the Touch-Tone phone.

"Did you hear nothing I said?"

"I heard." He held the receiver to his ear.

"And you would deliberately go against my wishes in this?" she challenged indignantly.

"I would. I don't intend to lose half our crop to mold the way we did a few years ago just because you can't see the advantage of a new method."

Stung by his open defiance, Katherine reacted sharply. "Hang up that telephone at once!"

"Hold on a minute, Murphy," Sam said into the phone, then lowered it, cupping a hand over the mouthpiece. "Are you making that an order, Katherine?" He studied her with a hard, level gaze. "Because if you are, I'm going to ignore it. It's my job to do what's best for the vineyards, and if that angers you, so be it."

The good of the vines. The phrase echoed from her past. She looked at Sam for another long second, then waved a hand. "Arrange for the helicopters if you must. We shall see how they do."

He lifted the phone back to his ear. "Murphy, this is Sam Rutledge. Looks like we might need your helicopters."

The high school, the thrift shop where she'd gotten nearly all her clothes, the crumbling brick tavern where her father had spent most of his time, the restaurants where she'd worked as a dishwasher — never slim enough or pretty enough to wait tables — Kelly drove slowly by all of them. Not running from the memories this time, but facing them. Remembering all the pain of not belonging, not wearing the right clothes, not being pretty or popular, not being asked out on dates, of being different, being ashamed of who and what she was, who her father was and what he was, the snickers, the snide remarks.

But there was the town library with its shelves of books that had given her so many, many hours of escape, the newspaper office where her article on the wine history of Napa Valley had been published, the house where her English teacher had lived, and there was her friendship with Ollie. Bright spots among all the darker memories.

Somehow they made it easier when Kelly turned off Main and traveled west on Spring Street. There was little traffic. The road was straight and clear, but she drove slowly, just the same. There was no hurry as she retraced the route by car that she had made so often on foot.

Near the outskirts of town, she came to the cemetery. A dozen long-stemmed roses, as red as the ruby wine from the valley's grapes, lay on the seat beside her, a yellow ribbon tying them together. Kelly gathered them up in her arms and left the car parked outside the entrance. She could have driven in, but she wanted to walk the last yards to her mother's grave.

The cemetery was as old as the town, a mixed collection of weathered gravestones, crypts, and family vaults. Now and then Kelly paused along the way to read familiar names chiseled in granite and marble.

Her steps slowed as she approached her mother's grave. A vase filled with a mixed bouquet of daisies, carnations, and baby's breath stood on the ground next to the marker engraved with the name REBECCA ELLEN DOUGHERTY and the epitaph BELOVED WIFE.

"*He* brought them, didn't he?" Kelly glared at the flowers. An anger swept through her, so hot and strong she shook with it. She wanted to pick them up and hurl them from her sight. She wanted to, but she didn't. Her mother wouldn't have liked it.

She crouched down and gently laid the roses next to the headstone. "Oh, Momma." Her voice cracked a little. "How could he do this to us? How could he?"

The minute she said it, Kelly knew what she had to do. Not for him. For her mother — and for herself.

Framed law certificates shared wall space with a photograph of the governor and the state seal of California. The chunky desk was cluttered with yellow legal pads, a haphazard stack of thick file folders, a black telephone, and a posed picture of two little dark-haired girls wearing glasses. A white paper sack sat squarely in the midst of all of it, a half-eaten ham and cheese sandwich on rye lying atop a matching white wrapper. The swivel office chair creaked when Ollie stood up to greet Kelly, hurriedly wiping his hands on a paper napkin.

Kelly saw the sandwich and hesitated. "Is it lunchtime already?"

"I was having an early one." He stuffed the sandwich back in the sack and shifted to a corner of his desk near the computer terminal. "I didn't have time to grab any breakfast this morning."

His remark reminded her of the reason she was here. She looked away, suddenly uncomfortable. "I didn't mean to interrupt."

"It's okay. Honestly." He smiled in reassurance, giving her a glimpse of the boy who had been her friend. "Have a seat, Liz. Sorry. It's Kelly now, isn't it?"

She sat down on the edge of the leather-backed chair facing his desk, the only one without papers stacked on seat cushions. "I had it legally changed nine years ago."

"You look great, Kelly." The swivel chair creaked again, taking his weight.

"Thank you. I . . ." She searched for something to say, something that would make this awkwardness go away. "You knew who I was right away, didn't you?"

"Your voice," he said with a faint shrug. "It's pretty unmistakable. Maybe because I listened to it so often."

"We used to talk a lot, didn't we?" She smiled in remembrance. "You don't know how many times I've thought about you, wondered where you were, what you were doing. I assumed you had moved away from here long ago. When I saw you today at . . ." She let the sentence trail off, unfinished. Now wasn't the time and this wasn't the place to reminisce or try to bridge the gap of intervening years. "Ollie, is it possible for me to see him?"

"I can arrange it." He nodded and studied her closely. "If you're sure that's what you want."

"It isn't what I want. It's what I have to do." She looked down at her linked fingers, then lifted her head. "Does he have a lawyer?"

"No. The court can appoint one for him."

"Yes, but the charge is murder." Unable to sit any longer, Kelly pushed out of the chair and walked over to the window, hugging her arms around her waist. "He'll need a good one, Ollie. I know it's improper to ask the prosecutor to recommend a defense lawyer, but I don't know who else to ask," she said tightly.

Kelly turned back around. For a long time Ollie was silent and she couldn't think of anything to break the silence. Finally he reached for one of the yellow legal pads on his desk.

"I'll give you some names. You can take it from there." He began writing on the pad, in that awkward upside-down way of left-handers. When he finished, he ripped off the sheet and held it out to her. Kelly hesitated, then walked over to take it from him.

"Thanks." She folded it and slipped it inside her clutch purse.

He adjusted his glasses higher on his nose. "You know I always wondered if we'd ever meet again. To be honest, I never thought it would be in a situation like this."

"Neither did I." Kelly ran her hand over the top of her purse, then sat back down on the chair. "Did he make a statement?"

"No."

"Are you sure —" she began, then stopped, shaking her head. "You must be sure or you wouldn't have charged him with murder."

"Do you want the facts, Kelly?" he asked gently. "An eyewitness puts him on the scene with the murder weapon in his hand. A gas-

oline can was found not three feet from the body. It was full. There
was a gasoline stain on the pants your father was wearing when he
was arrested. Three more cans were found in the trunk of his car.
And a receipt for four gallons of gasoline was found in the pocket of
those same pants. His grudge against Rutledge Estate is fairly common knowledge in the valley."

Slowly she put the pieces together. "So you believe he went there
to set fire to the winery; the baron caught him in the act; and he hit
him." Which meant it wasn't a deliberate act. Somehow that made
it easier to accept.

"Those are your words, not mine." But he didn't deny them.

"I understand." Kelly shifted her grip on her purse. "When can I
see him?"

He looked at her for a long second, then tossed his pen down and
rocked back on his chair. "Don't get yourself dragged into this. You
don't owe him anything. Walk away."

A smile of rueful amusement tugged at one corner of her mouth.
"Wouldn't the tabloids have a field day with that? 'Famous Daughter Deserts Father Accused of Murder.'" Kelly paused, sobering.
"But that isn't the reason I'm staying. If I walked away, then I'd be
just like he is. And I'm not."

"No, you aren't," Ollie agreed and reached for the phone. "How
soon do you want to see your father?"

Never. "As soon as possible."

Ollie took Kelly at her word. Fifteen minutes later she was ushered into a small, windowless room somewhere deep in the building.
It smelled of sweat, stale smoke, and not enough air. She sat at a
scarred, black-and-chrome office desk and waited, but not long.

In less than a minute a uniformed guard escorted her father into
the room, then stationed himself inside near the door. Her father
pulled out the wooden chair and sat down facing her, and Kelly had
her first really good look at him.

He was barely sixty, yet he looked ten years older. His hair, once
a dark shade of auburn like hers, was sparse and streaked with gray.
His green eyes were pale and watery and his complexion had a sal-
low, sickly look to it, broken blood vessels leaving a network of
tracks across his cheeks and nose. He seemed smaller, thinner, as
if he'd shrunk in the years since she'd last seen him.

"Got a cigarette, Lizzie-girl?" He fidgeted in his chair and she
knew it was whiskey he wanted more than a cigarette. It had always
been whiskey.

Wordlessly Kelly took a cigarette from her purse, lit it, and passed it to him, butt-end first. She lit one for herself and exhaled the smoke in a thin angry stream.

"My name is Kelly now," she said stiffly.

"Kelly was your momma's name before she married me. Rebecca Ellen Kelly." He smiled, but his smile was a little off center. "Made me feel good when I heard you using it. Have you been out to her grave?"

"Yes."

"I took some flowers to her, just yesterday it was."

She wanted to scream at him not to talk about her mother. He didn't have the right. But she hadn't come here to fight with him.

"I have the names of some defense attorneys," she told him. "I'll talk to them this afternoon and arrange for one of them to represent you."

"No need for that." His hand shook when he tapped the ash from his cigarette in the black plastic ashtray on the desk. "I can get a public defender. We'll need your money to keep the Rutledges from stealing my vineyard. Don't spend it on a lawyer."

"This isn't some little scrape. This time you won't get away with a fine and a few days in jail."

"You think I don't know that," he shot back.

"I'm hiring a lawyer to defend you." Kelly took a quick puff on her cigarette, then lowered it and flicked her thumbnail back and forth over the filter tip. "The vineyard isn't going to do you any good in prison, and that's exactly where you're going."

His rheumy eyes narrowed on her in accusation. "You think I did it, don't you? You think I killed that baron."

The guard looked on, his expression stoic, but he had to be hearing every word. That didn't stop her father, and Kelly didn't let it stop her.

"You tell me," she challenged coolly, realizing that because of him, she had learned to run early in her life. Flight had always been the best defense against his drunken abuse.

"I didn't do it." He searched her face, then something seemed to break inside him and he lowered his head, dragging a hand through his sparse, graying hair. "You don't believe me. Nobody believes me." He snorted a laugh. "You can bet she counted on that. That's why she told the police I did it. With me in jail, there's no way I can get my hands on the money to keep her from taking my land. I can't even get my grapes picked. She's a smart one, all right." He shook his head, and the ash tumbled from the end of his cigarette onto the battered desk top. "Cagey as a fox and cold as an iceberg, she is. She wants my land back. It doesn't matter to her that I'm innocent."

"Then why did you run?"

"Why?" He lifted his head, giving her a dumbfounded look. "What would you do if you stumbled across a body and somebody starts yelling at you? Are you going to stick around and pass the time of day?"

"I wouldn't run. Not if I was innocent."

He rubbed the back of his hand across his mouth and avoided her eyes. "Yeah, well, with as many run-ins as I've had with the cops, I wasn't about to hang around. I got the hell outta there as fast as I could." Silently Kelly conceded that he had been programmed to run as much as she had. "God, I'm dry. Do you have any gum? Some Juicy Fruit maybe? A couple of candy bars would be good, too. The food is lousy in here." He looked longingly at her purse. "You always did have a sweet tooth."

"Not anymore." She laid a hand over her purse, thinking of all the times her pockets and purse had contained Snickers bars, packets of M&Ms, or boxes of Milk Duds. Then his request sparked another memory — he had always craved sweets when he came off a big drunk. "You were drinking last night, weren't you?" She hadn't thought to ask Ollie that. Maybe she had subconsciously known the answer.

He bristled. "I had a couple."

"It was more than a couple, I'll bet." God, how she hated him. It was like bile in her throat.

"Okay, so maybe it was more than a couple." He stabbed his cigarette out, his hand trembling. He looked old and weak, lacking the strength to raise his hand, let alone deliver a killing blow. "I hadn't had a drop in two weeks. Not a drop in two weeks, I swear." But that was an old story to Kelly. "Then yesterday things went sour. I thought I was going to get the money to pay off the note she's holding. But his deal fell through and . . ."

"And you got drunk," she accused in disgust. "So drunk you probably can't remember half of what happened last night. You could have killed the baron and not remember it — just like you never remembered all the times you beat me."

She started to push away from the desk, but his hand shot out, his long, bony fingers clamping onto her arm with surprising strength. Reflex kicked in as Kelly raised her other hand to ward off the anticipated slap to her face. But he glanced quickly at the guard and immediately released her, pulling back.

"It wasn't like that," he insisted. "Not last night. A few parts are fuzzy, but I didn't kill him. I wasn't so drunk I would forget something like that."

If his voice hadn't been pitched so low, Kelly would have sworn he was saying that for the guard's benefit. "Of course you weren't," she mocked recklessly. "That's why you were stumbling."

Angrily he leaned toward her. "No, it was those goddamned gas cans." A wicked gleam suddenly sparkled in his eyes, and he leaned closer, dropping his voice even lower. "Oh, I had figured out the perfect way to get even with her for stealing my land, Lizzie-girl. Just imagine all of Madam's precious wines tasting like gasoline." He grinned, then moved his head from side to side in a rueful shake. "If I could have only gotten into those caves of hers, all I had to do was pour the gas over those oak barrels, drizzle some on the corks, and all of it — all of it — would have been ruined."

He had never intended to set fire to the winery, Kelly realized; his plan had been much more insidious than that, to taint every ounce of wine stored in the cellars of Rutledge Estate, to ruin vintages that spanned decades and more.

"How could you do that?" She almost breathed the words.

Frowning uneasily at her reaction, he lifted one shoulder in a defensive shrug. "If she takes my vineyard, I'm left with nothing. I wanted her to know what that feels like."

The walls seemed to close in; the air became suddenly stifling. She couldn't breathe. She had to get out. Seizing her purse, Kelly stood up and started toward the door.

"I'm ready to leave," she told the guard.

"Where are you going?" her father called.

"To get you a lawyer."

"You tell him I'm innocent. It was the wine. That's all I went there for. I swear I didn't kill him. You have to believe me."

But how could she believe him? How?

16

The late September sun blazed over the pool terrace, heating the afternoon air. With clean, rhythmic strokes, Gil Rutledge traveled the length of the pool, touched the side, and pulled up, his daily regimen of twenty laps completed. He scraped the excess water from his face and flashed a look at his son.

Clay stood near the pool's edge, nervously chewing at his thumbnail, something he hadn't done since he'd hit puberty and discovered sex. Nerves, which was another way of saying "fear," Gil thought. It was something neither of them could afford to show.

"There's a pitcher of martinis on the table. Why don't you pour a couple glasses," he told Clay and hauled himself out of the pool.

While he toweled himself down, he kept a covert eye on Clay and observed, with satisfaction, that his hand was steady. Not a drop of liquor was spilled, and none sloshed in the glass when Clay gave it to him. This nasty business might have shaken his nerve, but it hadn't broken it. That was good.

Under the circumstances, a toast would be in extremely poor taste. Gil didn't tilt his glass in Clay's direction before he sipped the martini in it. Taking a seat, he leaned back in the poolside chair, feeling a measure of pride in the firmness of his tanned flesh, the lack of flab. He was in better shape than most men half his age, and he knew it.

"Anything new?" He raised a silvered gray eyebrow at Clay.

"Not that I've heard." Clay sat on the edge of a chair, his elbows on the armrests, both hands holding his martini glass. "The police haven't been around to ask you any more questions, have they?"

"No. Why should they?" Gil countered evenly and took another leisurely sip of his martini.

Clay ran combing fingers through his blond hair and shrugged.

"When they took our statements last night, they said they might come around if they had more questions."

"There is nothing we can add to what we've already told them," Gil replied with a dismissing wave of his drink glass, then looked at Clay and said, with firmness, "At the approximate time Emile was killed, you and I were together. Dozens of people saw us. Besides, the police have caught their man."

"But on the noon news, they had a clip of Dougherty insisting he was innocent."

"And there isn't a guilty man in San Quentin either."

"You're right." Clay smiled in silent admiration of his father's calmness, his cool confidence. Some of it rubbed off, and he breathed a little easier.

"I thought it would be appropriate to pay a visit to the grieving widow tomorrow and offer our condolences." Gil idly lifted his face to the sun. "My sources tell me that it appears dear Natalie is Emile's sole heir. How unfortunate for Katherine that she failed to get anything in writing from Emile. It's possible Natalie might be persuaded to choose a different partner for her joint venture."

"I'd say it's more than possible." Privately Clay wondered how long his father had been thinking along those lines. But they had a tacit agreement: no questions. It was better that way.

"That's what I thought." This time Gil lifted his glass in a silent salute and downed a smooth swallow, releasing a gusty sigh.

But it was an earlier comment by his father that had started Clay thinking. He pushed out of his chair and wandered to the edge of the fieldstoned pool deck. "You say she's the sole heir." He glanced back at his father for confirmation.

"Assuming he's made no changes in his will the last few months. Why? What's on your mind?"

"Divorce. Barbara could be convinced it's best." He sipped thoughtfully at his drink.

"You're talking community property. That would be very expensive, Clay." He stood up, disapproval in his expression and his posture.

Clay just smiled. "I'd gladly give half of what I have now to get my hands on Château Noir. After all, Natalie is going to need someone to help her run it."

Gil stared at him for a startled instant, then threw back his head and released a hearty laugh. "By God, I like the way you think." He walked over and clapped a hand on Clay's shoulder. "We make one helluva team, son. One helluva team."

Grinning, they touched glasses and downed the rest of the liquor in one drink. Both silently recognized that as long as they stood together, there was nothing to fear.

The rental car bounced along the rutted track into the weed-choked yard. Kelly braked to a stop next to a Buick parked in front of the house. As impossible as it seemed, the house actually looked worse than she remembered.

The paint that had been cracked and peeling when she left ten years ago was completely gone, exposing gray and rotting boards. The roof sagged at one corner, probably leaked, too. Dust and grime coated the windowpanes. One was cracked, but she didn't see any that were broken.

Broken machinery parts, old tires, and odd pieces of junk poked their tops above the tall weeds around the house. If there was any trace of the flower bed she had once outlined with rocks next to the front stoop, it was hidden by the weeds.

At first glance, the vineyard didn't look much better. A wild tangle of jungle-thick vines. When she looked closer, Kelly could see places where the canes had been cut back to create the illusion of rows.

She switched off the engine and stared at the green-and-white Buick parked in front of the house, its bright chrome glinting in the sunlight. It looked out of place next to the weed-choked yard and the rundown house, all clean and shiny, its painted body waxed to a high sheen.

But it had always been like that; her father had always been very particular about his car. Just as his clothes had to be clean and crisply starched, his car had to be spotless. Keeping it that way had been her job. That old blue Chevy he'd owned when she was in junior high had been the worst, its royal blue color showing every speck of dirt and dust. Kelly remembered all the hours she'd spent laboring to wipe away all the wet streaks before the hot sun baked them dry. . . .

Almost done, she climbed onto the bumper and stretched to reach the top of the car's hood with the chamois. The front of her blue knit top was soaked. It clung to her skin, revealing the rolls of baby fat. A rubber band held her lank hair back in a ponytail, sweat plastering the few escaping strands to her face and neck and sliding her glasses down to the end of her nose.

The screen door banged shut, the sound freezing her for an instant and lacing all her nerves up tightly. The morning heat and her flagging energy were forgotten as she hurriedly wiped at the rapidly drying splotches of water on the hood, and cast a surreptitious glance at the door.

Wincing at the bright glare of sunlight, her father halted at the top of the steps and threw up a hand to shield his eyes from it. His face had that telltale pasty look of too much whiskey the night before. In his hand, he held a glass, half full of a pale brown liquid. She knew it wasn't iced tea he was drinking; it was more whiskey.

"Haven't you got that car done yet?" he demanded irritably.

"Almost." She scrambled off the hood, feeling as if the whole yard had suddenly become strewn with eggshells.

"Look at that." He came off the stoop, pointing a finger at the hood. "You left streaks all over it. What the hell is the matter with you? I buy you a new pair of glasses and you still can't see."

"Sorry." She hurried to rub the chamois over the area he'd indicated.

"You're always sorry," he jeered. "I ask you to do one simple thing, 'Wash my car,' I said, and you're too fat and lazy to do even that one thing right."

"I'll get it," she promised.

"You're damned right you're going to get it because I'm going to stand right here and make sure you do. Do you hear — or are you deaf as well as blind?"

"I hear." She flinched inwardly from the degrading slash of his words, tears stinging her eyes.

"You better," he warned, then erupted, "For chrissake, pay attention to what you're doing. You're leaving fingerprints all over the chrome. Clean them off," he ordered and she jumped to obey. "I'm not about to take this car into town with it looking like this. What will people think?"

She stopped, resentment flaring. "What will they think? Why weren't you worried about what they would think last night when you stumbled out of that bar? Or last month at the Fourth of July fireworks show when you started singing 'God Bless America' at the top of your lungs, waving that bottle around like some drunken —" She cried out as the back of his hand struck her cheek.

"Don't you smart-mouth me, little girl." He hit her again. Harder.

Staggered by the force of the last blow, she fell against the car, her hipbone colliding with its front fender, a numbing pain shooting up her back. She saw him coming at her again and threw the damp chamois in his face, a purely reflexive act of defense with the only weapon she had.

It slowed him for an instant as he swore and snatched the heavy cloth from his face. But it was just enough time for her to roll away and get beyond the reach of his punishing hands. But not from the whiskey glass in his hand. He hurled it at her. She ducked, but not quickly enough as the glass struck her forehead in a glancing blow.

Terror was stronger than the pain, and she started running, heading straight for the concealment of the vine rows, ignoring his shouts and the burning throb in her hip and face. Conscious of his feet pounding the ground in pursuit, she dived into the cover of the vineyard and scrambled along the ground, tiny sobs of panic escaping her throat with each breath. She didn't slow down until she reached the fence line.

Beyond lay a thicket of scarlet-stalked manzanita. She ducked under the wires and crawled into the brush. At last safe from him, she stopped, panting for air, sweat streaming down her face, her frantically beating heart clogging her throat. Her hip ached and her head throbbed. Gingerly she touched her face. The area around her cheekbone had already begun to swell and there was a hard knot on her forehead, the beginnings of a goose egg. But the skin hadn't been broken. She was lucky. *Lucky.* At that thought she began to weep softly and bitterly.

"Come out of there — do you hear me?" he shouted suddenly and she froze in fresh fear, brushing quickly at the tears sliding down her face. "Get your ass back down here and finish cleaning my car!"

The seconds ticked by, but she didn't budge from her hiding place. "Worthless, that's what you are," he shouted again. "You're nothing but a fat, lazy slut. No wonder your mother died. It killed her when she looked at you and realized this useless, fat thing was her daughter. She died because she couldn't stand to look at you anymore, you slut."

She clamped her hands over her ears to shut out his hateful words. Words that hurt more than his fists.

The sound of them still rang in her mind as Kelly stepped slowly out of the car, looking around and wondering what she was doing here. She should be finding a place to stay tonight before the tourists booked all the rooms. But she knew why she'd come — to face the rest of her ghosts. It was something she had to do. She'd run from them, denied them too long.

The rough, rock-strewn ground wasn't exactly meant for crossing in heels, but she picked her way carefully to the front stoop. With equal care, she avoided the rotted boards and tried the front door. The lock was still broken. It swung inward at a push of her hand.

Kelly walked in and stood for a minute in the airless living room, assaulted by the familiar smells — the sickly sweet odor of spilt whiskey, the lingering stench of dried vomit and old cigarette butts. Bright rays from the afternoon sun made a vain attempt to penetrate the grimy windows and throw light into the room, but they managed little more than the injection of a dull glow.

The end table next to her father's chair was half buried under dirty drink glasses, an overflowing ashtray, and a framed picture of her mother. An empty whiskey bottle lay on the floor beside his chair. More were probably under it.

She stared at the sofa where her mother had died. It was still covered with the same old Indian blanket, its once bright stripes now dingy and dull. By chance, Kelly happened to glance at the braided rag rug on the floor. She had an instant image of herself rolling on the rug with her father, giggling uncontrollably under his tickling fingers while he laughed just as loudly.

She was stunned by the memory. Laughter wasn't something she associated with this house, her childhood, or her father, until now.

Still frowning, she walked into the kitchen. The sink was piled with dirty dishes, and more spilled onto the counter. The linoleum on the floor, cracked and yellowed with age, peeled away from the scarred baseboard. But there stood the stove, and its oven that had once filled the house with delicious smells. Cakes, cookies, and her mother's specialty, rich chocolate brownies.

One more stop. Her bedroom, then she'd leave.

Nothing had been touched since she'd left. A thick layer of dust coated every surface, the cheap pine dresser she'd painted white, the flowered coverlet on her iron bed, and the old radio on her nightstand. Kelly flipped the knob. A mixture of music and static sputtered from it. She smiled, surprised it still worked, and turned it off.

Her old doll Babs lay propped against the pillow on her bed. *Waa waa,* it cried when Kelly picked it up. She blew the top film of dust from its plastic face and tipped it so its eyes would open, then touched the hem of the blue dress her mother had made for it, stitching it all by hand.

Babs had been a special gift from Santa Claus when Kelly was seven. They'd had a Christmas tree that year. Her father had brought it home the day before Christmas, and they'd spent the

entire evening, all three of them, her father, mother, and Kelly,
stringing popcorn, gluing paper chains together with flour paste, and
making cutouts of stars, candy canes, and snowflakes to decorate
the tree, topping it with a giant star made out of aluminum foil.
When her father had stolen some popcorn to eat, her mother had
laughed and slapped at his hand. He'd winked at Kelly and slipped
her a few kernels. The next morning there sat Babs under the tree.

Kelly rested her cheek atop the doll's dusty blond hair and closed
her eyes tightly, confused by these unexpected memories. She was
swinging her shoulders from side to side, absently rocking the doll,
when she heard a vehicle drive into the yard.

The police, she thought, probably armed with a search warrant to
look for more evidence against her father. She walked quickly back
to the living room and lifted aside the sun-rotted curtains in time
to see Sam Rutledge climb out of his Jeep. She froze for an instant,
afraid of how much more he'd learn about her roots, what he'd think
of her.

But it was a little late to worry about that. He was already walking
to the door. She reached it first and swung it open, still clutching
the doll in her arms. He swept off his weather-softened hat and
paused on the front stoop.

"I had a feeling I'd find you here." His brown eyes gently examined her.

"I wanted to look around." Self-consciously she gripped the doll
a little tighter, unnerved at having him there, and trying not to
show it.

He nodded, accepting her explanation. "I talked to Oliver Zelinski a short while ago. He told me you'd been to see your father."

For an instant she was back in that cramped interviewing room
sitting across from her father. "He hates Katherine. I don't think I
realized how much until today."

"I know." He came closer and touched the nylon strands of the
doll's hair with his fingertips. "This must have been your doll."

"I couldn't take it with me when I left. There wasn't room in my
suitcase." She moved aside, letting her action serve as permission
to come inside. The living room immediately seemed crowded with
Sam in it. She forced herself to face him, to confront him. "You
haven't asked why I lied about who I was."

His gaze made a brief circle of the room before it centered on her
again. "I think I guessed the reason."

"It didn't always look like this. When my mother was alive, she
was always cleaning and dusting, painting and sewing scraps of fab-

ric together to make slipcovers or curtains. After she died, I tried but . . ."

"How old were you when she died?"

"Eight. I didn't lie about that," she said and turned away. "She liked to bake, too. The house always smelled good then." Unconsciously Kelly shifted the doll in her arms, wrapping both arms around it and letting her glance roam the room, touching on the old sofa, the windows, the lamp, seeing it in her mind not as it was but as she remembered. "I remember Momma used to go from window to window, watching and waiting for him to come home. Sometimes she'd let me wait up with her and I'd bring my blanket and pillow and lie on the sofa. When he drove in, she'd hurry me off to bed, telling me I had to stay there, 'cause my daddy wasn't feeling good."

Sam listened more to her voice than her words. It reminded him of a quiet-running river, smooth on top with strong undercurrents hidden beneath. It washed over a man, pulling him into her. Just as it was now pulling her into the past. She looked small and alone, standing there, hugging her doll.

"He drank then, too," she told him. "Not as much, maybe, and not as often, but he drank. When I was little, I didn't understand what Momma meant when she said he wasn't feeling good. I just know I didn't like it when he came home with that funny smell on his breath, his face all flushed, his voice slurred, all mushy and loving one minute and angry the next. Momma tried to get him to quit drinking. She'd plead and beg, and he'd promise to stop. For a while everything would be all right, then he'd go off on a binge."

No response was expected from him and Sam offered none, watching as she wandered aimlessly over to the sofa and trailed her fingers along the back of it. Part of him wanted to get her out of this dirty, suffocating room, but he sensed she needed this.

Kelly lifted her head, staring into space. "Sometimes Momma and I would go and wait for him to get off work, especially on paydays. I think she did it because it made it harder for him to stop at a bar and have a drink with the guys at the end of the day. With him, one drink always led to another. He got mad at her a few times for waiting for him, accusing her of not trusting him, of spying and checking up on him." Pausing, she pulled her gaze from its study of nothing and fastened it on him. "He was working at Rutledge Estate then."

Sam knew what she wanted him to say, so he said it. "Which explains how you knew the layout of the winery."

"Yes."

Her gaze stayed on him. He loved the dark, black-green of her eyes, shadowed and deep like a lush forest of pines. But he didn't know what to do with what was behind them. In that moment, he was angry with his parents and Katherine for not letting him be close to them, for holding themselves away from him. If they hadn't been so distant, maybe he'd be able to see inside Kelly better, understand what was going on.

"Later, when I was older, she sent me to make sure he came straight home," she recalled idly. "I suppose she thought he was less likely to take a little girl into a bar. It was fun meeting him by myself, riding piggyback to the car, talking to him on the way home." She paused, a frown briefly pleating her forehead in vague puzzlement. "But sometimes I didn't do my job and we'd wind up at a smoky, noisy bar and I'd watch him change into a stranger."

He saw the darkening of her thoughts. Then she seemed to catch herself and lifted her head, throwing him a quick smile.

"I liked going to Rutledge Estate. I was fascinated by the winery and the cool cellars. When no one was looking, I used to sneak inside and wander around." Her gaze traveled softly over his face. "I saw you a few times."

"Did you?" He knew Dougherty had once worked at the winery, but he hadn't known much about him then. Or his family. "I'm not sure I even knew he had a daughter."

"Good." She set the doll on the sofa, not carelessly but without any real awareness of her action. "I'm glad you don't remember me. I was ugly. A tall, chubby girl with long stringy hair and glasses." She stopped and looked at him, then shook her head and softly laughed, at herself, Sam suspected. "Why on earth am I telling you all this?"

"Maybe because it's time you talked about it." He stood with one hand on his hip and the thumb of the other hooked in the back pocket of his khakis, his eyes quietly watching her. There was nothing challenging in his stance, just masculinity and a kind of easy strength.

"Maybe I don't think I should be telling you."

"I do."

He meant it. It wasn't pity in his eyes, but a desire to listen, to share in the past with her. No one had ever wanted to share anything, definitely not anything that might be unpleasant. She was off balance, her emotions ricocheting all over the place. She had to get control of them. She felt too vulnerable.

"Talk to me, Kelly," Sam urged, surprising himself with his gentleness.

"There isn't much more to tell." She moved briskly over to the end table and gathered up the dirty glasses, something automatic in the action that suggested to Sam she had cleaned up after her father endless times before, that this was a release for the restless energy crackling from her. "After my mother died, his drinking became worse. She wasn't there to stop him anymore. I tried. If he was working, I met him when he got off. I waited up for him, pacing from window to window, afraid every time the phone rang. I threw away any bottles I found. I did everything she did. But it wasn't the same."

When she carried the glasses into the kitchen, Sam followed, trying to keep his eyes off the easy sway of her hips. He only partially succeeded. The sink overflowed with dirty dishes. She stopped and stared at them for a helpless second, still holding the glasses with no place to put them. In the end, she shoved them onto the counter, clinking them against the rest.

Keeping her back to him, she walked over to the window and looked out. "He always found a reason to drink," she murmured and Sam noticed that she never called him Daddy or Father, always referring to Dougherty as *he*. "He drank because Momma died. He drank because he felt bad; he drank because he felt good. When it was hot, he drank to cool off; when it was cold, he drank to warm up. We never had any money because he was always pouring it down his throat. And when he was really feeling good, he liked to hit things."

"He beat you." His eyes sharpened on her.

Her shoulders lifted in a deliberately vague shrug. "A few times. Most of the time I managed to get away before he hurt me too badly."

But Sam saw the way she stroked her arm as if it hurt — as if remembering past pain. He clamped his mouth shut. She didn't need his anger.

"He was always sorry when he sobered up afterward. He'd plead with me to forgive him, beg me not to hate him. He'd promise it would never happen again, that he'd stop drinking. It was almost like living with two different people. When he was sober, he would act like a father. Did I have my homework done? Why was I late getting home from school? What was I doing spending so much time with that Zelinski boy? And when he was drunk, it usually wasn't safe to be around him, unless he brought a woman home with him. Then I didn't want to be around." Kelly looked up to the ceiling, suppressing a shudder of revulsion. "The walls of this house are so thin. . . ."

She didn't want to talk about the sounds she'd heard, the heavy breathing and the moans, the bedsprings squeaking and the obscenities they whispered to each other. For a long time, the sex act had been something ugly and revolting to her.

"Once he actually went six months and twelve days without a drink." Kelly strived for lightness, but there was a catch in her voice. "'This time it will be different, you'll see,' he used to say. He'd promise and I'd believe him. I wanted to believe him. I wanted it to be different." She heard her voice getting thicker, but for once she couldn't control it; she couldn't make it project the calm tones she wanted it to have. "I kept thinking if he really loved me, he'd quit drinking. But he kept drinking. He kept hitting me. And I hated him. I hated him."

Her voice vibrated with pain and anger. She had loved her father but he hadn't loved her back. That was something Sam understood. Kelly wasn't the only one with unmet emotional needs. He knew what it was like to feel unwanted and unloved, to call out in the night and not have the person you wanted answer your cries.

Kelly was only half aware Sam was still in the kitchen until she felt the comforting weight of his hand on her shoulder. Why did he have to touch her now? Now, when she was weak and vulnerable.

She wheeled around to face him. "What are you doing here?" she demanded, a strange hoarseness in her voice. "Why did you come?"

Lightly, very lightly, he trailed the backs of his fingers over her cheek, tracing its curve. "Because I didn't want you to be here alone." She wanted to believe what she saw in his eyes, but that old protective instinct flared and she turned her head away from his fingers. His hands simply drifted to her arms, settling warmly on them. "You didn't want to be alone, did you?"

"No one wants to be alone," she said. "Although *he* might, providing he was alone with a bottle."

"Don't think about him, Kelly." The pressure of his hands increased, drawing her to him, his arms sliding around to enfold her. "Think about me." His mouth brushed her forehead, the corner of her eye, and onto her cheek. "Right here." His breath was warm against her lips. "Right now." He rubbed his mouth over them once. "Just me."

Compassion. Kelly hadn't known a man's kiss could hold it. It was more than gentleness, more than tenderness; his mouth soothed and warmed even as his hands stroked away the tension, the stress, the pain. There was no demand as his lips roamed over her face, only understanding.

It became easy, incredibly easy to think of him and nothing else. He surrounded her, his warmth and his strength becoming one and the same. She had needed this, desperately, for a long time. Kelly relaxed against him and murmured his name, turning her head to stop his wandering mouth.

When he felt the sudden, soft give of her body, Sam struggled to check his own answering response. He reminded himself she needed comfort, not passion, but that didn't stop his hands from molding her against his chest and hips, letting her know what true sharing could be. And it didn't stop his mouth from enjoying the rich taste of hers.

But all his good intentions vanished at the reaction of her body to his, her hands drawing his head down, her lips boldly demanding more and more from the kiss and from him. He had to touch her. It was a pressure, a heat.

He ran his fingers down her neck, discovered the pulse hammering inside her throat, bent his head to explore it more fully. He felt the slickness of her blouse and the fabric-covered buttons that held it closed. He freed them and slipped his hands inside, pushing the blouse aside and encountering more silk. Sam almost smiled when he glimpsed the peach silk camisole edged with lace.

Bringing his mouth back to hers, he swallowed her gasp as he smoothed his hands over the silk nothing and discovered the ripple of her ribs beneath it. He rubbed his thumbs across the hidden peaks of her small breasts, felt the hardening of them, the arching of her body to end the teasing play.

Sam drew back, needing to see her, needing to see what was in her eyes. He took his time as his gaze traveled over her face. Her eyes were dark and cloudy, a hunger in them that matched his own craving. He looked down at her breasts and the pointy nubs that pushed against the fabric. He had to know if they tasted as hard as they looked.

Arching her backward over his arm, he bent and rubbed his lips over one of them, feeling the dig of her fingers into his shoulders, hearing the small breath she caught back. With a faint groan of his own, Sam closed his mouth around fabric and nipple, and breathed in the clean, fevered scent of her.

Her hands were on his face, drawing his mouth back to hers. He was lost. What little restraint he had left was fast disintegrating. The more she opened to him, responded to him, the deeper he fell. He ran his hands over her, cupping, stroking, molding, wanting to touch all of her and feel her tremble in response.

Suddenly she tore her mouth away, her hands stiffening in resistance, her breath coming fast and uneven. "Oh, God, no. Not here." The broken protest came out in a near sob.

Sam went still, the filth of the kitchen and the house hitting him instantly, along with his initial resolve to keep the embrace quiet and undemanding. He drew back, but he wouldn't let her pull away from him.

"No," he agreed quietly. "Not here. Not now."

Her eyes were wide on him, wary and uncertain, and still clouded by the desire they'd ignited in each other. Sam glanced at the wet circle his mouth had left on her camisole, and the clear outline of her nipple under it. He wondered if she knew that was a promise of what was to come.

"But it will happen," he told her. "We both want it. You know that as well as I do."

Standing there, conscious of his hands drawing the front of her blouse together, his fingers deftly refastening the buttons, Kelly couldn't deny it, but the sudden clutching in her stomach had left her momentarily speechless.

She wanted him, not just to hold, not just for a few heated kisses, and not just for comfort, though she'd taken that. She wanted him in bed. She wanted him in a way she couldn't remember ever wanting a man before. She had only to look at his sure hands, his broad chest, the hard length of his body, and imagine what it would be like to touch and be touched by him, to roll together on the bed in one tangled heap.

It was crazy, insane. She couldn't afford to be thinking like this. Her world was falling apart; her career was falling apart; her carefully crafted image was being tarnished by the past, blackened by her father's name. That's what she needed to focus on. Not Sam.

But when he stepped back, leaving her completely alone, beyond the touch of his fingers, the hard knot of pressure in her stomach didn't go away. She worked on steadying her breathing and carefully tucked the hem of her blouse inside the waistline of her skirt.

"You weren't planning on staying here tonight, were you?"

Kelly lifted her head at his question and drew in one ragged breath, self-consciously pushing back the stray strands of hair that had escaped her braid. "No."

"Then let's get out of here." He held his hand out to her, inviting her to take it. "There's nothing here for you anymore."

She hesitated only an instant, then slid her hand into the warm grip of his and let him lead her out of the house. She had forgotten the simple pleasure that could be found in holding someone's hand. When they stopped in front of her car, there was no more reason for their hands to remain linked. Kelly almost regretted that. She didn't want Sam to affect her this way, but it was something she hadn't been able to control almost from the moment they met.

After the dimness and staleness of the house, the sun's slanting rays were bright and the air smelled fresh. Kelly cupped a hand above her eyes, shielding them from the glare as she faced him. The sun was a blazing ball behind him, its brilliance darkening his face to a blur of strong features.

Overhead the sky was a flawless blue, unbroken by clouds. The vineyards seemed to stretch on forever around them, the ground beneath their feet ageless, the mountains silent. For a moment, he seemed part of the elements, a man born out of the hot sun, the sea fog, the rugged mountains.

"How long will you be staying now?" His low voice broke the spell.

"As long as I want."

"I thought you had to leave soon." His brows came together in puzzled surprise.

"Officially I've been given a leave of absence from the show." Kelly tried to pretend it didn't hurt.

"What do you mean, 'officially'?"

"I mean that in the next few days, the network's lawyers will probably start talking to my agent about buying out my contract so they can very quietly replace me with another host."

"Why?" His voice was sharp with demand. "What have you done?"

"I've committed the unpardonable sin of becoming headline news of the worst kind. My name is now associated with a murder case." She said it all very lightly, but some of the hurt, tinged with bitterness, came through.

"But you had nothing to do with it. They can't hold your father's actions against you."

Kelly looked at him, unable to remember a time when anyone had been angry on her behalf. But Sam was. Somehow it made everything easier.

"It isn't his actions. It's the notoriety that's rubbed off on me."

She recognized that, and the injustice of it. "In the public's mind, I'm the daughter of an accused murderer. That will inevitably color their thinking of me, and the network can't have the character and integrity of the host of their new prime-time magazine show called into question. That person has to be above reproach. I'm not. It's as simple as that."

"They'll forget." There was a harshness in his expression that touched her.

"In time," Kelly agreed. "But that won't be for a long while. A trial date hasn't even been set yet. Which means there's all that publicity still to be faced. It won't be a short trial either. He isn't about to plead guilty. He swears he didn't do it."

"Do you believe him?"

Sam didn't. She could hear that in his voice. She looked away, focusing on the jungle of grapevines and remembering a time when she'd ridden on her father's shoulders, sitting high above the vine rows, his hands gripping her legs to make sure she didn't fall.

"It isn't a case of whether I believe him," she said softly. "It's more that I don't want to believe he could kill a man."

"I know."

Those two words nearly broke her. She was suddenly and inexplicably tired, so very tired of struggling to make something of herself, tired of fighting to throw off the chains of the past. She felt the sting of tears, but she wouldn't give in to them. She hated weakness.

"Where are you staying tonight?" Sam's question provided the distraction she needed.

"At a motel somewhere. Probably in Napa or Vallejo."

"They'll find you." He meant the reporters.

"Probably."

"Do you want that?"

"No."

"Then come back to the house with me. I have guards stationed at the front gates to keep the press out. They won't bother you there, and the house has plenty of empty rooms." To Sam, even the ones that were richly furnished were empty.

Kelly shook her head. "I don't think so. I would be hiding again."

"Not hiding. Just on the sidelines instead of being a featured performer in the media circus."

His smile was irresistible. She laughed softly and gave in. "All right. I'll come."

"There's a side entrance. Do you remember where it is?"

"I think so."

"Then I'll follow you."

The reflection of the Jeep in her rearview mirror should have given her second thoughts. Instead the sight of it reassured her that she wasn't alone. When she pulled up in front of the house, Kelly did hesitate a moment, wondering how Katherine would react when she found out Sam had invited her to stay with them.

The woman didn't blink an eye. Katherine simply glanced at the stout housekeeper standing close by. "Mrs. Vargas, will you show Miss Douglas to the rosewood suite in the south wing," she instructed, then turned back to Kelly. "Dinner is at seven. I know you will wish to freshen up first, but it isn't necessary to change. We are quite casual here."

"Thank you." But that didn't alter the feeling that she had been living in this blouse and skirt for days. Kelly sent a brief smile at Sam and followed the housekeeper up the marble staircase to the second floor.

Later, when she came down for dinner, she had changed into a white blouse and tobacco brown dress slacks of sueded silk. The ubiquitous Mrs. Vargas appeared and showed her to a small salon adjacent to the formal dining room. Katherine was already seated at the table when Kelly walked in and immediately hesitated. There were only two place settings at the small table.

Katherine observed her reaction. "Natalie won't be joining us for dinner this evening. She is having a tray in her room."

The baroness. Kelly had forgotten she was staying here as well. "What about Sam?"

"I suspect he is still at the winery." Katherine unfolded her napkin and smoothed it across her lap. "There was some difficulty with two photographers who slipped onto the grounds. The police are here as well, to question several of our workers who live on the estate. I expect Sam will be tied up with them for some time."

"I see." Kelly sat down in the lone remaining chair and removed the rose-colored napkin from the table, drawing it across her lap.

There was no further reference, even obliquely, to the baron's death, and certainly none to the role Kelly's father had played in it. The perfect hostess, Katherine kept the conversation centered on safe topics, somehow managing to make a subject as dull as weather interesting by discussing the effects of the drought in California and the contradictory concern that a rain could be a danger to the valley's grape crop. Kelly was glad to have the dinner talk stay on mundane subjects. She didn't feel mentally sharp enough to handle anything else.

Shortly after dinner, she excused herself and went to bed early. If Sam returned to the house before she went upstairs, she didn't see him. She crawled into the rosewood four-poster and pulled the chintz coverlet over her, trying not to think of Sam or that her father would be sleeping in a jail cell tonight.

🔊 *17* 🔊

A pink satin sleeping mask lay on the nightstand next to Katherine's bed. She had removed it well before dawn when she had first wakened. She hadn't risen, but remained in bed, still wearing her man-tailored satin pajamas similar in style to ones she had worn as a bride when such a night garment had been considered quite risqué.

But it wasn't the delight she had known shocking and arousing her husband that was on her mind as Katherine stared at the morning sunlight coming through the gauzy sheers at the east window. Her blue eyes were dark and troubled. Worry lines creased her forehead while her idle fingers moved in a silent and nervous tap across the pages of the book lying open on her lap, the book itself forgotten like the lamp that uselessly burned on the nightstand.

A rap at her door roused Katherine from her fretting contemplation. Hurriedly she closed her book and concealed it beneath the plump pillows that propped her upright in bed. With equal haste, she smoothed a hand over the duvet encased in rose brocade, erasing any trace of the restless night she'd had.

Lastly, she switched off the lamp and called, "Come in, Mrs. Vargas."

She settled back against the pillows, tucking the duvet around her middle, as the housekeeper walked in carrying a lap tray. The tray held its usual glass of freshly squeezed orange juice, nestled in a silver goblet of crushed ice; a carafe of coffee; its accompanying cup and saucer; and a small dish of prunes. Something Katherine consumed privately or not at all.

"Good morning, Madam." Mrs. Vargas came straight to the bed and placed the tray across Katherine's lap.

"Good morning." She took the napkin her housekeeper handed her. "How is Madame Fougère this morning?"

"I couldn't say, Madam." She gathered up the water pitcher and glass she'd left on the nightstand the previous evening.

"Why?" Katherine turned a sharp glance on her. "You took a morning coffee tray to her."

"She refused it."

"Did you leave it?"

"The door was locked, Madam."

There was an instant of silence before Katherine began pushing at the tray that trapped her legs. A startled Mrs. Vargas quickly rescued it, nearly spilling the water pitcher in the process as Katherine threw back the covers and swung out of bed.

"Where is my robe?" she demanded, her dark blue eyes snapping with temper.

"On the chair, Madam." The housekeeper helplessly nodded at it, the lap tray she balanced making it impossible for her to retrieve it. Katherine grabbed up the quilted satin robe and shoved her arms through the sleeves. "Where are you going, Madam?"

"To end this nonsense." Katherine slipped her feet into a pair of flat-soled mules and marched toward the door, ordering over her shoulder, "Bring her tray."

"Yes, Madam." Mrs. Vargas cast a darting glance around the room, then deposited Katherine's tray back on the bed, and hurried to catch up with her.

Katherine never stopped until she reached the door to Natalie's suite, the one she had never had an opportunity to share with Emile. She rapped on the door twice, hard.

"Natalie? It is Katherine. Open this door at once." It was an order, not a request. One that tolerated no argument.

Almost immediately there was a whisper of movement from the other side of the door. Then the click of the lock turning.

"You may come in," came the muffled voice.

Without ado, Katherine walked into the room's disarray. Untouched trays of food, suitcases lying open, clothes scattered about, an evening dress thrown carelessly on the floor. Little sunlight filtered through the closed damask drapes. Katherine walked over and flung them open, then pivoted and motioned to the housekeeper.

"Bring the tray and take these out," she said crisply. "Later you will come back and clean this mess."

In quick order, Mrs. Vargas left the morning tray and removed the old ones, closing the door behind her. Only then did Katherine turn to the woman at the far side of the room. She was clad in a long, sliplike nightgown of ivory silk, her arms crossed in front of her, her hands rubbing at her shoulders and upper arms. Her dark hair fell loose and disheveled about her shoulders. Her dark eyes were tear-swollen, her face shadowed. Natalie turned away from Katherine's examining eyes.

"You cannot continue to shut yourself away in this room, Natalie." Katherine's voice was sharp with temper. She didn't soften it, not even when she saw Natalie flinch at it. "It solves nothing."

"You do not understand," she murmured in weak protest.

"While it is true I lost my husband, a man I deeply loved, I do not presume to understand the pain you are feeling at Emile's death," Katherine stated, her tone firm now, rather than sharp. "But you must put it aside and attend to the duties and obligations that are now yours."

"I cannot," Natalie sobbed and lowered her face, spreading a hand over it, her body trembling in more silent weeping.

"You have no choice, brutal as that sounds."

"It would have been better if I had died."

"But you are not dead. Emile is."

Natalie whirled about, showing a flash of anger. "Must you be so cruel?"

"If that is what is required, yes." Katherine allowed a hint of satisfaction to curve her lips. "Look at this stack of messages and telegrams on your tray. Your attorney in Paris has called five times. There are decisions that have to be made, papers that have to be signed, an endless array of details to be handled, and —" She paused to soften the pitch of her voice. "— you must begin to think about funeral services."

"Oh, God." She gulped back a sob and covered her mouth.

"These things cannot be postponed until you feel able to cope with them, Natalie. You do not have that luxury. You have a life to live and a winery to run."

She shook her head. "I know nothing of wines."

"Learn. I did," Katherine retorted, her impatience back. She stopped and sighed. "Emile has left you a legacy. If you cared for him at all, you will see that Château Noir continues its tradition of fine wines." When Natalie said nothing, Katherine moved toward the door. "I will expect you downstairs before noon."

Kelly slept late, a rarity for her. She found the tray that had been left in the sitting alcove of her room, but the coffee in the carafe was cold and the fresh juice had separated. Sighing her regret, Kelly picked up the tray and carried it downstairs.

Mrs. Vargas waited at the bottom of the staircase to take it from her. She took one look at the tray and said, "There is fresh coffee and juice in the morning room if you would care to follow me."

"Thank you."

The housekeeper led her to a cheery, east-facing room, decorated in the homey style of the French provinces with its wrought-iron table in verdigris, its fireplace of pickled pine, and side tables and chairs adorned with subtle hand paintings. The woman nodded in the direction of the silver coffee urn and juice tray on the ornately carved sideboard.

"If you would care to serve yourself," she said stiffly, then added, "there are croissants in the basket on the table and an assortment of preserves. Madam has already breakfasted. Would you like something more? An omelet, perhaps? Coddled eggs?"

"Some dry toast, thank you."

"Dry toast," she repeated.

"Whole wheat, if you have it."

"Of course."

Alone in the room, Kelly walked over to the sideboard and filled a glass with juice. She set it on the glass-topped table and went back for coffee. She was standing at the sideboard when Sam walked in. He paused to look at her, tall and slender in her slacks of hunter green and a ribbed cotton sweater, clothes that accented her long legs, slim hips, and slimmer waist. He noted with mild annoyance the gold clasp that caught her glossy hair together at the nape of her neck. Just for a moment, Sam let himself imagine that the only reason she was there — the only reason she had come to the valley — was to be with him.

Then she turned and he swept off his hat, giving it a toss onto the woven-rush seat of a chair as he walked the rest of the way into the room. "Good morning." He flicked a glance at her sleep-softened features as he crossed to the sideboard and the silver coffee urn. "Just get up?"

"Guilty." Chair legs scraped the floor under the pull of her hand. Kelly sank into it and looked at Sam when he dragged another chair away from the table, steam rising from the thick coffee mug in his hand. "I can't say the same about you though, can I?" There was a look about him, a kind of quiet vigor, that said he'd spent the morning outdoors. And a sense that, if she was closer, he would smell of sunlight and fresh air. "You've been up awhile, I think."

"Since about dawn," he admitted and sat down, leaning his arms on the table and wrapping his big hands around the mug. His posture was all loose-limbed and lazy, relaxing with an ease she envied. "I've been out in the vineyards. They're forecasting rain and I wanted to make sure enough leaves have been cut away from the grape clusters to allow air to circulate and dry them out in case it does rain. Otherwise mold can form and ruin half the bunch. Which means, come crush, we'll be faced with the time-consuming task of picking through each cluster of moldy grapes to remove only the good ones. We had to do that a couple years ago and, believe me, it wasn't fun."

"Didn't anybody tell you today is Sunday? It's supposed to be a day of rest," Kelly chided lightly.

"Ah, but the grapes don't know that, and Mother Nature doesn't pay attention to it." He lifted his mug, holding her gaze over the rim of it, a gleam of amusement in his golden brown eyes.

"I suppose not." She smiled faintly and saw the immediate shift of his gaze to her lips. When it lingered on them, the sensation was almost physical. She felt her pulse scrambling in response. She tried but she couldn't seem to steady it, not even when he raised his glance to her eyes.

"You look rested. Did you sleep well?"

"Very."

"I'm glad one of us did." His eyes were on her, making it clear she was the reason he had lost sleep. And making it equally clear that he wasn't through with her yet.

The attraction was there, undeniable, potent on both sides. But that's all it was. Attraction. Right now there was too much ahead of her, too many problems, too many uncertainties. This was a complication she didn't need in her life, so Kelly chose to ignore both messages.

"Yes, Katherine mentioned last night at dinner that some of the press had gotten on the property and that you'd probably be tied up until late." She noticed the sections of the Sunday newspaper loosely stacked on the table near his elbow. The front page of the top one carried her photograph, and another she couldn't recognize from this distance. "Anything in the Sunday paper?" She stared at it as she sipped her coffee, wanting to know what had been written yet afraid to read it.

"Just what you'd expect." He scooped it up and tossed it out of her sight onto an empty chair seat. "If you insist on reading it, leave it until after we've had coffee together."

There was a slight hardening of his features. Kelly understood the cause for it. Sam didn't want anything about the baron's death intruding on this moment. But putting the paper out of sight didn't put any of it out of mind. Unlike Sam, she recognized the futility of his gesture, but she let it pass.

"Yes, sir," she said and started to snap him a mock military salute as the housekeeper returned to the morning room with Kelly's wheat toast. She let her hand fall.

"That looks nourishing," Sam mocked lightly when Kelly picked up a diagonally cut slice.

"It is." But she nibbled disinterestedly on a corner, listening to the faint squish of the thick rubber soles on the housekeeper's feet as she exited the room.

"So, anything special on your agenda today?" Sam's question seemed to be an attempt to make things sound normal. Her world was far from normal.

"What agenda?" She looked idly at the dark toast in her hand and tore off a small bite from the corner, letting her fingers toy with it. "Two days ago, every waking minute would have been crammed with things to do. Now I have nothing but free time, and not much to fill it." Unconsciously she began crumbling the small piece of toast. "I've already retained a lawyer, a man named John Mac-Swayne. He's supposed to be a good defense attorney."

"I've heard that." Sam nodded, his displeasure at the turn of the conversation evident in the tightness around his mouth.

"He still has to visit the jail to make it official. He planned to do that as soon as he could. Definitely before I meet with him on Tuesday," she added, talking out her thoughts, only half aware of the things she was saying, and to whom. "After I talked to him, and told him the little I knew, he was convinced he could get the charges lowered. He said he didn't think Ollie could prove premeditation." Kelly saw the pile of crumbs on her plate and self-consciously brushed off the few dry particles still clinging to her fingers. "After I meet with him, there really isn't any reason for me to stay. Everything else can be handled by phone."

"Where would you go?"

"Back to New York."

His gaze stayed on her while he lifted the mug to his mouth, saying against it, "What will you do there?"

"A lot of things."

"Name two." He softened the challenge with a smile.

"For one, I can lobby to keep my job," Kelly replied, then

paused, smiling with a slightly grim humor. "In television, absence rarely 'makes the heart grow fonder.' More often it's 'out of sight, out of mind.' At least if I'm there, I can argue my case. Trying to do that long distance would be difficult, if not impossible."

"Okay, now what's the second?" Sam asked, unable to refute the logic of the first.

"Ever since I moved to New York, I've been active in a local child-abuse program, helping them whenever I could to raise funds and public awareness. I could devote more time to it now, become more involved. Lord knows those kids deserve everyone's help." Hearing her voice thickening with emotion, she stopped and threw a quick glance at Sam to see if he had noticed it.

His eyes were dark, almost black with anger, but when he spoke, his voice was softer, its tone gentler than she had ever heard it. "They do. Just as you did."

His quiet understanding was almost her undoing. Kelly had to fight to keep back the tears. "I guess that's why if I can help just one," she said huskily, "if I can keep just one child from suffering the physical and psychological abuse that I did, it will be enough."

"One won't be enough. I think we both know that. It's too personal."

And it was a subject she still wasn't comfortable talking about because of that. "Anyway," she said and took a deep, sobering breath, releasing it and forcing a smile. "Besides those two things, I have another: a Bentwood rocker I picked up at a flea market. It must have about twenty coats of paint and I've only managed to strip off half of them."

"It can wait. All of it can wait a few days. You don't need to leave yet."

She shook her head. "I need to work." Not wanting Sam to misinterpret that, she added quickly, "It isn't a question of money. I've managed to save quite a bit, enough to keep me going for a while and still pay the legal bills."

"Pretend this is a vacation," Sam reasoned. "Lie around. Give things a chance to die down."

He made it all sound very logical; still, Kelly hesitated. "I don't know."

"I want you to stay, Kelly."

He wanted more than that from her. She could hear it in his voice. She was disturbed by it — by the things it made her want.

"I'm not ready for this, Sam," she said, then realized she was being only half honest. "I'm not ready for you."

"I don't think I'm ready for you either. But what does that change? Nothing."

"But it should."

"Maybe. And maybe some things can't be changed. Maybe they just have to be accepted."

"I don't believe that."

"Don't you? Then believe this: right now I need you here with me. And I think you need to be with me."

"No." Her protest was swift and insistent.

"Deny it all you want, Kelly. But with you and me, it's not a matter of *if*. It's a case of *when*." He pushed the coffee mug away and got to his feet. "As much as I would like to continue this discussion, I have to get back out and see how the guys are doing." Pausing by her chair, he trailed the tip of his finger across her cheek. "I'll see you later."

"Right," Kelly murmured, unnerved by the certainty in his voice.

Not until his footsteps had faded was she able to shake it off, retrieve the newspaper from the chair seat, and begin to read.

The baron's death had not only rated front page, but it also stretched over two full pages on the inside. In all there were three related stories. The first, a factual account of the circumstances of his death and the subsequent arrest of her father for the crime. A second story was basically background on Baron Emile Fougère with quotes from various dignitaries and fellow vintners on the man and his contribution to the wine industry, including one from Gil Rutledge stating: "The world has lost a great vintner and a gentle man."

A photograph of Kelly headed the last story, although the article focused mainly on her father and relegated a recap of her career in television news to three small paragraphs. Some of the information on her father read like a police report, the dry facts fleshed out with interviews from people who knew him and vaguely remembered her, and gave a fairly comprehensive recount of his past misdeeds, proving again that small towns have long memories.

Sighing, Kelly pushed it away from her. Sam had been right; it was just about what she expected. There was consolation in knowing that by tomorrow's edition, the story would be little more than a short column, buried somewhere in the inside pages.

Her coffee was cold when she tasted it. Kelly made a face and got up to add more hot coffee to it from the urn. A set of light footsteps approached the morning room at a subdued pace. Kelly glanced at the archway, smiling in anticipation that it would be Katherine.

But it was Baroness Fougère who walked into the morning room and paused uncertainly. She wore a simple black sheath, no jewelry except her wedding rings. Her dark hair was drawn back in a smooth chignon. There had been a valiant attempt to mask her pallor with makeup and disguise the puffiness around her eyes, but nothing could hide the tortured look of grief in her eyes. They grew wide in their regard of Kelly, surprise and dismay in their haunted depths.

"You are the television reporter." Her voice was pained in its accusation.

"I was," she began, only to be cut off.

"How did you get in here?"

"I'm staying here. Sam invited me." Kelly couldn't go on letting the woman think she was only a television reporter. "Forgive me, Baroness, but you must know that I'm Leonard Dougherty's daughter."

Her frown had a blankness to it. "I do not understand."

Guilt. Kelly felt it, and try as she might, she couldn't rationalize it away. "He has been accused of killing your husband."

There was a paling of her face as Natalie half turned her head away. "I knew a man had been arrested. If I was told his name . . ."

There was no hysteria, no raging storm of accusations, no fit of weeping, just a deep, silent anguish that Kelly found unbearable. That half-formed conviction that it was a mistake to stay here crystallized into a certainty.

"I'm sorry, Baroness. My being here will only upset you. I'll go at once." Leaving her cup on the sideboard, Kelly moved quickly toward the door.

Before she'd taken three steps, the baroness raised a hand to stop her. "No, please."

Katherine walked in, her sharp eyes quickly taking in the scene. "Natalie. How good of you to join us. You remember Kelly Douglas, of course."

"Formerly Dougherty," Kelly insisted firmly. "I told her who I am."

Katherine smiled smoothly, showing no surprise. "Kelly has become the unfortunate victim of a great deal of media attention due to the actions of her father. Sam suggested she take refuge with us, and I agreed."

"And I'm grateful, but I think, under the circumstances, it would be best if I left."

"Nonsense." Katherine reacted strongly and would have said more, but Natalie Fougère's soft voice interposed.

"There is no need for you to go."

Kelly shook her head. "That's very kind of you, but my being here can only be a constant and unpleasant reminder of all that's happened."

The baroness seemed surprised by that. "How can you remind me of something I cannot forget? With each breath I draw, the pain of Emile's death is with me. Your presence cannot make it worse, but it would hurt me to know I am the cause if you would leave here."

Kelly tried to argue, but Katherine stepped in. "Natalie is right. You will stay, and we will hear no more of this talk about leaving."

Trapped, Kelly could think of no argument to make. She gave in, as graciously as she could, and made an excuse to go to her room on the pretext of penning a letter to a nonexistent friend. In her room, she felt even more confined and restlessly prowled its limits until she was summoned for the noon meal.

An ominous bank of clouds loomed on the western horizon, a fore-shadowing of rain in their darkness. The sun rode high in the sky, blithely ignoring them as it blazed over a valley of vineyards.

From the French doors in the main salon, Katherine gazed at the threatening clouds, their blackness matching her troubled mood. They were far off yet, always with the chance they would miss the valley altogether. It was true of other things as well, but that thought failed to comfort her.

She was getting old, she told herself. She'd started seeing things that weren't there. Seeing ghosts. And perhaps Natalie would see ghosts now. She thought of Emile's widow in the library, making all those distressing calls, handling so many tiresome details, dealing with various important matters that seemed so unimportant, just as she herself had once done so very long ago.

The air in the room suddenly seemed close, suffocating. Katherine threw open the doors and stepped onto the terrace. The splashing of water pulled her attention from the dark line of clouds beyond the Mayacamas. Following the sound to its source, she saw the slender shape of Kelly Douglas slicing through the water in the swimming pool, her long legs kicking, the powerful, reaching strokes of her arms driving her across the length of the pool. In a race with demons, Katherine suspected, and exhaustion the trophy. Once she too had worked until she was too tired to think, to feel.

She watched as Kelly made three more laps of the pool at the same killing pace before she stopped and hauled herself out of the water. A tall, wand-slim woman, her arms and legs glistening with moisture, her shoulders and chest heaving from the exertion, the gold swimsuit, one of several Katherine kept for guests, gleaming brighter than the sun. She slicked back her long hair and let it hang down her back in a dark curtain, faintly glinting with red.

Distantly came the chime of the doorbell. Katherine turned with a frown. No one was expected this afternoon. Who would arrive unannounced?

Her curiosity aroused, Katherine went back in the main salon and through to the marbled hall, arriving as Mrs. Vargas opened the front door. Katherine stiffened when she saw the distinctive silver-gray mane of hair that could belong only to her son Gil. A second later it was confirmed when she heard his voice inquiring after Natalie. His son, Clay, it appeared, was with him.

"Show them in, Mrs. Vargas," she instructed and walked the length of the marbled hall to the front door, her cane tapping the floor with each step.

She nodded to the housekeeper in dismissal and faced her son, noting his guarded expression and the watchfulness in his eyes. "You came to see Natalie. Is that wise?"

An eyebrow lifted smoothly. "Courteous, I believe. We came to offer our condolences, and our assistance."

"Of course." She accepted the excuse he gave, recognizing it for what it was.

"How is the baroness?" Clay inquired, his handsome face wearing an expression of appropriate concern.

"She has recovered from the initial shock of Emile's death," Katherine replied. "Time will take care of the rest."

"Will you let her know we're here?" Gil requested, his eyes silently challenging, his hostility carefully banked. Katherine longed to tell him it was wasted, but he wouldn't believe her, just as he had not believed her at the party the other night.

"She is in the library." She leaned heavily on her cane for an instant, then turned and led the way, listening to their following footsteps, one set quick and firm, the other slow and calculated. Yet in some way both were similar.

What was that banal phrase? Like father, like son. But Gil was nothing like his father, her beloved Clayton. That ambition, that single-minded determination to succeed, Gil had gotten from her He'd passed it on to his son, along with cunning and guile. Each possessed traits that could have been good if they hadn't become twisted. Was Gil right? Was the fault hers?

Her sigh was a silent sound as Katherine paused before the closed library doors. She knocked lightly and walked in. Natalie sat in the leather wing chair by the dead fireplace, as if seeking warmth from it. Her gaze was fixed on its blackened interior, her features pale and drawn, a sheaf of faxed messages gripped loosely in her fingers.

"Natalie." Katherine stood in the doorway, observing the startled turn of the woman's head, the blank look that was replaced by momentary confusion. "You have visitors."

"Visitors?" She rose uncertainly to her feet. Her hesitation increased, accompanied by a sudden rush of color to her cheeks, when she saw Clay and Gil Rutledge standing in the hall outside the doors. "I . . ." She fumbled with the papers, then turned away, touching her lips, then bringing her hand down to rest against her throat. "Please, show them in."

Katherine stepped aside to admit them, one hand staying on the brass doorknob. She was slow to leave, covertly watching as Gil approached Natalie first, clasping both her hands and raising them to his chest, murmuring words of sympathy. Yet it was Clay Natalie's glance went to. Katherine walked out, deliberately leaving the door open.

The music room was but a short distance down the corridor from the library. Drawn by the sight of the ebony black piano, Katherine walked in and moved slowly to it. She lowered herself onto the hard piano bench and ran a hand over the smooth black wood that concealed the piano keys.

She smiled faintly, remembering the hours of lessons both her sons had taken. It had been years since anyone had played the piano. No doubt it was dreadfully out of tune. Which wouldn't have troubled Jonathon at all, Katherine recalled, the curve of her lips increasing with amusement and fondness. The poor boy had been tone-deaf, completely unable to recognize when he struck a wrong note. Gil had taunted him unmercifully about it. But Gil had been so much more musically skilled, mastering the piano with the ease of a natural.

"Would Madam care for some tea and cakes?" The housekeeper's voice broke across her thoughts, scattering them.

"That would be fine, yes." Katherine flicked a hand in impatient dismissal, then lowered it to her lap. Once there her fingers fidgeted anxiously with the material of her dress.

Katherine stared at the piano, her eyes dark again, troubled again, the worry lines of anxiety and confusion back again. She longed to stop this wondering. She should have asked them, confronted them, but she was too uncertain in her own mind . . . and too afraid she wouldn't be able to distinguish between truth and lies.

She hated growing old. She hated this body that could no longer be trusted, this mind that kept wandering, these eyes that looked at the present yet sometimes flashed images from the past.

Voices, subdued and indistinct, drifted to her from the library. Katherine managed to separate the sound of Gil's from the others. A moment later she heard footsteps in the corridor. They belonged to Gil. Even after all these years she could recognize his quick, firm tread. He had always been in a hurry, always determined to get where he was going.

When they approached the music room, she suddenly wondered if he was coming to see her. Hope brought Katherine to her feet. And it was in her voice when she called to him as he drew level with the door.

"Gil?"

He halted, and glanced in the music room. Irritation flashed briefly in his expression, and brought Katherine abruptly down. "Any objections if I use the phone in the main salon? I have an important call to make."

"An important call?" she questioned, and murmured dryly, "How convenient for Natalie and Clay."

When she saw the angry flush that stained his cheeks, Katherine knew she had guessed right. His supposedly important call was nothing more than a ploy to leave Clay alone with Natalie. She found no satisfaction in the knowledge, and turned away as the sound of Gil's footsteps continued down the corridor to the main salon.

The minute Gil left the library, Natalie went to stand at the fireplace and stare into the fire-blackened chasm, her head bowed, her back turned to Clay, isolating herself from him. She had built some shell around herself that made it difficult for Clay to read what was going on inside. He could only hope it was as brittle as it seemed.

"Natalie," he began and took a step forward.

She stopped him in place with a softly harsh "You should not have come here."

"I couldn't stay away any longer. The thought of you alone,

knowing the anguish you were going through, it was more than I
could stand. I —"

"He knew." It was as if she hadn't heard a word he'd said.
Thrown by that, he withheld comment and waited, wondering if he
had misjudged her. She half turned, sending him a haunted look as
she hugged her arms tightly. "He must have known. Why else did
he follow us?"

"I've tortured myself with that same question." He moved closer
when she swung back to the fireplace. "But we have to face the fact
that we may never know the answer." Lightly, he curved his hands
over the fingers she dug into her arms. She shuddered at his touch,
but didn't pull away, and Clay knew he had nothing to fear. "I
wanted us to be free. I wanted us to be together. But not like this.
Never this way." He bent his head and lightly nuzzled his lips
against her hair. "I love you more than life. I couldn't stand it if you
hated me now."

With a small moan, she turned and melted against him. He held
her warmly, lovingly, not pressing her, not yet. Later, when he was
sure there would be no guilt, no recriminations, he would bring up
the subject of the merger.

The terrace doors to the main salon stood open. Kelly hesitated,
then walked through them, the shadowed cool of the house a relief
after the glaring heat of the sun. She paused and lifted her dark
glasses to the top of her head, poking the earpieces into the sides of
her nearly dry hair. She looked around for Katherine, but no one
was in the room.

Voices came from the marbled entry hall and Kelly went to inves-
tigate, her bare feet making almost no sound on the salon's Persian
rug. Before she reached the doorway, Mrs. Vargas walked in, her
eyes widening slightly, betraying a faint surprise at finding someone
in the salon.

"May I help you, miss?" Her gaze swept Kelly's bare feet and
legs, and the short terry robe she wore over the gold swimsuit.

"Not really." She had the distinct impression the housekeeper
found her attire inappropriate for the salon. "I was looking for
Katherine."

"I believe Madam is in the music room. If you —"

"No," Kelly quickly broke in. "I was just wondering what time
dinner is tonight."

"At seven, miss."

"Thank you." She made a brief detour around the housekeeper and headed once again for the doorway, reaching it as Katherine walked up.

"Did you enjoy your swim?" Katherine inquired. The words, the tone, and the smile, all held the politeness of a consummate hostess to her guest.

Kelly made a sound of agreement, then realized that wasn't enough. "I'm used to working out, but there hasn't been much time for any physical exercise since I arrived. The swim was just what I needed." She was about to add more when she noticed Katherine wasn't listening. Her attention had shifted to the front of the marbled hall and the quiet murmur of voices that came from there. "Is someone here?" Her hand slid up the front of her robe, drawing the lapels a little closer together.

"Gil and Clay are just leaving," Katherine replied. "They came to see Natalie and offer their condolences."

Kelly heard the front door open and stepped out of the salon to steal a glance at the departing pair, curious about this unexpected visit considering the less-than-friendly relationship between Katherine and her son. Both men had already stepped outside, Gil moving out of view and Clay turning back to the baroness who stood just outside, holding the front door open. He said something to her, then raised a hand to her cheek and slowly stroked it. Kelly stared, stunned by the gesture that could only be described as intimate. She glanced uncertainly at Katherine.

"Clay's version of the sympathetic touch, I would suspect," Katherine remarked with a definite chill in her expression that confirmed Kelly's initial impression.

Clay and Natalie Fougère were both more than acquaintances or friends. Yet her grief over Emile's death had seemed quite genuine. Kelly puzzled over that as she climbed the stairs to shower before dinner.

～ 18 ～

*T*he chandelier, dripping crystal, showered its light over the wide entry hall, driving off the night's darkness. The polished marble on the floor and the sweep of the stairs gleamed softly under its light, a warmth and a richness to it that contrasted with its cool, hard look in daylight.

Sam was too used to his surroundings to notice the change as he covered the hall's length with long strides and continued up the stairs at a quick pace. He had only two things on his mind, a cool shower and Kelly, and the shower didn't occupy much of his thoughts. Ever since morning, he had been waiting for the day to end and the night to begin. It finally had, a little later than he'd planned.

At the top of the stairs, he swung away from the deep gleam of the pewter-finished railing and headed down the hall to his room. When he neared the door to Kelly's, he automatically slowed his strides, hesitated, then went to it and knocked once.

"Come in." The heavy door muffled her voice, altering the rich texture of it but not the meaning of the words.

His hand circled the knob and turned it. With a push, he swung the door inward and walked into a darkened room. Not completely dark. A lamp burned in the small sitting alcove, but it was more decorative than functional, deepening the shadows in the rest of the room rather than chasing them off.

Then he saw her, standing at a window, her face a pale shine against the black of the night beyond the panes. She had on a silk robe and he noticed her hair was pulled back in a damnable braid again. She was too far away. He had to change that. Sam released the door, letting it swing shut, and moved toward her.

"Do you always stand around in the dark?"

"Not always." But tonight Kelly had wanted to become lost in the shadows, to hide in the darkness and let it keep her safe . . . as it had so often protected her from her father's drunken rages.

She watched the dark shape of him come toward her. Then the sound of his footsteps stopped and he was there, by the window, very near her. Too near. She should turn on more lights, but not yet. Not yet.

"Sorry I didn't make it back for dinner." His voice was pitched low, but she was more conscious of the quiet probe of his gaze. "I planned to, but every time I tried to get away, something came up. I'm afraid I haven't been much of a host."

"I don't know about that. We did have coffee together this morning." Casual. Keep it light and casual, Kelly told herself. It wasn't easy when she was so conscious of his presence and the way he smelled of earth and sun and something else that was male.

"True." Sam's voice matched her tone. "So how did you spend your day?"

Kelly made a slow turn back to the window and touched a hand to a cool pane. "I swam, soaked up some sun, and thought."

"About what?" She had been on his mind all day. Sam wondered if it had been the same for her.

"Dozens of things. Mostly about my job, though." She leaned into the window and rested her forehead against the glass, staring out. "I can't lose it. Not now. Not after I've worked so hard to get it. There has to be some way to keep this from happening, something I can say or do to convince them not to let me go."

"Don't you think you're borrowing trouble? You haven't lost it yet."

"But with this leave of absence, I'm very close to it. Too close to it," she insisted. "If I don't fight for it now, I will lose it. That's why it's so imperative that I come up with some plan of action."

"Such as?" Sam watched her mouth twist into a smile that wasn't a smile.

"I haven't come up with an answer to that question," she admitted, then sighed, something defeated in the sound. "I thought about going to the media with my story, try to generate public support. But how can I describe it to someone who hasn't lived through it? How can I make them understand what it's like to grow up with someone who drinks too much, who acts out against a child?"

"I got a pretty clear picture of what it must have been like when you explained it to me the other day," he reminded her.

"You also *saw* the house, the filth and the bottles. Your eyes told

you as much as my description did. Probably more," she added.
"I'm not good at putting my feelings down on paper, Sam. I know
because I tried. A little while ago, I tried to write an op-ed piece for
the *New York Times,* but it was no use." She pushed back from the
window and left her hand flattened against the pane. "It turned out
to be an exercise in frustration."

"It could be that you are too critical," Sam suggested. "Do you
mind if I read what you wrote?"

"Unless you're good at fitting pieces together, you can't. I tore it
up and threw it in the wastebasket."

"It couldn't have been that bad." He was half tempted to dig out
the scraps of paper and try piecing them together.

"It certainly wasn't that good. Television is my medium, not print.
I can get my message across when I can let pictures tell half of the
story."

"Then use television."

"But there aren't any pictures that can show the anger and the
hate and the pain that have been bottled up inside all these years,"
she protested, releasing her frustration in a sudden flare of temper.
"How can I get a camera inside my head to show that my earliest
memories are of being woken in the middle of the night by loud
noises — the slam of doors or voices raised in anger or the crash of
dishes and bottles being thrown? How do you show the confusion
and the terror of a child alone in a darkened room, hiding in her bed,
afraid to open the door, afraid of what was happening out there?"

"Kelly. It was hell for you; I know that." When his hand lifted to
her, she pulled back from it, but his voice and his movement provided the distraction she needed to regain control of her emotions.

"Hell is one way of putting it." Her voice was level again,
although tinged with bitterness. Kelly turned back to the window.
"Did I tell you about the first time he hit me, the first time I learned
how really mean he could be when he 'wasn't feeling good,' as
Momma used to put it?"

"No. No, you didn't."

"You'd think I would have forgotten it, repressed it. But I remember it very clearly, as if it was burned into my mind," she mused.
"It happened during my first year in school. I was in kindergarten.
My momma had made me a new yellow dress to wear. She called it
my sunshine dress, and I was so excited when she let me wear it to
school. Off I went, a roly-poly little girl eager to show off her new
sunshine dress. I thought I looked so special, but that's not what the

older kids on the bus thought when they saw me in it. They laughed and said I looked like a fat little butterball. I tried to make them stop, but the more I tried, the more they teased me. It was worse on the way home after school. I was in tears when Momma met me at the front door. She wanted to know what was wrong and I told her."

"I'm so sorry, honey." Loving fingers wiped the tears from her cheeks. "Don't you pay any attention to what those boys said. They were just teasing you. This is a beautiful dress and you look lovely in it."

"They said I was a fat butterball." She hiccuped back another sob.

"Well, you're not. You're my little sunshine girl." She gave her a hugging squeeze, then scooped her up and carried her over to the sofa. "Now, you sit right here and I'll bring you some brownies I baked specially for you. Okay?"

"Okay." But her voice wavered on the word, and her chin continued to quiver.

She watched her mother go into the kitchen, and another tear slipped from her eye. She was sniffling audibly when her father walked in from the bedroom, his T-shirt only half tucked inside the waistband of his trousers.

"What's this?" He stopped to peer at her, swaying a little. "Are you crying?"

She nodded as more tears spilled from her eyes. "On the bus, Jimmy Tucker and that boy named Carl were making fun of me and calling me names."

"Didn't you tell them not to do that?"

"Yes, but they wouldn't listen to me."

"Then you should have punched them in the mouth."

"They're too big," she protested, her lower lip jutting out in a trembling pout.

"That's no excuse." He picked her up and stood her up in front of the sofa, then got down on his knees, facing her. His face was close to hers and his breath smelled funny. "Come on. I'll teach you how to fight. Hold up your hands like this."

She looked at his raised fists and shook her head. "But I don't want to fight, Daddy."

"Well, you're going to anyway. Now, do what I say. Hold up your fists like this and knock my hand away when I try to hit you."

She tried to do as he said, but when his hand snaked toward her face, she wasn't quick enough, and his fingers tapped her hard on the cheek.

"You've got to be faster than that, Lizzie-girl." His hand shot out again, this time stinging her cheek with the sharpness of the hit.

"Ow!" She clamped a hand to her smarting cheek.

"Come on and fight. Hit me. Go ahead."

"No. I don't want to," she said again, growing more confused and frightened.

"You'd better fight back or I'll keep hitting you." First one hand, then the other struck at her jaw with hard, stinging slaps. When she raised her arms to protect her face from more blows, he jabbed her in the stomach. She cried out, half doubling over and clutching her stomach. Immediately he hit her in the face again.

Frightened into anger, she screamed at him. "Stop it!"

"Getting mad, are you?" he taunted with a nasty grin. "Then fight back."

He hit her again, harder than before. She fell back against the sofa's seat cushion, tears streaming down her face in earnest.

Her mother came hurrying out of the kitchen. "My God, Len. What are you doing to her?"

"He hit me, Mommy," she sobbed.

"It was just a little tap. I'm teaching her how to fight."

"She's only a little girl, Len." She scooped her up and rushed her out of the living room to the safety of her bedroom.

"Why did Daddy hit me, Mommy?" she sobbed. "What did I do wrong?"

"You didn't do anything wrong, sweetheart. Sometimes . . ." Her mother paused and hugged her close, resting her chin atop her head. "Sometimes Daddy forgets how strong he is. He didn't mean to hurt you."

" 'What did I do wrong?' " Kelly repeated softly. "When you're little, you can't understand. You just feel all this confusion and guilt when you're yelled at for no reason, and especially when ordinary roughhousing turns into sadistic abuse. When I think of how many times my mother rescued me from him." She stopped and shuddered expressively. "But she died and left me alone with him. Suddenly I had to grow up fast just to survive. I didn't really have a childhood. I was young, and the next minute I was old. Old and terrified. Not just of him," she added quickly. "I was just as terrified that somebody would find out what my life was really like. That's why I lied about the bruises and black eyes. I couldn't bear to have people know the truth. I was too ashamed, too humiliated."

"Ashamed," Sam exploded, unable to remain silent any longer. "There was no reason for you to feel ashamed or guilty. You didn't do anything wrong. It was him. He was the one who hit you, who beat you."

"How can I make you understand?" she said with a bewildered shake of her head. "If you are told often enough that something is your fault, you begin to believe it. You begin to think you must have done something. That's the worst part, the insidious part. It isn't just the physical blows. It's the damage that's done to your inner self, too. And you can't capture that on videotape."

Dougherty had done this to her. Sam had never despised another human being so passionately before. But he did now.

"For a while today," Kelly continued, "I seriously considered making the rounds on the talk shows. As you know, the trouble is my story isn't brutal enough. I wasn't sexually abused. His beatings didn't leave me crippled or maimed. The only thing that makes my story sensational to the press is the fact that he's been charged with murder. But even if I did go on the talk-show circuit, what would it gain me? A lot of publicity and the image of an abused child as well as the daughter of a murderer. It certainly wouldn't guarantee I'd keep my job."

"Would it really be so bad if you lost it?"

Kelly swung her head around, stunned that he would even ask such a question. "It's my whole life. All my friends are in television." Even as she said that, she remembered the exceedingly brief phone conversation she'd had with DeeDee that afternoon. Kelly had called to let DeeDee know where she was staying, and to see if DeeDee had any questions on the Travis material.

To be honest, she had also called because she wanted to talk to someone who would understand the deadly effect of all this on her career, someone who would commiserate a little, maybe become indignant at the way she was being treated. But DeeDee had been polite and aloof, as if wanting to distance herself from Kelly just as Hugh had done in case the corporate suits started viewing her as a potential liability instead of an asset.

The memory of that phone call brought an ache to her throat and took the stridency from her voice when Kelly finished with, "Landing a job with the network has been my dream."

"You must have had others," Sam suggested quietly.

Once, Kelly thought. Once she had dreamed about having a nice

home, children, and a man who would hold her and love her and
protect her. But that was long ago, back when she still had romantic
notions about life.

"Not really. Nothing but childish fantasies" was the answer she
gave Sam and turned back to stare out the window again. The moon
was a white sliver riding low in the sky's blackness, punctuated by
distant stars, their light so faint they made almost no impression on
the night. "They're still calling for rain." But the clouds that had
been visible at dusk were now lost in the darkness.

There was a whisper of movement, cloth brushing against cloth,
as Sam shifted and propped a shoulder against the window frame to
look out. "If it comes, we're ready for it," he said, recognizing that
she was seeking to change the subject to one less emotionally
charged. Right now he needed it too. "At least as ready as we can
be. We've cut away the leaves around each grape cluster so air can
circulate, and I have a helicopter service on priority standby."

"A helicopter service?"

"To hover over the vineyards and generate air to dry the grapes,"
Sam explained, his gaze turning to her and staying. "Then we have
to hope the vines don't carry too much moisture to the fruit and
dilute the flavor before it's ready to pick, which should be in a few
more days. Before this threat of rain popped up, everyone thought
this might be the best vintage the valley's seen in a good many years.
Now it's questionable."

"Maybe it won't rain." Kelly wasn't sure why his problems mattered to her when she was faced with so many of her own, but they
did.

He smiled, white teeth flashing in the shadowed blur of his features. "Maybe it won't, but a vintner learns to worry about the
things he can control, cope with the ones he can't, and move on."

"Wise words." There was a message in them, meant for her. "But
you stand to lose only one vintage, not your entire vineyards."

"Kelly, life has forced people to change their careers before.
Maybe you'll find another line of work you like better, a place,
maybe even people you like more."

"Maybe." But she felt surrounded by darkness, locked inside herself with nothing to turn to, nothing but this room and this moment.

"Kelly?"

She wanted to tell him not to say her name that way. The questing
warmth of his voice seemed to peel through the protective layers,
turning her toward him.

"Yes, Sam," she whispered.

But Sam couldn't say what he wanted. That he'd give anything to spend the night making love to her. Wordlessly, he straightened from the window and raised his fingertips to the smoothness of her cheek.

Kelly closed her eyes against the light touch, but she couldn't shut out the sensation of it or that Sam stood close to her, representing warmth and strength, and an end to being alone if only for tonight. And tonight, she ached to know what that would feel like, what it would be like to have strong arms around her, to be held and loved.

Impelled by that need, she brought her hand to his face and ran her fingers along his hard jawline, feeling the light stubble of a day's growth. Sam's hand drifted down her neck onto her shoulders. Through slitted eyes, Kelly watched as his hand glided lightly down her arm. His fingers circled her wrist, lifted it; his fingers slid up her palm until their fingertips touched.

Quick shafts of something quivered through her. It might have been desire. Kelly only knew she wanted more. So much more.

"Sam."

"Don't," he told her with a wisdom he hadn't known he had. "Don't talk. Don't think."

Kelly finally tipped her head to look at him, admitting in a taut whisper, "I don't want to think."

"Then tell me what you do want." He laced his fingers through hers. "This?" He lifted his other hand to her throat and trailed it slowly down to the swell of her breast. There was a wild scrambling of her pulse, her senses, her breathing . . . of everything. "Or maybe this?"

His hand traveled lower and fit itself to the dipping curve of her waist, drawing her closer to his warmth, his heat. Then his breath was in her hair, whispering onto her temple, skimming over her cheek, and the ache inside became something blind and primitive. Still Sam didn't kiss her, and she wanted him to. Yet she didn't try to stop the roaming of his mouth. She remained motionless, absorbed by the exquisite stroke of just his fingertips, the warm caress of only his breath on her skin, and the promise there would be more to come. There was no reason to rush, there was time. Time for everything, and she wanted everything, every touch, every whisper, and every second of this night.

She was all silk, wherever he touched . . . the sleeves of her robe, her skin, her hair. Despite the misery of her childhood, she was silk. Hot silk. Sam couldn't get enough. He wanted her, not just because

there hadn't been a woman in his life for a long time. It was more
than that, more than lust. Much more than lust. It was a tightness
in his chest as well as his loins.

Drawing back, Sam brought his fingers to the sides of her neck,
sliding thumbs under the point of her chin, lifting it to look in her
eyes. "Do you want what I want, Kelly?" he asked huskily and
watched her lips grow heavy and part. "Do you want this?"

With his fingers, Sam lifted the top edge of her robe and eased it
from her shoulders. It slid down her arms and fell, with a silky rustle, to the floor at her feet. Kelly shuddered lightly and answered
him by reaching for the buttons of his shirt. Sam stopped her, catching her hands and drawing her with him as he walked backward to
the bed.

There, he pulled off his own shirt and Kelly spread her hands over
his hair-roughened chest, at last touching him and feeling flesh, muscle, and bone, the strength of him, the power of him. He found her
mouth and rubbed his lips over it. It was impossible to do anything
but invite him in.

The heat and hunger were instant, driving the kiss, bringing an
urgency that hadn't existed before. She needed him, inside her,
becoming her, turning her into something new. She pressed into him,
restlessly running her hands up and down his back, needing to know
everything about him and wanting him to know everything about
her.

It was happening fast. Not fast enough, yet too fast. Sam wanted
to savor, explore inch by glorious inch of her. But there was no
gentleness in him now, no patience, not with the insistence of
her hands digging into him, her body pushing against him in
demand. A demand he was only too willing to answer and satisfy
his own.

The darkness was a cocoon that shut out the world. There was no
sound except the fevered rush of their breathing and the violent roar
of his speeding pulse. Her fingers tugged at the waistband of his
slacks and his stomach muscles quivered at the contact. Sam took
over, shedding the rest of his clothes that had become an encum-
brance, and watching when Kelly stepped back, pushed the thin
straps of her gown from her shoulders, and shimmied out of it. She
stood naked before him, like a wish all long and slim and pale in the
soft lamplight.

Sam admired her with his eyes. Then he saw the braid that fell
across one shoulder. "Let me," he murmured thickly and closed the
space between them to reach for it.

With deft fingers, he unplaited her hair, and Kelly felt the freed mass of it slide onto her naked shoulders. She shook her head to send it raining onto her back. Sam slowly ran his fingers through it and caught a strand between his thumb and forefinger, drawing it between them all the way to its smooth end. The return to gentleness, to tenderness, after the near-frenzy that had pushed them, was unexpected, and achingly wonderful. Kelly found it suddenly very hard to breathe.

"Why do you always confine it?" Again Sam ran a hand over her hair, his breath stirring it.

"It's practical, more professional."

"But it's beautiful like this."

Kelly felt the feathery kisses he brushed over her hair before he bent to graze the slope of her shoulder. Once again his hands were everywhere, barely touching her, just fingertips stroking along her arms, her hips, her waist, her breasts. Kelly discovered how exquisite agony could be. She began touching him, needing him to make the same discovery she had.

A moment later, still holding her, Sam flung back the bed covers with one hand and swung her onto the mattress, joining her and giving her a long, lazy, luxurious kiss. It left her wanting more, but Sam had already begun to give her that, with his hands and his lips.

Taking his devastating time, he worked his way down to her breasts and teased the tips with his tongue, ignoring the bowing arch of her body to take more and the fingers she dug into his hair to demand. Open-mouthed, he kissed them and flicked his tongue over each rigid nipple. Shuddering, Kelly writhed under him and he took more, ending the torment. She dug her fingers into his hair and felt the pressure deep inside, clenching and unclenching to the tempo of his clever mouth, building, layering, soaring until she thought she would weep from it.

The faint lamplight played against her closed lids. His skin was hot and damp beneath her hands, the taste of him rich and male. She clutched at him, certain if this went on forever, it would still end too soon.

For long minutes, Sam had fought the urge to take swiftly and greedily all that she offered. He had no more control, not with her hands urging him and her body poised and waiting, silently confirming she was aching as much as he was. One last time Sam brought his mouth down on hers and swallowed her stunned cry when he slipped into her.

It was like sinking into fire, all clean and hot and wild. He had known it would be like this — no restraints, no boundaries. Nothing and no one but the two of them, soaring higher and higher.

Across the room, the lamp continued to cast its pool of soft light and deepen the shadows elsewhere. Carved rosewood posts stood silent guard, tall and solid black shapes at the bed's four corners. Completely and thoroughly satisfied, Sam was content to lie in this tangle of arms and legs and enjoy the heat of Kelly's limp body against him, her skin still damp from their lovemaking.

In some distant part of his mind, Sam suspected he wouldn't find it so easy to lock his emotions back in their tight, dark compartment. Then Kelly stirred and shifted more comfortably against him, making him aware of the strength of her body and the amazing softness of it.

Lazy as a cat, Sam stroked a hand over her small breast. "If you had asked me before tonight, I would have said I liked full-breasted women. You changed my mind."

"I did?" Idly she rubbed her cheek against his shoulder, then tipped her head to look at him.

"You did." His mouth curving, Sam looked down at her and the smile faded from him, his eyes intent in their slow study of her. "How do you do it?" He brought his hand up to her lips and traced their outline.

"Do what?" She stopped his hand and moistly drew the end of his finger into her mouth.

"Make me feel strong and leave me weak. Empty me out and fill me back up again with just a touch."

"I do that to you? Really?" She seemed surprised, pleased.

"You do." He pulled her up level with him and tasted what his finger had already explored.

Sleep was a long way off yet. For both of them.

Kelly rolled over and discovered the bed beside her was empty. The sheets were cold beneath her reaching hand. Sam was gone. He must have been gone for some time. Frowning, Kelly sat up and tried to push the sleep from her eyes and face, telling herself it didn't matter, she was used to waking up alone. But it felt different this time; it felt lonely. She hugged her knees to her chest, drawing the sheet up with them, and rested her chin on top of them, fighting the tightness in her throat.

There was a knock at her door, sharp and insistent. Belatedly Kelly realized it was that same sound that had awakened her. "Who is it?" she called out, suddenly and vividly aware that her nightgown was a pool of shimmering silk on the floor and the thin sheet did little to conceal her nudity.

"Mrs. Vargas. I have your morning tray of coffee and juice."

Kelly grabbed for the coverlet and hauled it over the sheet. "Come in."

The door swung open and the housekeeper walked soundlessly into the room, balancing a tray with practiced skill. "Shall I leave it by the chair?" She nodded her graying head at the one in the sitting alcove.

"Please." Kelly felt awkward and thought how much more awkward she would have felt if Sam had still been in bed with her.

The minute the housekeeper left, Kelly slid out of bed and retrieved her robe from the floor by the window, leaving the nightgown lying on the floor. Overnight, the clouds had moved in, blanketing the morning sky with a dull gray. No rain yet, Kelly thought and slipped on the robe, then padded over to the tray.

The aroma of freshly brewed coffee rose from the carafe in a burst of steam when Kelly removed the covering lid. She poured some in a cup and raised it to her lips, breathing in the invigorating scent of it.

Suddenly there was this vague memory of warm lips brushing against hers and Sam's voice saying, "It's morning. I have to go." Had he touched her cheek then? It was all so dreamlike Kelly wasn't even sure it had happened. Hadn't he told her to go back to sleep? She couldn't have been even half awake yet.

Something else niggled at her mind. Kelly frowned, trying to remember as she stared at the black coffee in her cup. *Coffee,* that was it. Sam had said, "Come to my office when you get up. I'll have coffee on." She couldn't have dreamed that. It must have happened.

The smallest smile touched the corners of her mouth, a kind of secret pleasure in the discovery that Sam hadn't stolen off in the night without a word, somehow cheapening what they'd shared. Kelly set the cup back on its china saucer, deciding that she preferred to have her first cup of coffee with Sam.

Years ago Kelly had learned to shower and dress in a hurry, but she managed to break all records. She even succeeded in slipping out of the house without encountering either Katherine or the housekeeper.

She paused on the front steps and looked up at the thick cloud cover. There was a heavy stillness in the air, a faint smell of rain. Somewhere, not too far away, came the chopping drone of helicopter blades beating the air. Kelly guessed at the direction of the sound, but didn't see anything but clouds and trees and ridge tops.

Shrugging off the brief curiosity, she started down the drive, then spied the entrance to the bridle path, a shortcut to the winery and Sam's office. She hesitated only an instant, then changed course and headed down it.

Trees grew thick on both sides of the wide trail, their interwoven branches blocking out much of the light. The clouds added to the dark gloom and the sense of isolation. Listening to the reassuring sound of vehicles growling along the drive, Kelly tried to imagine how much darker, how much blacker it had been the night of the party.

But that thought started her wondering again what had prompted the baron to go to the winery. And to take this route. Had he merely sought to escape from the party for a little while? Probably. Kelly had only met him twice, but both times she had gotten the impression Baron Fougère didn't enjoy socializing; he preferred the company of books. So why hadn't he gone to the library in the house? It would have been quiet there; he would have been alone; and the atmosphere would certainly have suited him better than this thickly shadowed path.

Unless he'd been upset about something. Kelly thought immediately of the intimate little exchange she had inadvertently witnessed between the baroness and Clay Rutledge. Had the baron seen something similar? Something that made him suspect his wife was having an affair with another man? It might be the kind of thing that would send him down a dark and lonely path, eventually winding up at the winery and discovering her father there. Was it pure happenstance? Had he been at the wrong place at the wrong time? Was that all it was?

The questions kept buzzing through her mind. Kelly sighed and shook her head. She had spent the better part of the last ten years, first in college studying journalism, then later in her career, asking questions, ferreting out the answers. It had become second nature to her, a habit too deeply ingrained to be broken quickly or easily. Especially when this particular story involved her father and trapped her in its backlash.

The winery towered before her, reigning over the yard at the end of the bridle path. Without the morning sun to warm its color, the building's brick looked dark and dull. By contrast, the long band of bright yellow strung out from the building's far end stood out sharply. Kelly recognized the wide plastic tape as the kind police used to mark off a crime scene. She was surprised it hadn't been taken down before now.

There wouldn't be anything to see; any evidence would have been removed long ago. Kelly knew that. Still, she found herself walking over to look.

The ground was scuffed with prints. A faint outline remained, indicating where the body had been found. There were two more spots marked as well. Kelly decided one of them probably indicated the location of the murder weapon and the other the gasoline can her father had dropped, but she didn't know which was which.

She remembered the brief and unpleasant visit with her father. He had been scared and confused, hiding behind an angry bravado. He had probably been scared as well as drunk that night. When the baron had challenged him, he had probably struck out in panic.

But why with a mallet? Why not with the gas cans he was carrying? If he planned to ruin the wine stored in the cellars, what had he been doing here? The entrance to the cellar was behind the winery. Kelly frowned and glanced at the security light mounted high on the building. Why would he have approached them from this direction when the area was so brightly lit? Had he been so drunk he didn't notice that? Or so drunk he didn't care?

A small side door to the winery opened and the burly, grizzled figure of Claude Broussard stepped out. He cast a darting glance at the yellow tape. He started to look away, then jerked his head back to fasten his dark eyes on Kelly.

"Hello." Smiling, she took a step toward him.

Immediately he waved a big hand at her, a glower claiming his wizened, craggy features. "We do not allow reporters. You are trespassing. You must leave at once!"

Again Kelly found herself forced to explain her presence. "Monsieur Broussard, I am Leonard Dougherty's daughter."

"You?" His eyes narrowed on her in sharp suspicion, his thick gray brows drawing together to form a solid, bushy line.

"Me. You must have seen my picture on television or in the newspaper accounts of the baron's death."

"I have no wish to see or read such accounts." He came closer, continuing to eye her. "I remember his daughter. She was a tall, plump thing who wore glasses."

"And who used to sneak into the winery," Kelly added. "You caught me hiding in the cellars once."

"I did." He nodded, acceptance slowly forming.

"I was scared to death, certain you were going to beat me," Kelly recalled.

Old Claude shook his head. "I would never strike a child." Then he smiled. "I gave you a taste of wine."

"That's right," she murmured, suddenly remembering. "I thought it would taste like grape juice, but it was sour."

"Not sour," he reproved. "The wine was young, a bit puckery perhaps."

"More than a bit, as I remember," Kelly replied, her smile growing.

Claude Broussard smiled back for a moment, then sobered, a sadness entering his eyes. "Your father was not a good man. He had begun to drink at his work. I found a whiskey bottle he had hidden. I could not permit that to continue. I had to discharge him."

"I know." Kelly dipped her head, remembering how humiliated she'd been when she had come to meet him after he got off work that day only to be told that he had been fired. He had staggered into the house the next morning, roaring drunk. When he finally sobered, he had told her that he had gotten tired of being treated like a slave by the Rutledges and quit. But she had always known the truth. Without thinking, she turned her head and looked at the crime scene. "He was always drunk, always causing trouble."

"Let us come away from this place." His leathered hand gripped her arm, firmly guiding her away from the site. "It is not a good place."

Touched by the gesture, Kelly lifted her gaze to his face and studied the network of age lines that creased his leathered face. "How old are you?" He had seemed ancient to her when she was a girl.

He halted, his posture stiffening, his big shoulders going back. "What is the importance of this?" It was obvious he was offended by her question.

Kelly tried to shrug it off. "None. I was just curious."

Still full of pride, he looked her in the eye. "I am in my seventieth decade. My *grand-père* served as *maître de chai* here at Rutledge Estate until he reached his eighty-fourth year. His last years were good years and the wines were fine wines. These young people with their college degrees, their test tubes, and their meters, what do they know about making fine wines? Old," he repeated the word in disgust. "Like my *grand-père*, I have many good years left. I am not yet ready to be pensioned off."

"I didn't mean to suggest you were."

"*Non?*" His glance challenged her, then backed off, but a look of vague irritability stayed in his expression. "What was it you wanted here?"

"I came to see Sam."

"He left no more than five minutes ago."

"He did?" Disappointment. Kelly hadn't expected to feel it so sharply. She looked toward the winery offices, noticing for the first time that his Jeep wasn't parked in front of the long building. "Do you know where he went?"

"*Non.*"

She nodded, trying to pretend it didn't matter. "I'll see him later back at the house." But it wouldn't be the same and Kelly knew it. With a wave to Claude, she began the long walk back to the house.

19

*T*hrough a break in the trees, Kelly spotted a silver-gray Bronco parked in the driveway in front of the house. It seemed a bit early in the morning for visitors, she thought. Not until she emerged from the bridle path did she see the other vehicles in the drive — a marked police car, a plain sedan, and Sam's Jeep.

Something was wrong. She felt the prickles on her skin, the sudden tensing of all her nerves, turning them taut as wires. She faltered only a second, then lengthened her stride and cut across the grass to the front door. As she opened it, Kelly heard Katherine's voice.

"She is not anywhere in the house. She must have gone out."

Two uniformed officers, Ollie Zelinski, the defense attorney John MacSwayne, and Sam stood in a group at the bottom of the marble staircase, facing Katherine as she joined them. John MacSwayne was in his forties, a touch of gray at his temples, average in height, weight, and build. He had one of those fatherly faces, the kind that projected an image of a man who had dealt with a lot of bad boys but never had cause to lose his faith in the basic good he saw in them. He turned to Kelly, as did the others when they heard the front door shut.

"Were you looking for me?" She advanced slowly toward them, braced for bad news. The grimness of Sam's expression and the banked anger in his eyes only confirmed what her instincts had already told her.

Sam met her. "Your father has escaped," he told her. "I heard it on the radio and came to tell you. Then Zelinski and the others drove up."

"When?" There was a flatness in her voice. It was the only way to keep the anger — the fury — out of it.

She knew precisely what her father's escape meant: a full-blown manhunt complete with roadblocks, search teams, police swarming over the area, helicopters overhead. The kind of sensational story that would bring the news media out in droves. And her name would get dragged into it again, just when all the publicity had been about to die.

"About dawn this morning," Ollie replied, a silent commiseration in his eyes.

"How? How was that possible?" Kelly shifted away from Sam, inconspicuously rejecting the comfort he seemed to be offering by standing beside her. If he touched her, she might lose control. And she didn't want any of them to see what this was doing to her. She folded her arms tightly across her middle, a protective gesture against the rawness inside.

"He acted sick. There was a new trustee on duty. We're still putting all the details together." Ollie pushed the glasses higher on his nose, something he had always done when he was nervous.

Kelly recognized it, but it didn't make any real impression on her. "Why did you come? It wasn't just to tell me that."

Ollie's glance bounced off her, then came back, none too squarely. "This should never have happened. His arrest already caused enough problems for you and I wanted you to know how sorry I am." He paused a beat. "Do you have any idea where he might go?"

"Did you check the nearest bar or liquor store?" The bitterness came out. Kelly couldn't stop it.

"Do you think he would try to head this way or make for the Bay Area? Oakland or San Francisco?" one of the officers asked.

They were watching her. All of them. Waiting for an answer she didn't have. "I don't know." She gave a small, tight shake of her head and felt strands of her loose hair brush against her cheek. She dragged fingers through it, scraping it back from her face and wishing she had clamped it in a twist. "I don't know where he'd go or what he'd do. It would be easier for him to lose himself in a city. More places to hide, but I don't know if he'd think that way."

"What about the mountains?" the other patrolman asked. "Is your father much of an outdoorsman? A hunter?"

"No."

"Did he ever go camping?"

Kelly shook her head again. "Drinking was his only form of recreation."

"What about his friends?"

"I left ten years ago. I don't know who he has for friends or even if he has any. You'd have to check the bars he frequented. Find out who his drinking buddies are."

They asked more questions she couldn't answer. With each, her tension increased until her nerves were even more taut. Finally she couldn't take any more.

"If I knew anything — anything at all — don't you think I would tell you?" she snapped. "I want him caught as much as you do. The longer he's out there, the longer this will drag on —" Kelly broke off the rest of it, instantly regretting the flare of temper.

It didn't help when Sam slid a hand onto her back, again moving to her side. "That's enough questions for now, I think," he said while Kelly held herself stiffly, fighting to keep from swaying against him.

"Right." Ollie nodded. "I'm sorry we had to put you through this, Kelly, but it couldn't be helped. If you think of anything or remember anything that might be useful . . ."

"I'll call," she promised.

Through all the questioning, MacSwayne had remained a silent observer. When Ollie and the two officers offered their good-byes and crossed the hall to the front door, he stayed behind. He waited until the door closed, then turned to Kelly.

"I have only one thing to add to this unfortunate situation, Miss Douglas," he said. "If you should talk to your father, if he should contact you."

"He won't," Kelly inserted. "He doesn't know where I am."

"I'm afraid he does." MacSwayne's eyebrows lifted in silent apology. "You see, I told him you were staying here."

Sam swore softly and viciously under his breath, and demanded aloud, "Why the hell did you have to do that? There was no reason for him to know where Kelly was."

"At the time I thought there was." The attorney shrugged, as if to indicate the damage was done and debate over the right or wrong of it was pointless. "When I visited Dougherty in jail, he kept ranting about the Rutledges, you in particular, Mrs. Rutledge." He glanced at Katherine and received not a flicker of reaction. "He was making a lot of accusations, and I thought it might alter his opinion if he knew his daughter was staying with you."

"Did it?" Sam showed blatant cynicism and skepticism.

"Unfortunately, no. At that point, he became convinced you were trying to turn his daughter against him. But paranoia is frequently one of the side effects of alcoholism," MacSwayne stated and swung his attention back to Kelly. "Which is part of what I wanted to talk to you about."

With one arm outstretched directing her away from Katherine and Sam, and the other curved in a shepherding fashion, he guided Kelly off to the side where they could talk privately. She failed to understand what could be gained by discussing her father's drinking habit. She waited, tensely and impatiently, for the lawyer to explain.

"If, by chance, you do hear from your father," MacSwayne began, his voice low, his tone confidential, "make every effort to convince him to give himself up."

"He isn't likely to listen to me."

"Try. Things will go much better for him if he surrenders to the police," he explained, then went on. "When he was arrested the morning after the baron was killed, the alcohol level in his blood was considerably above the legal limit. He admits he had been drinking. It's very possible he was too drunk to really know what he was doing. I can argue diminished capacity, possibly get the charges against him reduced to involuntary manslaughter. But to do that, he needs to give himself up and we need to get him out on bail and enrolled in a rehabilitation program. We have to show that alcoholism is a disease and your father is a victim."

"Don't talk to me about victims." Kelly's voice vibrated with anger. "*I* was the victim! *I* was the one who had to live with him and deal with his lies. *I* was the one he beat up on when he got drunk. *I* was the one who paid the price. And I'm still paying it!"

Fighting the tears that burned the back of her eyes, Kelly whirled and walked quickly and blindly away. She didn't even hear Sam call out to her.

Before Sam could go after her, MacSwayne stopped him. "Let her go."

Sam turned on him. "What in hell did you say to her?"

"I'm afraid I upset her. I thought by now she had come to accept her father's drinking as a sickness, one she didn't cause, can't control, and can't cure." MacSwayne gazed thoughtfully in the direction Kelly had gone, then glanced at Sam. "There are programs for those whose parents are, or were, alcoholics. Al-Anon has one specially designed for adult children of alcoholics. Talk to her about taking part in one. At least she's beginning to get in touch with some of her feelings and releasing the anger she has stored inside all these years. That's a step in the right direction anyway."

* * *

Tears trembled on the ends of her lashes. Kelly hurriedly wiped at
them when she heard the firm, measured tread of Sam's footsteps
approaching. Her flight from the entry hall had brought her to the
library.

When Sam walked in, Kelly didn't turn around, but continued to
stand next to a leather chair, one hand resting on the back of it.
"Kelly?"

The instant she felt the warm pressure of his hands on her upper
arms, she walked away from it. "I'm fine." She'd had time, just
enough time, to pull herself together. She ran her fingers over the
pleated sides of a lampshade, needing to keep them busy or she'd
start twisting them together. "I could use a cigarette though. You
wouldn't happen to have one, would you? I left mine in my purse
upstairs."

"No. I don't."

"That's okay." She turned the lamp on, throwing some light into
the paneled room, darkened by the heavy gray clouds beyond its
windows. "With all that's been happening, I'm surprised I haven't
started smoking more."

A remote control lay on the table next to the lamp. Kelly picked
it up and aimed it at the television, pushing the power button. A
picture flashed instantly on the screen.

"Kelly, about your father," Sam began.

She held up a hand to silence him, her gaze fixed on the screen.
"There's a news bulletin. Maybe they've caught him." She sank
quickly onto the leather chair seat and hunched forward to concentrate on the reporter's words.

But the bulletin turned out to be a correction on a previous report
that the suspect had been sighted aboard a ferry bound for San Francisco, a sighting that turned out to be erroneous. The correction was
followed by a recap on the jailbreak and a rehash of the baron's
death.

"Let's go get some coffee," Sam suggested when the station
returned to its regular morning program schedule.

Kelly shook her head. "I'd rather stay here, see if anything
breaks."

"Even if it does, there's nothing you can do."

"I know that, but I want to stay just the same. It's something I
need to do. Try to understand that, won't you?"

She spent the rest of the day and most of the evening in front of
the television, flipping from station to station, catching a news bulletin on one and checking it against a report from another. There

were numerous reported sightings, most of which proved to be false and the rest couldn't be confirmed one way or the other. The police continued to state their belief that he was still somewhere in the city of Napa, insisting that roadblocks had been in place within ten minutes of the prisoner's escape.

There were scenes of SWAT teams searching an abandoned building, helicopters making slow sweeps over an area, officers at roadblocks opening car trunks and checking identifications, and long lines of cars backed up on the highways. There were interviews with various legal officials, residents in isolated areas afraid to stay alone in their homes, people on the street, and tourists. The coverage was extensive.

And all of it, every lead story began with some variation of the words: "The father of television news personality Kelly Douglas, accused of the murder of Baron Emile Fougère of France, remains at large . . . this morning . . . this afternoon . . . tonight." And nearly every report included a publicity still of her or a clip from a broadcast or a shot of her outside the city jail in St. Helena.

The next day, dawn came with no rain and no new developments. Leonard Dougherty was still at large. Around midmorning, there was a flurry of excitement with live coverage of police surrounding a small vineyard in the Carneros district where the suspect was thought to be hiding. One news crew in a helicopter showed TV audiences an indistinct figure huddled under thick vines. After twenty suspense-filled minutes, the man surrendered to the police.

The instant the man crawled out from under the vines, his hands clasped over his head, Kelly knew it wasn't her father. The black hair, the swarthy complexion; he looked Mexican. The reporter on the scene reached the same conclusion. A mug shot of her father flashed on the screen for the benefit of the viewers.

The noon broadcast included a follow-up report that explained the man taken into custody at the vineyard had proved to be an illegal alien. There was also a report that a house in a remote area of the valley's Stag's Leap district showed signs of forced entry this morning, although nothing appeared to have been taken. Police now admitted that it was possible Dougherty had managed to get past the roadblocks and was somewhere beyond the city limits of Napa; they were widening their search.

Late in the afternoon, a fine rain began to fall. Low clouds hugged the high ridges and peaks of both mountain ranges. The early eve-

ning newscasts showed reporters on the scene standing under dripping umbrellas, relating the latest facts on the manhunt and adding
a few suppositions.

The NBC affiliate carried a related story that had been taped earlier, before it started raining. When Kelly heard the anchor's lead-
in to the piece, she guessed at once she would be the focus of it. But
she was stunned to see Linda James, her enemy and rival, in the
opening shot, standing in front of her father's ramshackle house,
explaining to the viewers that this was the home where Kelly Douglas had grown up.

The green-and-white Buick was in the background, along with the
tall weeds and the scattered junk. Linda James walked up the steps
and opened the door. A slick edit showed her walking into the living
room. The clutter of it, the filth, the pile of ash and cigarette butts
next to her mother's picture.

Oh, God. Kelly cupped a hand over her mouth, choking back a
cry. There was her doll, in close-up, sitting forlornly on the dirty
couch. The grimy kitchen and the dishes, caked with dried food,
piled in the sink and on the counter, the moldy contents of the refrigerator. Why hadn't she cleaned it up when she was there?

Linda James sat on a bed. Kelly's bed. Dragging a finger over the
dust-laden top of her dresser, touching the iron headboard, standing
at the window gazing up at the bleak sky.

The two-and-a-half-minute piece ended outside, with Linda
expressing sympathy and closing with, "We haven't been able to
reach Kelly Douglas for comment, although we understand she is
staying in the area. No doubt monitoring the latest developments in
the hunt for her father. With mixed feelings, I suspect. Linda James,
Napa Valley."

Professionally, Kelly recognized it was a good story. Personally,
she felt devastated, exposed. Her privacy invaded. Angry and
ashamed, she bolted from the library. That was never going to happen again. Not a second time.

She faltered only an instant when the front door opened and Sam
walked in. His shirt was soaked, the wet cotton sticking to his skin
and outlining the muscled contours of his chest. His tan chinos were
rain-spotted and wet around the cuffs. He didn't immediately see
her as he swept off his hat, scattering droplets of water over the
marble floor. She took a deep, steadying breath and unclenched her
fingers, meeting his gaze when he finally noticed her.

"The rain has started coming down in earnest out there," he told
her with the smallest of grimaces.

"It looks that way." She moved toward the stairs.

"Going up?"

"Yes."

"I'll walk with you. I need a hot shower and some dry clothes." With long strides, he crossed to the staircase, leaving drops of water in his wake. He fell in beside her as they mounted the stairs. "Anything on the news tonight?"

"Nothing new. He's still hiding out somewhere."

A sigh came from him. "I'm sorry. I honestly thought they would have caught him before now."

"So did I," she admitted.

He halted when they reached the door to her room. "Are you okay?"

She wasn't sure she had ever felt *okay*. "I'll make it," she told him.

"I know you will." He smiled. "See you in a bit."

Kelly nodded, but didn't answer as she pushed the door open and Sam continued down the hall. Wasting no time, she grabbed her purse and yanked her Burberry's raincoat from the closet. Then she was out the door and running down the steps.

Fifteen minutes later, the rental car splashed through the water puddling in the rutted lane and rolled to a halt in front of Kelly's old home. Rain had stained the exposed wood siding a near black and turned the windowpanes into dark shiny mirrors. Kelly stared at it for a long minute, then switched off the headlights and killed the engine.

She stepped from the car into a steady rain and made it to the front door without stepping into any deep puddles. The living room was pitch black when she walked in. She groped along the wall for the light switch, hit it, and the overhead light lit the room with a dull glow. Shrugging out of her coat, Kelly looked around and decided trash first.

Miraculously, she found plastic garbage bags in the cabinet under the sink. She filled the first one with spoiled food from the refrigerator, containers and all. She emptied the kitchen wastebasket into the second one and topped it with empty cartons lying about. The third bag she carried from room to room, emptying ashtrays, picking up empty bottles, stuffing in old magazines and newspapers and anything else that resembled trash. By the time she finished, four garbage bags were piled next to the front door.

Kelly tackled the sink of dirty dishes next, scraping off as much of the dried food as she could, then soaking and scrubbing, soaking and scrubbing. Thirty minutes after she started, Kelly dried the last pan and stored it in the stove drawer. With the sink filled with fresh soapy water, she scoured the kitchen table, the range top, and the counter, then wiped down the front of the cupboards and the refrigerator, inside and out.

When she was through, the fifth garbage bag was partially full. She hauled it into the living room with the others. Outside the rain had slowed to a drizzle. Taking advantage of it, Kelly dashed to her car, turned on the headlights, then one by one carted the bags outside, and hoisted them into the back of a rusted-out trailer near the shed.

Finished, she turned and surveyed the junk visible in the headlight beams. The stuff she could lift, she threw in the back of the trailer; the rest she let lie. Tomorrow she'd come back and figure out what to do about it. And the weeds as well, if it stopped raining.

But there was still furniture to dust, floors to sweep and mop, and a bathroom to clean. She turned the car lights off and went back inside. She started to close the door, then changed her mind and left it open to air out the house.

Her fingers were on the last button of her raincoat when Kelly heard a noise. A clink, like silverware. Frowning, she pulled off her coat and draped it over a chair as she walked to the kitchen.

She froze in the doorway, staring at her father. He sat in one of the kitchen chairs, calmly shoveling dry cereal out of a box into his mouth. His thinning hair was wet and flattened to his head in a dark gray cap, but he had on dry clothes.

The anger, which never seemed far away lately, came back. "What are you doing here?"

"Eating." He poured another handful of Frosted Flakes into his mouth and chewed noisily. "Cold wienies, cheese and crackers, a couple candy bars, and some chocolate chip cookies, that's all I've had for the last two days. You've cleaned the place up some. It looks good." He dug his hand in the box again. "Why don't you fix some coffee? I got chilled to the bone out there in that rain. It took me a while to figure out you were alone. Remember, I like lots of sugar in my coffee."

Kelly wanted to slap the cereal box out of his hand. Instead she walked over to the sink, washed her hands, and filled the old electric percolator with water. "I meant why did you come back here?"

"To get some food, dry clothes, blankets, and anything else I might need."

She added two scoops of ground coffee to the basket, pushed on the top and plugged the pot into the wall socket, then gripped the edge of the counter and leaned against it, keeping her back to him. "Why did you have to break out of jail?"

"What did you expect me to do? Stay in there and get convicted for something I didn't do? Not a chance." There was the rustle of dry flakes. "I had to get out, figure a way to get my hands on some money and keep those Rutledges from stealing my land. They were clever blaming me the way they did. Those grapes out there should have been picked yesterday. With this rain, I'll probably lose the whole damned crop to mold. I won't get a penny out of them. Which means I'll need that much more." He chomped on more flakes. "You have to help me, Lizzie-girl. I need to raise enough money to pay that bitch off before she takes my land away from me."

"Give yourself up and I will help." Kelly stared at a chipped spot on the cupboard door. "You said once you needed thirty-five thousand dollars. I have it. I have that and more. Surrender to the police and I'll pay off the note. The land will be yours, free and clear."

"The Rutledges put you up to this, didn't they?"

Kelly swung around to face him, her hands seeking their previous grip on the counter's edge. "No. This is my idea. Strictly mine." The cereal box was on the table. His hands were empty of all but crumbs as he stared at her with suspicious eyes. "I'll go with you when you give yourself up. I'll drive you myself."

"No. I won't give myself up. I'm not going back to that jail."

"They'll catch you sooner or later," she argued.

"No, they won't. Not if you help me."

"Help you? How?" The percolator began to gurgle behind her.

"By slipping out, meeting me every so often, bringing me food and stuff."

She couldn't believe she was hearing this. "You're asking me to become an accessory after the fact. Aiding and abetting an escaped prisoner."

"Dammit, I'm innocent." He glared at her. "You can bet if your mother was still alive, she'd do it. She'd help me. And she would want you to help."

"Don't talk about her!" Raw with anger and old pain, Kelly swept forward and grabbed the back of the nearest chair, her fingers digging through the ripped cheap vinyl and into the crumbling foam padding. "I'm so sick of hearing you go on about her. About how much you loved her. How much you miss her. You killed her. You killed her just as surely as if you'd put your hands around her throat and strangled her." There were the tears again, burning her eyes,

blurring her vision. "I told you she was sick. I told you we needed
to take her to a doctor. But you said you didn't have the money to
spend on doctor bills. 'It's just a summer cold,' you said. But you
had enough money to throw away on whiskey, didn't you? You took
off. You took off and left me there to take care of her. And I didn't
know how! I didn't know what to do!"

Kelly barely managed to swallow back a sob. The air seemed to
have been squeezed from her lungs. She tried to draw more in as
her father leaned his arms on the table, bowing his head slightly and
turning it away. The coffeepot gurgled and sighed in a quickening
rhythm that seemed to match the aching pound of her heart. As
much as she wanted to turn and walk out the door, she couldn't.
She'd started this; now she had to finish it.

"You were so drunk when you came home that night you passed
out before you ever got to the door. She had tried to wait up for you
just like she always did. She was too sick and too weak to do anything but lie on the sofa. I slept on the floor beside her and when I
woke up — she was dead."

"I know." He brought his hands together on the tabletop, a faint
tremor in them. "I let her down. I was always letting Becca down.
God knows I loved her, but I wasn't much of a husband." His whiskey voice was thick with regret and his eyes were shiny with wetness
when he lifted his head, not quite able to meet her eyes. "I guess I
wasn't much of a father either."

"Not much of a father? My God, that has to be the understatement of the century," Kelly declared, disbelief and outrage warring
for supremacy. The latter won. "Have you forgotten how you broke
my arm and all the times you beat me, all the times I went to school
with bruises and black eyes, all the nights I spent here alone, scared
that you wouldn't come home and more scared that you would? The
real truth is I never had a father. I lived in this house with a drunk.
A child beater."

"It was the whiskey," he protested.

"Then why didn't you quit? Why did you have to drink? Why?"

"You never understood, did you? Becca, your momma, she
always knew."

Self-pity. How many times had she heard it in his voice? So many
that the same old disgust came back. "Then make *me* understand."

"It's because I'm weak. Because I could never be strong like your
momma. Like you." He kept his eyes centered on his clasped
hands. "She always knew I was nothing. That I'd always be nothing.
But the whiskey made me feel big and powerful. I could brag about

how someday I was going to take the grapes from my vineyard and make my own wine. Wine that would be as good as anybody's in the valley. And when I had whiskey in my belly, I could believe it. Then I'd come crashing back to earth and know it would never happen. Because I couldn't do it. I didn't have what it took. Inside, I mean."

Kelly stood looking down at him, at the coarse thinning hair on his head, at sagging skin yellowed from too much alcohol for too long and aged beyond its years. Once his shoulders had been broad and muscled; now they were bony and slumped in defeat. This tired and broken old man was the fugitive the police were hunting with helicopters, dogs, and drawn guns.

"This land was the only thing that made me somebody," he went on, his voice low and throaty. "That's why I have to hang on to it. That's why I can't let those Rutledges take it." He finally lifted his gaze, his eyes pleading with her. "Don't you see? Without it, everyone will see I'm nothing."

"I see," Kelly murmured and turned away, going to the cupboards, taking down two clean cups, filling them with coffee while her mind raced.

All those years. All those years of pain and anger and . . . fear. All those years of hating and wanting and needing. Now, she just wanted it to end, to be rid of it and him forever.

She reached for the sugar canister and spooned three teaspoonfuls into his coffee cup, then carried the cups to the table and set one down in front of him. "Drink some coffee. It will warm you up." She pulled out a chair and sat down at the table, opposite him. "You can't keep running," she said finally, watching as he lifted the cup with both hands and slurped the coffee hot from the cup. "I talked to MacSwayne yesterday. He's a good lawyer. He can help, but only if you give yourself up to the police."

"Help me go to prison, you mean," her father grumbled. "The Rutledges have got me framed good for this. It's my word against hers, and who's gonna believe me?"

"But if you're innocent —"

"*If.*" He paused and expelled a fragment of a humorless laugh. "See? Even you don't believe me. My own daughter, and you think I killed that guy."

Kelly wanted to believe him, but that meant trusting him, something that had never brought her anything but pain and heartache.

She released a long tired breath and said, "Then answer some questions for me."

"What kind of questions?" There wasn't any trust in the look he gave her either.

"You said that night you went to Rutledge Estate to get in the cellars and ruin the wine." Kelly curled her fingers over the cup, the steam rising to heat her palm as she idly turned the cup by degrees. "If you wanted to get into the cellars, what were you doing by the corner of the winery building?"

"I heard voices, people talking. I knew there was a party going on up at the house. I got worried that maybe it was shifting down there, that she was planning to take them through the cellars and show off her wines. I thought I'd better check it out. Wait until later if I had to."

That made sense, Kelly conceded, a little reluctantly. "When you went to check, what did you see?"

"Nothing. At least not until I saw that guy stagger into view and crumple to the ground."

"You never told me that before." The rain had picked up again, becoming a steady patter on the roof. "You said the body was already lying there."

"It *was* lying there when I got to it," he insisted with a touch of indignation.

Semantics, Kelly thought. Only politicians and bureaucrats were supposed to twist such fine points to their benefit. "Okay." She pulled in another breath and pushed on. "What did you see before that?"

"Nothing. I told you that. All I heard were voices, some people talking, arguing."

"About what?"

He blew on his coffee and took another drink of it. "I don't know. I couldn't make out what they were saying." He frowned, becoming irritated by her questions. "I probably wouldn't remember anyway. I'd been drinking. And it was the first time in more than two weeks. You don't have to believe me. Just look at the cupboards," he challenged. "You won't find any bottles stashed away."

"The voices you heard, how many were there? Two, three, four? More than that?"

"For chrissake, how do you expect me to remember?" He got up in a huff and stalked over to the counter to refill his cup and add more sugar.

"Try."

He was a long time answering. "Two. Maybe three. I'm not sure."

"The voices, were they male? Female? Or both."

"One was definitely a man's, wasn't it?" He snickered a little that he'd been clever enough to remember the victim had been male.

"What about the other one? Or ones?"

"I don't know." He poked his head in the refrigerator, looking for something else to eat, then raided a can of peaches from the cupboard. "The one talking loud, like he was mad or upset, it was definitely a man's voice." He rattled through a utensil drawer and came up with a can opener. "I think I figured they were men, but . . . I'm not sure now. It's all fuzzy. One of them could have been a woman, I guess."

Which could be the truth, or a convenient way to try to convince her someone else had been there. Kelly rubbed her fingers across her forehead. She had no idea how long this headache had been building, but it was a steady, pounding pressure now.

"When you reached the body, did you see anyone else around?"

With a fork from the silverware drawer, her father walked back to the table and began spearing out peach slices. "Just the great Katherine Rutledge herself, looking at me like I was some kind of vermin." He washed down a mouthful of peach with hot, sweet coffee. "Who's to say she isn't the one that knocked the guy off?"

The suggestion was ludicrous. Katherine was a formidable woman, even at ninety, but she had neither the size nor strength to hit a man, nearly a foot taller than she was, over the head with enough power in the blow to kill him.

"And you didn't see or hear anything before that?"

"Not that I remember." He jabbed the fork into another slick peach slice.

"No footsteps?" Kelly persisted. "No sound of someone running, or anything like that?"

"How many times do I have to tell you it isn't clear to me?" he said, half in anger and half in frustration. "Maybe you want me to lie and say I did hear something? Don't you think I want to? Don't you think I've been racking my brain trying to figure out some way to make somebody believe me? Hell, I'm smart enough to know that if I get caught in one lie, *one lie,* nobody will believe anything else I say about that night."

The rain lashed at the windowpanes while the silence between them thickened. Kelly had run out of questions and she was still trying to decide whether she believed any of his answers. She watched him drink down the juice in the can. His coffee cup was already empty.

He got up, saying, "I have to get some food together." He took a plastic garbage bag from the box under the sink, stuffed a couple of extras into it, then began emptying the cupboard shelves of their canned goods. "Bring me a couple pairs of pants and shirts to take with me."

"Where will you go?" The police were searching everywhere. There was no safe place that he could hide. Not for long. "Where will you be?"

"Why? So you can sic the law on me?" he jeered, like the father she remembered rather than the stranger who'd sat at the table with her. She opened her mouth to deny his accusation, then closed it, realizing that of course she would report it. He must have read it in her face. "I knew those Rutledges would turn you against me."

"Will you stop going on about the Rutledges!" Angrily Kelly pushed out of her chair, her hands balling into fists at her sides. "You always try to find someone to blame for your problems. But no one got you into this mess but yourself. And if I don't believe what you tell me, it's because you have lied to me too many times in the past, and broken too many promises. You. Not the Rutledges."

He dropped his gaze and looked away, mumbling, "I'll get my own clothes."

A low rumble made itself heard above the sound of the rain. Kelly thought it was thunder, but the pitch of it stayed steady, only the volume of it increased. With a start, Kelly realized it wasn't thunder; it was an engine.

"I think someone's coming." She breathed the warning to her father and dashed into the living room in time to see a pair of headlight beams slash a path through the falling rain.

She crossed to the front door she had left standing open. A vehicle was easing to a stop next to her rental car. For an instant, she was blinded by the headlights. The back door slammed with a bang as the headlights went off. There was silence except for the sound of falling rain. Kelly waited for a car door to open, an interior light to come on and show whether the driver wore a uniform.

The darkness revealed the vehicle's black, square shape. It was a Jeep. Sam's Jeep. Some of the tension flowed out of her, then came right back. Bareheaded, he ran through the rain and the puddling water to the front steps. Kelly backed away from the door to let him in.

He stopped just inside the living room and shook the excess water off his hands and arms, his glance slicing over her with more than a touch of impatience and irritation. "You could have told someone where you were going."

"It didn't occur to me," Kelly admitted, then wondered, "How did you know I'd be here?"

"I didn't. It was just the first place I could think of to look." His hands shifted to his hips as his chest lifted in a deep breath that was released in a weary sound. "Do you mind telling me what you're doing back here?"

"Cleaning up." She should tell him about her father, that he'd been there, that she had talked to him, yet the words wouldn't come. It was as if they were choked off by some crazy, misplaced sense of loyalty. "One of the stations did a segment on the house in their newscast tonight. They had a camera crew out here. They came inside. . . . The place looked like a pigsty." She glanced at the living room. It was shabby still, but an improvement over what it had been. "I didn't want some other crew coming out here and seeing it like that."

"They won't. I'll post a guard here to make certain it doesn't happen again. I'm sorry I didn't think of it before," he said, a gentleness back in his voice. "So? Are you ready to go?"

"I still need to dust and mop. I —"

"I'll send someone over tomorrow to clean the place for you." His hand moved onto her shoulder, turning her into the room while he waved his other hand at the chair. "Go on. Get your raincoat. I'll turn off the lights in the kitchen."

Almost too late, Kelly remembered the coffee cups and cereal box on the table. "No, I'll do it." Guilt over her previous silence regarding her father had her breaking into a quick, running step toward the kitchen.

Sam trailed after her. Kelly reached the kitchen first, but not in time to hide the evidence that someone had been there with her. With a puzzled look, he glanced at the cups she shoved into the sink.

"Who was here?" Then his eyes narrowed in sharp suspicion. "Your father?"

She breathed in, then nodded. "Yes."

"When? How long ago?"

"He went out the back door when you drove in."

Sam broke off a muffled curse and charged to the door, yanking it open. But her father was long gone. He closed the door with a rough push of his hand and wheeled around to glare at Kelly. "Why the hell didn't you keep him here?" he muttered, shoving chairs out of his way as he cut across the kitchen back to the living room.

"What was I supposed to do?" she shot back and jerked the cord to the coffeepot, unplugging it from the wall socket. "Tackle him and hold him down until you came in? I didn't even know it was you. I didn't know who drove up."

Kelly followed him into the living room and watched as he picked up the black telephone on the table next to her father's chair. It was an old, rotary-dial phone. Kelly knew it didn't work, but she let Sam find it out for himself. When he didn't get a dial tone, he dropped the receiver back in its cradle and turned to her.

"This has to be reported, Kelly."

She had never seen so much hardness in his face, his eyes, his jaw, his whole body. "I know."

Moving with a swift economy of motion, he grabbed her raincoat off the chair back and shoved it into her hands, then took her arm in a vise-like grip and steered her to the front door. She bundled the coat against her, not putting it on when they walked outside. The fast-falling rain was cool on her hot face and his fingers were tight on her arm.

"Why didn't you tell me he was there?" The question sounded like it had been forced from him as he continued to look straight ahead, not at her.

"I didn't know how." Her voice was small, like she felt. But she wasn't a child anymore; she was an adult.

"You didn't know how? When you saw it was me, all you had to do was call out that he'd run out the back door. I might have been able to catch him." He released her and opened the driver's-side door to her car, holding it for her, his gaze fastening on her again. "I thought you wanted him caught. I thought you wanted this to be over."

"I do." She faced him, the rain falling in sheets between them, running down his face and hers.

"Then why didn't you say something? Did you think you could keep it a secret?"

"Of course not!"

"Where was he going?"

"He wouldn't tell me."

"Did you see which way he went?"

"No. I went to see who drove in. Then I heard the back door shut."

"What did he tell you, Kelly? The police will want to know."

Her chin started to quiver. Kelly tipped her head down to conceal it, conscious of the rain dripping off the end of her nose. "He told me he hadn't been much of a father. He told me he didn't do it, that he didn't kill Baron Fougère, that somebody else was there."

"And you believed that?" The cynicism, the mockery in his voice, spun her away. "Have you forgotten what he did to you? What he cost you?"

"No, I haven't. And I never will."

She slid behind the wheel and jerked the car door out of his grasp. The engine growled to life at her first hurried turn of the ignition key. She had a glimpse of Sam as he climbed into his Jeep. Then her headlights cut a bright track through the falling rain, showing her the narrow rutted lane.

Tears mingled with the leftover rain on her cheeks. She wiped at the wetness and drove faster than she should. She wasn't even sure what she was running from this time: the past or the present.

❧ *20* ❧

Soaked to the skin, Kelly ran into the house straight to the stairs. She was halfway up them when the front door opened. She glanced back as Sam walked in, a cellular phone in his hand.

"Kelly, wait." But the sharpness in his voice just quickened her steps.

Sam went after her, taking the steps two at a time. He reached her room just as the door was about to swing shut. His hand shot out and caught it, then shoved it inward. Kelly backed away from the door when Sam walked in. He took one more step toward her, then saw the flicker of fear in her eyes. It brought him up short. He was angry. More like furious. Sam tossed the phone on a chair cushion and clamped down on his temper.

"We need to talk, Kelly," he said, making his voice as level as he could. There was a good five feet between them, but he made no move to shorten the distance.

"Not now. I'm wet and cold. I need to change into dry clothes. So do you." Her arms were crossed in front of her, her hands gripping her shoulders, but the gesture seemed more protective than warming.

"Yes, now," Sam stated. "I left you alone last night. I'm not going to do it again."

"What is it you want? An apology? Okay, I'm sorry I didn't tell you he was there. I don't know why I didn't. I was confused, all right? I can't explain." She half turned away, plainly agitated. "I can't even explain it to myself."

"Then he didn't hurt you, or threaten you."

"No." Kelly shook her head, then threw it back to stare at the ceiling, pressing her lips tightly together for an instant. "We talked. Argued, really. I tried to convince him to surrender to the police, but it was a waste of breath." She brought her head down and sighed heavily. "He kept swearing he was innocent, that he wasn't going to prison for something he didn't do." She stopped, swinging her face toward him and shooting him an angry look. "And don't ask whether I believe him or not. I know better than you all the lies he's told. It's just . . . a part of me keeps thinking, *What if he's like the little boy who cried wolf? What if this time he's really telling the truth?*"

"Kelly." He took a step toward her.

Immediately, she swung away. "My God, why am I telling you all this? It has nothing to do with you. Nothing at all."

"I think it does."

She whirled around, moisture shining in her eyes, making them overly bright. "Will you stop it? Will you just stop it, Sam? I don't need your pity. I don't need you or anyone else feeling sorry for me."

Her anger touched a spark to his own temper. "For your information, I don't feel sorry for you. Dammit, Kelly, I care!"

"Why should you?" she demanded, unconvinced.

Sam studied her grimly. "Did it ever occur to you that it was possible I've fallen in love with you?" A look of shock flashed in her eyes. She retreated a step, the color draining from her face. "I can see the possibility just thrills the hell out of you," he muttered.

"You can't possibly know what you feel. We haven't known each other long enough."

"How long does it take to fall in love with someone?" Sam challenged. "A day? A week? A month? Two? What's the time frame supposed to be?"

"I don't know. I just think —"

She was turning away from him and Sam wasn't about to let her get away with it again. In two strides, he closed the space between them and grabbed her wrist, spinning her back to face him.

"Don't tell me what you think. Tell me what you feel."

There was a clash of eyes, and of wills. "You want to know what I feel, do you?" She hurled the words at him, her body rigid in resistance. "That I don't want to care about you. That it was a mistake to get involved with you in any way. Whatever it is that's between us, it won't last."

"Is that right? Then maybe we should make the most of it while it does." Sam hauled her against him and wound his fingers through the wetness of her hair, pulling her head back as his mouth came down to capture hers.

Kelly strained against him, hands pushing in protest, fingers clutching in need. She resisted the power of his arms and sought the hunger of his lips. She wanted to fight him, but it meant battling herself. Losing a fight had never been easier or more satisfying.

Driven by anger and frustration, Sam crushed his mouth to hers again and again. If only for tonight, he would prove to her that what they had together was something special, something unique, something right. She would think of nothing, remember no one, just him.

When her response came, it was total and complete. Her lips softened without yielding, parted without surrendering. He caught the soft, helpless sound that purred from her throat. Thunder rumbled and lightning flickered beyond the bedroom windows, but the storm was all within, sweeping both of them into its vortex.

Sam felt her fingers dragging at the front of his shirt. He began stripping away the layers of wet clothes, from him and from her, not caring what he tore. It was all heat and hurry as he tumbled her onto the bed, rolling with her, his mouth running impatiently over her rain-slick face, his hands relentless in their greed to touch and explore.

With a new aggression, Kelly rolled onto him, taking her lips on a frantic race over his body. But it wasn't enough. She moved onto him, gasping in sharp delight as Sam gripped her hips and sheathed himself in her, filling her. Not just physically. Even in her confusion, Kelly understood that.

She threw her head back, her body bowing in slim arch with the strain and the wonder. One sane part of her mind registered the thought that she didn't want to love him, she didn't want to need him. Then her hands were sliding over his chest and she was bending down to his lips.

Closing her eyes, Kelly let him take her away to a place where reality slid out of focus, and where love was more than just a word.

When the last shudders left them, Kelly lay half draped over him, her head pillowed on his chest, moving with the gradually slowing rise and fall of it. Her own breathing had begun to level out, the vague stirrings of misgivings starting to return. But for the moment, she was lulled by the idle stroke of his hand over her damp hair.

"What do you feel now?" Sam murmured, his voice a low rumble in his chest that vibrated against her ear.

"Satisfied," Kelly admitted. "Very satisfied."

There was nothing for a long minute except the soft patter of the rain against the windowpanes. She thought he had accepted the answer she had given him.

"But?" Sam challenged, a faint edge to his voice. "I think I heard one at the end of that."

"Touching, kissing, making love. Maybe that's all there is," she said as his hand stilled on her hair. Levering herself up on one elbow, Kelly pushed her hair back to look at him, seeing the impatience and the denial in his eyes. Yet she argued softly, "Maybe it doesn't go any deeper than that."

"Speak for yourself." Smoothly Sam rolled her onto her back, following to prop himself above her. "As for me, I don't deny I love your body. I love your breasts." He touched one. "I love having your long legs wrapped around me." He ran a hand from her hip to her thigh. "Half the time, more than half the time, I only have to look at you to want you. But, listen close, I love the woman inside this body more."

The conviction was there, in his eyes, his voice, his expression. "How can you be so sure?" Kelly wondered, frowning slightly.

Tenderly he touched a finger to the small crease between her brows and smiled sadly. "How can you be so unsure?"

"Very easily. Sam, my life has been turned upside down in the last week. I'm not sure I have a job, maybe not even a career, and you come along." She smoothed a hand over the ridge of his jaw, liking the hardness of it, the strength that was there, an innate part of him. "I could be grabbing at you for security. If that's all it is, it wouldn't last. I need to get my life in order, Sam. I need to sort things out."

"Sort away." He caught her hand and pressed a kiss in the palm of it, his gaze never leaving her face. "Just make sure you keep me in mind."

"It will be impossible not to." Kelly smiled, very aware of his hard length molded to her side.

"Good. But there's something else you should know."

"What?"

"I want to have children and see if I can't do a better job of raising them than my parents did raising me. I want you to be the mother of them. I want you in my life. And I want to be in yours so you'd better make damn sure you make room for me." An eyebrow arched in mild warning.

But Kelly shivered all the same. "You scare me."

He dropped a kiss on her lips. "That makes two of us then,

because you scare the hell out of me." He rolled away from her and off the bed, all bronze skin and tapered muscle.

"You don't really expect me to believe that, do you?" Kelly sat up.

Their clothes lay in sodden piles on the floor. Sam scooped them up and glanced back at her. "I certainly do. I've never let myself get close to anyone before. Never let myself care. If you don't care, you don't get hurt. If you don't want too much or expect too much, you aren't disappointed. It was safer that way." He paused a beat, holding her gaze. "Maybe you and I are two of a kind in that respect. I know I never wanted to care about you. I resisted it every time I was around you. I was so busy fighting against caring that I fell in love with you . . . and gave you the power to hurt me." Sam waited another beat and then grinned. "Be kind."

But Kelly couldn't smile back. She was too stunned by the way he had exposed his feelings to her, made himself vulnerable. Sam Rutledge vulnerable — the combination seemed contradictory and yet it made her feel warm inside, almost at peace.

Sam carried the wet clothes into the bathroom and paused when he saw the array of feminine items arranged along the counter next to the porcelain sink. Makeup, brushes, hair spray, combs, lotions, it was all there. His ex-wife had probably left her things sitting out on the counter of their bathroom, but Sam couldn't recall noticing them. He picked up a jar of cleansing cream and smelled the edge of the lid. It was Kelly, fresh, silky, subtly sexy.

A rivulet of water from the wet clothes in his arms trickled down his thigh. Turning, Sam dumped them all in the tub. Mrs. Vargas could think whatever she liked in the morning. He spotted a swatch of torn lace in the wet heap and smiled. Whatever she thought, she'd be right. He grabbed a towel off the rack and went back to rejoin Kelly.

Kelly wasn't surprised when Ollie Zelinski and a lieutenant from the team heading up the manhunt for her father arrived at the house to question her the next morning. Anticipating it, she had written down, in detail, everything that had happened the night before, omitting only the personal parts about her mother's death and the reasons her father gave for drinking. She had finished her notes shortly before Sam returned to have a cup of coffee with her.

"Any objections if I stay?" Sam asked after Mrs. Vargas had ushered Ollie and the lieutenant into the morning room.

"No," the lieutenant replied, a man by the name of Lew Harris, in his fifties with a paunch and a tired look. "In fact, I'll probably have some questions for you."

"There's coffee in the urn," Sam said. "Help yourself."

The lieutenant did, but Ollie sat down. "I'm sorry about this," he said to Kelly.

"It's routine, I know. I've been a reporter long enough to know about police procedures." Kelly could guess why Ollie had come along, and it wasn't to offer sympathy or moral support. They had been friends in the past and she suspected that he hoped she would trust him enough to tell him things she might be reluctant to tell someone else. He was doing his job. She recognized that.

"Here." She passed him the sheaf of notes she had made. "I wrote down everything while it was still fresh: what he said, what he'd eaten, what he was wearing when he left, anything I thought might be significant."

Ollie glanced through them, then handed them to the lieutenant. Automatically, Harris reached inside his jacket and took a pair of reading glasses from his shirt pocket. He slipped them on, then sent a quick smile at the others.

"The eyes are the second thing to go," he said, then patted the bulging line of his stomach. "The waistline is the first."

It was an old joke, but Kelly managed to smile at it. He began reading her notes. She sat and watched, conscious of the tension building. Finally he tapped the papers on the table to even out the edges and glanced sideways at Ollie.

"At least now you know what Dougherty's defense will be," he said. "He's going to claim someone else was there arguing with Fougère."

"Is that so impossible?" Kelly challenged smoothly.

"Impossible? No. Unlikely? Highly. Am I surprised that he would make such a claim? The only thing that surprises me is that he didn't include some sort of vague description of this alleged third party."

The rain had stopped sometime in the night. A shaft of sunlight came through the window in the morning room, penetrating the broken cloud cover. Kelly could hear the muted, chopping drone of a helicopter, one of several inching their way over the vineyards on the estate, whipping up air to dry the wet grapes before mold could set in.

"Then you think he's guilty." Kelly didn't have long to wait for a response.

"As sin," the lieutenant stated, then shrugged, a little self-consciously. "Sorry, I know he's your father, but that's my professional opinion."

"Lew took part in the investigation into the baron's death," Ollie explained.

"I see," she murmured.

Sam shifted in the chair next to hers. "Kelly doesn't want to believe her father is capable of murder. I guess no daughter would, regardless of what kind of man her father was."

"Let's just say I still have one or two doubts," Kelly suggested, aware she was the only one in the group who did.

"Miss Douglas, where your father is concerned, we have motive, opportunity, and the proverbial smoking gun." Harris ticked them off on his fingers and explained the last. "The murder weapon, seen in his hands and bearing his fingerprints."

"Were there other fingerprints on it?"

"Of course."

"Have you identified them?"

"We have one set of prints we haven't identified," Ollie admitted. "The other two belonged to workers here at Rutledge Estate. The mallet is a tool of their trade, so to speak."

"Wouldn't it be ironic if the third set belonged to the person who really killed Baron Fougère?" Kelly suggested, more to irritate than out of any real belief they would.

"Kelly, we have a preponderance of evidence against your father," Ollie began patiently.

"All of it circumstantial. You have a witness who can place him on the scene beside the body with the murder weapon in his hand. But you have no one who actually saw him commit the crime. Your so-called motive is the assumption that Baron Fougère caught him in the act of willful destruction of property. Which suggests he was surprised. If that's the case, why didn't he hit the baron with one of the gas cans he was carrying? Why did he put them down and pick up a mallet?"

"Maybe Fougère had it. He heard a prowler and picked it up for protection," the lieutenant theorized. "Then the two struggled over it. Your father took it away from him and hit Fougère with it."

"Or maybe there was a third person there. Someone who argued with the baron, then hit him." Kelly returned to her father's story with growing stubbornness. "Have you been able to determine the whereabouts of all the guests at the party at the approximate time of the baron's death? Were any of them absent from the terrace then?"

"You and I were gone," Sam reminded her. "I took you home."

"But I can't swear you were with me when he was killed," she countered. "I don't know what time we left the party. I wasn't wearing a watch that night and I didn't look at the clock when I got to my room. For all I know, you could have driven back to the winery instead of the house, seen the baron there, argued with him, then hit him."

"You're reaching for straws," Sam said roughly. "What possible reason would I have to kill him?"

But she had a point to make and she was determined to make it. "You tell me. I know when Baron Fougère announced before dinner that Fougère and Rutledge would be uniting in California, you looked far from happy about the news."

"It came as a surprise." The hardness was back in his features. "I knew it was being discussed, but I hadn't been informed an agreement had been reached."

"And you were unhappy about it," Kelly persisted.

"I wasn't entirely pleased, no." The answer came out clipped, curt as the demand that followed it. "What the hell are you doing, Kelly?"

"Trying to prove a point." She swung her gaze from him back to Ollie and the lieutenant. "There might be others who had reason to want the baron dead, who might have profited from it in some way. But it's much easier to accuse a known drunk, isn't it?"

Ollie found the diplomatic path. "His guilt or innocence will be for a jury to decide."

"Beyond a reasonable doubt," she reminded him. "And as of now, I still have reason to doubt."

"I'm sorry you feel that way, Kelly," Ollie said and meant it. He pushed back from the table. "I think we're finished here, Lew."

"Right." The lieutenant sounded almost relieved and quickly gathered up his things.

"I'll walk you to the door." Kelly stood, already regretting some of the things she had said. Sam went with her when she accompanied the pair to the entry hall. "No hard feelings?" She extended a hand to Ollie, more to make peace than as a parting gesture.

"None." He gripped it warmly.

"I guess somebody has to be the devil's advocate," she said in defense of the unpopular position she had taken.

"Why not the devil's daughter?" Ollie smiled.

"Thanks. I should have known you would understand." She smiled back, relieved that she hadn't alienated her childhood friend.

Sam added his good-byes to Kelly's and closed the door when the two men left. Smoothly he turned back. Kelly stood motionless against the backdrop of the hall's gleaming marble, her attention already inwardly absorbed by her thoughts. Yet, for all her stillness, there was an energy about her, restless and contained. It seemed to vibrate from her and make the house feel alive.

"Care to tell me what that was all about?"

"What?" She frowned blankly, then flashed him a faintly impatient look. "You surely didn't think I was serious when I suggested you could have killed Baron Fougère. I told you I was only trying to make the point that there might be others who had both motive and opportunity. I don't, for one minute, think you did it."

"I'm more concerned that you are starting to believe your father is innocent. You're heading for a fall, Kelly," he warned.

"It isn't that I *believe* he is. It's more that I have to find out whether he is or not, for my own sake, for my own sanity. I can't keep wondering."

"What is it going to take? A confession?"

"I don't know." She lifted her hands in a mixture of frustration and irritation. "I just know that right now there are holes in the case against him."

"You hired a lawyer to defend him. That's MacSwayne's job. Not yours."

"Have you ever taken a good look at the figure of Justice, Sam?" she asked, her lips curving in a faint smile. "Not only is she blindfolded but the scales are tipped, too. We both know he'll make a lousy witness in his own defense. And if I'm called to the stand, I'll have to testify that he got violent when he was drunk. What jury in the world will believe a man like that is innocent, even if he is?"

"So what are you saying?" His eyes narrowed on her.

"I'm saying he was a terrible father, and he isn't much of a man, but I don't want him convicted for that. If he goes to prison, I want it to be because he's guilty. Is that so difficult to understand?" She was half angry with him and showed it.

"No. What's difficult to understand is how do you propose to go about proving it? And why do you feel you have to be the one to do it?" he countered, matching the sharp edge in her voice.

"Who else will? And the only way to prove anything is by eliminating all other possibilities. The only way I know to do that is by asking questions."

Katherine paused at the top of the stairs. "Asking questions about what?" One delicate hand slid along the rail as she began her descent.

"About who might have killed Baron Fougère." Turning to face the staircase and Katherine, Kelly was once again in control of her emotions, something she had difficulty with around Sam.

Her reply had Katherine pausing in midstep before resuming her descent. "What a question. As painful as it may be for you to accept, it was your father."

"He insists he didn't. He says someone was with the baron, that they were arguing."

Something flickered in her expression, but when Katherine spoke, her voice was smooth as glass. "That is ridiculous."

"So everyone keeps telling me." Kelly was still angry enough to want to provoke some kind of reaction. "But if he didn't, who did? Someone named Rutledge, maybe?"

Katherine stiffened. "I hope you don't expect me to reply to such an absurd question."

"Are you satisfied now, Kelly?" Sam murmured.

Suddenly all the confusion and uncertainty came flooding back. What on earth was she doing? She sighed and shook her head. "I don't know what's the matter with me. Sam is right I owe you an apology."

"Nonsense." Katherine touched her arm. "You have been under considerable strain these past few days. In such situations, we all tend to act and speak out of sheer desperation."

Kelly wondered if Katherine knew what a powerful motivation desperation could be. She certainly did. Too much hinged on what would happen these next few days. Her job, possibly even her future. She couldn't sit silently by and wait. She had to act.

⨾21⨾

A playful wind tugged at the hem of Kelly's skirt when she stepped from the car onto the roadside's grassy verge. Her heel sank briefly in a small mound of gravelly soil before she moved to firmer ground and closed the car door. The solid thunk of it was a harsh interruption of the vineyard's peaceful stillness.

Then all was quiet, dominated once again by the rustling wind whispering through the vine leaves and the distant hum of traffic. Kelly glanced at the Jeep parked in front of her rental car, a pair of large, smoke gray sunglasses masking her eyes from the brightness of the morning sun. A scarf of raw silk, patterned in golds and rusts and greens, covered her hair, the long ends of it wound around her neck and knotted at the back to secure the scarf in place.

Kelly ran a finger along the inner edge of it where the silk brushed her cheek, and turned to look across the sea of vines. The setting was almost Edenlike, the bright sun shining from a crisp blue sky to warm it, and the ringing mountains to isolate it. There, in the middle of it, stood Sam wearing that old brown felt hat.

She reached inside the open window of her car and pushed on the horn once, twice, three times. When Sam turned to look, Kelly waved, then picked her way across the shallow drainage ditch, angling toward the end of the vine row he was in. There she paused and watched him come striding toward her, walking with that assured male gait, his arms swinging loose and easy by his sides.

"Hello." His voice reached out to her, warm and rich. "What's up? Did something break?"

"No. He's still out there somewhere. No one's seen him." Her father had become a touchy subject between them. Kelly switched to a safer one. "How are the grapes? Dry, I hope."

"The ones I've checked seem to be." Sam lifted a vine branch and revealed a cluster of tightly packed berries with purple-black skins.

With his finger, he probed the center, seeking traces of lingering moisture. The grapes were bunched so thickly on the stalk there seemed to be no opening that would permit any air to reach the center. Sam plucked one of the grapes from its stem and crushed it between his thumb and forefinger, then rubbed them together, testing the stickiness of the juice for an indication of the berry's sugar content.

"I'll have to test to be sure, but I think in another couple days this vineyard will be ready to harvest." Small weather wrinkles deepened about his eyes as Sam turned his head to idly survey the vine rows.

"Which means crush will begin and you will be busier than ever."

"Definitely busier than I want to be right now." His gaze came back to her, a warm light in his eyes that made something intimate out of the moment. "Want a taste?"

Without waiting for her answer, Sam picked another grape from the cluster and carried it to her lips, his gaze shifting to them, his eyes darkening in a way that had her pulse skittering in reaction. Obediently, Kelly opened her mouth and he slipped the fruit between her parted lips, letting his juice-stained fingertip linger on the lower curve.

Kelly bit into the grape and felt the burst of tangy sweet juice even as her fingers curled over his hand to keep it there near her lips. It was something she did not consciously, but instinctively, a response to the feeling of intimacy that whispered around her, around them.

The pulpy juice and mashed skin slid down her throat. "Mmmm, good," Kelly murmured automatically, then drew his finger into her mouth and let her tongue lave the juice stains from it. Finished, she gave the same attention to his thumb with all the innocence of a child licking icing from a spoon. Not until she looked into his eyes did the simple action become something else. Oddly enough for her, she felt neither self-conscious nor sorry.

"Damn you," Sam said softly and with a smile. "Did you come out here to deliberately drive me crazy?"

"That was an afterthought. An unconscious one," Kelly admitted and gave his fingers a last light kiss, then lowered his hand, releasing it.

"Why did you come out?"

"I was too restless to sit in the house another day, watching the

reports on television and doing nothing." It was the "doing nothing"
part that bothered her the most. But that was something Sam
couldn't, or wouldn't, understand.

"I was sure they'd catch him yesterday," Sam remarked. "He
couldn't have gotten that far from the house, not on foot. Although
that is rough terrain east of his place. I hear they're combing it foot
by foot today. Maybe they'll flush him out."

"Maybe." Kelly nodded and took in a breath. "Anyway." She
released it. "I came by so you wouldn't get all excited when you
went to the house and discovered I was gone. I'll be back, so you
don't have to come looking for me. Okay?"

"Okay."

"I'll see you later." She took advantage of the opening to head
back to her car.

"You never said where you were going," Sam called after her.

Kelly turned and forced herself to laugh. "Wouldn't you like to
know?" She waved and half ran the last few yards to the car, mentally crossing her fingers that he wouldn't press her for a more specific answer. She didn't want flatly to lie to him.

"Look me up when you get back."

"I will," she promised and climbed in the rental car. She waved
to him one last time as she drove away.

Less than a mile from the estate, Kelly encountered her first roadblock. The line of cars was short and the delay no more than five
minutes. When a pair of uniformed officers approached her car from
two sides, Kelly fought off the spate of nerves and reached for the
car-rental papers and her New York driver's license she had lying
ready on the passenger seat.

One of the patrolmen stopped by her door, tall and unsmiling,
dark glasses hiding his eyes and reflecting a distorted image of her.
"My papers and identification." Kelly handed them to him before
he could ask.

He took them, saying, "Open your trunk, please."

Conscious of the second patrolman peering through the rear side
passenger window, Kelly reached across and opened the glove compartment to push the trunk-release button.

"You are Kelly Douglas?" the first officer asked, her driver's
license in his hand.

"Yes." She knew he couldn't fail to recognize her name or be
unaware that she was the daughter of the fugitive.

"Remove your sunglasses please."

Nerves jangling, Kelly did as she was asked and waited interminable seconds while he compared her face with the driver's license photograph.

"Where are you going, Miss Douglas?" The question was quietly issued, but the suspicion behind it was obvious to her.

"To The Cloisters winery," she replied, making certain her fingers maintained their loose curl around the steering wheel, not gripping it tightly as they wanted to. "I have an appointment with the owner, Mr. Gil Rutledge."

There was silence while he thoughtfully considered her answer. Kelly could only hope he wouldn't call to verify it. Kelly Douglas had no appointment; Elizabeth Dugan did. The trunk lid closed with a solid thud and shook the frame a little. The rearview mirror reflected the second patrolman as he gave a one-fingered signal to the first, indicating he had seen nothing suspicious and it was okay for her to pass.

"You can go on, Miss Douglas." The patrolman returned her papers and identification.

"Thank you." She tucked them on the seat next to her and drove off, but in her rearview mirror, she saw the two men conferring, then one walked over to the cruiser and reached inside.

She could only guess that he intended to radio his superior and inform him she had passed through his checkpoint, just in case she hadn't been telling the truth about going to The Cloisters and planned to rendezvous with her father.

At the next roadblock, Kelly had the impression the officers had been expecting her. There was little reaction to her identification and only a cursory search of her car. She arrived at The Cloisters one minute before her scheduled appointment.

In contrast to the gray austerity of the abbeylike structure that housed the offices of the winery, there was a subtle luxury to the interior. The luxury was even more evident when Kelly entered the spacious executive office of Gil Rutledge.

A Persian rug in muted hues of burgundy, gold, and blue covered much of the flagstoned floor. An ancient tapestry graced one wall, sharing space with old paintings depicting vineyard scenes. At the end of the room, mullioned windows stretched from floor to ceiling and looked out on a rolling vineyard scene. A massive antique desk of gleaming mahogany stood before them. Behind it Gil Rutledge sat in a tall, ornately carved, thronelike chair.

"Miss Dugan." Smiling with typical charm, he rose from his chair and came around the desk to greet her. "I believe Mrs. Darcy said you are from Sacramento, with the health department, was it?"

"No. As a matter of fact, I'm not with any governmental agency and I'm not Elizabeth Dugan." Kelly took off her sunglasses. "I'm Kelly Douglas."

"Of course. I recognize you now." His smile faded slightly, his expression changing to one of puzzled curiosity.

"I'm afraid I lied to your secretary. I wasn't sure you would see me and I didn't want my own name on your appointment calendar for one of your office staff to see and possibly leak to the press. I don't think either one of us wants a horde of reporters camped outside your building."

"That's true. Please, have a seat." He motioned to a pair of carved wooden chairs upholstered in a short-napped velvet. Kelly chose the closest one while Gil Rutledge made the long walk around the desk to his chair. "What do you want to see me about?" Immediately he held up a hand, stopping her. "If this is in regard to the wages your father has coming for the last few days he worked here, the way our pay periods fall, it won't be issued until the end of this week. I don't think, legally, it will be a problem to release it to you. However, I will check that out."

Her father had worked here? Kelly carefully schooled her expression to show none of the surprise she felt. She remembered that when she had visited him in jail, he had mentioned that he had a job in a winery, but he hadn't named it. Neither had any of the news stories.

"I believe he worked for you as a security guard," she recalled.

"The job title is a bit of a misnomer. As I told the police, his role was more that of a glorified baby-sitter for the tourists, to make sure they didn't wander into areas of the winery that are off limits to the public," he explained. "I must admit, according to our records, we never had any trouble with him. He was sober every day he worked here as far as I know. We certainly never received any complaints about him." He breathed out a heavy sigh. "Which makes the subsequent events so much more tragic."

"Yes, I suppose it does." She was missing something here, something she should be picking up on. "You were at the party that night, weren't you?" Kelly already knew the answer; it was a stall tactic to give herself time to think without allowing any dead air.

"Yes. Both Clay and I attended. I admit I was surprised to receive an invitation. It's no secret Katherine and I haven't gotten along for years now. I expect it was courtesy. After all, Baron Fougère had initially come to the valley at my invitation. It was only polite to include my name on the guest list. And if nothing else, Katherine is scrupulously polite. I suspect she didn't think I would come. Which was the very reason I went." His smile had a touch of a naughty little boy in it.

"As I recall, you and Katherine were competing with each other to work some sort of joint-venture arrangement with Baron Fougère, weren't you? His announcement at dinner that night must have been a surprise to you."

"Not at all. Emile had called me that afternoon to inform me of his decision. I anticipated there would be an announcement that an agreement had been reached. Of course, there wasn't time for it to be committed to writing before his tragic death."

"Then it's all up in the air again?"

"In theory, I suppose." His shoulders lifted in an idle shrug. "The final decision will obviously rest with his widow. She may choose to abide by Emile's decision." He paused, then smiled in silent commiseration. "This must all be very distressing for you."

"It is, yes." Kelly nodded readily. "More so, I suppose, because I had been to the party, but I left before . . . You were still there, weren't you?"

"Yes. Clay and I had decided to leave. Actually you provided the impetus for our decision, Miss Douglas." His eyes beamed at her from across the desk. "Pride wouldn't permit me to be the first to leave. When I saw you go, there was no more reason to linger. That's when Clay and I began making our rounds, saying our goodbyes. That can be such a lengthy thing when you're at a party where you know practically everyone. I know I chatted awhile with the Fergusons. We have a croquet tournament coming up soon at Meadowwood," he added as an aside. "I remember noticing the baroness sitting alone in the rose garden. We were working our way in her general direction. We hadn't gotten around to the point of looking for Emile. As a matter of fact, we were talking with Clyde Williams and his wife when we heard the police sirens. That was the first we knew something had happened."

Despite the names of other guests that he'd thrown in, his alibi for the time of death was his son, and vice versa. Kelly thought that was very convenient, possibly even highly suspicious. But then, she wanted to think it was suspicious.

"I suppose it was shortly afterward that you learned the baron had been killed. Did the police mention who they thought was responsible for his death?"

"There was no announcement as such, but a friend of mine in the department told me there was an all-points out on Leonard Dougherty." A thoughtful look stole over his face as he leaned back in his chair and gazed at the silver wine goblet on his desk. "I remember at the time thinking how ironic it was that of the two deaths that occurred at Rutledge Estate, both involved a Dougherty. Discounting my brother's untimely demise from natural causes, of course. An aneurysm according to the coroner's report."

"I'm afraid I didn't learn anything about the baron's death until the next morning." Kelly carefully steered the conversation back, still nagged by this vague feeling there was something she was missing, something she needed to remember.

"It must have been a terrible blow, especially for someone in your position," Gil sympathized.

"Sometimes I feel as if I'm still reeling from it," she admitted, trying to think of something more to say.

"I'm sure you do."

"I'm sure you've heard that he swears he didn't kill the baron. He's convinced Katherine has pinned it on him to prevent him from raising funds to pay back the money he owes her. He put up the ten acres of land he owns as security. If he doesn't pay, she gets the land."

Money. That was it. Her father had told her that someone was going to give him the money to pay Katherine off, but his deal fell through. That's why he had started drinking that night. Had it been the loan that fell through, or Gil Rutledge's deal with Baron Fougère?

Taking a wild stab, Kelly said, "He was sure you were going to loan him the money to pay Katherine off."

"He said that?" Gil Rutledge did a credible job of looking surprised. She might have believed him if he'd left it at that. But he laughed shortly, a hint of nerves in the sound. "He did ask to borrow some outrageous sum of money from me. Even if I was in the business of loaning money, I wouldn't have considered it. I don't mean to offend, but your father is an extremely poor risk. I may have brushed him off with some vague answer like, 'I'll think it over.' But I assure you, I never had any intention of loaning him a dime. I'm afraid he was indulging in some wishful thinking."

"But you might have had some satisfaction in keeping that land out of Katherine's hands."

"If I could have stolen it from her for thirty-five thousand, I might have considered it. But the price was too high when there was nothing more to be obtained than satisfaction."

Kelly noticed he mentioned the amount her father needed. Why would he remember it unless he had given serious thought to loaning her father the money? Maybe he had even agreed to make the loan, then backed out when the baron reached an agreement with Katherine.

"It would be expensive." She stalled, trying to remember anything else her father had said.

"Very. As I said before, your father was indulging in wishful thinking."

Another thought occurred to her. "He told me he went to the winery the night of the party to pour gasoline over the barrels in the aging cellars. He knew it would soak through the wood and taint the wine inside."

"My God, what a diabolical way to obtain revenge. I never guessed your father had such a devious mind."

"Assuming it was his idea —" Kelly paused deliberately for effect. "— and not yours."

Anger darkened his whole face. "Are you suggesting I put him up to it?"

"Did you?"

"Katherine's behind this, isn't she?" In the blink of an eye, he was on his feet, rage mottling his face, the veins standing out in his neck. "That sanctimonious bitch! She is not going to get away with dragging my name into a murder case. If she thinks to ruin me and kill any chance I have to make a deal with Fougère's widow, she'd better think again." He began shouting, vibrating with the force of his anger. "I know the truth about the legend of Madam. I know the secrets she's kept locked in the wine library all these years. I know about the accident that was no accident. She tries this and, by God, I'll blacken the name of Madam and her wines forever!" He slammed his fist on the desk and Kelly jumped at the explosive sound of it. "Now get out. Get out before I throw you out!"

Without hesitation, Kelly stood up and walked swiftly from the office, more frightened by the fury of his wrath than she cared to admit.

Gil Rutledge stood behind the desk, slow to regain control of himself. Still breathing heavily, he raised his shaking hands and smoothed them over his head, then gripped the back of his neck. When he had calmed himself sufficiently, he reached for the phone and punched Clay's extension.

When Clay came on the line, Gil wasted no time with preliminaries. "Katherine is trying to involve us in the murder case."

"My God, did she —"

"Right now she's only trying to link us with Dougherty. I want you to start putting pressure on Fougère's widow. And get her the hell away from Katherine. I don't trust her. I don't trust either of them." He slammed the phone down and stalked to the wall of windows, staring out.

All the way back to the estate, Kelly ran the scene in her mind over and over again, trying to make sense of the obscure statements — accusations, really — that Gil Rutledge had made. Finally she started with the first and analyzed it.

I know the truth about the legend of Madam. What was the legend of Katherine Rutledge? That she had carried forth the dream she had shared with her late husband to make wines in California that were equal to the finest from France. That she had replanted all her vineyards with cuttings of wine grapes at a time when others in the valley were tearing theirs up to replant with either hard-skinned shipping grapes or walnut and prune trees. That she had kept the winery going during Prohibition by making sacramental and medicinal wines. That she had kept the memory of her husband alive. That basically she had fulfilled her lifelong dream and the wines of Rutledge Estate were considered by many experts to be the equal of the best from Bordeaux.

That was the legend, but Gil's statement implied that was not the truth. All of it or part of it? It had to be part of it. Too much of it was documented fact: the vineyards had been replanted; many experts had rated the wines of Rutledge Estate in print; she had devoted her life to the winery; she had sold sacramental and medicinal wines during Prohibition. Where was the lie?

Confused, Kelly moved on to the next. *I know the secrets she has kept locked in the wine library all these years.* He had to be referring to the wine library in the cellar that housed a collection of all the wines Rutledge Estate had produced over the years. *Secret* implied something was hidden in there; *secrets* implied there was more than one. *All these years* implied they had been placed there quite some time ago. But what could be hidden there? She had been in the wine library. It was rack after rack of bottles stacked nearly to the ceiling. Nothing of any size could be concealed there. Could it?

The last one was a little simpler. *I know about the accident that was no accident.* Kelly knew of only two accidents, assuming Gil had meant the word in the context she was taking it. Katherine's husband, Clayton Rutledge, had been killed in a motoring accident in France, and Kelly's grandfather Evan Dougherty had died in a freak accident at the winery. If something wasn't an accident, then it was deliberate. If a death was caused deliberately, that made it murder. Whose? Committed by whom? Katherine?

Why was she driving herself crazy trying to figure it out? This had nothing to do with her father or the baron's death. Did it? It certainly had to do with Katherine, and Katherine was the one who had seen Kelly's father bending over the body of Baron Fougère.

Avoiding the gated main entrance to the wine estate, Kelly took the back road and drove straight to the winery. The wine library was the only lead she had. She parked in the shade of the cinnamon-barked madronas. There was no sign of Sam or his Jeep.

The receptionist was away from her desk when Kelly went inside the office complex. She hesitated only a moment, then went behind the desk to the slim metal cupboard mounted on the wall. Hung on hooks inside it were duplicate sets of all the keys to the various locks on the estate. Kelly located the key to the wine library, removed it, and left without being seen.

With the key in hand, Kelly circled the winery building to the aging cellars. She entered the shadowed cool of the caves and paused, removing her sunglasses and pushing her scarf back. There was a silence, so absolute it was almost eerie. There were no voices, no sounds of workers, nothing. Just the lights strung along the walls of the hand-hewn tunnels, the mammoth shapes of the aging barrels and the racks of kegs lined along the walls.

The silence magnified the sound of her footsteps as Kelly made her way to the grated door of black iron, emblazoned with a scrolled *R*. Beyond its lattice of bars was the wine library, layer after layer of bottles lying on their sides.

Kelly inserted the key and turned it. A pull, and the door swung silently open on its well-oiled hinges. She walked in, closing it behind her, and paused, making a visual search of the long and narrow underground room. Bottles, hundreds and hundreds of them, lined the opposite wall, from floor to the curve of the arched ceiling. There was a small wooden table and chair, racks with empty slots for future vintages, a sturdy-looking stepladder; otherwise the room was bare.

A walk around it confirmed the walls were solid. There were no concealed side rooms, no obvious hiding places. Kelly scanned the bottles again and sighed. If anything was hidden in here, it had to be small. Had some sort of documents or papers been secreted away here among the bottles? But that would be risky, dangerous. There were probably half a dozen workers, winemakers and their assistants, who would have reason to be in here, not to mention the visitors who were commonly brought here to view the collection. Any of them could accidentally discover the papers. And if the papers were somehow incriminating, why hadn't they been burned?

Why hide anything here at all? This room was strictly for storing the collection of wines the estate had bottled. If anything else were found among the bottles, it would arouse instant suspicion.

But something was hidden here. Kelly started working on the premise that if she wanted to hide something in this room, where would she put it? Not among the bottles. People were always pulling ones out to look at the labels. Inside a bottle? Yes.

"Locked away all these years," Kelly murmured, repeating Gil's phrase. "How many years? Thirty years? Forty? Fifty?"

She tried to remember her dates — Katherine had married Clayton Rutledge sometime near the end of World War One, and Gil had left Rutledge Estate in the early sixties. A span of roughly forty years.

Kelly shifted to the section of the collection that contained wines bottled at the end of the first war. She began pulling them out, checking to make sure they were filled with wine. When she reached the decade of the twenties, the era of Prohibition, she began to slow her pace as a nagging suspicion started to form.

Abruptly she skipped ahead to the latter part of the twenties, *after* Clayton had died. She pulled out a bottle and studied it. It looked the same as all the rest. But was it? There was only one way to find out.

Kelly took it over to the table and removed the cork. She smelled the contents and wrinkled her nose at the strong vinegary odor that advised her the wine had turned. She tried another bottle, with the same results. Uncertain now, she turned back to the rack. What if her suspicions were wrong? She didn't dare open every bottle trying to find that one.

One more. She would try just one more.

The leather strap dug into her shoulder, the weight of the two bottles Kelly had tucked inside her purse pulling it down. She held it close to her side to keep the bottles from clinking together as she walked into the house. The housekeeper was at the other end of the entry hall, moving noiselessly away from the terrace doors.

"Mrs. Vargas," Kelly called to her. "Where's Katherine?"

The woman stopped. "Madam is having lunch on the terrace."

"Is Natalie with her?"

"Madame Fougère had a previous engagement."

"Is Sam there?" Kelly walked quickly forward.

"Yes, miss. Will you be joining them?"

"Yes, but not for lunch. Will you bring some wineglasses, please?"

"Of course."

Sam stood up when Kelly walked onto the terrace. "I was beginning to wonder what happened to you." He pulled out the chair next to his.

"I told you I'd be back." She sat down, careful to swing her purse onto her lap.

"You had an enjoyable outing, I hope." Katherine smiled pleasantly and slipped a bite of poached salmon on her fork.

"Actually I had a very busy morning."

"What did you do?" Sam's glance was idly curious.

With impeccable timing, the housekeeper walked onto the terrace with the wineglasses Kelly had requested. She saw the questioning frown on Katherine's face. "Miss Douglas asked me to bring these."

"I thought we should have wine for lunch," Kelly explained and took the wine bottles from her purse. "I stopped at the cellars before I came to the house and picked up these." Kelly set them on the table, making sure the labels faced Katherine.

Katherine blanched slightly when she saw them. "Your choice is extremely poor. Take them away, Mrs. Vargas."

"No." Her fingers circled the neck of one bottle as Kelly firmly but quietly challenged, "I think we should try this wine. Will you open one, Sam?"

"I have no intention of trying it and there certainly is no reason to open that bottle," Katherine stated sharply. "I know the wines of Rutledge Estate as well as I know my own children. This particular vintage went out years ago."

Sam looked at the label. "Katherine is right, Kelly. This was a blended red wine, meant to be drunk when it was young. Like a Beaujolais, it has a very short life. It will be vinegar by now."

"Let's open it and see. What's the harm?" Kelly reasoned. "If it isn't any good, we won't drink it."

"This is pointless," Katherine insisted, holding herself almost rigid.

"You're wrong, Katherine. There is a point." Kelly kept her gaze leveled at Katherine. "You know it and I know it."

Sam looked from one to the other. "What is this all about?"

"Do you want to tell him or shall I?" Kelly asked and received a small, trembling shake of the head from Katherine. "It's all about Prohibition, Sam, and a term paper I did years ago in high school about the history of the wine industry in Napa Valley. It was so good the local newspaper published it. To write the paper, I interviewed people who had lived through those years. They told me a lot of stories about bootleggers and the methods they used, everything from wild night rides to shipping jugs of wine in coffins. The wineries involved also had to find ways to account to treasury agents for the loss of inventory. Sometimes the owner would claim a hose broke and a hundred gallons of wine were spilled, or that a fire destroyed wine casks, and sometimes . . . sometimes barrels were filled with colored water so they would sound full when they were tapped by federal agents. When you open that bottle of wine, Sam, you'll find it's filled with colored water."

"Is that true, Katherine?" His look was narrow and sharp.

"Yes." Her voice was barely above a whisper. She was pale, her eyes were a watery blue, bright with pain. Somehow she managed to keep her head erect, but she looked old, very old. "How —" Her voice broke.

"How did I find out?" Kelly completed the question. "I talked to your son this morning. I know about the so-called accident, too."

"It *was* an accident." A veined hand came up, slender fingers clenched to form a fist. "You must believe that. Evan's death was a horrible, tragic accident."

Evan. Her grandfather. Kelly looked down at her own hands. "Maybe you should tell me your version of what happened?"

"It was so long ago. So very long ago." Katherine shook her head faintly. "I never knew our wine was being illegally sold . . . not until that night."

Her voice grew flat and brittle, the way she looked. "Evan Dougherty was the estate manager. He was in charge of everything — the accounts, the hiring, the purchases, the sales, everything. When Clayton was alive, Evan reported to him. Later, to me." She lowered her hand to her lap. "Was a photograph ever taken of him?"

"I never saw one."

"Evan was a handsome man, in an arrogant, almost brutish way, all muscle and cocky charm, and intelligence. Evan was a very clever man. When Prohibition came, it must have been quite easy for him to take wine from the estate and sell it on the black market, then cover his tracks with false entries, false records. Even now, I have no idea if he began his illicit operations before Clayton and I went to France, or during the more than two years we were there. When I returned, with Girard Broussard and his grandson, Claude, I cared only about the new vineyards. I took little interest in the arguments between Evan and Monsieur Broussard. It was easier to tell Claude's grandfather that he must let Evan handle things as he always had. I thought it was best. Claude's grandfather spoke almost no English. How could he deal with the inspectors, the forms? Why should he when Evan could?"

A sigh broke from her, full of regret. "I never questioned what he did at the winery. Perhaps I wondered at a few things, the amount of grapes we bought from other growers, but I preferred to avoid his company. He had made suggestive remarks in the past, and what his remarks didn't suggest, his eyes did. Evan Dougherty was that type of man. When my sons' nanny became pregnant and I learned he was the father, I was outraged and insisted that he marry her. He did, but it hardly changed his philandering ways. I think he saw every woman as a conquest to be made." Her voice trailed off into nothing, her gaze fixed on some distant point in the past.

Sam set the wine bottle on the table. "What happened that night, Katherine?" In that moment a subtle shift occurred. The confrontation was no longer between Kelly and Katherine. It was between Sam and Katherine.

"That night?" She swung a blank look in his direction, then stared at him for several seconds, recognizing that Sam would settle for nothing less than the whole truth. "It was late. I went for a walk. I felt lost, lonely that night, and worried. There had always been money. I never had to watch what I spent before. But after the crash, I had so very little left. The first year, it was difficult. I resented it, you see. I tried to deny it, but that night, I think I finally realized I would be dependent on the small income the estate made."

A cloud passed in front of the sun, throwing its shadow over the terrace. The breeze picked up and tugged at the scarf loosely wound around Kelly's neck.

"When I saw Claude hurrying home through the darkness, I knew I wanted company, even that of a young boy. I called to him, asked him why he was out so late. He told me he had been walking, but he seemed troubled, unusually quiet. I thought perhaps something had happened at school and I asked him what was wrong. He was reluctant to tell me at first, then he admitted he had seen Evan loading wine from the cellars into his truck. He was very confused by that. I remember he said, 'Should Monsieur Dougherty be doing that?' I tried to think of a reason Evan might load wine at night when there were no workers about to help. But none made sense. I told Claude to go home to his grandfather and not to worry, that I would go and talk to Evan. I finally found him in the cellars. I heard him whistling before I actually saw him. He was carrying wine jugs. . . ."

"Where are you going with those?" Katherine halted squarely in the center of the aisle, flanked by racked kegs.

"Well, well, well." His mouth curved in that lazy, insinuating smile of his while his bold, bottle green eyes made their sweep of her. She felt her skin heat despite the cool of the underground cave. "If it isn't the widow herself, and all alone, too. You finally got lonely and came looking for company, did you?"

"I asked you a question."

"The cellars are pretty chilly. You should be wearing something warmer than that thin blouse." He set the jugs on the floor. "You'd better put on my jacket before you catch your death."

He shrugged out of it, the action stretching the plaid material of his shirt until Katherine could make out the definition of his smooth muscles. She hadn't meant to notice that.

"I have no need for your jacket." Katherine deliberately put a frost in her voice and her eyes.

But it had no effect on him as Evan advanced toward her. "Of course you do." Katherine stood her ground, trapped by the feeling that if she backed up, she would be relinquishing her authority over him. "Come on, now. We'll just slip it around your shoulders and warm you up."

When he reached out to draw the jacket around her, the urge was strong to retreat out of his reach. She controlled it and remained impassive while he draped it around her and drew the collar together at her throat. The jacket held the heat from his body and the musky male scent of him. She felt smothered by it.

"There. Isn't that better?" Holding the jacket closed, he tapped the point of her chin with his thumb, then stroked it lightly.

Katherine kept her expression icy cold. "I want to know what you were planning to do with those jugs and the wine in your truck." She refused to be distracted by him, or unnerved.

"Sell it, of course." His slow smile was cocky as his gaze moved lazily over her face.

"To whom?"

"A man I know in San Francisco." Letting go of the jacket, he trailed a finger along her cheek. "I always knew your skin would be smooth to the touch. All over, I'll bet."

This time she slapped his hand away. "What man in San Francisco?"

He pulled a smile. "You know, I can't remember his name."

"You are selling it illegally. You are taking my wine and selling it on the black market. I should have realized that." She was furious.

"Now, now, it's nothing for you to be getting yourself upset about," he chided in a crooning voice. "You take too much on yourself. You work too hard. It's a way to get through the loneliness, I know. The nights must be worse with no man to hold you in his arms. You must be aching."

His hands moved to her shoulders. "Stop it." Katherine angrily twisted sideways away from them. "You have involved me in a bootlegging operation. Do you realize what will happen if you are caught?"

"Don't you be worrying your pretty head about that. It isn't going to happen. Not after all this time." He shifted around to keep facing her head-on.

"All this time?" The anger came first, then the fear of the consequences his activities could bring down on her. Katherine backed up, not from him, but from the thought of what could happen. "Do you realize that if they catch you, my permit to make wine will be revoked, they will confiscate the winery, I will lose everything."

"I'm careful." He moved toward her, his voice as smooth as honey. "I promise you I am very careful. You can count on Evan to handle things just like you always have. Don't you know that? How do you think this place has been showing a profit these last few years? Not from the sale of that church wine, that's for sure. No, I've been making sure you received your share of the profits."

"You have to stop this. The risk is too great." She started to take another step back and came up against the solidness of the wine kegs.

"You're worried about me. I like that." He braced his hands against the oak barrel, trapping her inside his spread arms. "I like a lot of things about you."

Katherine flattened her hands against his chest to keep him at a distance. "I'm not worried about you," she said, angry again. "I'm worried about me!"

"Your eyes, they look like hot blue flames. I always knew there was a fire under all that ice." He cupped a hand to the side of her face.

She tried to turn her head away from it, without success. "Stop it. Leave me alone." She tried to push him back, out of her way, and get distance between them again. But he simply slid his other arm behind her back.

"You don't really want me to leave you alone, do you?" he murmured confidently.

"Yes!" She threw her head back to glare at him, and realized her mistake instantly as his hand imprisoned her head and his mouth came down.

She struggled, closing her lips tightly, but he ate away at them, nibbling in little bites and taking them whole, all the while ignoring the push of her hands and the strain of her body to arch free. When she started hitting at him, he just laughed in his throat.

"A little wildcat, aren't you? They always purr the loudest. Let me hear you." Effortlessly, he pinned her hands between them and nuzzled at her neck, licking at the pulse he found pounding there.

Moaning at her own helplessness, Katherine closed her eyes, hating him, despising him, loathing him — for reminding her of all the times she and Clayton had made love, all the times Clayton's mouth had roamed her face and neck, exciting her, arousing her, all the times his hands had molded her to him, showing her the perfect way a man and woman could fit together. She longed to know it all again, the fever and the greed, the pain that could become unreasonable pleasure.

Lost in the memory, she wasn't aware of her fingers digging into his shirt to cling tightly. She wasn't aware of her body straining to seek a greater closeness. She was aware of nothing until she felt the cold rush of air against her breast an instant before his rough hand closed over it.

"No!" She struck out, hitting and kicking, trying to claw free. "Let me go. Do you hear? Let me go!"

"You heard Madam." It was the voice of a boy trying to sound like a man.

"Claude." Katherine almost cried with relief when she saw him standing there, a tall, strapping boy, big for his age and wearing his sternest expression.

Evan looked over his shoulder. "Your puppy dog followed you again, I see. Better send him home, don't you think?" Turning back, he grinned at her. "He's too young to understand how it is." He pushed his hips against her, making sure she felt the hard ridge in his pants. "Go on, boy," he said, keeping his eyes on her. "The lady doesn't want your help."

Katherine frowned in stunned surprise at his total indifference to Claude. Recovering, she shot back, "Nor do I want you." Again she tried to wrench free of his hold, only to hear him laugh at her attempts.

Suddenly Claude was there, launching himself between them and trying to tear Evan from her. Evan turned and, with one shove, pushed him backward, sending him sprawling to the cellar's hard floor. Then he caught Katherine's wrist before she could escape.

"Get out of here," he told Claude. "Before I send you home with your tail between your legs." He laughed as Claude scrambled to his feet, his face dark and angry. "Now we've got some privacy." He yanked Katherine back against him, smiling. "A little panic is natural. It's been a long time for you. I'll take it slow."

"No." It was more a sound than a word as she tried to use her arms as a wedge.

There was a dull, cracking noise, and he went still, a look of shock on his face. Katherine stared as his eyes rolled back in his head and he sagged to the floor. Claude looked at her, panic in his young eyes.

"Claude had struck him," Katherine explained. "In defense of me, and Evan was dead. Claude had never meant to kill him. It was a horrible accident and I knew I had to make it look like one."

"Why?" Sam leaned forward, trying to understand. "Why couldn't you have called the police?"

"And endure the scandal of an investigation?" Katherine shook her head. "How could I explain why I had gone to the cellars so late? How could I say I had gone to speak with Evan Dougherty at that hour of the night? We both knew what people would think. It is that way yet today, and it was worse then. And how could I risk the police discovering he was bootlegging? It would have meant losing everything. And Claude . . . Claude was only sixteen years old. It would have ruined his life."

"So you rolled a barrel off the rack to make it look like an accident," Kelly guessed and thought of her father, wondering if Katherine had given any thought to other lives that had been forever changed by her actions. Evan Dougherty's death meant he had been raised without a father, and she had been deprived of a grandfather.

"Yes, I did that. I had to make his death appear accidental," Katherine said, giving a slow nod, appearing somehow shrunken by exhaustion. "Afterward, I turned and saw Gil, staring at me with such cold, accusing eyes." She rubbed her arms as if chilled by the memory. "I never learned how he got there. He had liked to stalk

people, sneak up on them. Perhaps it was a game he played that
night. He would never talk of it." She looked across the table at
Kelly, her expression humble and her eyes begging for understanding. "Evan's death was an accident."

"Yes," Kelly agreed softly, regretting that she had ever wanted to
know the truth about the legend of Katherine Rutledge.

"If you will excuse me," Katherine murmured as she reached for
her cane. "I am very tired. I think I will lie down for a while."

Sam was there, drawing her chair back and tucking a hand under
her arm, assisting Katherine to her feet. A gesture of solicitous concern; Kelly hadn't seen it from him before. "Will you be all right?"
he asked quietly.

Her white head came up, a ghost of its former confident tilt. "Of
course."

All this, Kelly thought, and she had gained nothing that would
prove her father's guilt or innocence. "Katherine." She waited until
the woman turned. "I never asked you — the night of the party, did
you see anyone else at the winery?"

"Anyone else?" Pain flickered in her eyes.

Or was it alarm? "You did, didn't you?"

Dullness clouded her eyes. "When I checked to see if Emile was
still alive, I looked up and saw only a ghost. A little boy with cold
accusing eyes. He vanished even as I looked at him."

Kelly felt Sam's hard stare as Katherine moved slowly to the terrace doors. "Did you have to ask?" He came back to the table.

The vague lift of her shoulders was a nonanswer. "Do you think
she saw Gil that night?"

"I think she saw exactly what she said she saw. A ghost."

He sounded very certain. The trouble was that Kelly didn't
believe in ghosts, unless they were living ones.

22

The library's paneled walls gleamed in the morning sunlight that flooded through the windows. Kelly prowled the room, trailing a finger over a collection of leather-bound classics and touching a brass magnifying glass on the desk. The soft burr of the telephone intruded on the silence. She ignored it; Mrs. Vargas or Katherine would answer it. Restless and hating this feeling of being at loose ends, she wandered over to a window.

A dispirited sigh slipped from her. Yesterday had accomplished nothing. With a rueful pull of her mouth, Kelly recognized that wasn't quite true. She had gained possession of family secrets and she didn't like the burden of them.

"You have a telephone call, Miss Douglas." The soft-footed housekeeper stood in the doorway.

"Thank you, Mrs. Vargas." Kelly crossed to the desk and picked up the extension. "Kelly Douglas speaking."

"Kelly. This is Hugh."

"Hugh." A thousand things Kelly hadn't let herself think about rushed through her mind. "How's everything going? What about DeeDee's interview with John Travis? How did it go?"

"It went fine. The reason I called . . ."

"Yes?"

"You need to contact your agent, Kelly. There are discussions that have to take place now, and I understand he feels reluctant to talk until he has spoken with you."

"What kind of discussions?" Unconsciously Kelly tilted her chin a little higher, certain she already knew the answer.

"Kelly." Hugh sighed her name in a voice thick with reproval, and regret. "Surely you don't need me to spell this out for you."

"But I do."

A long pause was followed by another heavy sigh. "Dear God. 'Quickly, bring me a beaker of wine, so that I may wet my mind and say something clever.'" Hugh muttered the quote.

"Forget clever, Hugh, and try the truth."

"I thought it would be obvious to you, Kelly."

"It is. As they say back in Iowa, it's as obvious as a brass tack in a hog's ear," Kelly replied curtly. "They want to replace me on the show, isn't that right?" She didn't wait for Hugh to confirm it. "You can tell them for me that I will fight them, loud and strong, every inch of the way. My father has caused me enough grief in my life. I am not going to let him cost me my job — or my career."

"Kelly, this isn't personal."

"You are wrong, Hugh. This is very personal."

"Try to understand. Your image, your credibility, has been badly damaged by all this."

"I am well aware of that. I am also aware that it can be repaired."

"How?" Skepticism riddled his voice.

She didn't have a pat answer for that. "Maybe if less time was spent trying to figure out who to get to replace me, and more on trying to correct the problem, a way would be found. I am far from the only person who has endured the physical and emotional abuse of an alcoholic parent. Maybe I could interview some well-known personality with a similar background who has succeeded in living down the notoriety of a parent. That way the public perception of me may be influenced by the story of that individual. There has to be something that can be done, Hugh."

"Perhaps," he murmured, his tone less skeptical and more thoughtful.

"In any case, Hugh, I will call my agent — to hire a PR firm to start doing some damage control and repair. If the powers that be want to discuss that with me, I will. But nothing else."

"I understand."

"I hope so, Hugh. I hope so." She hung up, and felt an instant, urgent need for fresh air.

In the entry hall, Kelly flung the terrace doors wide and walked out. Seeking the warmth of the sunlight, she moved out of the building's shade. The screaming wail of a siren pierced the morning quiet. Kelly refused to think it had anything to do with her father.

She left the hard fieldstones of the terrace and walked onto the lawn, the thick grass cushioning each step she took. Halfway to the concrete balustrade that guarded the land's steep slope, Kelly heard voices coming from the rose garden. She pulled up when she saw Natalie Fougère in the arms of Clay Rutledge.

Abruptly the baroness broke off the kiss and pushed at him, arching against the band of his circling arms. Clay said something and Natalie shook her head and pulled free to walk quickly toward the terrace, head down, totally unaware of Kelly. Clay spun angrily away and stalked off, cutting through the garden to circle around to the front of the house.

Only feet separated them before Natalie saw her. She gave Kelly a startled look, threw a glance at the rose garden, then swung back, pale and apprehensive.

"You saw," Natalie murmured.

"I saw you and Clay together. I wasn't surprised. I suspected all along the two of you were having an affair." Kelly watched the discomfort and guilt grow in the woman's expression as Natalie avoided her eyes.

"Please, it is not what you think. It is over. I cannot bear to have him touch me anymore." Her small shudder of revulsion seemed genuine. "I have told him this, but he refuses to listen."

"You weren't in the rose garden when your husband was killed, were you?" Kelly guessed. "You slipped off to meet Clay."

"We were together, yes." She rubbed a hand over her forearm in an agitated motion.

"And Emile followed you, didn't he?"

Natalie looked at her with brown, haunted eyes, not answering. Not needing to answer. "I should never have met him. It was a mistake."

"What happened? Did your husband catch the two of you together?" Kelly kept the questions coming soft and fast. "Was there an argument? A struggle? Did Clay hit him?"

"No. No!"

"She was frightened, Sam." Kelly sat on the wide, molded rail of the concrete balustrade that overlooked the valley floor.

The setting sun rode the rim of the western mountains, throwing an amber tint over the land. The view of vineyards, scattered valley oaks, and buildings had the look of a yellowing tintype in the light. Sam stood next to Kelly, one foot on the grass and the other propped on the railing, his arms folded across his raised knee.

"Frightened of what?" he asked because it was what she wanted.

"I don't know." She picked at the pieces of crumbling concrete along the lip of the railing. "Maybe she's afraid of Clay because he killed the baron. Maybe she's afraid because she did. Or maybe she's just afraid people will find out she was unfaithful to her husband. Maybe it's something she honestly regrets." Kelly lifted her head, narrowing her eyes to look at the scarlet-turning sun. "Who knows what her reason is? But somebody's lying, Sam. She claims she was with Clay, and Gil said the same. What if Clay wasn't with either one of them when Baron Fougère was killed? But how do you prove that?"

"*You* don't." Sam angled his head at her. "You tell the police what you've learned and let them check it out. That's their job."

"Right, add the spice of sex and infidelity to a story that's already sensational enough," Kelly countered. "And what do I tell the police? That Natalie Fougère admitted to me she had been having an affair with Clay Rutledge, that she had slipped off to meet him, and Emile followed her. All she has to do is deny it and Clay already has an alibi. It's my word against theirs. I have no proof of any of this."

Sam let that pass. "The police think they've found where your father's been camping out, in a ravine over by the old Bale mill. One of the rangers discovered the campsite after a tourist reported seeing some smoke."

"Where did you learn that? I didn't hear anything about it on the news."

"I talked to one of the park rangers this afternoon. He told me. That's some rough and wild terrain over there. They're trying to seal it off now and box him in. In the meantime, they've taken the dogs there to see if they can pick up his trail from the campsite."

"Are they sure it's him?"

"They found a plastic garbage bag with some canned goods in it, and a shirt like the one you described. They think he left in a hurry, maybe when he heard the ranger coming. With luck, they'll have him back in custody by tomorrow."

Which was a polite way of saying "back in jail." On murder charges. Kelly looked to the north where the cone-shaped peak of Mount St. Helena crowned the skyline.

"You should be glad." Sam kept his voice very cool, very even.

"I am." Wasn't she?

"You don't sound it."

"I'll do my celebrating when they actually catch him. Until then" — Kelly brushed the fragments of cement from her fingers — "there's still the question of his guilt. And who's lying and why?

I've got to think of some way to shake the truth out."

"Leave it alone, Kelly."

"And do nothing? Sam, he may be innocent."

"And he may not." He dragged his foot off the railing, straightening. "That isn't for you to find out."

"But no one else is trying. They've already decided he's guilty."

"That is no reason for you to get involved in this. It has nothing to do with you, and I don't want to see you get dragged into the middle of it."

"Why?" Kelly was on her feet, his words turning her cold. "Because he's a drunk and a troublemaker?"

"You said it. I didn't. What if he does go to prison for something he didn't do, Kelly?" Sam challenged. "After the hell he's put you through, he deserves whatever he gets. You're out of it. Stay out of it."

"I can't. He's my father," she shot back.

He gave her a long, grim look. "That's the first time you've ever called him that."

"What does it matter? It doesn't change anything."

"It should. Kelly, you, of all people, know he's not worth the trouble. Leave it alone."

"I can't. And I won't." She started to walk past him, but he stepped into her path.

"Why?" Sam challenged. "Do you think if you prove he's innocent, he'll thank you? The minute he got out of jail, he'd go get drunk. Don't you know that? Or do you think if you do this, he'll finally love you?"

She shoved past him, tears springing to her eyes. All the way to the house, Kelly fought them, her lungs burning with each breath she took. Emotions crowded her, but anger was uppermost. Three steps into the entry hall, Kelly swung toward the library.

There, she went to the desk and searched through the drawers until she found the telephone directory. She flipped to the *R*'s and ran her finger down the names, then stopped and picked up the phone. She punched the numbers in rapid succession and waited.

"I want to talk to Mr. Rutledge," she told the voice on the other end of the line.

"Who's calling, please?"

"Miss Douglas." She sat on the edge of the desk and waited again.

At last Gil Rutledge was on the line. "Yes, Miss Douglas. What can I do for you? But please make it brief. I'm entertaining guests this evening."

"This will be very brief, Mr. Rutledge." She kept her voice clipped and cool, betraying none of the anger that simmered below the surface. "First, let me make it clear that Katherine knows nothing of this. This is strictly between you and me."

"What is?" He was abrupt.

"I know you weren't with your son when the baron was killed. If my father is going to take the fall for this, it's only right that he receive compensation."

"What are you saying?"

"At the moment I'm not saying anything to anyone. That can change, of course."

His voice dropped to a low, angry murmur. "This is blackmail."

"A harsh word, Mr. Rutledge. I had a business arrangement in mind. Think about it. We'll talk again." She hung up, then paused, a rawness sweeping aside the anger. Lightly Kelly ran her fingers over the phone. "I found one liar, Sam," she whispered. "Next I'll find the truth. I have to."

She had lived too long with lies. Lies that she had told about the bruises her father had inflicted on her, the arm he had broken. Most of all the endless lies her father had told her. She had to find out if he was lying to her again. She had to find out if he was guilty or innocent. It was the only way she could stop being a victim — the only way she could finally be free.

She was doing this for herself, not her father. But Kelly didn't know how to make Sam understand that. And it hurt that he didn't; it hurt much more than she cared to admit.

It was late when Sam climbed the stairs to go to bed that night. All evening he had expected Kelly to come to him, seeking to make peace. He had been certain that after she thought it over, she would recognize that he was only trying to keep her from getting hurt again by expecting too much from Dougherty, by wanting something the man couldn't give.

When he drew level with her door, Sam paused in the center of the hall. If they hadn't argued, he would be in there with her tonight. He still could be. All he had to do was walk over to that door.

No. He wasn't about to apologize for one damned thing he'd said. He was right. Dougherty had caused her nothing but pain. By now, she should have learned he hadn't changed. The man was a habitual liar and a drunk. It was time she woke up to that.

Sam pushed off in one long stride toward his own bedroom.

❧ 23 ❧

Nearly a dozen pieces of luggage, a mix of gleaming black leather and floral tapestry, sat on the marble floor next to the front door when Kelly came downstairs the next morning. She looked at it and immediately sensed the significance of it.

"Good morning." The familiar tap of Katherine's cane accompanied the greeting.

"Good morning." With her hand, Kelly gestured toward the suitcases. "I see Natalie is leaving."

"Yes. A car will be here to pick her up in a little over an hour. The coroner has finally released Emile's body for burial," Katherine explained. "Natalie intends to accompany his coffin to the airport. From there, she will fly to New York, then on to France."

"I see." But Kelly hadn't anticipated that Natalie might leave quite so soon.

"Would you mind running down to the winery and letting Sam know? A new telephone system is being installed at the offices and the line is temporarily out of service. I know Sam will want to see Natalie before she leaves."

"I don't mind," she told Katherine, but Kelly wasn't sure she wanted to see Sam yet. Or maybe she just wanted to see him too much.

As she walked out the door, Kelly realized it was time for her to leave. Not the valley, but definitely the house. Sam didn't understand and didn't approve of what she was doing. If she stayed here, there would be more arguments, more angry words. It was going to end between them anyway. Wasn't it better to pick the time?

A car door slammed, startling Kelly out of her thoughts. She was at the opening to the old bridle path. Turning, she saw Gil Rutledge. He looked the picture of vigorous health, casually dressed in sky blue slacks and a polo shirt, his leonine mane of silvered hair meticulously combed in place.

The phone call last night — it had worked. Why else was he here? This was what she had wanted, the result she had hoped to get, but Kelly hadn't expected him to contact her this soon.

He lifted a hand in greeting and came toward her, smiling easily. "Out for a morning walk, Miss Douglas?"

"I'm on my way to the winery." Kelly worked to gather her wits, recognizing that she was going to need them.

"I thought over our telephone conversation last night, as you suggested. It's time for us to talk."

"All right. When?"

"Now."

"As I said, I'm on my way to the winery. You're welcome to come along or wait until I get back."

"I'll come with you."

Kelly lifted her shoulders, indicating the choice was his, that it made little difference to her. When she set off down the trail, he fell in beside her. They walked for several strides without talking.

Finally Kelly said, "You surprise me, Mr. Rutledge."

"I do?" His smile was smooth and challenging.

"Yes. A businessman like you has to know that it isn't smart to appear too eager to make a deal. It's a sign of weakness." The trail's deep shade closed around them, broken by scattered patches of sunlight.

"Maybe I've decided I don't want to enter into any kind of business with you."

"That's entirely up to you." There was a tension, a kind of excitement, lacing her nerves.

"Maybe I think you're casting blind to see if you can get anything to rise to the bait."

"I attracted something, didn't I?" Kelly directed her smile at a squirrel darting among the tree branches. "You're here."

"I made some phone calls this morning, Miss Douglas. I understand that you are in danger of losing your job."

"Ah, but I still have my contacts in the media, Mr. Rutledge."

"And I have attorneys who specialize in libel cases. I wouldn't go around making false accusations if I were you."

"They wouldn't be false," Kelly assured him, smiling as smoothly as he did.

He halted. "Prove it."

Kelly shook her head at him in mock reproval. "That isn't the way it works, Mr. Rutledge. My father stands to go to prison for a very long time if he's convicted."

"I never enter into any business deal until I know what I'm getting for it, *and* what my partner is bringing to the table. Personally, Miss Douglas, I don't think you have anything but a lot of hot air."

"Enough to burn you." Kelly resumed her strolling pace, forcing him to join her.

His expression was stern. "I am not amused."

"I didn't think you would be." She heard a vehicle coming up the drive, but the thick woods concealed it from view.

"I think you had better start talking."

"What would you like me to talk about? The affair between the baroness and your son? Or I could talk about how she slipped away from the party to meet him. Unfortunately Baron Fougère must have been suspicious, because he followed her."

"Speculation."

"Oh, it's more than that, Mr. Rutledge. That is fact."

"That hardly rates my time. If you don't have better proof than that . . ."

"I do." They were approaching the bend in the trail. Not far beyond was the winery. "It could be I have a witness."

"Katherine?"

Sam climbed out of the Jeep and glanced thoughtfully at the slate blue Mercedes parked in the driveway. A frown creased his forehead as he ran lightly and easily up the steps to the front door of heavy Honduran mahogany. He walked into the marbled hall and noticed Katherine coming down the staircase.

"Sam." A pleased smile curved her mouth. "Good. Kelly gave you my message."

"Kelly?" Sam halted, his frown deepening. "I haven't seen her."

"Really? I sent her to the winery not ten minutes ago. Perhaps she took the bridle path and you passed each other on the way. I wanted to be sure you knew Natalie is leaving this morning."

"Is that why Gil is here?" Sam glanced at the luggage by the door. "Is he taking her to the airport?"

"Gil?" Katherine looked puzzled. "Why would you think that? He isn't here."

"His Mercedes is parked in the drive."

"How odd." She walked over. "He never came to the door. I wonder if he is with Kelly."

The minute she said it, Sam knew Kelly was with him. "Damn that woman," he muttered and tightened his grip on the ignition key. "I told her to stay out of it. To stop asking questions."

"Questions? About Emile's death? You think she is asking Gil about it?"

"Probably." Sam swung around in irritation and reached for the door. "I'm going back to the winery and see if they're there. I need to talk to Kelly."

"Wait. I want to come with you."

"Why?" He paused, the door halfway open, his eyes narrowing when he saw the confused and troubled look on Katherine's face.

"Because —" She broke off the rest of the answer and impatiently waved at him to hurry.

"Dammit, Katherine, did you see someone else that night?" Sam demanded, suddenly angry with her. "Did you see Gil?"

She looked hesitant, unsure. "I . . . I may have."

Swearing, he jerked the door the rest of the way open and charged outside.

"Katherine?" Kelly echoed Gil's question and shook her head. "Katherine says she saw Dougherty, my father, . . . and the ghost of a little boy with cold, accusing eyes."

He stiffened slightly at that, then demanded, "Then who is this mysterious witness?"

"Did I mention I visited my father in jail before he escaped?" They rounded the curve. At the end of the tunnel of trees, the morning sun glowed on the rose brick walls of the winery. "Naturally we talked about what happened that night. He told me he heard voices, people arguing. He snuck along the building to see what was going on."

"Are you telling me it's your father?"

Kelly ignored the contempt in his voice. "Of course, he was very drunk that night. He might have trouble remembering what he saw."

"Is that what you're bargaining with?" Gil Rutledge shook his head in cold amusement. "You have nothing, Miss Douglas. You and I both know no jury in the world is going to convict my son of murder on the testimony of a drunk."

Clay. She had to fight to conceal the sudden swell of elation. She had been certain when Gil showed up this morning that her father was innocent. But she had needed to hear it. Unconsciously she quickened her pace.

"But they would convict him if there were corroborating evidence, wouldn't they, Mr. Rutledge?"

"What evidence?" He pushed the words through a tightly clenched jaw.

"You're getting ahead of yourself, Mr. Rutledge. This is the place where you show me what you're bringing to the table."

"How much?"

"I won't be greedy." They had reached the clearing. The corner of the winery was not twelve feet away. "You tell me."

He stopped. "I can't come up with more than twenty thousand in cash."

Kelly swung around to face him. "Your son's not worth very much to you."

"Later. I can get you more later."

"The installment plan. Not bad." Kelly nodded smoothly. She was pushing it. She could see the anger building, and she had no desire to see another display of his temper. "I'll tell you what."

"No, I'll tell you." He caught her wrist when she started to back up away from him. "The evidence. What is it?"

"When I get the cash, you'll get the evidence." Hopefully by her next meeting with him, she would have convinced Ollie to wire her. The tape might not be admissible, but at least he would have to recognize her father's innocence.

"Not good enough."

"Too bad." Kelly tested his hold on her wrist. "That's all you're going to get for now."

"Like hell it is." He jerked her closer.

"Let go of my arm," she ordered curtly. "You're hurting me and I don't like to be hurt."

"I'll hurt more than your damned arm if you don't tell me what the hell you've got." He gave her wrist a hard turn and Kelly gasped at the pain that shot up her arm.

"Let go of her."

Kelly looked in surprise at the burly, bristling figure of Claude Broussard. But the fingers around her wrist didn't loosen their grip.

"Miss Douglas and I are having a private discussion. You're interrupting it. Now get out of here. Go on." Gil jerked his head to send Claude on his way.

"You will release her. Then, I will leave."

"Listen, you stupid old man."

"Old?" It was a roar. "You say that I am old? Me? Claude Broussard." He launched into a tirade in French as he moved slowly but steadily closer to them.

Kelly stared at the wooden mallet Claude gripped like a weapon in his hand, and never saw the Jeep swing into the yard, making straight for them. Voices, her father had heard voices arguing, but he said he couldn't understand what they were saying. He couldn't understand, Kelly realized, because they had been arguing in French.

The mallet. Ollie had said two sets of fingerprints had belonged to workers at the estate. If one of them was Claude's — dear God, she had *proof.* The Jeep's engine was switched off, bringing a new silence to the yard.

"You," Kelly murmured, then repeated it in a stronger voice, her gaze lifting to Claude's face. "You were the one arguing with Baron Fougere that night, weren't you, Claude?"

"What?" Gil's voice was small and dazed as his hand fell away from her wrist.

"Weren't you, Claude?" Kelly insisted, watching as the old man faltered, his face graying a little. In her side vision, she was conscious of two figures swiftly approaching — Sam and Katherine, she thought, but she didn't take her eyes off Claude.

"He said . . . I was too old." There was a look of confusion, regret, even pain, in his dark eyes. "He said he would bring a younger man to take my place. He would not listen. I tried . . ."

"You killed him, didn't you?" Kelly said it gently, carefully, trying to pry the admission from him. A breath was drawn in sharply by someone. Kelly refused to be distracted by the sound.

"He said it was decided. He was too busy. He put his hands on me to push me out of his way and I —" He seemed to choke on the words.

Kelly said them for him. "And you hit him?"

He nodded once, then his eyes misted with tears as he swung his big head toward Katherine. "Madam, it was an accident. I did not intend to strike him so hard. I . . ."

"Say no more, Claude." She moved to his side, laying a hand on his arm and looking up, her own eyes brimming with tears. "Say nothing more please, Claude, until I can obtain an attorney for you," she urged in a voice that commanded.

It was over. Kelly felt the draining of tension, the sagging of relief as she half turned and met Sam's gaze. The silence between them lengthened, growing heavy with strain.

"It seems your father was telling the truth," he said at last. "He is innocent. This time."

"I had to know that, Sam. I don't expect you to understand, but I couldn't live with any more lies." She took a step toward the office building. "I'll go call the police."

"Kelly." His hand reached out, as if to stop her. "I went to the house to tell you, I heard on the radio a few minutes ago, they caught your father."

"Is he all right?" She looked at him sharply, thinking she heard something that said otherwise in his voice.

"Other than being dirty and tired and scratched up from scrambling around in the brush, he's fine."

Kelly nodded, and glanced back at Claude. "I'll need to see him, tell him about this, and arrange to get him released."

"There isn't any reason for you to see him, Kelly," Sam argued. "The police will eventually release him. MacSwayne can handle it. You don't need to be there."

"Yes, I do." Without another word, she walked off.

"He isn't going to thank you, Kelly," Sam called after her, angered that she couldn't see that, that she had to go through the pain of finding out herself.

Within minutes the police arrived and Claude was taken into custody. As soon as his statement was taken, Sam went looking for Kelly, determined that if he couldn't convince her to change her mind about going to see her father and personally arranging for his release, then he was going with her. He wasn't going to let her go through it alone.

But he was too late. She'd already left.

Sam reached the Jeep as the police car drove away with Claude in the backseat. Katherine and Gil stood next to the Jeep, both staring after the departing cruiser. Neither seemed to notice Sam when he walked up.

Gil's expression was still faintly dazed, confused. "It was old Claude," he murmured as if he needed to say it to believe it. "All along I thought Clay —" He clamped his mouth shut on the rest of it.

"We are a pair, Gil." Katherine gave him a wise and sad look. "I thought it was you. I thought I saw you there."

His mouth curved without humor. "You did. I came to warn Clay that Emile had followed him. I cut through the woods to find Clay before Emile did and got lost. When I finally made it here, there you were . . . beside Emile's body."

Gil shook his head, remembering that when he had caught up with Clay, he had said only, "Emile is dead." Clay had gone white with shock, and he had assumed his son's guilt from that, without asking any further questions. He almost laughed when he realized Clay had probably thought he had killed him.

Sobering, he glanced at Katherine again, his eyes narrowing in veiled suspicion. "If you thought you saw me, why didn't you mention it to the police?"

"Why did you fail to tell them about Clay?"

"He's my son."

"Exactly."

Uncertainty flickered through his expression. After a moment, he nodded to her, a hint of a smile about his lips. Then he turned and walked off, automatically taking the old bridle path back to his car.

Turning, Katherine glanced at Sam, age and a weariness of heart pulling at her. "Take me back to the house, Sam."

Silently he helped her into the passenger seat, then walked around the Jeep and slid behind the wheel. The key was in the ignition but Sam didn't reach for it. Instead he turned to study her.

"You thought Gil killed the baron, yet you never told the police. Why, Katherine?"

"I thought I'd imagined Gil there that night," she began, then stopped and sighed. "No, that is a lie. I wanted it to be my imagination. Just as I wanted it to be Dougherty who had killed Emile. Not my son."

"Your son hated you — and probably still does. There has been a cold war between the two of you for as long as I can remember. Why protect him, Katherine?"

"If you had children, you would not ask that question."

"That's your reason. Do you think he would show the same loyalty to you?"

"Possibly not." She dismissed the importance of that with a lift of her hand. "It hardly matters, though, does it?" Through a break in the trees a vineyard became visible. "I understand the grapes are drying nicely. It would seem the helicopters served their purpose."

"I don't think there's any question that they did."

"I have been blind to a great deal lately . . . Sam." She paused deliberately before stressing his name. "Age, I suspect. In any case, it is time I stepped down. From now on Rutledge Estate is in your charge."

He glanced sideways at her, a smile tugging at one corner of his mouth. "You can't let go, Katherine. You don't know how."

"I may surprise you. After all, Claude will require a great deal of my time and attention over these next weeks and months," she stated.

Of course she would stand by old Claude; he should have realized that. Right or wrong, Katherine would be at his side. Just as he should have been there for Kelly. He had been wrong, and all the best intentions in the world couldn't change that. How could he explain that to her? How could he make her understand?

*I*t was late afternoon when Kelly pulled up in front of her old house. The weeds had been cut down all around and all the junk had been hauled away. Anything usable was stacked by the old shed. New boards replaced the rotted ones on the front step. They were minor things that did little to improve the looks of the house, but she noticed them all as she stepped out of the car.

The passenger door was slammed shut. "Would you look at that?" her father demanded and waved a hand at the vineyard. "Ruined, the whole damned crop is probably ruined, every cluster full of mold. If it hadn't been for those damned Rutledges trying to pin that murder on me, I could have had those grapes picked before it ever started raining. Now I'll be lucky to get anything."

Ignoring his tirade, Kelly reached in the backseat and lifted out the grocery sack. "Here."

He looked at the sack, then at her. "Aren't you coming in?"

"No."

"But I thought that's why we stopped at the store." He took the sack from her, frowning. "I thought we were coming back here to have dinner and celebrate my release."

Celebrate. The all-too-familiar sound of that word acted as a flash point to her temper. "With what? A bottle of whiskey?" Kelly challenged hotly. "You are a free man. It's the perfect excuse to get roaring drunk, isn't it? It so happens that I'm free, too. Free of you and your drinking."

Indignant and angry, he protested. "I said dinner. I never said anything about drinking."

"No, you didn't. But it really doesn't matter because I don't care whether you get drunk or not. Nothing you do can ever hurt me again." Remembering that, Kelly stopped before this escalated into a full-blown argument. She reached inside her shoulder purse and took out a business card, handing it to him. "MacSwayne wanted me to give you this," she said stiffly.

"What is it?" Still frowning in irritation, he tried to read it over the top of the grocery sack.

"It's a name and phone number for the local chapter of AA."

"What are you giving me this for? I'm no alcoholic."

"But you are," Kelly insisted, anger vibrating beneath the surface of her voice. "Why don't you stop lying to yourself and admit it? Maybe they can help you. I can't." She swung away and climbed back in the car.

"Where are you going?"

"I'm not sure. I'll talk to you tomorrow." Kelly closed the door and started the engine. When she drove out of the yard, her father was still standing there.

Tense and tired, her head aching, Kelly drove back to Rutledge Estate. She saw the Jeep parked in front of the house and mentally braced herself for another round with Sam, vowing it would be the last round.

He opened the front door before she ever reached it. "You're back."

"Yes."

"Did they release your father?"

"Finally." Kelly brushed past him into the hall. "And no, he didn't thank me, if that's what you're waiting to hear," she said over her shoulder as she crossed to the marble staircase.

"No, that isn't what I want to hear. That isn't even what I want to talk about." He came after her.

Kelly ran quickly up the steps. "Everything has already been said."

"Dammit, you're not making this easy."

"That's too bad. But why should I make it easy for you? Nothing has ever been easy for me. Face it, Sam. I'm not the kind of person you want me to be, and that's that." In her room, Kelly went straight to the closet and dragged out her suitcase.

Sam caught her arm, stopping her. "Will you listen to me for one minute?"

"I have listened to you," she shot back, needing the anger to protect her from the hurt. "All my life I have listened to someone. From now on, I'm going to listen to myself."

"The way I should have listened to you all along."

Halted more by the soft pitch of his voice than the restraining hand on her arm, Kelly looked at him warily. "What do you mean?"

His grip loosened, his eyes gentling on her, regret shadowing them. "Those things I said about your father — I know how much he's hurt you in the past, and I don't mean just the physical abuse. I didn't want you to get hurt again. I was trying to protect you."

"You can't protect people from things like that."

"No, you can't." He paused and seemed to grope for the right words. "Kelly, I don't know much about families. I was never close to my parents. I taught myself not to care because it was easier."

"If you don't care, you don't get hurt." Kelly remembered Sam telling her that.

"Maybe that's not the right attitude. Maybe you shouldn't give back everything you get, especially when what you get is nothing. Maybe sometimes you have to do things just because you believe they are the right things to do."

"Maybe." She was afraid to read too much into what he was saying.

"Kelly, I'm not perfect."

She moved away, out of his reach. If she didn't, she knew she would touch him. "None of us are." She laid her suitcase on the bed and opened it.

"Where are you going? Back to New York?"

"In a day or two, yes." Kelly nodded. "That's where my work is." She crossed to the closet and removed the clothes that were on hangers. "I spoke with Hugh while I was in MacSwayne's office waiting for my father to be released. His innocence has gone a long way to salvaging my credibility — and my career." She carried them back to the bed. "Enough that the network feels an aggressive PR campaign will take care of the rest."

"I'm glad." His voice sounded closer. "I know how much your job means to you."

She had thought it meant everything, Kelly remembered as she laid her clothes on the bed next to the suitcase. But she had learned a few things about herself in the last days. Once she had believed a career was all she needed to feel fulfilled. It wasn't enough. As much as she loved her work, she wanted a husband, children, a home — a family. She knew that now.

Kelly took a deep breath and slowly let it out. "You may as well know that I will be paying off the note my father owes you. Mac-

Swayne is drawing up an agreement for my father to sign tomorrow." She took a blouse off its hanger and began to fold it. "Assuming he stays sober, of course. I'm going to lease the vineyard from him, hire some workers to get it back in shape this winter and take care of it next year. Properly tended, it should produce a good income and provide a more than adequate return on my investment."

"Then you will be coming back." Sam stood directly behind her.

"Probably every weekend." Kelly knew what he was thinking, and wouldn't let herself even consider it. Instead she concentrated on laying the folded blouse neatly and precisely in the bottom of the suitcase, then picked up a skirt. "I thought I could catch the red-eye flight out on Friday, have Saturday to check on the vineyard and handle any business related to it, then fly back on Sunday to New York, or wherever we're taping the show."

"I want to see you when you're back, Kelly."

She felt the sting of tears and closed her eyes against it. "I'll be on a tight schedule. I doubt if I'll have time."

"Make time. That's what I will have to do, especially now that Katherine is stepping down and I'll be taking over the winery." Sam was impatient with her. It was in his voice.

But Kelly deliberately focused on the content of his statement. "Katherine is retiring?"

"Yes."

"Congratulations."

"Don't change the subject." His hand seized her arm and turned her around, forcing Kelly to meet his probing gaze. "I told you once that when you started making plans for your life, you had better make room for me in them. I meant it, Kelly."

"I know, but I don't think it would be wise for us to see each other for a while. Maybe not for a long while." She tried, but she couldn't keep the ache out of her voice. He couldn't possibly know how hard it was for her to say that, how hard it was to ignore the warm weight of his hands on her arms, and to see the pained look of confusion in his eyes. "Don't you see, Sam? Too much has happened. There are still too many things I need to sort out. About myself, I guess. I have the name of a support group in New York that's made up of people with alcoholic parents. I think they might be able to help me understand some of my feelings — some of my anger. Maybe I'll even be able to forgive my father someday for all he's done to me."

"What does that have to do with us? With seeing me?"

"Everything," she insisted, then attempted to explain. "I need to learn to trust again. I've been hurt so often that it's going to take time. And no relationship can exist and grow without trust. Try to understand that."

"Understand?" His smile was warm and totally unexpected. "You're talking to a vintner, Kelly. I know all about grafting a vine shoot to a rootstock. There is never any way to be certain in advance that the pairing will take. It has to be tended, watered, nourished, and even then, there are no guarantees it will flourish. But that's all I'm asking for — that knowing and growing time for us. Will you give us that, Kelly? The time together to find out if we can make it work?"

She looked at him for a long, hesitant moment, then smiled, a radiance spreading across her face. "Yes," she said, realizing she wanted that as much as he did.